Praise for Bonnie K. Winn

"This vibrant, amazing story has two romances that show that love doesn't die...but the heart always has room for one more."
—*RT Book Reviews* on *Lone Star Blessings*, 4.5 stars, Top Pick

"A poignant romance imbued with marvelously drawn protagonists, stirring moments, and a charming supporting cast."
—*RT Book Reviews* on *Substitute Father*

"A delightful romance of lovers reunited, where both need to exhibit forgiveness and understanding."
—*RT Book Reviews* on *Return to Rosewood*

"In *Vanished* Bonnie Winn creates a realistic, fast-paced thriller enhanced by the seamless relationship between Gillian and Brad."
—*RT Book Reviews*

BONNIE K. WINN

Jingle Bell Blessings
&
Family by Design

H HARLEQUIN® LOVE INSPIRED®CLASSICS

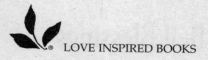

LOVE INSPIRED BOOKS

Recycling programs for this product may not exist in your area.

ISBN-13: 978-1-335-00673-8

Jingle Bell Blessings & Family by Design

Copyright © 2018 by Harlequin Books S.A.

The publisher acknowledges the copyright holder of the individual works as follows:

Jingle Bell Blessings
Copyright © 2010 by Bonnie K. Winn

Family by Design
Copyright © 2011 by Bonnie K. Winn

www.Harlequin.com

Printed in U.S.A.

CONTENTS

An author of over thirty-five historical and contemporary romances, **Bonnie K. Winn** has won numerous awards for her *USA TODAY* and Amazon bestselling books. *Affaire de Coeur* named her one of the top ten romance authors in America. Fourteen million copies of her books have been sold worldwide. Formerly an investment executive, she shares her life with her husband as well as her son and his family, who live nearby.

Books by Bonnie K. Winn

Love Inspired

Rosewood, Texas

A Family All Her Own
Family Ties
Promise of Grace
Protected Hearts
Child of Mine
To Love Again
Lone Star Blessings
Return to Rosewood
Jingle Bell Blessings
Family by Design
Forever a Family
Falling for Her Boss

Visit the Author Profile page at Harlequin.com for more titles.

JINGLE BELL BLESSINGS

Behold, children are a gift of the Lord.
        —*Psalms* 127:3

For our beautiful Liberty Winn
Born April 18, 2010

Chapter One

Chloe Reed gripped little Jimmy's hand as much to stop her own shaking as to reassure him. Everything was on the line. The boy's future, her own. Swallowing, she tentatively raised the brass knocker on the massive front door.

Silence.

She bent down to encourage Jimmy, and whispered, "It'll be okay, I promise."

The door whipped open suddenly and she nearly teetered. Unnerved, she looked up, way up, to meet a dark pair of unpleased eyes. Set in a rugged face with a determined chin, his eyes swept over her in uncompromising dismissal.

Awkwardly, Chloe straightened up, expecting to meet him face-to-face, but he was tall, unusually tall. "Um…hello."

"Yes?"

"I'm here to see Evan Mitchell."

"You're looking at him."

"Oh." She'd held a wild hope that she'd knocked on the wrong door. Despite her boss's warnings, she had wanted to believe that Evan Mitchell would be approachable, reasonable. "I'm Chloe Reed." Wishing she could shield the little boy, she squeezed his hand again. "And this is Jimmy Mitchell."

Eyebrows as dark as the man's thick hair swooped downward. "What are you doing here?"

Wanting to protect the seven-year-old, Chloe beseeched the man with a pleading glance.

Relenting, Evan opened the door wider. "Come in."

She and Jimmy both stared as they walked into the circular, two-story-high entry hall, their steps echoing on the marble floor of the impressive house.

Evan hadn't expected his late cousin's son to appear on his doorstop, but he didn't want to hurt the boy. Raising his voice, he called for the housekeeper. "Thelma! Can you come out here?"

Wiping her hands on a cheery gingham apron, a pert woman in her sixties dashed into the hall. "What is it? I'm in the middle of pie making and..." Her voice trailed off when she saw Chloe and the boy, her face easing into a smile. "Who do we have here?"

"Spencer's boy," Evan replied briefly.

Thelma's eyes widened, then warmed in understanding as she spoke to Jimmy. "Do you like apple pie?"

Uncertain in his new surroundings, Jimmy looked at her warily, taking a step backward, leaning against Chloe.

Thelma walked toward him, extending her hand. "I've got lemon meringue, pumpkin, cherry and banana cream, too. I sure could use a taster."

Jimmy looked up at Chloe, who nodded. Accepting Thelma's hand, the pair disappeared in the direction of the kitchen.

Evan wished he could whisk the woman away as easily, but he knew that wasn't going to happen. Instead he gestured toward the parlor, observing the swing of her long, wavy, caramel-colored hair as she walked. Once in the room, she turned, her large green eyes questioning.

"Have a seat."

As she did, he wondered what his late cousin's attorney was up to now. Sending a pretty woman was novel, even for Holden Wainwright.

"Miss…?"

"Reed," she supplied nervously. "Chloe. Call me Chloe, please. I work for Holden Wainwright. I'm his… that is, I'm the estate representative for Jimmy's parents."

He'd guessed as much. "What are you doing here?"

"Mr. Wainwright wants what's best for Jimmy. Your cousin and his wife didn't have any immediate family who could take care of him. And Mr. Wainwright himself is an old bachelor—he doesn't have a clue about raising a young boy. That leaves you."

"Wainwright knows how I feel about that."

Her face filled with distress, darkening her already unusual eyes, pulling down the edges of her full lips. "He does?"

"Oh, come now, Miss Reed—"

"Chloe," she corrected, staring at him in shock.

"Miss Reed, we aren't going to get to know each other well enough to worry about first names. I told Wainwright I wasn't going to change my mind. And I'm not." The thought of growing close to another child… The pain nearly choked off his breath. And his voice was gruffer than usual because of it. "You've come on a fool's errand. I can't say whether you're Wainwright's pawn or a schemer yourself. Doesn't matter. You can sort that out with Wainwright when you're back in Milwaukee."

Chloe found her voice. "It's taken us forever to get out here. The flight from Milwaukee to San Antonio took two plane changes. Then driving way out here to Rosewood…and you expect us to just turn around and head back?" Some of her distress had vanished, leaving fire in its place. "And I'm supposed to tell Jimmy what? That the only relative he has on this continent doesn't even want to get to know him?"

Evan watched as the quivering in her neck spread to the hollow at the base of her throat.

She stood abruptly, pressing her hands together. "How do you live with yourself?"

Bleakly. "We aren't in the time of Dickens, Miss Reed. There are no workhouses, no orphanages. Spencer left the boy a trust fund that'll guarantee his future."

"The *boy's* name is Jimmy. And all the money in the world can't replace his parents." She gestured toward the rest of the comfortable room. "Since your father is alive and living here, you obviously can't understand that kind of trauma."

Evan's throat was so tight it was a wonder any oxygen could pass into his lungs. *Trauma.* A trendy term, like *closure.* As though such a thing existed. The hole in his heart would never heal, certainly never close. Not since he'd lost Robin and Sean. He crossed the room so he could look out the tall, wide window. A rental car was parked in the circular drive. So that much was true. "And what do you know about trauma, Miss Reed?"

"Enough," she replied evenly.

Turning his back to the faceted panes of glass, he

watched the sunshine illuminate Chloe's face. Wainwright was playing hardball. Sending a woman Evan couldn't ignore. At least that's what the old horse trader thought. "I doubt that. What are you, twenty-four, twenty-five?"

"Actually, I'm twenty-seven. But—"

He held up one hand. "No need to get in a one-upmanship contest. Not even the most tragic tale's going to change my mind, Miss Reed. I'm surprised you didn't learn more about the situation before you agreed to bring Jimmy here. I haven't seen Spencer since we were teenagers. Hardly a close relationship that would warrant any reason to appoint me the boy's guardian."

"*Jimmy,*" she emphasized. "And to repeat myself, Jimmy doesn't have anyone else." Chloe took a breath. "He's alone. You're his parents' choice as guardian. Have you no compassion?"

Evan met the woman's unrelenting stare. His compassion had drowned along with Robin and Sean. But he didn't feel the need to spill those details to a stranger. The deaths of his wife and son were sacred, not to be bandied about for this woman's benefit.

Chloe stood as well, crossing the room, planting her petite frame in front of his. "I'm not suggesting it's an easy obligation. But surely you can see the sense in having Jimmy stay for a while, to see if the arrangement will work." She steepled her fingers together, the crisscross pressure making them whiten. "The estate will pay for my services during the transition."

His humorless chuckle was bitingly sarcastic. "Two for the price of one? Am I supposed to believe that's a good deal?"

Thunder clashed across her face and for a moment

it looked as though she was about to launch a tirade. Instead, she tugged at the jacket of her prim, navy blue suit, then tightened her hands further. "I don't believe you should be thinking of Jimmy in terms of a deal. But if that's the only emotional barometer you possess, then I'll tell you that it is a first-rate deal. Jimmy's kind, unspoiled, loving. And he's just had both of his parents blown to smithereens in a factory explosion."

Not stopping to let him speak, she held up her hands, ticking off her points. "One grandfather's dead. One grandmother is in a nursing home with Alzheimer's. His other set of grandparents are on a dig in Egypt and suggested we put him in a boarding school.

"You knew Spencer. Do you think he'd want his son to have the same kind of lonely life he did? Crying himself to sleep because the other boys went home to their families for holidays and he stayed behind, hurt and alone? Spencer told Mr. Wainwright that his only good memories of growing up were here, in Rosewood, with you and your family. Don't you think his son deserves to be happy?"

Evan's gaze narrowed, his suspicions growing as he studied her. "Sounds like you're pretty chummy with Wainwright."

"I'm in his employ. You should know that Mr. Wainwright was more than Spencer's attorney. He and Spencer's father were best friends. After Spencer's father died a few years ago, Mr. Wainwright did his best to step into a father's role, to give Spencer *some* semblance of a parent."

Evan still didn't know what she had to gain by talking him into a guardianship, but it wasn't going to happen. "Then perhaps he ought to step into the grand-parent role now."

She quieted for a moment, then her ocean-green eyes held a clashing combination of sadness and ferocity. "Mr. Wainwright's health is not…" Chloe took another breath. "He's had heart problems—three surgeries so far. He doesn't think it would be fair to Jimmy to take him in and then…" Clearing her throat, she met his gaze. "And regardless of his health, Mr. Wainwright doesn't know anything about little boys. He's never had children of his own. However, he does know that Jimmy needs more than an ailing elderly acquaintance or a soulless boarding school to be happy."

Evan knew the amount of love little boys needed. He didn't want or need a reminder. Five-year-old Sean had filled his heart and life. The emptiness was a piercing, never-ending reminder. Looking away from Chloe, he saw the shadows on the front lawn lengthening. Chloe could hardly drive to San Antonio in the fast-approaching darkness. And Rosewood's only bed-and-breakfast was full because of the approaching holidays.

Holidays. Little boys and holidays. The combination used to fill him with joy. Now the dread was inescapable. Still, he couldn't, in good conscience, turn Spencer's boy and this woman out in the night. "Dinner should be ready in about an hour. Thelma will show you to a guest room."

Chloe's delicate features brightened.

"Just for the night," Evan cautioned. "I haven't changed my mind and I'm not going to." Wainwright could send a dozen beautiful women and it wouldn't matter. His ability to love a child had died with his son. And there was no resurrecting it.

* * *

Chloe found herself tiptoeing as she wandered past the entry hall. After Evan Mitchell's rather abrupt dismissal, she wasn't quite sure what to do with herself. He had mentioned dinner and staying the night. Should she bring in their suitcases? No, she told herself. Plunking them on the floor of the immaculate entry or parlor seemed like a terrible idea, especially since hers was a Salvation Army classic. And she wasn't sure where the back entrance was.

Jimmy hadn't emerged since the kind-looking woman had led him away. The scent of sweet fruit and browning pie crust melded with savory vegetables and something else. Beef? Maybe it was stew.

Chloe's stomach growled. "Just like one of Pavlov's dogs," she muttered to herself. She could read a highway sign announcing the next Dairy Queen and suddenly be swamped with a craving for ice cream.

"Chloe?" Jimmy questioned, his voice floating out from deeper in the house. Even from the distance, she could hear the anxiety coating his words.

"We're in the kitchen," Thelma added in a louder voice. "Down the hall to the left. Just pass through the dining room."

Chloe followed her directions, pushing open a swinging door at the end of a long passageway. For a moment she thought she'd stumbled into the kitchen of the Keebler elves. Bright bursts of color caught her attention, pulling her gaze to the limestone counters, the cozy eating nook, the massive stove.

Several pies cooled on the wood sideboard in front of the slightly opened window. Despite the charm of the room, Chloe wanted only to see Jimmy, to make sure he was all right.

She placed an arm over his shoulders. "How we doing, big guy?"

He scooted close to her without replying.

And Chloe wished she could make everything better for him.

"That young man is a super worker," Thelma told her, winking at Jimmy. "Helped me roll out the pie dough."

Chloe squeezed his shoulder. "That's great, Jimmy! I've never been able to make a decent pie crust."

"Cold water's the secret," Thelma continued as though they were old acquaintances. "Ice cold. Otherwise the shortening melts down, makes it tough and the crust falls apart."

"I'll try to remember that." She bent down, closer to Jimmy. "You getting hungry?"

"I'm afraid I've given him quite a few samples of the pie fillings," Thelma confessed. "I knew something was off with the banana cream. So we had to taste that one at least three or four times."

"It was good," Jimmy finally offered.

"It smells delicious," Chloe agreed with a smile for the older woman. "Do you always make this many pies at a time?"

"We have a bake sale every year to raise money for the Angel Tree." She paused, then quieted her voice. "It's for the holidays, you know."

Chloe guessed the fund was to buy toys for children who wouldn't get them otherwise. And she appreciated Thelma's discretion around Jimmy. He'd had more than his share of untimely discoveries.

"Since Evan didn't introduce us, I'm Thelma, the

housekeeper. My husband, Ned, is the… well… he's pretty much the everything-else man. Keeps up the gardens, the cars, whatever needs fixing."

"I'm Chloe Reed. I work for Holden Wainwright."

Thelma started to reach out her hand, then realized it was covered in flour. "Pleased to meet you. And I've thoroughly enjoyed meeting Jimmy. Ned's eaten so many of my pies over the years, he automatically says they taste good no matter what I put in them. The Mitchell men don't like their pies too sweet and Jimmy here helped me balance out the lemon meringue."

Jimmy wasn't distracted, though. His expression was pensive, anxious, worried. And Chloe felt sure he must be exhausted. As kind as Thelma seemed, she was another stranger.

"Would you mind if we walk around the grounds?" Chloe queried.

"Fresh air might do you both good." Thelma dusted the flour from her hands, then wiped them on her apron. "Back door's right over here. You'll find doors in most every room on this level—French doors open out from the front room. And upstairs, there's even a door that leads out and down the staircase from the bedrooms. There's three sets of stairs in the house." She pointed to the one in the kitchen. "We call this one the back stairs. Used to be just for the servants. As for all the doors, I guess a few hundred years ago people felt they might need to get away in a hurry." She chuckled. "There I go, running off at the mouth. Takes a little while to get the feel of the place, but then it seems right homey."

"I'm sure it is," Chloe agreed, edging toward the door.

Thelma smiled. "There's a nice swing out back. Actually two. One on the porch, another under the oak tree. Can't miss either."

"Thank you." Chloe still gripped Jimmy's hand as they stepped outside. The air was clean, tinged with the faint aroma of burning leaves. She guessed that out in the country people didn't have to worry so much about air pollution.

"Let's find the one under the tree," Chloe suggested. As Thelma had said, it was easy to see the glider swing. It sat beneath a tall oak tree that had already lost many of its leaves. Jimmy clung to her hand as she guided him to the cozy-looking spot.

Once seated, Chloe gently urged the glider into motion. "We can rest before dinner if you'd like to."

"Then what?"

Immediately, she wondered if the child had guessed or overheard Evan's intentions. "Then we'll be all stuffed and we'll get a good night's sleep."

"Here?"

"Sure, big guy. That's where we are."

Shoulders hunched, Jimmy's head dropped forward, his shiny hair nearly obscuring still-childish features. "I like sleeping in my own room."

A room he would never again occupy. The house was being sold, along with the majority of its contents. Only photos and sentimental items were being boxed up for storage. All of Jimmy's life, all of his memories. The thought dried her throat, stung her eyes. But Jimmy didn't need sympathy. He needed someone strong to lean on. If that wasn't going to be Evan Mitchell, that left only her. Despite being solely responsible for her mother's care, Chloe couldn't abandon this boy. Even if it meant taking on a forceful, obstinate man like Evan Mitchell.

* * *

Dinner was more formal and somber than Chloe expected. Thelma served them in the dining room, then retreated to the kitchen to eat dinner with her husband. And Evan Mitchell wasn't a very entertaining host. He sat at the head of the table, while she and Jimmy faced each other across the long, banquet-sized table.

Thelma had served them each generous helpings of stew, along with freshly baked biscuits.

"Thelma's oven must stay busy," Chloe ventured. "She was making pies and now these biscuits."

"Umm," Evan replied so sparsely, he might not have even spoken.

Chloe smiled encouragingly at Jimmy, then tried again. "I understood that your father lived here with you."

"It's the family home. We share it."

"Isn't he joining us?"

Evan looked annoyed by her questions. "He's hunting quail with friends out near the Markham ranch. They make a day and night of it."

Chloe dipped her spoon into the savory stew. "This is delicious. Don't you think so, Jimmy?"

He scrunched his narrow shoulders together, the sweep of his dark hair hiding his eyes. "Guess so."

Trying to lighten the glum atmosphere, Chloe took some butter for her biscuit. "Have Thelma and her husband been with you long?"

"Curious, aren't you?" Evan replied. Then he glanced over at Jimmy. "They've been here as long as I can remember."

"Came with the house?" she questioned, hoping to infuse some cheer into the conversation.

Evan looked at her as though she'd suggested swallowing a bucket of mud.

"Just kidding, of course," she tried to remedy. "I haven't had any experience with household employees."

"They're not just employees," he replied sharply. "They're family."

Chastened, Chloe stirred her spoon aimlessly. "Of course." If not for Jimmy, she would have fervently wished for a hole to appear in the floor so she could vanish.

Silence reigned, interrupted only by the scrape of spoons against the bowls. The clinking of china when a coffee cup was returned to its saucer. The last time Chloe had felt this uncomfortable at a dinner table, she'd been twelve years old and painfully aware of the boy sitting across from her. He was fourteen and she had a terrible crush on him. In turn, he considered her a complete nuisance. Seemed she hadn't progressed much from then.

Thelma eventually cleared their dishes and then brought in dessert plates. "Lemon meringue," she announced. "Had some good help making this one. Wasn't hard to decide which one to keep for dessert."

Jimmy glanced at the housekeeper, a furtive, slightly pleased look.

Thelma winked back at him.

Chloe wished the width of the table weren't so broad. She would have liked to squeeze his hand in encouragement. Instead, she smiled at him. Lifting her gaze she caught Evan studying them.

He didn't blink. The woman didn't act like a mere estate representative. Which made him that much more distrustful. Evidently, she stood to profit if she convinced him to accept the guardianship. Wainwright had the funds.

And the old guy had always held a soft spot for Spencer. After the explosion in their newly refurbished factory, Spencer's wishes had been presented. And Wainwright had pled his case as though Spencer were a son rather than the son of a friend.

Committed to placing Jimmy in the Mitchell home, Wainwright may have offered Chloe quite a sum to succeed. Why else would the woman have traveled across the country with no guarantee of how she would be received?

Thelma rustled around the large bedroom as Chloe stared first at the tall ceilings, then the intricate moldings and charming bay window. She gently touched the delicate lace curtains as she admired the four-poster bed and marble-topped dresser. "The room's lovely," she murmured. "It's really a guest room?"

"Evan's mother decorated every room on this floor. The men didn't want her changing the rustic stuff in the den and the parlor's stayed pretty much the same for generations."

"She's passed away, hasn't she? Evan's mother?"

Thelma stopped plumping the pillow she held. "Adele died… several years ago, now. And…" She stopped abruptly.

Chloe knew that Evan was single. Mr. Wainwright had given her a brief sketch about him. Evan ran the family business, in fact, devoted all of his time to it. Could that be why he was so insistent about not taking on Jimmy?

Thelma laid the pillow at the head of the bed, then

checked the growing flames in the fireplace. "Gets chilly this time of year. Family had central heat installed back when Mr. Gordon, Evan's father, was a boy. But when the wind's howling, it's awful nice to have a fire."

Standing next to a wide chaise that was angled by the fireplace, Chloe agreed. "I love a good fire and I haven't had a fireplace of my own in... well, a long time." *Not since the family home had to be sold.*

Thelma crossed the room to an archway containing a door. "This opens into Jimmy's room. It used to be the nursery."

Chloe peeked inside, seeing that he was still fascinated by the interesting little room with its slanted ceiling, nooks, arches and cushioned window seat that overlooked the widow's walk surrounding the upper story. "He may have trouble sleeping tonight. He's had a lot of... changes."

"Mr. Gordon told me all about Jimmy when the lawyer wrote. Poor little tyke. We all hoped Evan..." Thelma sighed. "Mr. Gordon's too old to take on raising the boy himself. Wouldn't be right for Jimmy if...well, if Mr. Gordon couldn't see him all the way through 'til he's old enough to be on his own."

Chloe thought she heard a thread of worry in the woman's voice. "Is Mr. Mitchell ill?"

Thelma shook her head. "He wouldn't retire until a few years ago. Worked hard all his life. Too hard. A boy needs parents who can keep up with him."

"That's how Mr. Wainwright feels, too. When I'm taking care of Jimmy, I have to stay on top speed myself."

A knowing smile lit Thelma's eyes. "I'm guessing you don't mind that too much."

"He's a wonderful little boy." So much so that Chloe knew she would have to rein in her feelings. A huge part of her wished she could just take him back to Milwaukee, raise him as her own. And that was impossible. "Thelma, would it be too much trouble to make some hot cocoa?"

"Course not. I'll bring it up directly."

She didn't want to cause the woman more work. "I'm happy to come and get it."

Waving her hands in dismissal, Thelma tsked. "Don't want to hear another word about it. You just get the little one settled."

Chloe exhaled in relief. Thelma was proving to be an ally. "Thanks." As Thelma left, Chloe knocked lightly on the connecting door frame to Jimmy's room. "Mind if I come in?"

"Uh-uh." Jimmy sat on the edge of the bed, staring out the large window. Still dressed in his best clothes, as though waiting for something that would never happen, he looked completely, inescapably alone.

"Know what I was thinking?" she asked in an encouraging voice.

He shook his head.

"We could get in our jammies, scrunch up on this amazing chair in front of the fireplace in my room and tell stories." Chloe wriggled her eyebrows. "Might even be some hot cocoa in the deal."

"My dad used to read me a story every night and Mommy would sing."

Chloe sat down beside him, putting her arm around his shoulders. "You know, I seem to remember packing a few of your favorite books."

Leaving him to change into his pajamas, Chloe did

the same. By the time she'd tied the sash on her thick, fluffy robe, she heard a light knock on the door. Expecting Thelma, she whipped open the door with a smile.

Evan Mitchell's muscular frame filled the doorway and his forbidding expression sent her smile plummeting.

"If you need anything," he began uncomfortably. "Just ask Thelma."

Chloe clutched her pink robe, excruciatingly aware of the matching bunny slippers on her feet. Trying to tuck them backward just pulled his attention toward the embarrassing footwear.

Straightening her shoulders, she tried to look as businesslike as possible. "We're fine, thank you."

He didn't reply.

Unnerved, she tried to think of something else to say, to distract him, to remove his all-too-male presence. "Thelma's making us some hot cocoa."

"Right." He glanced down the empty corridor.

Chloe fervently wished Thelma would make an appearance.

But the hall remained empty.

"I'll say good night then," Evan finished.

"Good night." Rattled, Chloe shut the door and retreated to the burgundy velvet chaise. Not that she needed the heat from the fire. Touching her cheeks, she confirmed they were warm and no doubt bright red. Oh, yes. Evan Mitchell had seen past her professional facade. All the way to her pink bunny slippers.

Chapter Two

The fire was dying down and their cups of cocoa were empty. Chloe had read three of Jimmy's books, told him several of her favorite stories and he was finally nodding off. It had been an eternally long day for her. She could only imagine how it had tired him. But the little guy didn't complain. Instead, he had cuddled close on the chaise, listening to the stories, and trying to stay awake.

Certain that he was ready for bed, she scooped him up from the lounger.

"I'm not sleepy," he mumbled, his head falling on her shoulder.

"I know, big guy. We'll just rest for a while." Chloe carried him through the adjoining door into the nursery. Thelma had made up both the child's bed and the single bed nearby. Chloe gently deposited him on the smaller bed. Then she grabbed his stuffed dog, Elbert, and laid it close. Pulling the sheet and handmade quilt up to his chin, she kept her voice low. "Snug as a bug in a rug."

Jimmy's eyelids were drifting closed, but he struggled to keep them open. "Don't go."

"Okay." She sat on the edge of his bed, softly singing one of the Irish lullabies her mother had sung to her when she was little.

Chloe hummed the chorus again, watching until finally the gentle rise and fall of his chest told her that Jimmy had nodded off. Quietly she returned to her room, leaving the door to the nursery open. Warmed by the dwindling fire, she crossed over to the bay window. Old-fashioned streetlights—that she guessed had been converted from oil—softly illuminated the brick-paved street below. She hadn't imagined such quaint places still existed. As she studied the engaging landscape, she spotted a lone figure walking up the lane. When the man reached the Mitchell home he turned and headed to the tall oak on the knolled rise of the lawn.

Unable to take her eyes from the man, she glimpsed his face when he stepped beside the gas light in the yard. Evan Mitchell. She shouldn't be surprised. After all, it was his home. Continuing to watch, she saw him sit on a stone bench that curved around the tree. Evan just didn't seem like the sort of man to take solitary night-time walks. Fleetingly she wondered if he was cold.

Not that it should matter to her. His behavior had been utterly frigid. Still, she wondered why he sat alone, what drove him out in the chilly night. Wisps of clouds drifted, allowing some moonlight to filter downward. Evan looked up in the direction of the light. His expression was so bleak, Chloe's hand flew to her mouth to stop an automatic cry of distress. What was troubling him so deeply?

Not that he would confide in her. Nor should she want him to. Evan was the enemy, the man who decided Jimmy's fate. But the part of her that always reached out to others refused to stay quiet. Was it possible that Evan had issues that she needed to learn? Issues he had to resolve before accepting a child in his life?

The questions stilled. Because Evan Mitchell dropped his head in his hands. And Chloe couldn't intrude on his private moment any longer.

Even though the soft feather bed was incredibly comfortable, Chloe couldn't sleep. Literally tossing and shifting in the bed, she'd twisted the sheets and lace crocheted coverlet into a tangled mess. But sleep was impossible with the mass of conflicting thoughts racing through her mind. Hearing a sudden cry, she bolted upright. Remembering the small set of wooden stairs beside the mattress for climbing in and out of the tall bed, she clicked on her lamp so she could find them. Untangling herself from the covers, she grabbed her robe and raced into the adjoining room.

Jimmy was sitting up in the bed, looking terrified.

Immediately, Chloe reached out to pull him into her arms. Rocking him back and forth, she imparted all the comfort she possessed. "It's okay," she murmured. "You're safe. I'm right here." He shook with a convulsed sob and Chloe's eyes filled. If only she could take his pain for him. Rubbing his back, she held him until he was finally still. Pulling back slightly, she smoothed the dark hair from his forehead. "Was it a dream?"

He nodded, a jerky motion. "And when I woke up I didn't know where I was."

"I wasn't having much luck sleeping either. I'd probably go to sleep faster if I wasn't alone." She rubbed her chin as though in deep concentration. "Do you suppose

I could sleep on the extra bed in here? It would really help me out."

This time when he nodded, he looked up at her with relief in his big brown eyes.

She eased the tears from his cheeks with her fingers. "I know I'll feel safe in here with you."

He sniffled.

"Okay, better get that bug snug again." He dutifully laid back down and she tucked him in. "If it wouldn't keep you awake, I'd kind of like to keep the little light on."

"It's okay," he agreed gratefully.

She smoothed his hair once more. "Thanks."

Climbing into the bed she guessed once belonged to a nanny, Chloe actually did feel better. She had been worried about Jimmy being alone, frightened in the strange house. She smoothed the blanket in place, leaving her arms out. Now, if she could just get Evan Mitchell out of her thoughts. Sighing, she realized that wouldn't be nearly as easy.

Early morning sunlight invaded Chloe's face. Scrunching her eyes, she reached for the sheet to cover them. Awareness hit at the same instant. Immediately, she looked at Jimmy's bed. It was empty. Fear filled her chest. Surely he hadn't run away. He didn't know anyone in Rosewood.

Blinking, she focused again and saw his pajamas thrown across the bed. Next to them was his stuffed dog, Elbert. Jimmy wouldn't have left his treasured friend behind.

Although reassured, she dressed quickly so she could

look for him. Evan Mitchell wouldn't welcome a curious, roaming child in his house.

Once downstairs, she headed toward the kitchen,
but paused when she heard voices in the dining room.
Walking slowly, she approached the group.

"You must be Chloe," a gray-haired man boomed in
a deep voice. He stood up, keeping Jimmy close to his
side. "I'm Gordon Mitchell, Evan's father. Sure pleased
to have you here."

Surreptitiously glancing around, she didn't see Evan,
and relaxed. "Thank you."

Thelma poured another mug of coffee and handed it
to Chloe. "Morning. How'd you sleep?"

"Very well, thanks. It's a beautiful room." She
glanced at Gordon. "A beautiful house."

"Too empty, though." He patted Jimmy's shoulder.
"Need some young energy to fill it up again."

Unwilling to discuss Evan's refusal in front of
Jimmy, Chloe sipped the bracing brew.

Jimmy knelt down. "Did you see the dog, Chloe?"

A calm golden retriever seemed delighted by Jimmy's attention, waving a beautifully plumed tail and
pushing his muzzle into Jimmy's hand.

"I don't remember seeing him yesterday," she mused.

"Bailey was with me," Gordon explained. "Hunting.
But he pined for Evan the whole time."

"He's Evan's dog?" Chloe asked in surprise.

"Bailey's usually camped out by Evan's side, clinging like thistle. Jimmy's pretty special to have tempted
him away."

"French toast this morning." Thelma winked at
Jimmy. "Thought I might find somebody who'd like it."

"Sounds great." Chloe slipped into a chair. "How did your hunting trip go, Mr. Mitchell?"

"Best part of it is the guys. We tell the same stories we've told each other for the last fifty years, and now that we're getting on, some of 'em even sound new again." His dark eyes crinkled with kindness.

Although she could see the resemblance between the two generations of men, Gordon exuded warmth, friendliness. Chloe wanted to relax, but she was still facing a major confrontation.

The thought apparently conjured up the man in question. Evan stalked into the room, crossing over to the sideboard to pour a mug of coffee. Bailey jumped up and ran to his side. Evan rubbed the dog's head. As he did, Evan turned, his gaze narrowing first on Chloe, then Jimmy and finally his father.

Thelma pushed open the door from the kitchen, holding a large platter. She placed the French toast in the middle of the table. "Eat it while it's hot."

Chloe turned to Jimmy. "Looks good, doesn't it?" Hoping Evan wouldn't open with an argument, she speared one piece.

Gordon passed the pitcher of warm syrup. "Thelma dusts the toast in powdered sugar, but I still like my maple syrup. How 'bout you, Jimmy?"

"I like syrup," he replied in a tiny voice.

Knowing Jimmy was nervous, she patted his leg. "Me, too."

Evan continued to stare at his father.

Gordon met his son's gaze, his voice deceptively casual. "I was just about to invite Chloe and Jimmy to stay for a while. Won't be long 'til Thanksgiving. Holidays are always better with children, more family."

A vein in Evan's muscular neck bulged, while his lips thinned into an angry line. He pushed back his chair, scraping it loudly over the wide planked floor as he rose. "I have to get to work."

His boots rang loudly as he left, and the sound of the door slamming echoed through the house. Bailey whined, then laid down next to the front door, apparently waiting for his master.

"Did I make him mad?" Jimmy asked in an even smaller voice.

"Of course not!" Chloe rushed to reassure him. "He probably has problems at work that are on his mind, that's all." She glanced at Gordon. "It's a family business, isn't it?"

Gordon nodded. "Mitchell Stone. My great-grandfather started the quarry with not much more than a land claim and a box of dynamite. A few men agreed to work with him in exchange for shares in the company. A lot of their descendants are fourth-generation employees now."

Chloe glanced upward at the elegant chandelier, just one of the impressive fixtures in the obviously expensive home. "So your family built all this up themselves?"

He chuckled softly. "First house wasn't much more than a tar shack. The way I heard it, my great-grandmother threatened to dig enough stone out of the quarry herself to build a decent house. But in time, they built a small wood cottage—it's the carriage house we use for a garage now."

"I think Thelma mentioned that you're retired?"

"Yep. Evan's in charge now."

Chloe swallowed, hating to pry, but needing to know as much as possible about Evan. "Is that a good thing?"

"He lives and breathes work. Since the recession, Evan's done everything he can to keep the place together so no one loses their jobs. It's a Mitchell trait, I suppose." Gordon absently tapped his fingers against the tabletop. "Feeling responsible. Can't let go when…"

Chloe waited quietly.

But Gordon glanced up, reined in his memories and lifted a mug of coffee. "So, it's settled. You and Jimmy will stay here. I'd like to show you around town. See the school, the church. People are friendly in Rosewood. Not much like a big city."

"Milwaukee's not small, but it is down to earth," Chloe replied. "Kind of the best between a small town and a big city."

"You have family there?"

Chloe nodded, thinking of her mother, worrying about her. "My father passed away when I was in junior high school. My younger brother, Chip, is in the army—he and his family are stationed in Germany. And my mother lives in an extended care facility. She has COPD—it's a chronic pulmonary condition. Because of it, she can't live on her own. If she had a bad episode and no one was around, it could be…" she glanced down at Jimmy, then up to meet the understanding in Gordon's eyes. "Since I work full-time, it's safest where she is."

"Much extended family?"

"They all live pretty far away in the rural part of the state. But Milwaukee still clings to its ethnic roots. We have areas that are primarily German, Romanian, Hungarian. Makes neighborhoods friendly."

"Sounds familiar."

"Rosewood has neighborhoods like that?"

He smiled. "Pretty much the whole town. We're a dying breed, but we don't cotton to superstores, tourist traps. So far, we've been able to keep them out. The news always says mom-and-pop businesses can't survive, but they do here." Gordon chuckled. "Sounds like I'm about a century old with my reminiscing."

Chloe was liking him more and more. "I noticed the town was pretty when we were driving through." She lowered her lashes, trying to hide some of her anxiety from Jimmy. "But I was too nervous…driving in an unfamiliar rental car to pay very much attention."

"Then we need to take care of that." He turned to Jimmy, who was adding even more syrup to his plate. "What do you say? After breakfast, we check things out?"

Jimmy appeared shy but pleased.

While she was looking forward to their tour, Chloe didn't know how it was going to help matters. The look in Evan's eyes that morning had said it all. He wasn't about to change his mind.

Evan studied the latest financial report. Mitchell Stone was sinking as though pummeled by its own boulders.

Perry Perkin, their chief financial officer, shoved both hands in his pockets. "Numbers won't get any better by staring at them."

"Yeah." But he had to turn around the profits. The employees depended on him, most were like family. "Construction business is picking up. Got two new orders this week."

"Small ones. Evan, you know they aren't going to carry the payroll."

"Recession hit everyone, Perry. It'll take time for bigger deals to roll in." Mitchell Stone had operations all over the hill country and in other parts of the state. Even though most of Texas hadn't been hit as hard by the recession as the rest of the country, new construction was still down. And many of their orders had been national as well as international, customers that still remained on shaky ground. "We'll make the payroll."

"If you keep putting your personal money in the business, you'll tank when it does."

"*If,* not when." Evan plowed his fingers through his hair, then looked out the window at Main Street. "You know we've had our offices in this building more than a century. My great-grandfather didn't want to confine himself to one quarry, so he insisted on having an office right in the middle of town. That's why he kept looking for more sources, staking more claims all his life. Then my grandfather and my father. And there was a little thing called the Great Depression that happened along the way. But Mitchell Stone never closed its doors. I don't intend to let it happen on my watch."

Perry was empathetic but realistic. "You know as well as I do, that the first decade of this millennium wasn't hit by just a recession. It was a depression."

"Plattville is accepting bids next month on their new courthouse. If we can get a lock on who wins the job…" Speculating, Evan knew Mitchell Stone would be one of dozens interested in supplying the limestone.

Perry sighed. "Look, I've got some savings. More than my shares in the company. I'll cut my salary down to just enough to cover my health insurance."

"You can't do that."

"I'm in charge of payroll. Be pretty hard to stop me. And, I can just about guarantee that everybody else would understand a cut in pay. In fact, they would support the idea, so we don't have to close."

"No. Let's take it slow. Holidays are just about here. I'm not taking Christmas dinner out of any mouths."

"You're a good man, Evan." Perry sighed. "I'm just not sure you know when to say no."

Chapter Three

"No!" Evan looked exasperated as he spoke to his father.

Gordon put his hand on Jimmy's shoulder. "If you don't have time now to show Jimmy the quarry, we'll do it another day."

Chloe held her breath, hoping the men wouldn't argue.

"Course I could do it myself..." Gordon continued. "Not sure I still have my keys to the outer gates, though."

Evan rolled his eyes heavenward. "I'll fit it in this week or next. Don't you have enough to keep busy today?"

Gordon rubbed his chin in thought. "Well, I do have a doctor's appointment...."

Chloe choked back unexpected laughter, coughing to cover the sound. Gordon had told them he had a checkup scheduled with the foot doctor. He sure was milking the excuse for all it was worth. And clearly it was working.

Concern filled Evan's face. "You didn't tell me."

Gordon shrugged, his face on the verge of woeful. "You've already got a lot on your mind."

Evan glanced at his father, then plunked a pile of papers down on his desk. "You want me to take you to the doctor?"

Clearing his throat, Gordon shook his head. "Not necessary."

Reluctantly, Evan shifted his gaze to Chloe. "I'll show them around the quarry. But I can't spend all day."

Chloe knew his last words were directed at her. "I've never been to a quarry before."

"I've never met any women who wanted to before."

Tension bubbled through the air like hail stones.

"So that's settled." Gordon turned to leave. "I'll see you all back at the house."

"I told you I can't..." Evan didn't bother to complete the sentence since his father was walking away without listening.

"Spend all day," Chloe completed for him. "Jimmy and I understand, don't we, big guy?"

Jimmy, looking intimidated by Evan, nodded tentatively.

For the briefest moment, Evan's countenance turned utterly bleak. He shook the expression off as quickly as it had formed, then picked up his phone, punching in a few numbers. "Perry? Push the meeting with Alsom back two hours." He listened a few moments. "Oh yeah, I'll definitely be back in time for the bank."

Chloe got the message. The visit would be brief, but any time Evan spent with Jimmy would help.

Outside, parked in front of the building, were a few shiny new SUVs and three double-cab trucks. At the end of the row was a beat-up pickup truck. Since all of the vehicles were emblazoned with Mitchell Stone logos, Chloe trailed behind Evan waiting to hear the chirp of doors unlocking.

When he paused in front of the ragged old beater, Chloe couldn't help staring.

Evan walked to the passenger door and opened it.

Jimmy immediately tugged on her hand. "You get in first, please?"

Since he drew out *please* like a deathbed request, she reluctantly scooted over to the middle position in the single cab.

While Evan slid in front of the steering wheel, Chloe scrunched over as close as possible to Jimmy.

Glancing in the rearview mirror, Evan backed out on to the lazy Main Street. Even though it was near noon, not much traffic flowed through the quaint downtown area that looked as though it had stayed primarily the same since Victorian times.

"Swell truck," she commented.

He darted a glance, obviously gauging her sarcasm. "It was my grandfather's."

"It's nice."

The corners of his mouth curled down.

"That you kept it, I mean," she added hastily. "A lot of people just want the newest model. I think sentiment's more important."

"Hmm."

Chloe had already figured out that he wouldn't be easily convinced of anything. Apparently, Evan was equally economic with his words.

As they rolled out of town toward the quarry, the old truck bumped considerably. One especially large bump thrust her against Evan's shoulder. Feeling as though she had hit heated rock, Chloe drew back, immediately scooting toward the passenger-side door.

"Ouch," Jimmy squeaked.

"I'm sorry! I was...concentrating too much on the landscape." At the moment she couldn't have guessed if they were surrounded by mountains or desert.

"You mean the trees?"

Feeling smaller than the child at her side, she tried to look unaffected. "Pretty aren't they?"

Actually they were. Leaves had transformed into clusters of color. Standing next to sentinel green pines, this was the beautiful Texas hill country she'd heard so much about. But the squiggle in her stomach didn't have anything to do with the surroundings—the non-human ones, that was. Still feeling the impression of Evan's shoulder against her arm, she wanted to touch the spot, to see if the fire she'd felt was external. Ridiculous, she knew. A grown woman practically melting by the accidental brush of a man's arm. A very handsome man's arm.

"We're not far," Evan announced.

Still ruminating on her reaction, again she overreacted, jumping when he spoke. "Well... that's good then." At this rate she would reduce her conversational skills to a first grader's level.

"Look!" Jimmy poked her as his voice threaded with something close to excitement.

Chloe followed his gaze. A beautiful horse trotted in a field, lifting its head in a royal motion.

Evan didn't take his eyes from the road. "He's an Arabian. Belongs to the Markhams."

"That's a neat trick," she commented. "How did you know without looking?"

"This is my home," he explained simply.

"Still...."

"At the curve, there's an old oak that's got more notches on it than an outlaw's gun. One of them's mine. Most everybody in town's hit that oak when they were learning to drive. Luckily, the tree's over far enough that no one's run into it straight on."

How could a man who obviously cared about his home and employees have absolutely no compassion for a parentless child? Burdened with the thought, Chloe didn't ask any more questions as Evan drove farther from town. Jimmy, still intimidated, didn't speak either. And Evan clearly wasn't going to initiate a conversation.

In the quiet, Chloe saw much more of the gently rolling hills, the yellowing of wild grass, the last wildflowers struggling to survive despite the bite of late autumn. The hill country really was a beautiful place for the holidays.

Back home, they would have a wintry cold Thanksgiving and a guaranteed white Christmas. She wasn't missing the weather. Or her job. Just her mother. And Barbara Reed had been insistent that Chloe accept this assignment. Still, she was so used to caring for her mother...visiting her in the long-term recovery facility, spending every spare minute with her. Intensely aware of the thousand-plus miles that separated them, Chloe sighed.

"Something wrong?" Evan asked.

Again, his unexpected speaking startled her. This time her hand flew to her throat to disguise the rapid pulse that must be visible. "No... of course not."

"Hmm."

How did the man run a business when he barely

spoke? Feeling the opportunity, she cleared her throat. "Actually, I was thinking about my mother. Missing her."

Evan took his eyes from the road. "Then why'd you come all the way out here?"

Because she needed the money Mr. Wainwright had offered to continue paying for her mother's care.

Jimmy looked up at her and she smiled for his benefit. "I wouldn't miss this adventure for anything."

Evan snorted. "Adventure?"

"Sure, neither of us has ever been to Texas." Chloe struggled for something benign to say. "Or a quarry."

This time when he glanced at her, she met his dark eyes, sustaining the gaze. Despite the disbelief lurking in their depths, she felt the same as she had when she'd bumped into his shoulder. Silly but....

Chloe swallowed. She hadn't experienced that kind of reaction to a man since her ex-fiancé, Derek, had dumped her. Must just be nerves, she told herself. That, and knowing how much was riding on her swaying Evan Mitchell to change his mind.

Still, she straightened up, holding her body rigidly in place. And kept herself in that position until they neared a large sign indicating the quarry. Unexpectedly excited, Chloe leaned forward when Evan turned off the main road.

Bumping over the rutted dirt road, dust billowed behind them in a dark cloud. Evan didn't slow down. Clearly the pitted road was familiar to him, so familiar he knew its ups and downs, its twists and curves.

Not surprisingly, the small office, barely more than a shed, was built of limestone.

"Is the quarry in that building?" Jimmy asked in a disappointed voice.

Evan chuckled, startling Chloe and Jimmy. "Nope. It's the big pit we're driving to when we switch vehicles."

Transfixed by the difference in Evan when he smiled, Chloe didn't pay attention to the quarry until Jimmy poked her arm, pointing out the large slabs of stone literally everywhere.

Chloe tried to think of something intelligent to say; she reverted to the familiar. "Do you sell stone from this office?"

"Small jobs like home remodels. All the commercial orders come through the main office." He pulled the truck up close to the small building.

"Is the quarry nearby?" Chloe asked, as curious as Jimmy.

"We'll grab a buggy to get over there." Evan got out of the truck and disappeared.

Chloe wriggled her eyebrows at Jimmy. "Sounds cool."

He loosened up slightly. "Evan doesn't even sound mad at me."

Chloe's heart pinged and she impulsively wrapped her arms around him. "He isn't mad at you, honey. If anything, he's mad at himself."

"How come?"

Yes. Why? "Because he's the sort of man who's used to being in control, in charge, like at his company. And, when Evan's in unfamiliar territory…he's confused. And that makes him mad. Let's get out of the truck and be ready when he brings the buggy around, okay?"

Evan appeared shortly in what resembled a golf cart. "Hop in."

When Jimmy hesitated, Chloe climbed in, taking a spot in the back so Jimmy could ride up front next to Evan.

When Jimmy continued to hesitate, Evan's impatient expression relented a fraction; he shrugged his head to one side. "Come on. You ride shotgun."

Once Jimmy was onboard, Evan didn't speed off as Chloe imagined he wanted to. Instead, he drove slowly, pointing out various formations.

"This quarry is limestone." Evan pointed to a newly excavated vein. "See the different colors? The clay and the iron oxide cause that." He drove past the open pit to a second pit. "Now, this limestone's been weathered a long time, about a hundred and forty years. That's why the color's different than the new vein. Subtle change, though. Takes stone thousands of years to form, sometimes more to change."

Jimmy's big brown eyes grew even larger. "How do you grow more, then?"

Evan's mouth curved as though about to smile. As quickly, he pulled his eyebrows together in a serious expression. "We can't. Have you heard about taking care of the environment?"

Solemnly, Jimmy nodded. "Daddy and Mommy said we have to take care of the earth. That it's our job, so that's why we have to use green things." He looked up at Evan. "That doesn't mean the color green."

"So I've heard. Which is why we use every part of the stone we dig up. After the big slabs are cut, we use the small pieces for all kinds of things—cement, mortar, it even goes in toothpaste."

"We brush our teeth with rocks?" Jimmy asked, forgetting his fear, completely intrigued.

Evan's lips definitely twitched. "Helps that they flavor it with mint. Oh, and bubble gum for kids."

Bubble-gum flavored toothpaste? Funny thing for a single man to know about. Mr. Wainwright had told her that Evan was an only child. So no nieces or nephews. Of course he could have seen the product in a commercial.

Chloe had wondered if Evan's stubborn refusal to even consider taking Jimmy in was because of being an only child. Never having to share. Maybe he hadn't left the trait behind with his childhood. Maybe he didn't want to share his life, either.

She found that terribly sad. Even though Chloe had felt the impact of financial problems for years, she wouldn't trade caring for her mother. Not for a zillion dollars. But the money Holden Wainwright had promised her if she succeeded in placing Jimmy with the Mitchells would change their lives. There would be no more angst-ridden moments of worrying whether she would be able to pay the rising costs of the care facility.

"Are most of the rocks for toothpaste?" Jimmy was asking Evan.

"Nope. Most of it's used in architecture. Have you heard of the Great Pyramids? They're in Egypt where your grandparents are. Anyway, they're made of limestone."

"I didn't know that," Chloe blurted out, belatedly realizing she had verbalized her thought.

"Castles in medieval times were made from it, too." Evan replied, unperturbed by her question.

"With dragons?" Jimmy asked with the first note of genuine, full-out excitement she had heard in his voice.

Evan scratched his head. "Hard to say. We don't carry dragons at our quarries."

Chloe nearly giggled aloud, not something she would have ever anticipated doing with Evan.

The thought had barely formed when he turned around. "I have to get back to the office soon. Where did you leave your car?"

"The house," she admitted, belatedly realizing that hadn't been a well-thought-out plan.

Evan glanced at his watch, then scowled. "Have to head back now, then."

By the time they returned the cart and switched back to the truck, Evan was impatient to get to his meeting. He pulled into the driveway at the house, leaving the engine running. Jimmy hopped out immediately. Chloe started to follow, but Evan caught her arm.

"We have to talk. Soon." He met her eyes, his own making her shiver unexpectedly. "When we're alone."

Chapter Four

*A*lone. Evan waited through dinner, then coffee and cake in the parlor. Chloe had managed to keep someone within a foot of her the entire time. He wouldn't be surprised if she super-glued Jimmy to one of her hands.

And his head was throbbing. The meeting with the bank president had gone so poorly he didn't expect a follow-up visit would change a thing. Evan, like the rest of his family before him, had kept his business with the local bank. No connections to any of the large multinational banks. He couldn't blame his local banker. Loans, especially big commercial loans, still weren't the flavor of the day. And Mitchell Stone had been operating in the red for the last three years.

It hadn't helped that during the meeting, he couldn't forget his other immediate problem. Sending Chloe and Jimmy back to Milwaukee. The boy resembled Spencer too much, making him remember too much...about too many things.

A sudden image of Sean seared his thoughts. His son would be seven now, too. Sean should have been the one sitting in the cart beside him as they toured the quarry, learning as Evan had, from a young age to appreciate both the family business and the blessings of the earth, what it gave up to us.

Sean had wanted to learn—every waking moment of every day. What kind of bird nested in the tall oak out front? Why did Grandpa's hair turn gray? How did the dew form on the grass? A million questions, he had thought at the time, hoping he wouldn't run out of answers. He had never dreamed it would be Sean who would run out of time.

And his beautiful Robin... The Lord had never made a sweeter woman. She had lived her life for her family, and ultimately died trying to save Sean. If only.... If only he hadn't chosen Hawaii to vacation. But Robin had always wanted to visit there and he had delighted at the surprise on her face when he had given her a dream vacation for her birthday. She and Sean had counted the days until they flew to the beautiful islands.

Evan would give anything to turn back the calendar, to change that one dreadful decision. He swallowed, knowing life didn't work that way.

"Son?" Gordon repeated.

Evan shook his head, then lifted his gaze. "Sorry, Dad."

Gordon's eyes filled with empathy and understanding. "I'm going to teach Jimmy how to tie some flies. Thought we'd go fishing Saturday. How does that sound?"

Like another painful reminder. "Whatever you want."

Concern lingered in Gordon's eyes.

And Evan didn't want to worry his father. "Be good to go before winter sets in." Thanksgiving was right around the corner; Christmas would descend in seeming days.

"That's what I was thinking. Chloe says her father used to go ice fishing up in Wisconsin. Makes my bones shiver to think about it."

Evan glanced in her direction. "Doesn't your father ice fish anymore?"

"My dad died when I was in junior high school," she explained. Although Chloe's voice was steady, he glimpsed a flash of pain in her eyes.

"Sorry." Evan knew the words were inadequate. He had heard the phrase often enough in the past two years.

"It's been a long time."

But never long enough. Time heals all wounds. He had heard that one so much it made him sick. That and *the Lord never gives us more than we can bear.* But there had been no reason to take Robin and Sean. Again his throat swelled and Evan couldn't speak around the lump it caused.

Chloe glanced down, then patted Jimmy's knee. Clearly, she knew that the discussion could upset him, might have already done so.

Evan wondered how Wainwright had found this woman. Someone as pugnacious as a bulldog, yet obviously sensitive to a child's needs.

Gordon stood and clapped one hand on Jimmy's shoulder. "Let's go in the den. Those flies aren't going to tie themselves."

They had barely begun walking from the room when Chloe rose. When she passed his chair, Evan snagged her arm.

Startled, Chloe pulled back, her hand immediately brushing the spot where he had touched her.

Funny, he felt a strange tingle at the touch himself. Ignoring it, Evan waited until Gordon and Jimmy were out of hearing. "We need to talk."

"In here?" she asked weakly.

"No. Too many interruptions." He stood, grabbing her hand. Again the feeling shot clear through his body. Again he ignored it. He led her through the kitchen, out the back door. The wide, wrap-around porch was lit by soft gas lights.

"The days are shorter," Chloe commented, sounding nervous. "Gets dark so early." She pointed toward the sky. "Good there's moonlight."

"Are you a stargazer, Miss Reed?"

"Chloe," she insisted. "Yes, I suppose I am. Not that I've had time to—"

"How *do* you spend your time? Convincing people to make bad decisions?"

Anger flashed in her sea-green eyes. She was right. The light from the moon aided the gas lights enough to read her expression. Chloe's mouth opened, then she firmed her lips into a resolute line as she pulled her shoulders back. "I work, if you must know."

"That's what you call it?"

The anger in her face intensified. "What did you want to talk to me about?"

So, she had a temper. "Surely it's clear, even to you, that Wainwright's plan isn't going to work."

"Why are you so negative? You act as though Jimmy has some sort of disease. He's a wonderful child!"

"I didn't say he isn't." The boy seemed like a good kid. On the quiet side, but Evan didn't expect anything different after what Jimmy had been through.

"Then what is it?" Exasperation spilled into her voice.

"I told you my answer is *no.*"

Chloe paused, tilting her face so that the moonlight enhanced the beguiling heart shape of her face. "Your father seems to have a different opinion."

Evan tried to ignore the unwanted feeling her proximity caused. "It's not going to work, regardless of what my father says. There's no room in my life for a child. I'm fighting to keep the business alive. I have twenty-seven employees who depend on me for their livelihood. Do you expect me to forget about them?"

"Of course not." The exasperation had left her voice. Concern replaced it. "But that doesn't mean you can't do both. You have help—your father, Thelma and Ned."

"What is it about *no* that you don't understand? This isn't like a pet rescue. I can't turn Jimmy out in the yard with Bailey if I don't want him close to me. He needs parents, not a guardian."

"But with time—"

"There isn't going to be any time." Evan's constant anguish flared so fiercely it felt like a physical blow. The back door opened and Jimmy ran outside, followed more slowly by Gordon.

"Guess what?" Jimmy asked Chloe with a glimmer of excitement. "Tomorrow we're going to see the school."

All four adults looked at one another. Chloe seemed uncertain. Gordon was determined. And Evan knew he had to stop this from happening. At all costs.

Chloe and Jimmy had disappeared upstairs. Evan made certain of it before he confronted his father.

"What were you thinking? Telling the boy you'll show him our school?"

Gordon knocked the ashes from his pipe into an ash-tray. "Why shouldn't he see it?"

"You know exactly why. Jimmy will think that means he'll be staying on for a while."

"Son, he needs us."

Evan snorted. "There are thousands of orphaned children who need homes. Are we going to take them in as well?"

Gordon packed cherry tobacco into the bowl of his worn pipe. "He's family."

Evan felt his chest heave with pain. Family would never again mean the same thing for him. "Are you planning to take care of him?"

"We had that talk when Wainwright first called."

Slumping into a deep leather chair, Evan sighed. "Why are you doing this to me, Dad?"

Gordon stopped tamping down the tobacco, which didn't really matter since he never lit the pipe. "It's not *to* you, son. It's *for* you. When we first lost Robin and Sean, I knew it would take you a long time to accept that you still have a life. It's natural."

"*Accept* it? I'll never accept it. There was no reason for them to die."

"You did everything you could to—"

"But the Lord didn't!" Furious, he rose.

"We don't always understand—"

"I've heard it all before. And I don't want to hear it again."

Gordon sighed. "This boy is another chance for you, son. The Lord knows of the hole in your heart."

"A replacement?" Evan laughed bitterly. "A cosmic reparation? No. I lost the only son I'll ever have."

"Evan, you—"

"If you persist in having them stay here, he's your responsibility."

"Son, it doesn't do you any good to be angry at the Lord."

Sadness and pain settled in Evan's heart. "I'm not angry at Him. I'm disappointed. And that won't ever change."

"All the grades go together?" Jimmy asked in a hushed voice, tightening his grip on Chloe's hand as they stood in the main hall of Rosewood Community Church's school.

"Not in the same room," Chloe explained, although she wasn't certain just how the school was organized.

Gordon nodded. "That's how it was when I was a boy."

Jimmy looked at him in awe, as though the older man had said he had attended school with the dinosaurs. "*You* went to school here?"

Chloe and Gordon both chuckled.

"Yep. We'd invented fire by then." Gordon clapped one hand on Jimmy's shoulder, giving him a small hug while he exchanged an amused glance with Chloe.

Just then a pretty woman walked out of the office.

"Well, hello, Grace."

"Gordon!" She smiled, a generous smile that lit up her blue-gray eyes. "I heard the hunting went very well."

He turned to Chloe. "Ah, the bane of small towns. Can't get by with much that everybody doesn't know about."

"Afraid that's true," Grace agreed.

"I'm forgetting my manners. Grace, this is Chloe Reed and Jimmy Mitchell."

"So good to meet you," she said to Chloe, then extended her hand to Jimmy. "Always glad to meet another Mitchell man."

Pleased, but shy, Jimmy grinned.

"I don't have a class this hour," Grace continued. "Can I help you find anything?"

"Thought it'd be nice to show them around. You know, a little tour, before they meet the principal," Gordon explained.

"I'd be glad to help. I teach part-time in the upper grades, but I know all the buildings." She leaned down slightly toward Jimmy and confided, "The kids call me *old lady Brady.*"

Chloe couldn't restrain her laughter. "We're probably close in age. Didn't realize I was in that category yet."

Grace laughed with her. "Came as quite a shock to me, too. Teaching is my second and best career. Didn't realize it would age me so!"

Gordon groaned. "You kids are killing me."

"You are a sweetheart," Grace declared as she turned to Chloe. "See why I love the Mitchell men?"

Chloe had seen plenty of reasons, even in Evan. Because for all his protests, she suspected he was covering a deep and grievous hurt.

Grace led them down the main hall. "We're in the administration building. Besides the office, the cafeteria, library and auditorium are in this building. There are separate buildings for elementary, junior high and senior high. Since it's a church school, we're not funded by the government but we have private donors. I imagine you'd like to see the elementary building."

The cheerful building was filled with colorful banners and posters. "Kindergarten through fifth-grade classes," Grace explained as they passed individual classrooms. "There's also a smaller, all-purpose room for the youngest grades. The plays and larger performances are held in the auditorium. More room for all the doting parents and grandparents." Grace paused in front of one classroom. "This is a first-grade class."

"Is there more than one?" Chloe asked, liking the positive energy in the school.

"That depends on enrollment. Our elementary teachers are certified to teach two or three grades. That way we can adjust to make sure class sizes aren't too large."

"Sounds like you've thought of everything."

"Are you a teacher, too?" Grace questioned.

"No. I'm a sec… I work for a legal firm out of Milwaukee."

Gordon looked at her strangely, and Chloe fiddled with her purse handles, worrying about her near slip.

"A fellow big-city native! I'm from Houston."

Chloe was immediately curious. "How do you like living here?"

"It's perfect," she replied in a soft voice. "I love it."

"Met her husband here," Gordon added.

Grace blushed, a gentle pink. "Yes. You'll meet him at church. He's the choir director."

"A musician?"

She smiled widely. "Actually, Noah's a plastic surgeon who happens to love music. Works out well because I do, too."

"Do you teach music?"

"Actually, I teach English." Grace laughed again. "You probably think you've wandered into the land of Oz where nothing is as it seems. A choir director who's a doctor and a musician who teaches English."

Chloe liked Grace's infectious smile and laughter. "I'm enjoying Oz just fine."

"Are we in Oz?" Jimmy asked in a confused tone.

Chloe met Grace's glance and broke into another round of laughter. Then she knelt down next to Jimmy. "Oz is a pretend place. It's very colorful and full of surprises."

With a child's understanding, Jimmy nodded. "But the school's real?"

"Very," Gordon replied. "Do you like what you've seen?"

Jimmy nodded. "I don't like big schools."

"Me, either," Grace confided. "I was kind of scared when I started teaching, but at this school, all the people are nice and welcoming. In no time, I felt right at home."

Grace might teach upper grades, but she had the perfect touch for young children. Chloe was glad they had run into her. She mouthed *thank you* above Jimmy's head.

"I know how it is to be new to Rosewood," Grace continued. She reached into her pocket, pulling out a pen and notepad. She scribbled on one page quickly, then handed it to Chloe. "This is my cell number. I'd like to help you settle in."

Chloe felt at a loss as to how to answer. Her position was so tenuous.

Gordon replied for her. "That's mighty nice of you, Grace. And, of course, we'll see you at church Sunday."

Church. Because she spent every Sunday visiting

her mother, it had been a long time since Chloe had been in a church. But their pastor visited at the care facility, mostly seeing her mom. Chloe's faith had never wavered. Which was comforting, because she would need it now more than ever.

Chapter Five

Evan could scarcely believe he had been dragged into this fishing trip. With mountains of work waiting on his desk, he was standing on the shore of the river, casting into the flowing currents. He glanced over at his father. After breakfast, as the others were readying for the trip, his father had sat down suddenly, seeming out of breath. Gordon insisted he was all right. So much so that it worried Evan. Was it a ruse to make him go fishing as well? To spend more time with Jimmy?

His father refused to call the doctor or stop by the clinic, which was open Saturday mornings. Ruse or not, Evan couldn't let him drive out to the river with only Chloe and Jimmy. She didn't know the area. If something happened, they could be stuck, far from help.

Gordon's last checkup had gone well, but he wasn't a young man anymore. The thought chilled him. Once his father was gone, Evan would be the only one left. Feeling his gaze pulled as though by a strong magnet, Evan looked at young Jimmy. The only one left in his family.

Why had Spencer and his wife insisted on reopening that abandoned factory? Wainwright had told Evan that the newly refurbished machines ran on clean energy, apparently a fervent cause of Spencer's. And, he intended to employ people who had been jobless through no fault of their own. It was a noble cause. But the cost?

Bailey nudged his muzzle into Evan's hand. Absently, he petted the golden's head. Next to the shore, Jimmy stood between Chloe and Gordon. The boy had taken a shine to Gordon. But then Jimmy hadn't really had a grandparent relationship before. His maternal grandfather had died when Jimmy was a toddler, that grandmother suffered from late-stage Alzheimer's.

And, Evan wondered if the child had ever even met his paternal grandparents. Obviously, Spencer's parents hadn't changed since Spencer was a child. Devoted to their archeological dig, they had tunnel vision when it came to anything else in life. He supposed they loved Spencer in their own way. But they had seen nothing wrong in letting him grow up virtually alone. When Evan was young, he had overheard his parents disparaging over why they had ever had a child since they didn't seem to want to be parents.

His gaze roved toward Chloe. He had expected her to be a typical city woman, squeamish and ill at ease. Instead, she eagerly baited Jimmy's hook and now stood next to the hill country river as though she'd done so a hundred times before. In the sunlight, her long hair gleamed like spun honey. And Chloe's laughter was easy and often. Yet she still wore her mother-bear persona, keeping Jimmy under her watchful eye.

Only a week and a half before Thanksgiving, the mild hill country weather was holding true. The changing leaves proved autumn had arrived, but the bite of winter wasn't yet in the wind. It wouldn't be long though, bringing the holidays he now dreaded.

As Evan watched, his father sat down in his camp chair, something he usually didn't do until he had fished for several hours. They'd only been at the river about two hours. Although Gordon's fishing rod still rested in the river, he wasn't casting it any longer.

Frowning, Evan studied his face. The niggling worry resurfaced. He walked casually over to Gordon's side. "River's running low. Probably won't catch much today."

Gordon nodded toward Jimmy. "Never know."

Clearly, his father wanted Jimmy to have a good time and Evan knew better than to suggest they go home early. His father would dig his feet in and not budge. But if he helped Jimmy catch a fish...

Sighing, Evan reached for the thermos, poured a hot cup of coffee and handed it to his father.

"Thanks, son." Gordon's voice sounded weary.

There was a second thermos with hot cocoa for Jimmy, but the youngster was so absorbed in the new sport that Evan could tell he didn't care about refreshments at the moment. Manners drilled in by a determined mother couldn't be ignored. "Chloe? Coffee?"

Chloe turned, her mouth wide with a smile, sunshine illuminating her face. "Thanks, no." Their gazes still connected, she hesitated for a moment before turning back to the river.

It was a terminally long moment, yet not nearly long enough.

Evan frowned, then shook his head. Trick of the light, he decided. Nothing more.

Yet he continued to watch as she gracefully arched

her back as she prepared to cast her line into the river. It plopped into the water perfectly. *She must have gone fly fishing with her father as well as ice fishing.* It took time to learn to cast like that. Which was why they'd given Jimmy a pole instead. Although the boy had helped tie flies, he was still too young to master casting. Maybe in the spring when there was plenty of warm weather ahead.... Evan jerked his thoughts to an abrupt halt. No. Jimmy wouldn't be here in the spring.

Reminded that the boy needed to catch a fish so they could get his father back home, Evan paused. His own gear lay in the yellowing grass. He had brought it along only to appease his father. But it gave him an excuse to help Jimmy.

Evan walked to the shore quietly so he wouldn't startle the boy. Studying his wobbling line, Evan remembered his own father teaching him to fish. Then he remembered the times he had brought Sean to this very shore, the bubbling excitement of his son's animated face. Evan had expected someday to be the one sitting in a camp chair while Sean taught his own child the sport.

Evan felt a light tug on his arm and looked down.

Jimmy's upturned face was quizzical. "Do you want to use my fishing rod?"

A sweet gesture. Evan swallowed and pushed away the emotion. "Thought maybe I could watch awhile. You using worms or minnows?"

"Uncle Gordon said I could use his best fly, but Chloe said I'd better start with worms."

Uncle Gordon? Evan pushed past the moniker. "That's how I began. Takes a while to learn how to cast."

"Like Chloe and Uncle Gordon?"

"Yep."

"Uncle Gordon must be a neat dad."

The remark caught him completely off guard. "You had a pretty neat dad yourself."

Pain flooded Jimmy's eyes. "We were going to go on a boat next summer. Mommy, too."

Chloe met Evan's gaze over the boy's head.

She knelt down so she was at the child's level. "They would be so proud of you. How you've been so brave about starting a new school. And now, learning a new sport!" Chloe's clear green eyes beamed with empathy and Jimmy's expression started to clear.

Paralyzed with shared grief, Evan couldn't speak. But there was no condemnation in Chloe's eyes. It was almost as though she understood what he was going through. But that couldn't be.

Gathering his senses, Evan watched quietly for a while. When Jimmy's line snagged, Evan could tell it wasn't a fish. "Looks like you're caught up in some brush."

Jimmy frowned, then tugged on the rod, but it didn't yield.

"This is the good part of fishing with bait. No big deal to lose a worm, but when you lose your favorite fly...."

"Oh." Jimmy's eyes widened. "I'm glad I didn't lose the fly."

He was so serious that Evan wanted to pat his shoulder, tell the boy to relax. Instead, he cut the line and reached in the tackle box for a small hook and bobber.

"Is it bad to lose a hook?" Jimmy asked in a near whisper.

Evan couldn't stop his smile. "Nope. That's part of

fishing—the worms, hooks and line. We don't waste them on purpose, but it's not bad when we lose some."

Jimmy visibly exhaled.

"What do you want to use for bait this time?" They had stopped by the bait shack and picked up leeches, worms and minnows.

Jimmy shrugged his narrow shoulders, his eyes still anxious. "Which one should we pick?"

"In the spring, you can find all the earthworms you need right in the yard. I used to collect them to sell to the bait store. Don't suppose kids do that anymore."

"They don't?" Jimmy's expression remained sober.

Evan knew the child shouldn't have to always be so cautious and serious. "Let's try a minnow this time, okay?"

"Okay."

Evan showed him how to slip the tiny fish on to the end of the hook. Jimmy's small hands were practically hidden under his while the youngster tried to imitate the process. "Go ahead and drop your line in the water."

Jimmy obliged, watching eagerly as the sinker took the bait under the surface. "Will the big fishes see the little one?"

"They see your bait move. They're attracted to the colors, too. That's why fly fishers spend so much time making their lures."

"We used feathers," Jimmy confided. "Yellow ones."

Gordon made an art of tying flies. Evan hid a smile as he imagined the ones the pair had created. Glancing to his other side, he watched Chloe whisk her fly into the air, then back over her shoulder, finally casting it forward in a perfect motion. "You've had a lot of practice."

"My father was an avid fisherman. We learned how to tie a fly about the same time we learned how to tie our shoes."

"Big family?"

"One brother. Chip and his family are stationed in Germany."

"Your mother?"

Chloe looked straight ahead, not meeting his gaze. "Mom lives in an extended-care facility."

He frowned, wondering at this aspect. "She's ill?"

"COPD. It's a chronic pulmonary disease. She has to be on oxygen, among other things. So she can't safely live on her own. If she were to lose consciousness while she's alone…" Chloe glanced down at Jimmy who was concentrating on the bobber on his fishing line. "Fortunately, she's surrounded by people."

"Allows you to have a life of your own."

Chloe's head jerked sideways as though it, too, were connected to a string. Indignation was written on every feature. "You really believe that?"

"Isn't that why people use nursing homes?" He wasn't sure why she was so indignant. She was more than a thousand miles from Milwaukee.

"It's *not* a nursing home." Seeing that Jimmy was staring at her, Chloe quieted her voice. "My mother's living where she's safe. Not all of us have the means to stay home and employ others so that our loved ones have constant care."

Evan caught the barb in her words, but still didn't understand her injured expression. He certainly hadn't asked her to cross the country, leaving her mother behind. In fact, he couldn't understand why she had. Especially when she was prepared to dig in and stay as

long as it took for him to give in about Jimmy. And all
the while her mother was left on her own. Cold-blooded,
Evan decided. To choose whatever amount of money
Wainwright was offering over the welfare of her mother.

The chill of Evan's words superceded the late autumn
weather. Chloe could scarcely believe his accusation.
She had sacrificed everything to care for her mother.
Working as a legal secretary barely covered the cost
of the extended-care facility. As the rates continued to
rise, Chloe despaired about how she would be able to
afford it. For herself, she lived in a cheap one-room, efficiency apartment. Not that it mattered. She spent all
her weekends visiting with Mom. And days at the law
firm were long. Since Chloe's fiancé had dumped her,
she had virtually no social life. Derek couldn't understand her devotion to family and Chloe couldn't understand how she could have been so wrong about him.

When Mr. Wainwright offered to pay her way
through law school, along with a full salary, Chloe
couldn't turn down his proposition. As an attorney,
she would be better prepared to afford a lifetime of
payments to the care facility. And, she had promised
herself she would never put her mother, Barbara, in a
state facility. Her younger brother's military pay was
barely enough to support his growing family. Besides,
Chloe had promised her father she would look out for
the others.

All she had to do was happily settle Jimmy in with
Evan Mitchell. It would probably be easier to push a
rock across the country with her nose. She hadn't imagined anyone could turn away a child like Jimmy. Even
though Derek had proven to be the wrong choice, Chloe

longed for the family she had dreamed of having with him. She was twenty-seven years old. Much longer and her biological clock would run out of batteries.

Trying not to be obvious, she checked on Jimmy. He was watching Evan's every move, trying to imitate the tall man's every motion. Bailey's plumed tail thumped happily against Evan's endlessly long legs.

Keeping her eyelids down, Chloe tried to hide her interest. Clad in jeans, boots and a casual Western shirt, Evan cut an impressive figure. Not many men in the city could have pulled off the look. And there was something about the rugged image that had always intrigued her. True, she had often been in the Wisconsin countryside where plenty of men wore jeans. But not quite the way Evan did.

Chloe's fishing line jerked suddenly. Having relaxed her grip while stargazing, the rod slipped right through her hands. She hadn't done anything so amateurish since she was a kid.

Evan reacted before she could, reaching a long arm toward her escaping fishing gear. Chloe found herself duplicating Jimmy's reaction as they both stared, open-mouthed at him.

"Got it." Evan turned back, holding the fishing rod, water dripping from his strong fingers.

And Chloe swallowed, unable to think of a single word to say. Realizing her mouth must be practically flapping open, she snapped her lips shut.

"That was neat!" Jimmy declared, impressed.

"Yes…." Chloe cleared her throat. "Thank you. I don't know what I was thinking." But she could tell what Evan was thinking. That she surely *hadn't* been thinking.

He handed her the rescued rod. "No problem."

Right. It wasn't even her own gear she had almost lost.

Gordon waved to her from his chair. "Don't worry, Chloe. It's just a fishing rod."

One of his favorites. He'd told her so when he had insisted she use it that day.

Chloe met Evan's startled gaze. His eyes narrowed.

That wasn't a good sign.

When Evan spoke, she nearly dropped the pole again. "Better keep a good grip on what you don't want to lose."

She swallowed. "Right."

"Let's check your bait," Evan said, turning to Jimmy.

While he helped the boy put fresh bait on the hook, Chloe suddenly felt a million miles from home. Was she crazy for accepting this assignment? The holidays were around the corner. Even though Mom had insisted she would be surrounded by friends at the care facility, Chloe hated the thought of not being there for her.

Jimmy plunked his freshly baited line back in the water just as Evan instructed. Only moments later his float bobbed, then disappeared beneath the water's surface.

"A fish!" Knowing not to, Chloe didn't raise her voice. But inside she was shouting. Jimmy needed a victory. Even one as minor as catching his first fish.

"You've got him," Evan encouraged.

Jimmy's hands shook as he hung on to the pole.

Evan moved behind him, reaching forward to grasp Jimmy's hands, adding his strength.

The fish flopped as together, they reeled him in.

Shades of silver glinted in the sunlight while Evan dipped the net beneath the struggling fish.

"Wow," Jimmy breathed. "We really caught it."

"You did," Evan amended. "I just helped. Now we have to decide what to do with him. No one else has caught anything. And, big as he is, this guy isn't enough to feed everyone. So, do you want to keep him or let him go back in the water?"

Jimmy pinched his lips together in concentration. "He probably wants to go back."

"Good decision." Evan removed the unbarbed single hook from the fish's jaw and quickly tossed it back in the river. The frantic creature wiggled and dove before swimming away. "They have to get back in to the water real fast to survive."

"Will he be okay?" Jimmy asked, staring where the fish had disappeared.

"Looks like it. Good job."

Chloe stared at Evan, wondering if the man had any idea of how good he was with Jimmy. He was a natural. And, if Evan wasn't so stubborn, he would at least *consider* accepting guardianship. Instead, he acted like an old man set in his ways. Well, that wasn't exactly true. Gordon had welcomed Jimmy with open arms. What could have slammed Evan's mind completely shut?

Chapter Six

With Thanksgiving only days away, Chloe was torn. Even though Jimmy had begun shadowing Evan whenever he was home, she still had no idea whether Evan would change his mind.

Sitting in the den with her cup of hot tea, she watched Jimmy through the large window. He was running and playing with Bailey, the dog eager to fetch and retrieve endlessly. If Evan had been home, both boy and dog would be tagging behind him. And Evan would still be telling her that Jimmy's attention wasn't going to change his mind. Overcome with indecision, she sighed.

"That's a mighty big sigh for a little lady," Gordon commented as he entered the room.

She turned. "Sorry. Just thinking."

"No need to apologize for your thoughts. Sounds like you have plenty on your mind."

Chloe met his kind eyes. "I'm trying to decide whether I should take Jimmy back to Milwaukee before he gets too attached."

Gordon took his time to settle into a deep leather chair. The aged cowhide was as supple as a lambskin glove. "You know, I've lived in this house, in this town, all my life. I met my wife here. Raised my son. Buried my parents, my brother." He paused. "More people than I want to count. Retired from my business because it was time... because it was Evan's turn. He's done well by the quarry. I wouldn't have wanted to be in his shoes with the economy these past years." Gordon glanced down, quiet for a few moments. "He doesn't ask, my son. He tells. But I ask because I've learned sometimes it's the best thing a person can do. I asked the Lord to give Evan some peace... happiness. And He sent you. You and Jimmy."

Chloe didn't speak, overcome by the emotion in Gordon's words, wondering what he meant. Evan's happiness? His peace?

"You don't seem like a quitter, Chloe."

She struggled for an answer. "It's difficult."

"If Thanksgiving wasn't this week, would you still feel like you need to go home?"

Chloe's mind had been filled with family, the fact that this would be the first Thanksgiving she'd left her mother on her own. "You get right to the heart of things, don't you?"

"It's hard to be away from family this time of year. But, this one time, don't you think it's worth it?"

Chloe stared down at her hands for a few moments, thinking about both Jimmy and Evan. "Can you tell me if there's something...bothering Evan? Something that's keeping him from accepting Jimmy?"

"He'll have to tell you that in his own time. But I can tell you that Evan needs Jimmy as much as the boy needs him."

So the bleak pain she'd seen on Evan's face was

genuine. But did that make him more or less likely to change his mind?

Gordon shifted, reaching for his pipe, going through the quiet ritual of filling it with his favorite cherry tobacco, then tamping it down. "Do you believe in prayer, Chloe?"

"Yes," she answered without hesitation. "Before my mother got sick, church was a big part of my life. Since then…well, it's been difficult. But my faith's still strong, if that's what you're asking."

"Evan's isn't anymore. His faith has been shaken to the core. But, if he can reconnect to the Lord, I believe he'll look at Jimmy's guardianship in a whole different light."

Chloe felt the enormity of what Gordon was saying. Absently, she rubbed her forehead, remembering all the prayers she had uttered when her father was ill. When he died, she had been utterly bereft and confused. But Mom had made her understand that the Lord listened to our prayers and understood our hearts. That the illness hadn't been a punishment or a betrayal. Rather, they needed to cling even more tightly to their faith, to believe they would be reunited one day. Slowly, she raised her face. "What makes you think I can help?"

"Faith," Gordon replied simply.

It had buoyed Chloe at her lowest moments, when life had been so overwhelming she had been close to despair. She couldn't imagine living without it…or the pain Evan must feel without this most important anchor. Still… "I've been thinking about myself as well as Jimmy. About being away from my mother. But, even if I take that out of the equation… well, what if Evan never accepts Jimmy?" She gestured out the window to where Jimmy and Bailey continued playing. "You've seen Jimmy follow Evan around like a puppy. He'll be crushed."

"And if you take him back to the city?"

Chloe paused. Even though she had become too attached to Jimmy herself, her situation made it impossible for her to raise him. "I don't know."

"Do you think Evan would be good for Jimmy?"

Strangely, she didn't feel a moment's hesitation. Evan grumbled and continued to be formidable. But his dedication to his employees and family told her he was a good man. Chloe glanced again out the window. Bailey was utterly devoted to him. In her experience, children and pets seemed able to sense a person's character. "I don't think that's the issue," she answered honestly. "He has to *want* Jimmy."

"Which will take time. Repairing his faith won't happen in a few days."

Gordon was right. Fleetingly, she thought of her mother, how she had insisted that Chloe needed a life of her own. That was why her mom had urged her to help Jimmy. She was afraid Chloe was sacrificing her youth, her happiness. Her mom had also prayed about the issue and felt certain Chloe was meant to do this. She would be disappointed if Chloe returned prematurely. In fact, she had repeated that in their last phone conversation the day before.

"Chloe, I know what I'm asking isn't easy. You're miles from home at the most special time of the year. And, Evan isn't making our task any more pleasant."

She smiled faintly.

"Only the Lord knows our hearts."

"That's what my mother always says."

"Smart woman," Gordon declared. "Will you think it over?"

She could say no. Justify it even. But Chloe felt the Lord's urging. "Yes."

"Then we can get ready for Thanksgiving," Gordon declared.

Confused, she looked at him in question.

"Oh, we would have had the dinner. But now we have more reasons for giving thanks than I can count."

Evan helped Ned carry in the extra chairs. They had already extended the banquet-sized table as far as it would go. They would have their usual number of guests this year. Several people from the retirement home, plenty of others who were simply on their own. Employees, longtime friends, the table always overflowed with guests. This year, as many before it, they put up a second table to accommodate everyone.

The first Thanksgiving after his wife and son died, Evan hadn't wanted the dinner tradition to continue. But Gordon had prevailed on him to think of the people who were on their own who didn't have his choices.

Irrationally, Evan wished he could keep Robin's and Sean's chairs empty, knowing no one else should fill them. But his father's gentle guidance helped him accept the inevitable. Two retired employees, both widowers, now occupied those seats. It would have been difficult to see anyone in places once occupied by Robin and Sean, but these old, and now alone, friends helped ease the transition. Since his life now revolved around business rather than family, Evan was able to welcome everyone to Thanksgiving that year and the next.

Evan frowned. *Almost everyone.* Chloe and Jimmy

didn't belong among old and trusted friends. He still had to learn the woman's true motive for sticking like a thorn. Jimmy... The boy needed family, but Evan wasn't that family.

How many more years could he offer a full Thanksgiving table to his employees? If the business failed, he would no longer have the resources. And all of his people would be without jobs, possibly losing their homes. The weight settled in to a knot in his shoulders. He had to keep them solvent, keep them from losing everything.

Thelma pushed open the door to the kitchen. "You two hustle! I still have to set the table."

Evan had grown up with Thelma bossing him and didn't mind her orders. "Sure you don't want us to set it for you?"

Thelma plopped work-worn hands on her hips. "That's the first helpful thing you've said today."

Ned rolled his eyes, then followed his wife into the kitchen.

Evan angled the last chair into position.

"Wow. I didn't know there would be so many people," Chloe murmured from behind him.

He should have made his escape with Ned. "It's a tradition."

"Nice one. My family's small so we didn't have big celebrations."

"No extended family?"

"Not close by. My parents moved to Milwaukee before I was born. Their families stayed in rural Wisconsin."

"For a job?"

She nodded. "My dad's parents owned an apple orchard, but Dad was an engineer. So he had to go where the jobs were."

"Wisconsin makes me think of cheese, not fruit."

"We have a little of that, too," she replied drily. He silently acknowledged her subtle rebuke. "So what's rural Wisconsin like?"

"A lot like here, actually. Gentle, rolling hills, fruit orchards. More lakes than you can count." Reminiscing, she walked closer. "I spent my summers in the country with my grandparents. The city's great, but the country's...special."

When Chloe spoke, her eyes brightened, taking on the hue of green sapphires. It was the clear, clean green of fresh apples. Ironic, he mused, since she'd just spoken of the orchards. He remembered that her eyes could also ripen from jade to emerald. His gaze drifted to her mouth. Caught in her memories, Chloe's lips were almost like a kewpie doll's. The same lips that widened easily into a big smile. Catching himself, Evan stopped ruminating.

"Can I help?"

He frowned. "What?"

"With the table. I heard Thelma when I was coming in."

"Shouldn't you be watching Jimmy?"

"Your father is."

Evan searched for another excuse. Next to him, Bailey thumped his tail helpfully. "The plates are in the sideboard."

"Now I know why Thelma's been bustling around all week," Chloe mused. "All the baking, chopping..." Her voice turned nostalgic. "A real family gathering."

"Yeah. Well." Uncomfortable, Evan opened the silver chest, digging through pieces that had been in the

Mitchell family for generations. Thelma wouldn't appreciate his actions. She had just polished all the flatware. Retrieving forks, spoons and butter knives, he piled them on the table.

Thelma pushed open the swinging door from the kitchen, assessing his actions. "You have to put the tablecloth on first."

Chloe smiled, then turned back to the sideboard.

Not that he cared about her opinion. Yet Evan snuck a quick look to see if she was still amused. She had one of those faces that looked perpetually happy. Oh, he'd seen a few angry expressions, but on the whole...

Chloe placed a stack of plates on the sideboard and turned to him. "Where do we find the tablecloth?"

"It's probably in the side kitchen."

She looked at him blankly.

"It's what city people call a butler's pantry where all the kitchen stuff is stored. It's next to the washroom. Thelma always washes and irons the tablecloth so it'll be fresh for the dinner, then lays it out in the side kitchen."

"Oh. I'll get it then." Chloe disappeared into the kitchen.

A few minutes later she reemerged, her petite figure nearly hidden by the huge tablecloth.

"You could have asked for help," he told her, lifting the linen cloth out of her arms. For a moment, he was face to face with her. Close enough to see the light sprinkle of freckles over her nose, the creamy smoothness of her skin.

Her gem-like eyes darkened to a near emerald shade. And he noticed the thready pulse at the base of her throat. Nerves? Or something else?

Long, dark lashes framed her eyes. Details he hadn't noticed? Or had ignored?

Abruptly, Evan stepped back. He had no need for these thoughts. Nor did he want them. His attraction to women had died with Robin. She had been the only woman for him and he had vowed to love her forever.

Echoing his movement, Chloe retreated as well, turning to the sideboard. "I don't know how many more plates to take down."

He cleared his throat, but his voice still sounded rusty. "Thelma has the exact count."

"I'll ask her then." In a rush, Chloe practically ran from the room.

Evan exhaled. His face felt warm, flushed. And he didn't intend to let it happen again.

By two o'clock the house was full of people. Chloe hadn't known exactly what to expect, but she was surprised by the variety of guests. Several elderly people, eager for the company, chatted nonstop.

Thelma's appetizers were a huge hit. Crab puffs, stuffed mushrooms, bacon-speared water chestnuts, red pepper cheese straws, tiny German onion tarts, spinach squares, mini pastries stuffed with locally made sausage. The enticing trays contained more food than Chloe could remember at any of her family holidays.

She recognized the man she had met at the Mitchell Company offices. "Mr. Perkin?"

"Miss Reed?"

"Chloe." She extended her hand. "It's nice to see a familiar face."

"Crowd gets a little bigger every year."

"Do many people from the company come for Thanksgiving?"

"The Mitchells collect strays. People who are alone, or don't have the means to buy a decent holiday dinner. And then just old friends."

"It's nice."

"Gordon started the tradition. Evan expanded it."

She was surprised. "Evan?"

Perkin nodded. "Where's the little boy?"

"With the older Mr. Mitchell. He's really taken a shine to Jimmy."

The man seemed to be appraising her. Chloe felt like she had on job interviews and had to fight the immediate desire to try and look more professional.

"Gordon's always been good with children."

Sensing no judgment in his words, she relaxed a fraction. "Jimmy's a great kid. He's fitting right in at the school."

Mr. Perkin popped a hot crab puff in his mouth. "Leaves you with a lot of time on your hands, I suppose."

"Yes, actually it does. I'm so used to being in an office ten hours a day—"

"Office?"

"Yes." She studied him, wondering at his interest. "I've had plenty of experience. I started while I was in college. Took all my classes in the evening." Chloe hesitated. "I'm sensing you asked for a reason."

"Not really. Just that we're shorthanded at the moment. One of our regulars is out on maternity leave. And, frankly, we can't afford a temporary replacement. We need to hold the job open for Melanie because her husband lost his job. He stays home with the kids, at least until he finds something else."

"I'd be happy to help." The words flew from her mouth before she gave them thorough consideration. "I do have a lot of time on my hands. I would need to leave every day in time to pick up Jimmy from school, but in between…"

Mr. Perkin studied her again. "I might just take you up on that offer."

"I hope you will." As she spoke, Chloe realized it was true. Accustomed to being busy, she was restless between the time she dropped Jimmy off at school and then picked him up. Without anything concrete to fill the time, she found herself worrying about him. What if the other kids didn't treat him kindly? What if he got scared? Each day when Chloe picked Jimmy up, he felt more and more comfortable.

But the idle time allowed her thoughts to drift. And often in directions she didn't want—Evan intruded constantly on her thoughts. Chloe rationalized that it was because he was the one she had to convince, the one standing between Jimmy and his happiness. But, today, as she had stared into Evan's eyes, she'd wondered.

Drawn by her own thoughts, Chloe raised her face, trying to casually gaze around the room. But when her gaze stopped on Evan, she felt a peculiar pit in her stomach. Her breath shortened. Not wanting him to see her reaction, she turned suddenly. Fortunately, she turned in Jimmy's direction. Even though he stood next to Gordon, he looked overwhelmed by the crowd of strangers. Especially since Gordon spoke in turn with his guests.

Needing to reassure Jimmy, Chloe wove between the crush of people until she reached him. He immediately grabbed for her hand.

"Hey, big guy. I hardly know anyone here and I'm feeling a little lost. Mind if I hang out with you?"

He pressed closer. "It's okay."

Thelma raised her voice, and the crowd hushed. "Turkey's on the table!"

As people segregated into different parts of the dining room, Chloe anxiously looked for where she and Jimmy had been assigned to sit. She wasn't above switching some place cards if they had been separated. However, she was relieved to see that Jimmy had been seated on Gordon's right and her spot was beside her charge.

Gordon and Evan stood behind the chairs at each end of the table as their guests seated themselves. Chloe was relieved when Perry Perkin sat beside her. She guessed that Thelma had ferreted out the few people Chloe had met. Smoothing a linen napkin in her lap, she then helped Jimmy with his.

Glancing up, her gaze rested on Evan as he walked around the table, then paused behind two elderly ladies, stopping to talk to them and making both smile, then giggle.

Perry followed her gaze. "That's Gertrude Heine and Matilda Depson. Both are widowed."

"Did their husbands work for the Mitchells?"

"No. Evan knows them from church. Gertrude and Matilda are great friends, but as they've gotten older, their circumstances declined. Neither drives and they lived more than two miles apart. Physically, they couldn't walk that distance any longer. And living on only Social Security, they didn't have much money. Evan suggested they move to Orchard House, the Rosewood retirement home. But neither of the ladies could afford it. So, Evan insisted on paying their monthly fees."

Chloe knew how much that could be, what a relief it must be for the elderly widows. It was an incredibly generous gesture on Evan's part.

"Matilda and Gertrude worried constantly about their houses. And, neither one could physically or financially cope with keeping them up. Evan handled turning both places into rentals. He arranged for Gertrude and Matilda to have their favorite pieces of furniture moved to their rooms in Orchard House. Once they got settled there, Matilda and Gertrude had the best of both worlds. Enough that was familiar so they wouldn't feel they had left their entire lives behind. But now they don't have to maintain yards, and aging houses with a million problems."

Chloe admitted it was a brilliant plan. "And I suppose the rent helps pay for their fees at the retirement home."

"You'd think so, but Evan insisted they keep the rent money for themselves. He said he knew that ladies enjoyed buying a bauble or two every now and then."

Having trouble processing Evan's generosity, Chloe frowned. "What about their children? Don't they help?"

Perry shook his head. "Gertrude's daughter moved to California to pursue her music. She struggles just to support herself. Both of Matilda's sons are in the military. They do what they can, but being stationed thousands of miles away, it isn't enough."

"My brother's in the military so I understand." The pay was low, the responsibilities enormous.

"Matilda and Gertrude are happier than either one's been in years. The home organizes outings to all sorts of places. Twice a year they go to San Antonio, visit the Riverwalk or the missions. There's always something to do there. They went to a Spurs game last time."

Chloe grinned, imagining the widows in the midst of their enthusiasm at an NBA basketball game. They probably waved foam fingers and wore team ball caps and T-shirts.

"There are plenty of Mitchell employees here, though." Perry glanced toward the end of the table. "The two older men sitting next to Evan are brothers who worked for the company until they retired. Then they fell for a scam targeting the elderly. Lost all their pension money. Evan helped them connect with the state's attorney. But they only recovered a fraction of what they lost. So, Evan insisted we keep making full pension payments to them. It's the right thing to do, he said. I admire Evan's honor and ethics, but as the financial officer, I have to admit his generosity is responsible for me going gray before my time."

Chloe glanced down, trying to absorb all that he had told her about Evan. Trying to compare it with the shell he had built around himself. To all appearances, he was all business, all shut away.

Then she wondered about Mr. Perkin himself. "And you? Is your family here?"

"I'm divorced." Although his voice remained calm, his eyes revealed a flash of pain. "My wife moved out of state, took our two children. I see them when I can, but this is her year to have them for the holidays."

"I'm sorry."

He sighed. "Me, too."

Impulsively, she touched his hand. "We don't always have to be in the same room, even the same state, to know our family loves us." Thinking of her mother, Chloe's throat clogged.

His voice was rugged, too. "I know."

Within a few minutes, Gordon and Evan both sat down and the group quieted.

Gordon bent his head to offer the blessing. "Dear Lord, thank you for each of these your children, our dear friends and family, gathered here today. Thank you for bringing us together, allowing us to be part of each other's lives. We are grateful for all the bounty you provide, the love you give us, the hope you keep constant. We ask that you let us remember and appreciate the true thanksgiving of each and every day, the blessings that surround us. Please bless and keep each of these dear friends safe and whole. We say these things in the name of your Son. Amen."

Amens chorused down the length of the big dining room table and carried over to the second.

Voices blended as platters were lifted, bowls were passed. Chloe couldn't stop thinking about Perry's words. And Evan's. About how the company was having financial worries. She took a scoop of mashed potatoes for herself and one for Jimmy. "Mr. Perkin—"

"Perry." He speared a piece of ham, then held the heavy dish for her.

"What would you think of Monday?" She picked up the meat fork. "For me to start helping out at the office?"

"I'd think that was the best offer I've had in some time."

Next, Chloe accepted a bowl of stuffing, offering it first to Jimmy, then taking some for herself. Unable to stop herself, she glanced down the length of the table at Evan. Her thoughts were in confusion as she wondered about him, the real Evan.

"Perry, is there something about Evan's past? Something that…" She paused, seeing a sudden defensiveness in the man's eyes.

"What you want to know about Evan will have to come from him," Perry replied, circling the wagons around Evan like Gordon had done.

Chloe swallowed, wondering if Evan would ever tell her. Wondering if she dared ask.

Despite Thelma's protests, everyone insisted on helping with the cleanup. Dishes were scraped and stacked next to the huge porcelain double sinks. They had filled the dishwasher, but it would take at least a dozen loads to accommodate all the dinnerware and serving bowls. It was more efficient to hand wash most of them. Besides, Thelma insisted the good china wasn't to even get near the dishwasher.

They all carried platters and bowls of food into the kitchen, lining the counters and filling the table. Since Thelma knew where everything should go, she was in charge of wrapping the leftovers. And there were plenty despite sending everyone home with an overflowing plate of goodies.

But then Thelma had been cooking for days. She had roasted two golden twenty-five pound turkeys and a huge ham, prepared three kinds of potatoes, gravy, two kinds of dressing, yams, green beans, creamed pearl onions, homemade cranberry chutney, fruit salad, then baked plump yeast rolls and enough pies to outfit a bakery. Not to mention the slew of appetizers.

They set up an assembly line to do the dishes. Evan insisted on washing, Chloe was assigned to rinse, then Ned dried and handed the stacks of plates to Gordon who shuttled them into the dining room. Thelma had instructed Gordon to place the dishes on the table and not to try putting things away where she couldn't find them. Meanwhile, Jimmy ran underfoot, fetching and carrying.

One side of the sink was filled with hot, sudsy bubbles, the other with rinse water. Evan wasted little time digging into the mountain of dinnerware. Chloe kept up, swiping plates and saucers swiftly through her side of the sink. A few soap bubbles collected in the rinse water and she reached for the plug to drain the sink and fill it with fresh water.

As she did, Evan plopped a plate in her side of the sink. Realizing at the same moment, that it would fall to the bottom of the sink he grabbed for it. Having seen it coming, Chloe reached out at the same time. Evan's fingers closed around hers as they touched the plate. Chloe froze.

So did Evan.

Time stopped as their fingers grazed, the water swishing around, encasing their hands in a liquid pool of sensation.

"Be careful with my crystal serving dishes," Thelma warned from behind them as she wrapped potatoes in plastic cling film at the counter.

They didn't jump apart. Instead, Chloe felt as though she moved in slow motion as she tightened her grip on the plate, then looked at the sink, the last of the draining water, the plug, anything but Evan.

He turned, immediately busying himself with another handful of saucers.

Ned and Jimmy talked in the background.

Gordon thumped down in one of the straight-back, oak chairs. "Thelma, you use more dishes every year."

"And you invite more people every year," she retorted mildly.

The buzz continued, but all Chloe could absorb was Evan's touch and the way it softened her bones, weakening them clear to her toes.

The porch out back was lit by soft gas lights and warmed by the round, full-bellied woodstove. Evan quietly walked across the aged oak planks, his thoughts confused, his emotions splintered.

Night was near silent, everyone and everything sated and tucked away. The sound of footsteps on the yellowing grass led to the broad steps of the porch. Instinctively, Evan stepped back into the shadows.

Chloe climbed the first stair. Sighing, she lifted her face. Platinum beams of moonlight cascaded over her face, enhancing her beauty. But also revealing her tears.

Evan emerged from the darkness. "What's wrong?"

Surprised to find him there, she looked embarrassed, then hid her eyes. "I'm missing my mother. I know it sounds foolish."

"If it's foolish to miss family, then the world's mad." Evan took her elbow and led Chloe to the porch swing where generations of Mitchells had retreated for comfort. He sat beside her, easing the swing into a gentle motion.

Chloe sniffled, another tear slipping down her face.

Unable to stop himself, Evan eased his thumb over her cheeks, wiping away the tears. Her skin was incredibly soft, just as soft as it looked. Unable to stop, his fingers cupped her chin, then tipped it upward.

Despite the dim light, he saw the confusion in her gem-like green eyes. Emeralds, he thought vaguely. So dark they resembled the finest of emeralds. When he didn't draw away, she quaked slightly beneath his touch.

Which made him wish to continue. Caution fled and he dipped his mouth to hers. Tender, welcoming, she kissed him back and he breathed in her clean vanilla scent. Tangling his fingers in her long, silky hair, he lengthened the kiss.

His conscience slammed into gear and he abruptly pulled away. *What was he doing? He had vowed to remain faithful to Robin forever.*

Chloe stared back at him, her lips trembling, her chest rising in short gasps.

Digging his heels in, he sprang from the swing. Not looking back, he disappeared out into the darkness. The comfort he had thought to offer had become his own. And now, it rose up in challenge.

Tempted by a harvest moon, he had betrayed the woman he had vowed to love forever. And he could never let it happen again.

The annual holiday bazaar was held on the Saturday after Thanksgiving. Established to raise money for those in need during the Christmas season, the craft fair filled Rosewood's park. People used the occasion to buy Christmas gifts, knowing the money was going to a worthy cause.

Chloe and Jimmy strolled through the mazes of booths, display tables and games. Not surprisingly, Jimmy wanted to play the games first. A scaled-down basketball toss appealed to him the most. Concentrating fiercely, Jimmy sunk three out of eight hoops. As a result, he had his choice of the second level of prizes. Again, his small face scrunched in thought. Finally, he picked a mug with the picture of a fish on its side. It seemed like an unusual choice for a small boy, but Chloe didn't want to say so. Maybe it reminded him of their fishing trip.

Their next stop was at the hat booth. From ball caps to an eccentric jester's hat with its jingling bell-tipped, floppy purple and gold arms, the shelves were crammed with novelty gear. Chloe tried on a sparkly green top hat that would be perfect for St. Patrick's day. Modeling it for Jimmy, she tipped to one side and bowed. He giggled and asked the vendor if he could try on a giant cowboy hat. The man obliged with a wink to Chloe.

Jimmy stuck it on his head, but the hat dwarfed his head, completely covering his face. "Nah, don't fit," he mumbled through the felt sides.

Laughing, Chloe spotted a smaller version. "How 'bout this one, pardner?"

The second one fit perfectly.

"Do you like it, Jimmy?"

"It's cool!"

Chloe dug in her wallet, handing the vendor some money.

"Don't we have to win it?" Jimmy asked.

"Not at this booth," she explained, accepting her change.

They walked on, pausing to toss pennies into glass milk bottles. Next, when they watched a balloon being twisted to resemble a dog, she cringed at the grating squeak, but smiled at Jimmy's grin when the clown handed the dog to him.

Reaching the area with handcrafted gifts, Chloe gazed around in delight. Piles of afghans, crocheted booties, children's clothing, knitted blankets, embroi-

dered tablecloths and hand towels filled several tables.
Booths displayed handmade jewelry, carved wooden
boxes, metal sculptures, paintings, custom-molded candles, cakes, pies, cookies, ribbon-tied bags of homemade chocolates and other candies.

And the aromas! Every spare inch of the perimeter
was crammed with food vendors of all kinds. Good
old American hotdogs, cotton candy, popcorn, pizza,
corn dogs, frozen bananas dipped in chocolate, ham-
burgers, funnel cakes, candied apples, and even deep
fried dill pickles.

There was a long line at the bratwurst booth. Homemade sausage and sauerkraut in a bun was tempting,
but then Chloe spotted kolaches advertised across the
aisle. Milwaukee had also been settled in large part by
German and Czech immigrants. Some of the German,
Romanian and Hungarian areas still retained their ethnic identities. The Czechs had introduced their flavorful
sweet and savory filled pockets of dough, kolaches, that
remained popular. The savory sausage or ham kolaches
made a meal. Various fruits as well as a cheesecake-like
cream cheese filled the sweet ones. Apparently, they
were equally popular in the hill country.

Her stomach rumbled, alerted by her inner cravings
radar and they wandered closer.

"Jimmy, we have to try one." She read the selection.
"I don't know how I'm going to decide." Eventually,
they settled on cherry for Jimmy and cream cheese
for her.

Finding one of many benches dotting the park, they
settled down to eat their treats.

"Good?" Chloe asked.

He nodded vigorously.

They savored the kolaches while Chloe indulged in people watching. Lifting her gaze from a pair of adorable preschool-aged twin girls, she spotted Grace Brady approaching.

"Look! It's the nice teacher lady!" Jimmy exclaimed.

And she was. Grace had been kind, helpful and non-judgmental about Chloe's mission to place Jimmy with an unwilling Evan. Grace saw them and waved. Jimmy hopped up, Chloe only seconds behind.

"Hi, you two! Enjoying the bazaar?"

"Completely! We just devoured kolaches. Honestly, I can just read the menu and I'm starving. It was terrible trying to pick just one."

Grace groaned, holding one hand to her stomach. "Same problem. I just left the popcorn booth. There are about a jillion flavors. I started out with cheddar cheese, then wound up stuffing myself with the white chocolate kind."

Chloe laughed. "Looks like we're going to have to visit there, Jimmy."

"Oh, and don't miss the booth with the oil essences. They mix whichever one you like into a natural sea salt scrub. My hands are so soft." She held them up, revealing a long, jagged scar. "Even around the scar tissue," she added unselfconsciously.

Gordon had told her about Grace's past after they met her at school that first day, moving Chloe to tears. Grace had been involved in a horrific car accident, resulting in devastating injuries. She had sacrificed herself by driving into a concrete barrier when another driver drifted into her lane, coming at her head on. If she hadn't, he and his family would have been killed. But Grace had paid a terrible price. In addition to internal injuries, one side of her face had been destroyed and her hands shattered. That was how she had met her husband, plastic surgeon Noah Brady. Fortunately, the multiple surgeries she had endured were successful. Grace's face showed no sign of what she had been through. All that visibly remained was the scar on her hand. Gordon said she had chosen to leave it to remind herself of what it had taken to bring her back to the Lord. Chloe thought it took an incredible person to come to that conclusion instead of self-pity.

Grace bent down to Jimmy's level. "How are you liking school?"

"It's okay," he replied with a shy smile.

"You know, I'm kind of new there, too. I just started teaching again when my little girl, Susie, was old enough for kindergarten, and that was the beginning of this school year." She straightened up, speaking to Chloe. "The school administration's been so great about it, adjusting my schedule to fit with Susie's. And it's nice to be able to peek in her classroom every little bit. Although she's just like her father, ready to tackle anything."

Chloe appreciated her new friend's kindness. Grace had peeked into Jimmy's room as well to make sure he was adjusting all right. At church, she had assured Chloe that he was getting on as well as he claimed. It put a portion of her anxiety to rest.

"Did you see Evan's booth yet?" Grace asked Jimmy.

"He has a booth?" Chloe was amazed. And uneasy. They had avoided each other since Thanksgiving night. But she couldn't rid her thoughts of their kiss. Replaying the moment over and over, she shivered each time at just the thought.

"It's for Mitchell Stone, but Evan always mans it. Except, of course, when…" She stopped abruptly, snapping her lips closed. Her look was apologetic.

Another circled wagon. Chloe longed to ask what Grace had left unsaid, but she couldn't in front of Jimmy.

He tugged at her sleeve. "Can we see Evan's booth?"

"I suppose so." She forced her voice to brighten, deciding she would act as though the kiss had never happened. "I'm sure we'll find it easily enough."

"Great to see you." Grace bent to Jimmy's level again. "Have a good time today."

Chloe and Jimmy strolled down the paths between displays, booths and vendors. It didn't take long to find Evan. A chronological history of Mitchell Stone in pictures papered the wall behind him. Generations of Mitchells, from a man standing next to the quarry with a pick ax to the present-day corporation. A wide shelf held a collection of exotic-looking gems. And all sorts of rocks filled the tables. Raw, beautiful chunks of amethyst sat next to elegantly carved onyx bookends.

Evan accepted the money for a set of intricately carved jade figurines from a pleased-looking couple, then stuffed the bills in a cash box. Glancing up, he saw them. His expression wavered between surprise and caution.

"We came to see your booth," Chloe began.

"Cool! Rocks!" Jimmy declared, pressing close to the stone display.

"Nice hat," Evan replied. He had taken a break to grab a soda when he'd seen Chloe and Jimmy trying on hats. She was completely natural and unaffected as she modeled some crazy green number, grinning and making faces at the youngster. Without the serious agenda she usually wore like an ever-present overcoat, Chloe appeared younger, more fun. It was a side to Chloe that Evan had never seen.

Jimmy plunked down a mug with the picture of a magnificent trout on its side. "Look what I won you, Evan!"

Taken aback, Evan looked at the boy. Apparently equally surprised, Chloe stared at them both.

"That's awful nice, but don't you want it for yourself?"

"Nuh-uh. It's 'cause you helped me catch the fish."

The boy grinned, waiting for a response.

"Nicest mug I've ever seen," Evan declared, his voice husky. "And I'll think about you whenever I drink a fish, I mean some coffee."

Jimmy giggled.

Not knowing what else to say, Evan placed the mug on the top display shelf where it wouldn't get damaged.

Chloe apparently sensed the awkward gap. "Look at this pretty rock, Jimmy." She gestured toward a huge amethyst.

Back on familiar ground, Evan touched the raw edge which had been cut to reveal the beauty of the stone's interior. "That's a fine example of amethyst. See how deep the purple color is?"

Fascinated, Jimmy nodded.

Evan turned and picked up another heavy rock, lifting it as though it weighed no more than an egg. Chloe watched the play of his muscles beneath his shirt. He might work in an office, but the fact couldn't be proved by his physique.

"This is the same kind of stone." He pointed to the pale lavender striping. "This color isn't as valuable as the deeper purple."

Brow furrowed, Chloe studied the rock alongside Jimmy. "I didn't know that."

"Amethyst is a fairly common gem—it's a form of quartz."

Unaccountably nervous, trying not to think of their time together during Thanksgiving evening on the porch, Chloe fiddled with some small stones he had scattered around the table. Her fingers closed around a green one.

"That's a moss agate," Evan told her.

"Because it's green?"

"Could be red or black and still be classified as moss. There are several types of agate." He picked up a rust-colored stone cut and polished into an egg shape. "This is banded agate. See the distinct layers?" He indicated the white stripes that went around the carved egg. Then he turned, pointing to the large bookends she had admired. "Onyx is a form of agate."

Chloe shifted the stone in her hand, wondering if she could identify it again.

"Are those ones for sale?" Jimmy asked hopefully, looking over the array of small specimens.

"Which one do you like?" Evan queried.

Jimmy carefully studied each rock, finally settling on a smooth, polished, oblong-shaped stone.

Evan picked it up. "Good choice. Obsidian."

"Because it's black?" Chloe asked.

"They're usually black, but they can be red, brown. Green is rare." Evan studied the stone. "But actually they can even be clear."

"Do they come from your quarry?" Jimmy asked, palming the smooth stone.

"Nope. The quarry you saw is limestone. We own

granite quarries, too. When granite is mined, it comes out in big, heavy pieces that are cut in to slabs. Obsidian comes out of lava flows and can be massive. Most precious jewels aren't that big."

"From lava flows?" Chloe asked, intrigued.

"It forms when viscous lava from volcanoes cools rapidly. It's about seventy percent silica."

Impressed, Jimmy stared up at him. "How do you know that?"

"In college, I studied geology. That's an earth science."

"We have science in school!"

"I loved science, and my dad taught me all about the rock business."

"So, you're a geologist?" Chloe questioned, as drawn in as Jimmy.

"I graduated with a double major—geology and business administration."

Made perfect sense. Impressed, Chloe toyed with the stone she still gripped. "Why do you have a booth at this fair?"

"To raise money for the town. People are always looking for unique gifts." Evan shrugged. "We like to do our part."

So much about this man was pulling Chloe in. Dangerously so. She had seen sides of him she wouldn't have believed existed only a few short weeks earlier. But which one was he? The hard man who could brusquely say no to a child? Or the one who took an interest in anyone who needed help?

And, what was his secret? The one everyone guarded so ferociously. A chill raced through Chloe. Could his secret be enough to convince her Evan wasn't the man who should take Jimmy in?

Chapter Seven

On Monday morning, entering Mitchell Stone, Chloe felt as nervous as she had on the first day of her first job. Jimmy was safely at school, she reminded herself. And, at the moment, Chloe wished she could join him.

"Chloe!" Perry Perkin greeted her cheerfully. "So, you didn't get scared off the idea over the weekend, I see."

"I need to keep busy," she replied, verbalizing the self-talk she had been reciting all morning.

"What's the majority of your background?"

She hesitated briefly. "Legal."

His eyebrows lifted a fraction. "What we need isn't nearly as exciting. To begin with, there's a mountain of filing."

"That's what I started out doing years ago. I don't mind." Actually, it was a good way to discover what the company was about. Learning the in and outs of filing systems had helped her leapfrog from general clerk to receptionist and eventually executive secretary at the law firm. A lot of businesses didn't employ secretaries as much any more. But, fortunately, in the legal profession, they were still in demand.

Perkin led her down the wide hall to a good-sized room. "Company started out with a half a dozen file cabinets, then moved the records into one cramped room. Even though we're supposed to be going paperless in this country, it hasn't happened yet. In addition to this file room, there's one upstairs on the second floor as well." Perry turned down another hall. "Let's head over this way." First he pointed out his own office and reminded Chloe where Evan's was. Then Perry showed her the cozy employee break room which had a microwave, dishwasher, snack machines, tables and comfortable-looking chairs. A long, overstuffed couch lined one wall. Perry opened the refrigerator, which was stocked with soda and juice, all free to the employees. As was coffee and tea.

"This is generous," Chloe commented, noticing a box of donuts on the counter.

"Treat people like you want to be treated and they're happier employees."

"Too bad all companies don't feel that way."

Perkin smiled with a touch of bemused exasperation. "Not even the economy tanking a few years ago could make Evan cut down any employee benefits or perks. I admire his ethics, but as the financial officer it does keep me up nights."

So, Evan had been completely truthful when he had told her about the company's financial difficulties. Initially, she had thought it was a convenient excuse—but, once again, the fact was reaffirmed.

Perkin showed her around, introducing Chloe to the

receptionist, account managers, clerks and the office manager, Viola, who was going to train her.

"You'll meet production employees as they happen by," Perry explained. "Even though they work at the quarry, most stop by once in a while. Did you meet anyone on your tour?"

"Not really," she admitted, trying to tactfully phrase her explanation. "It was a rather quick tour."

He grinned, then glanced down the hall. "Here comes Viola now. If you need anything, let me know. You know where my office is and my extension is two-fifty-nine. There's a phone on every desk. We appreciate this, Chloe."

"My pleasure."

Viola, a cheerful woman in her early forties, made it clear she was delighted with the help. "You are a real trouper agreeing to tackle this filing."

"I can practically file in my sleep." Chloe grinned. "Not that I will."

Viola spent more than an hour outlining the basics of the system, then providing sorters so Chloe could begin to organize the tall stacks of invoices and correspondence. Then she showed Chloe to a desk near the window in the file area. "There's plenty of room to stow your purse and anything else you want to in the bottom desk drawer. Melanie cleared out her things before she left. I know she'll appreciate this. She really needs the job."

"That's what I heard. Since I'm in the same position with my own job, I completely understand."

Viola studied her for a moment. "Good then. There's a hook behind the door for your coat. I know Perry showed you around, but if you can't find something, just holler, okay?"

"Absolutely." Accustomed to working on her own for the senior partner of a large firm, Chloe had no problem understanding the system. And, as she sorted correspondence, she read Mitchell Stone's recent history. It seemed that Evan was working on a large deal that might be important. She hoped so. Not just for his sake, but for his employees. Chloe hated to think of anyone losing their job. She knew Evan wasn't the only employer who worried about his people, but too many cut employees rather than profits.

Several hours passed as Chloe categorized papers, dividing invoices to be filed in the numbered sorter by date, and correspondence to fit in an alphabetical one. It was a fairly big job and would probably take several days. And, of course, more paperwork was constantly being generated. She glanced at her watch. Time to go pick up Jimmy.

Gathering her purse and sweater, Chloe stopped by Viola's office to let her know she was leaving. "Oh, and I left the sorters on the desk so I can pick up tomorrow where I left off."

Viola looked relieved. "I should have explained that the rest of us are sharing Melanie's job. So, there is more to do than just filing, hopefully something more interesting."

"No complaints. I've yet to have an office job with absolutely no filing. I still file private and privileged correspondence in my job."

Viola looked at her strangely. "As an estate representative?"

Chloe bit her lip, wishing she didn't have to conceal

her real job. "Estate work involves legal work, so…" She shifted her purse. "Anyway, I'll see you tomorrow."

"Good. And thanks again."

It took all of her control not to rush from the building. She had no talent for guile. Growing up with strict guidelines about telling the truth, misrepresenting herself was straining her nerves. Mr. Wainwright had articulated her mission as part of her ever-evolving job. But she didn't want to deceive these people. All of them had been kind and open with her.

Well. Almost all of them.

No one wanted to tell her about Evan's secret, perhaps from his past. She shouldn't be thinking of his past. She needed to concentrate on Jimmy's future. But Chloe had a strong feeling that the two were inescapably entwined.

"We're going to put stars and sprinkles and stuff on cupcakes," Jimmy told Chloe. "Then we get to go to the house where the old people live."

Evan noticed that Chloe seemed distracted.

"Chloe," Jimmy repeated.

"Yes. Um…cupcakes?"

"Can we get special sprinkles to put on them?"

She tried to collect herself. "I'm sure we can."

"When?"

"When do you need them?"

"Tomorrow." Jimmy's eyes glowed with excitement. The boy was gradually losing that pinched, anxious look.

Chloe blinked. "Tomorrow?"

Evan chuckled.

Drawing her eyebrows together, she frowned at him.

Coughing to disguise his laughter, Evan realized that for Chloe, not having children of her own, being with Jimmy day and night was a baptism by fire.

Chloe glanced at her watch. "We'd better go now, then, before everything closes. I guess the grocery store would have them—"

"And the bakery if you're in a pinch. You know where both are, don't you?"

She looked blank.

Evan wanted to smirk but the hopeful expression on Jimmy's face stopped him. Wasn't the boy's fault Chloe had dragged him to Rosewood. "We can go in my truck."

Looking relieved, Chloe grabbed her purse. As they piled in the truck, she encouraged Jimmy to get in first. So she wouldn't have to sit next to him?

The grocery store wasn't very busy, but the aisle with baking supplies was pretty crowded. Apparently, a few other kids in the first grade hadn't told their parents about cupcake decorating until the last minute as well.

Robin used to make the holiday season stretch out as long as possible. She baked over a dozen different kinds of cookies, but the most special times had been the ones when Sean helped her decorate. They'd had an entire arsenal of decorating supplies from chocolate sprinkles to pearl nonpareils. Robin had amassed a large collection of cookie cutters for every holiday of the year, but the copper Christmas ones were the most special. Lofty stars, elegant angels, and all the members of the nativity. Her cookie crêche had always been a marvel. Just as she had been.

Despite the time that had passed, the loss pierced fresh and new. This was the time of year for Evan to count his blessings, to be grateful to God for all he'd been given. If he hadn't been standing in the middle of the grocery store, Evan would have asked the Lord yet again why He'd had to take them. Unexpectedly, Evan felt a tug on his cuff.

"What's your favorite?" Jimmy asked.

Evan tried to concentrate. "I like the dragees—the little silver balls. But the colored sugar's good, too."

"I used to eat the little red cinnamon dots when we decorated cookies," Chloe confessed. "By the time we got to the gingerbread men, my mother would pull out the extra bag she had set aside, well, actually hidden, because she knew I'd nibble on too many every time."

"The sprinkles fall off sometimes." Jimmy looked suddenly worried.

"We'll buy enough to have plenty of extra ones," Chloe assured him. "They still have lots of colors left in the sugars. My mother said they used to only have red and green."

"How come?"

"People keep finding out new ways to make our favorite things even better. Personally, I like the pink-colored sugar."

Evan withheld a chuckle.

Chloe looked over a woman's shoulder at the display. It was a good selection. Bottles of sprinkles, lots of kinds—stars, hearts, confetti, tiny nonpareils. Then she had a thought. "Are we supposed to bring the frosting?"

Jimmy shrugged his thin shoulders.

She scratched her head. "I'd better get cream cheese, powdered sugar, butter, vanilla—"

"I imagine Thelma has most of that in the pantry," Evan interrupted.

"Even so, she may have plans for her ingredients. This *is* the baking season."

So it seemed. Women were studying most every product in the aisle. A few men acted baffled as they searched for items on their lists.

"Could you stay with Jimmy while I collect the frosting ingredients?"

Evan wanted to refuse. Intended to. Then Jimmy looked up at him expectantly.

"Sure."

While Chloe disappeared into the land of cream cheese, he and Jimmy debated the merits of the decorating options, ultimately choosing almost every single kind. All but the pink. Then Jimmy's hand strayed back toward the bottle of pink sugar crystals. "Maybe I should make a pink one for Chloe."

It was the kind of gesture Sean would have made. Evan resented the sudden lump in his throat.

"Is that okay?" Jimmy asked.

He could only nod. Even though his father had opened the family home to Chloe and Jimmy, Evan wondered how much longer he could bear it. The memories flooded more often, more completely each day. After the accident, Evan had immersed himself in memories, clinging to each and every one. But then he had begun to push them away, to escape the pain. The pushing allowed him to cope, to function. Yet he didn't want to forget a single detail about either of them. But he had found himself studying Robin's photo more often lately, realizing her face had begun blurring in his memory. How, he couldn't understand. Yet it had.

"My goodness!" Chloe announced. "I thought you were going to *choose* some decorations."

Evan felt the need to get away. From Chloe. From Jimmy. From everything they were making him feel. "We did," he replied shortly.

She looked surprised. Not waiting to hear if she had anything to add, he wheeled the basket toward the checkout stand.

Refusing the guardianship, once and for all, couldn't wait any longer. He was going to speak to his father. And make him understand.

The following morning Gordon slept in. When Evan had returned from the grocery store with Chloe and Jimmy the previous evening, Gordon had already gone to bed. It was almost as though his father had some sort of radar alert. At the same time, Evan couldn't dispel his worry. What if his father's health was wavering?

Still, they had to talk. But Evan couldn't wait around the house until his father was up and around. First, he had a phone conference with their newest and now biggest customer. TEX-INC had just given them the largest order they had received in more than three years. TEX-INC was building several commercial complexes around the country that would house retail stores and restaurants, with a top floor of high-end condos. The consolidated concept appealed to people looking to reduce the time and cost of commuting. TEX-INC had targeted several big cities, purchasing land adjacent to the business districts. Since TEX-INC was based out of Houston, they were close enough to inspect Mitchell's materials and also have face-to-face meetings when needed.

The profit from this one order could offset more than three years of doing business in the red. Just staying even was a success, because the smaller orders were trickling in more often now. Coupled with a few more large deals, Mitchell Stone would be back on solid footing. And, with this order, Evan hoped to get one of the large national banks onboard.

Evan clicked off the phone conference, raising two thumbs in victory. Now, Perry could make an appointment with the national bank they'd agreed on. Skirting his desk, Evan whistled as he made his way to Perry's office. Glancing in the file room, Evan thought he caught a flash of long, caramel-colored curls. He was going to have to make sure he and his father had that talk right away.

Chloe trudged through the front door of the Mitchell house, tired after a long walk. She had left Jimmy playing in the backyard with Bailey, watched over by Thelma. Hours of filing invoices and receivables that day had given Chloe a clearer picture of Mitchell Stone's financial state. It was even worse than she had imagined. No wonder Evan was tense. While she hadn't yet seen any ledgers, she could add quickly enough to tell the outgoing far outweighed the money coming in.

Shrugging out of her sweater, Chloe paused, surprised to hear raised voices upstairs. Although the situation with Jimmy had caused plenty of tension, this was the first time she had heard any arguing. Uncomfortable about being able to overhear, she knew she couldn't go up to her room to change for dinner.

Chloe ran chilled fingers through her windblown hair. Thelma wouldn't mind what Chloe wore. The older woman was too down-to-earth to care about trivialities. Quick, hard boot steps hit the wooden stairs, reverber-

ating throughout the entry hall. Chloe wanted to turn
and escape through the kitchen, but whoever was coming down the staircase would see her.

Heart sinking, she was fairly certain those stri-
dent steps belonged to Evan. Still uncomfortable, she
glanced up, hoping to remain unseen.

Evan looked livid. Brow furrowed, lips thinned, his
neck flushed, Evan exuded anger. Unconsciously, Chloe
took a step backward.

"There you are!" Evan accused.

"I was taking a—" she started to explain.

"Stay right there." He hit the last step with a forceful thud. "I want to talk to you."

Chloe had a strong feeling he wasn't going to just
talk. Not with all the anger spilling out of him.

"Did you talk to my father today?" Evan demanded.

She opened her mouth.

But he cut her off. "Don't bother denying it. He was
all ready for me."

Chloe could easily guess what they had been arguing about.

"Which part of *this isn't going to work* don't you
understand?" He stepped even closer. "I've heard all
your reasoning, but I told you mine. That isn't going
to change."

Perplexed, she wondered what had set him off just
now. "Did something happen?"

"You barged in here. After I'd told Wainwright no."

Chloe looked around uneasily. "Do you know where
Jimmy is?"

She hadn't thought it was possible, but Evan looked
even angrier. "Am *I* supposed to be keeping up with
him now?"

Chloe lowered her voice. "I don't want him to hear us."

He threw up his hands. "You still can't seem to remember this is my house."

"I just—"

"Look, I've been patient. Now it's time—"

A muffled cry caught Chloe's attention and she turned.

"What—"

"Shush."

Evan jerked his head back in disbelief.

But Chloe was following the sound she had heard. Reaching the dining room, she spotted something on the floor and knelt to retrieve it.

"What…" Evan repeated. But his protest trailed to an end when he saw what Chloe had found.

A fully decorated cupcake dropped so that it had landed on its side and smushed the frosting.

Grimly, Chloe picked it up, glaring at Evan angrily. She had asked him to stop.

Glancing around, Evan wondered when the boy had come in to the dining room. "You think Jimmy heard?"

"You think there was any way he could avoid it?" Anger warred with disappointment in her face.

Guilt swamped Evan. He had never intended to hurt Jimmy. How had he allowed himself to get in this position? He pushed through the swinging door to the kitchen, but the room was empty. "Did you leave Jimmy by himself?"

Indignation mounted on Chloe's face like a wind-whipped flag. "Of course not! He was playing out back with Bailey. Thelma was watching him."

Evan yanked open the door leading out to the porch, crossed it rapidly and searched the yard, spotting

Thelma deadheading the last of the autumn chrysan-themums. "Thelma, do you know where Jimmy is?"

She turned around. "He's right…" Her watchful gaze swept the yard. "He was here just a minute ago. He must have gone inside."

That was what Evan was afraid of. Immediately, he ran through a mental inventory of all the places he had used as a kid to hide. Not wasting time explaining to Chloe, he strode toward the old carriage house. There was still a loft intact above where they now parked their vehicles. Once it had held hay. Now he hoped it held a small, seven-year-old boy. He quickly climbed the built-in wooden ladder. These days, only a few trunks were stored in the loft. Evan's breath shortened. A few of them were large enough to hold a small boy. But was there enough air in them for that same small boy?

Yanking open the lids, he quickly discovered that Jimmy hadn't climbed inside any of them. Nor was the child anywhere else in the loft. Evan descended the ladder quickly.

"He's not down here in the garage," Chloe told him, her eyes filled with worry.

"He can't have gone far." Evan headed next to the storage shed. In addition to practical items like a lawn mower and gardening tools, the shed held an array of implements that dated back to his great-grandfa-ther's time. Plenty of places for a young child to wrig-gle under. But Jimmy was nowhere to be found. "He couldn't be in the attic," Evan muttered. "We would have seen him going upstairs."

"I thought the house had three staircases."

"Right. Still…" Evan stepped out of the shed, listen-

ing to the sounds carried in the light breeze. Abruptly,
he turned, striding in the opposite direction.

Chloe's shorter legs pumped to catch up to him.

Evan skirted the back porch, sprinting to the side of
the house where the wraparound porch continued. The
yard sloped near the end of the porch, creating a nook
beneath the wide planks. Evan remembered plenty of
times as a kid when it had been his sanctuary. Like the
day when, while playing in the Little League cham-
pionships, he struck out, and his team lost. The times
when a beloved pet had passed away. When his grandfather died.

Chloe caught up with him, walking by his side as
they neared the secluded retreat. The spot was the farthest away from everything without leaving the property. The sound of muffled crying nearly stopped Evan
in his tracks. Waves of memories hit. Sean's tears, his
own. The ones still unshed mixed with both.

His hesitation allowed Chloe to shoot past. Kneeling
down, she crawled beneath the porch, her petite frame
easily fitting inside. Jimmy hugged his knees to his
chest. Lips wobbling, he swiped at the tears running
from red-rimmed eyes.

Instantly, Chloe gathered him close. "Oh, sweetheart,
what is it?"

He cried even harder and Chloe glanced back at
Evan. Then, she dug in the pocket of her jacket, retrieving a handkerchief. She gently dabbed Jimmy's cheeks.

Jimmy allowed her to wipe his face, then buried it
against her shoulders, sobs rattling his small frame.

Evan felt horrible, utterly guilty. Kneeling down, he
couldn't begin to fit his tall body beneath the porch, but
he could reach in with his long arms. He patted Jimmy's

back awkwardly at first, then in a remembered comforting way as he had done with his son.

Eventually, Jimmy's sobs slowed down until he was dragging in deep gulps of air. When he was quiet enough, Chloe stroked back the damp hair on his forehead, speaking quietly. "Did you hear something you didn't understand?"

He nodded against her shoulder.

"Sometimes grownups don't agree about things. That's all it was."

"Evan doesn't want me here."

As his gut knotted, Evan caught Chloe's loaded glance.

"Oh, honey, that's not true. We were talking about some grownup stuff, nothing to do with you." This time when she looked at Evan, her gaze was a hybrid of pleading and glaring. "Right, Evan?"

He swallowed. There was only one answer. Only one his conscience would allow. "Right." Evan couldn't stop looking at the hurt in Jimmy's eyes. "I've been worried about the business. It's on my mind all the time. Guess it just got to me today."

"Especially since I was working in his office today," Chloe added helpfully.

Startled, Evan jerked his gaze toward her.

"You know, like Perry suggested," she explained rapidly, inclining her head to tell him to agree.

"Right." *She had been in the office today?*

"Remember? I go there after I take you to school," she reminded Jimmy.

He looked up at Evan, a tiny bit of hope struggling to bloom in his face.

"To do… " Evan struggled "…office stuff."

"When I picked you up from school, we talked about

it," Chloe continued explaining in a soothing tone. "I filed lots and lots of papers."

Whose brilliant idea was that? Still, Evan was incredibly relieved to see Jimmy's tears stop.

"You know what? I was just about to go upstairs to change for dinner. Do you want to go up, too? Maybe splash some cold water on your face?" Chloe studied him hopefully.

Jimmy looked at her, then at Evan.

"Why don't you go ahead," Evan suggested. "We guys can wash up downstairs, right, Jimmy?"

Anxiously, Chloe watched for Jimmy's reaction.

He looked cautiously at Evan and sniffled. "I guess."

Chloe didn't look completely convinced. "Okay, big guy. I'll be down in a flash."

Evan extended his hand to Jimmy. When the small fingers curled in his hand, Evan had to quash the protective feeling that exploded. He held out his other hand to Chloe, helping her stand. Though he allowed her to take the lead in returning to the house, she dawdled, as though afraid to leave him alone with the boy.

The boy. He had to keep thinking that way or Jimmy would slip past his defenses. Once Chloe disappeared upstairs, he led Jimmy to the washroom in back of the kitchen. It was a plain, utilitarian space with a deep sink, soap and white cotton towels. The shelves held supplies, along with Thelma's own home-concocted soap they used when nothing else would clean motor oil or grease from their hands. "No frilly girl stuff in here." Evan grabbed a fresh washcloth and turned on the tap, letting cool water flow. Then he pulled out the stool that had been stored in the room since before Evan was born. "Hop on up."

Jimmy did, sticking his hands under the cool water, then splashing some toward his face. Evan smiled, seeing that the youngster had missed most of the tears, in fact most of his face. Still holding the washcloth, Evan placed it under the faucet, then wrung out the excess water. "Okay, turn toward me."

Obeying, Jimmy waited. Evan carefully wiped his face, removing all traces of his tears. Only the redness remaining in his eyes indicated his distress. "Sorry about arguing before. Like Chloe said, grownups make mistakes, too. I've sure made my share." Evan smoothed Jimmy's hair which was sticking out in every direction. "So, how'd your cupcake project go today?"

Jimmy ducked his head. "I brought you one, but it's probably all messed up now."

Evan remembered the dropped, now crushed cupcake. "You think you might want to decorate another one? Or maybe some cookies? I'll bet we could talk Thelma into whipping up a batch."

"Would she be mad?"

Hating that this child had to worry about such things, Evan shook his head. "Nah. She bakes lots of cookies during Christmas. She makes a killer frosting to put on them, too. We could ask her, then head over to the grocery store and grab a few more bottles of sprinkles."

Jimmy sniffled, then looked down as though studying his sneakers.

And Evan could feel his insecurity. "We can see if Chloe would go with us."

Jimmy lifted his face. "Okay."

"Now, we'd better go sweet-talk Thelma."

Chapter Eight

Chloe could scarcely believe they had wound up back on the baking aisle in the grocery store. She was even more stunned to realize Evan was planning to participate in the decorating. While they had been picking up supplies, Thelma had indeed whipped up a pan of sugar cookies and a large bowl of buttercream frosting. This was in addition to finishing dinner and serving it. Now a pan of gingerbread men was in the oven.

The first batch of sugar cookies cooled while they ate dinner. And somehow, Thelma had cleaned up the mess and also managed to arrange all the bottles and little plastic cups of assorted sprinkles, colored sanding sugar, dots and silver balls. Chloe didn't remember buying the little silver balls, but she did remember Evan saying they were his favorite. No doubt Thelma had a bottle of them tucked away in the pantry.

Freshly made frosting was divided in several small bowls so it could be tinted various colors. Bailey sat beside Evan, wagging his tail, staring hopefully at the cookies.

Jimmy's eyes widened when he saw the preparations. "Wow!"

Thelma chuckled. "We've had many a good time decorating cookies in this house." She affectionately batted Evan's arm. "And this one ate them almost as fast as he decorated them."

Chloe couldn't picture Evan as a boy. She couldn't imagine all his hard edges covering what had once been soft spots. But this house exuded warmth. Gordon was a loving father and she had never heard anything negative about Evan's late mother. Something must have changed him....

She watched as Evan reached up with one long arm to pluck a basket from the tall shelves.

His face went peculiar for a moment, then he seemed to shake it away, putting the basket on the table so that Jimmy could peek inside. "Next time, Thelma will let you pick some cutters and make the cookies in special shapes, if you promise to help clean up the mess."

Jimmy plucked a star-shaped cookie cutter from the basket. "Mommy had one like this."

That same peculiar look crossed over Evan's face again.

"We made cookies lots," Jimmy continued.

Seeing the bleak tension on Evan's face, Chloe stepped forward. "Then you'll know all about cleaning up the mess when you get to use these special cutters. What do you say we start on the first cookie?"

Jimmy didn't have any trouble deciding he wanted four colors of sugar. After he smoothed them in place, he heaped on sprinkles and dots. "Can we make another?"

Chloe glanced over at Evan, seeing he still looked upset. "Of course. What do you want to start with?"

Jimmy reached for a bowl of frosting.

"What color do you want to make it?"

His small eyebrows pulled together as he thought. "Can it just be white?"

"Sure."

Jimmy picked up the small offset spatula and carefully spread white frosting over the entire surface. Then he reached for the silver balls and carefully placed them so that they sparkled in all the right spots to form a star. As soon as he finished, Jimmy hopped off his chair, going to Evan's side, then tugging on his sleeve. The motion seemed to bring Evan back from wherever he had mentally traveled.

Jimmy looked up at him. "This one's for you, 'cause you like Thelma's frosting and the little silver things."

Evan stared first at the cookie, then at Jimmy. And something in his face changed. The hardness that never completely left his eyes dimmed. Though Chloe couldn't really believe it, she thought she glimpsed vulnerability there, too. "Well…" His voice was husky, almost gravelly. "That's fine…." He knelt down and accepted the cookie. "Mighty fine."

Chloe tried not to gape. It was a huge reaction for a small cookie.

Gordon strolled into the kitchen. "I can smell gingerbread men all the way to the den."

Pulling her gaze from Evan, Chloe glanced at the timer. "They'll be ready soon. Right now, we're decorating sugar cookies. Would you like to join us?"

Gordon glanced at Evan, then Jimmy. "I think I'll wait until the gingerbread men are done—they're my favorites." He took a glass from an upper cabinet and filled it with water. Turning back around slowly, he spoke to Chloe. "You know, the company hayride's this Friday night. Everyone brings their whole families. I thought maybe you and Jimmy would like to come along."

Chloe dared a peek at Evan. But she sensed he hadn't quite returned to normal. "It sounds nice."

"We always have a good time. The Markhams have a huge wagon and a strong team of horses. Someone usually brings a guitar, which we sing along with. Off-key, of course."

She smiled.

"Afterward there's a bonfire. Kids always like the whole shebang."

"The kid inside me thinks it sounds fun, too." Chloe realized she was growing nearly as fond of Gordon as... Her thoughts screeched to a halt. That train of thought had to be derailed fast.

After Gordon ambled out of the kitchen, she sat at the table and eventually both Jimmy and Evan joined her. She had thought Evan would disappear once the decorating began again. But he sat quietly, helping Jimmy tint the frosting green, then outlining a tree shape on the cookie with toothpicks.

Entranced, Jimmy carefully smoothed on the frosting, staying within the design for the most part. Then he embellished his Christmas tree with jimmies and multicolored nonpareils. His last touch was a small clump of silver balls for the star at the top.

"That's lovely," Chloe told him quietly.

"I wanna make an angel next. A Christmas angel."

Evan blinked. And the pained expression returned to his face.

Instinctively, Chloe realized Evan couldn't continue. "I'd like to help you with that, Jimmy. I think stars and angels are the very best designs for the season."

Evan's head rose, his guarded eyes meeting hers. He didn't speak.

Nor did she.

But, Chloe sensed that somehow they had just communicated more in the past hour than since she and Jimmy had arrived in Rosewood.

Full moons had their advantages, Evan reasoned, as the hayride began. But so did partial ones, like the slice of moon that lit the dirt road. At the same time, there wasn't so much light that every nuance of a person's expression could be read. Normally, it wasn't a concern. But he had been overly emotional since Jimmy had presented him with that special star cookie. Even though the child felt emotionally battered, Jimmy had reached out to him again. And Evan had nearly come undone.

It wasn't as though he hadn't faced any emotional encounters since his young family perished. Life hadn't stopped for everyone else when it had for him. But none of the others had been orphaned with only him as a possible guardian.

Equally unsettling was Chloe's surprising sensitivity, her understanding. Just when Evan thought he might crumble, she had reached out, diverted the disaster. She should have taken advantage of his sudden weakness, striking when he was vulnerable if she wanted to press her case, to accomplish what Wainwright had sent her to do.

Why hadn't she? The thought rolled around in his

mind like a ceaseless pinball, striking curves, hitting flat out, but never disappearing. The few days before the hayride he had actually hidden out at his own office, unwilling to run into Chloe. Not certain what he would say if he did. But she had remained low-key as well, mostly staying in the file room. He overheard her speaking with the office manager, but left before Chloe could see him.

Hardly cold-blooded professional behavior. She could be off her game, but he didn't think so. Chloe continued to nurture and encourage Jimmy, and to further her relationships with everyone else in the house.

The clip-clop of horses' hooves blended with the quiet voices and occasional bursts of laughter from the wagon's passengers. He glanced over at Chloe and Jimmy, who were wearing newly purchased jeans and casual cotton shirts. He had heard her consult with Viola about what the attire should be. In addition, Chloe had made sure Jimmy was warmly dressed, insisting on a jacket and hat. But she wore only a light sweater.

The nights got nippy this time of year. Not the fierce cold of the northern midwest, but still cool enough to chill the bones. Everyone else on the wagon had been raised in and around Rosewood and knew the peculiarities of their own weather and had dressed accordingly.

Jimmy pointed toward the sky. "I can see really big stars."

Chloe smiled. "They're all big and bright in Texas." She leaned close. "*Everything's* supposed to be bigger in Texas."

"I'm bigger," he announced.

She laughed. "Probably nearly a foot taller."

Jimmy grinned, then looked over at a group of kids his own age on the other side of the wagon.

Chloe followed his gaze. "Do you want to sit over there?"

"Can I?"

"Just remember what I told you. Have fun, but don't hang over the sides or back of the wagon."

"Okay." He took off like a shot.

Her smile turned tender. Jimmy had gotten to her. Why couldn't she have been the one with the opportunity to raise this loveable child?

Evan watched Jimmy scramble away, then studied Chloe's dreamy expression. "Think he'll mind you?"

"He's a good kid." She stared up toward the sky.

Evan couldn't ignore the sweep of Chloe's long lashes, the curve of her cheek, the fullness of her lips. His gaze lingered overly long at the last spot. "I know."

"I was teasing Jimmy," she said in a muted tone, "but the stars truly do seem brighter."

"The sky looks different everywhere. Altitude, air quality, proximity to artificial light…."

"That's the scientist in you. But as a Texan?"

"Definitely bigger and brighter."

Chloe laughed quietly. "The sky reminds me of how it looks back home at the lakes. Very different from the city."

"Which do you like better?"

"That's like asking which is cuter—puppies or kittens."

Amused, he relaxed a fraction. "Guess it *is* the scientist in me. Never compared newborn animals with astronomy."

"Surely you've seen them in the clouds," she protested mildly.

"Not during the night."

"Ah, so technical," Chloe teased. "I've seen every living thing in the clouds."

"Even microbes?"

She groaned. "You do know how to take the magic out of the night skies."

No. The romance. That's what he was obliterating. And, the fact that he needed to, alarmed him. Yet he didn't pull away. If anything, he slid the tiniest bit closer. "Magic is in the beholder."

"I thought that was love."

The word dangled between them, hovering like a harbinger of danger, perhaps even more.

Chloe shifted first, ostensibly to check on Jimmy who was laughing with the other kids, paying no attention to two tense adults.

It was ridiculous, Evan reasoned. Just because he was a man and she was a woman. He couldn't quite complete the thought.

The wagon hit a bump, jostling Chloe, pressing her against his side. She didn't straighten up immediately, instead holding her breath. Lurching the other direction, the wagon took her away almost as quickly. Evan immediately missed the contact.

She hugged her arms, shivering.

"You should have worn something warmer."

"I didn't pack a coat. I thought…"

That he would have already said yes to keeping Jimmy. That she wouldn't be in Rosewood long enough to need winter wear.

"Why didn't you buy one when you got the jeans?"

Chloe glanced down. "I'm fine." There wasn't extra money in her budget for a new winter coat. Not until she received the raise Mr. Wainwright had promised if she fulfilled her mission. She had received an email from the administrator at her mother's retirement home. The rate was going up again, starting the following month. If Chloe was very, very careful she could squeeze it out of her budget. Fortunately, her utilities would be less since she wasn't home. But what if Evan stuck to his guns? What if she failed?

And what if she never forgot the solid feeling of his muscled body beside hers?

Chloe knew he was strong. She had seen the muscles flex beneath his shirt sleeves, and she could never have missed the endless length of his legs. Her breath was so short, she wondered if it would return to normal.

Even if Evan wasn't off limits because he was a client, she couldn't trust her judgment any longer. She had actually believed her fiancé, Derek, had loved her, that they shared the same dreams and values. How could she have missed what must have been colossal clues?

And then there was Mom. Chloe could never leave her. Chip wouldn't be back in the states for at least two years. Then he could be stationed on the other side of the country or world. No, she was the only constant in her mother's life, the one Mom depended on.

The evidence was conclusive, inescapable and it made her heart ache.

Surreptitiously, she peeked over at Evan. He, too, looked as though he had more than stars and hayrides on his mind.

There was something so basic, so appealing about bumping along a country road in the dark, wrapped in the comforting warmth of good people. For the briefest moment, Chloe let herself imagine how it would be if these were her friends, her family. Evan and Jimmy… family? The tender part of her heart twinged.

And she couldn't stop herself from lifting her face to meet Evan's eyes. Despite the dim light of the night sky, she watched his eyes darken, shifting to another place, another mood. She swallowed. The wagon lurched and Chloe allowed herself to slide with the motion, her arm pressing against his. Although reluctant to lose contact, she twisted until she faced him.

His eyes darted to her lips.

Throat dry, mouth drier, she could only continue gazing at him.

Tilting his head ever so much, he leaned close. So close she felt his breath whisper over her. The chill of the night fell away.

Evan's mouth met hers, searching, settling into her lips, soft and strong, intoxicating and powerful. Somewhere, drifting in her thoughts, was the notion that she should pull away, remind him that this could go nowhere. That she was a completely temporary fixture in his life. Perhaps remind herself…

Instead, she waited until he ended the kiss, until he leaned back so that she could see his face. The regret.

Shakily, she inhaled. Was she doomed to go from mistake to worse mistake?

Evan looked as though he wanted to say something. Even though she had been hoping since she met him that he would speak more, now she couldn't bear a word. Not one single word.

Chapter Nine

Evan retreated to the den, warming his hands on a mug of coffee. Guilt filled, overflowed, brewing like the fresh coffee he'd just made. No worry that it would keep him up. There wouldn't be any sleep for him this night. He couldn't believe he had kissed Chloe again. Having almost convinced himself that it was an unintentional slip and vowing never to repeat it, all reason had fled when she lifted her face.

Sinking into a deep leather chair, Evan placed his coffee on the side table, staring at the portraits lining the wall. His great-grandparents, grandparents, then finally his father and mother. Each had taken the vow till death do us part. And each had kept it.

He and Robin had planned to sit for their portrait on their tenth anniversary. No longer newlyweds, but still early in what they assumed would be a decades-long marriage.

And he couldn't even keep the vow a single decade. What was he thinking? Kissing another woman? The shame was overwhelming. He had ignored the Lord's voice since that fateful day when Robin and Sean had been killed. Now all Evan could hear was His censure. Dropping his face into his hands, Evan hated the other truth prodding him. That he had enjoyed the kiss. That he might even be developing feelings for Chloe. He groaned aloud.

"That's a mighty heavy load, son." Gordon's voice reached out from across the room.

Evan wasn't terribly surprised. His father had always seemed to know when he was needed. Slowly, he lifted his face. In the quiet, he could hear the tamping of fresh tobacco in his father's pipe. Not that Dad ever smoked it. He had given that up thirty years earlier. But he still enjoyed the ritual, the smell of his favorite blend.

"When you were a kid, you'd fall asleep in here, reading books about rocks, dinosaurs, and the Hardy Boys. Remember?"

Evan nodded.

Even though only one dim lamp lit the room, Gordon recognized the silent gesture. "Life's not quite like one of those Hardy Boys' mysteries. Not so easily solved, sure not wrapped up all tidy."

Evan sighed. "I know, Dad."

Gordon stood, relocating to the chair adjacent to Evan's. "I never wanted you to suffer so. When you were two days old, I promised you I'd never let anything hurt you. At the time, I thought I had the power to keep that promise. Took a lot of maturing to realize I couldn't. Only the Lord can hold you in His hands. And He does."

Assaulted by guilt and indecision, Evan doubted it. But hurting his father wouldn't help. "That's what you raised me to believe."

"Belief's a funny thing. It's easy when things are good."

Evan's defenses stirred. "You think I'm a rainy-day believer?"

"No man should outlive his child. And nothing hurts more than your child's pain. You're my child, Evan. Your pain is mine. I've felt it every day since you lost Robin and Sean. It's not belief you need to seek. It's acceptance, the reinforcement that you will see them again."

Staring at the floor, Evan wondered, as he had done since the accident. "Why them?"

"I don't know, son. But when the cancer took your mother, it was my faith that made it bearable, made me realize I could go on. Without it…" Gordon glanced up at the portrait of himself and Evan's mother. "I loved her all my life and I couldn't imagine life without her. Didn't want to."

"I'm sorry, Dad."

"We both lost her." Gordon tamped the unlit pipe again. "But I sure can't lose you."

"Don't think I'm going anywhere."

"Without your faith, you'll die inside a little bit at a time. One day you'll wake up and nothing's left."

Evan picked up his cooling coffee. "I'm having a tough enough time just getting through today." The kiss he shared with Chloe pricked his conscience again.

"The hayride." It wasn't a question.

Evan blinked. "Did you intentionally push us together?"

"Good parents don't push. They lead."

And that wasn't even an answer.

"Got any more hot coffee?" Gordon asked.

"It'll keep you up."

Gordon smiled, his concern evident. "Thought you might like some company."

Acceptance. Was it a concept or a reality?

Rising, Evan carried his coffee into the kitchen, dumped out the cold dregs, filled his own and a second mug. He paused. Thelma hadn't closed the kitchen curtains. Staring into the darkness, he continued to wonder. What if? What if he hadn't booked the vacation? What if Robin and Sean had survived?

What if he hadn't met Chloe?

Hadn't kissed her?

Evan's hand strayed to his lips, remembering the softness, the scent of her. What if, Lord?

What if?

Chloe devoured the new stack of correspondence that had been plunked into the *To Be Filed* tray. Letters to and from TEX-INC, apparently a new customer. They painted a hopeful picture. The enormous order could put Mitchell Stone back in the black.

Bells jingled in the doorway. Viola popped through a few seconds later. "Time to decorate. Actually, past time."

Her mind filled with what she'd just read, Chloe frowned.

"For Christmas," Viola explained. "We usually put everything up right after Thanksgiving. Being short-handed and all, we waited." She shook the string of bells again. "We all fix up our own areas, then a few of us tackle the reception area. You game?"

Chloe had been thinking about the tiny tree she usually set up in her mother's room. The home would have one in the communal television room, but it wasn't the same. She put down the letter in her hand. "I'm game."

Viola led her to the break room where open boxes were scattered around the tables. Plastic holly trailed from one, wooden strings of cranberries from another. One box in the corner remained closed.

"That's the nativity set," Viola explained. "We set it up in reception. Gordon and Adele brought it back from the Holy Land. It's really special."

"Ours always was, too."

"Was?"

Chloe bit down on her lower lip. "We sold our family home a few years ago. My mother's in a care facility. And my brother and his family are stationed overseas. He's Army. So there's no place to set up the nativity. I kept it, though. That and the ornaments we made with our father." Ridiculously, she felt the sting of tears that she blinked back.

"It's an emotional time of year," Viola said quietly. "It's supposed to be. Would you help me set up the nativity this year?"

Chloe's lips trembled. "I'd love to."

"Good. And pick anything you want from the boxes to make the file room area festive. We all do, so stuff gets switched around each year. Everything except the nativity."

"Thank you, Viola."

The older woman paused, searched Chloe's face, then nodded. "See you in a bit."

Chloe chose a few simple pieces to arrange on her desk and the incoming records table. Her mind swirled with memories and anticipation. Memories of Christmases past, the kiss she had shared with Evan, the expression on his face....

And the anticipation of setting up a nativity for the first time in several years.

For Jimmy's sake, she also considered the reverberations of Mitchell Stone's new customer. If Evan felt his employees' futures were secure, maybe he would rethink his decision. Perhaps he would decide that his life would be fuller with Jimmy in it.

Then, of course, she could go home. No more missing her mother, no more endless images of Evan's regret, his distaste for her. No more Evan.

Chloe pushed back the hurt, reminding herself it was for the best. That, even if Evan had been attracted to her, they could have no future. She expected the rationalization to make things better, to make the hurt go away. Yet it lingered, and it grew.

The day dragged along. Chloe popped into Viola's office to ask when they would be setting up the nativity. Learning it was just after closing time, she left to pick up Jimmy from school and get him settled before returning.

The days were growing shorter, the sun setting earlier and earlier. Driving down Main Street, Chloe felt nostalgic as she saw the lights, which were strung across the road, flicker on. A huge star dominated the middle of Main Street. Alongside, on the sidewalk, living Christmas trees were placed about every twenty-five feet. How long had it been since she had taken time to enjoy the signs of the season? Always in a rush from her job to the apartment or retirement home, she never noticed anything but red lights and stop signs.

Pulling in one of the diagonal spaces in front of

Mitchell Stone, Chloe parked. She could see Viola and the receptionist, Jackie, through the large plate-glass window.

Once inside, she shrugged out of her jacket. "Hope I'm not late."

"Just on time," Viola replied cheerfully. The box containing the nativity was perched solidly on the counter. "We keep this area simple, tasteful."

Jackie, who had been humming "Joy To the World," set up a brass easel. "This holds our greeting cards."

A simple wooden table, topped by marble from Mitchell Stone's own quarry, had been placed between the two leather couches. Chloe tried to remember where she had seen the piece of furniture before.

Viola opened a package of dried moss, then pointed to a small box. "The straw's in there. Do you want to set up the stable and arrange the straw? You'll have to take out the other figurines first."

Taking a deep breath, Chloe realized she was being given the privilege of opening the nativity box. Carefully she reached inside, removing the first of several pieces wrapped in tissue. One by one she unwrapped the glorious wood figures. She paused when she held the manger. The quality of the carving was exquisite, replicating the rustic resting place of the Christ child.

Chloe took out small handfuls of straw, placing the chaff inside the stable. She centered the manger, then placed Mary on one side, Joseph on the other. As she finished placing the holy family, the entire scene came to life.

Chloe added the shepherds, then the Magi. Oxen, sheep and camel completed the last semicircle around the stable. Now, to place the babe in the manger. A lump stuck in her throat.

"Looks beautiful," Viola said quietly. "Every year, when it's set up, I'm moved all over again."

"My mother would be pleased," Chloe murmured. "Thank you for letting me be part of this."

"It's gotten cliché, the saying that people who work together are like a family. But we really are, have been for four generations. My great-grandfather was one of the originals. And, someone in my family has worked here ever since."

"It's rare—this complete devotion to the welfare of the employees. I'm lucky. I have a good boss, too. But this... You're right. It is family." Brow furrowing, Chloe frowned.

"What is it?"

"Just that family is so important to the Mitchells, yet Evan's so resistant to Jimmy."

Viola studied her and Chloe wondered at the doubt in her eyes.

"You've put it in a nutshell," Viola finally replied. "Family is everything to Evan." She walked to the light switch and flipped on the exterior one. Soft white lights surrounding the main window flickered, then settled to a gentle glow.

And Chloe knew she wouldn't learn anything about Evan's past from Viola. It was frustrating, yet she had to admire the loyalty of his friends, family and employees. Perhaps there was one person who would tell her. One person who had once been new to the town herself.

Grace's free hour was at ten in the morning and she had readily agreed to meet Chloe at the café on Main

Street for coffee and pie. Although Chloe loved coconut cream pie, she didn't pick up her fork.

Finishing a sip of coffee, Grace's eyes lingered on Chloe's untouched dessert. "It's wonderful getting out for a while and I love the pie, but I'm guessing that's not why you asked to meet."

Chloe hadn't dared tell Grace what she wanted over the phone. "You're the only person I've really talked to in Rosewood who isn't related to or works for Evan."

"Hmm…" Grace listened, holding the mug close to her lips, but not drinking.

"And I think you know what I want to ask. Everyone keeps alluding to some sort of secret about Evan… his past or some event. I don't know what it is, but I feel that it's what could be keeping him from accepting Jimmy." She leaned forward. "Yes, I'd like to know for myself, as well. I admit it. But Jimmy's entire future is at stake, his happiness. I wouldn't ask if I…well, I could ask Evan. But he's not going to open that door for me."

Carefully, Grace set her cup in its saucer, staring down at the table. "It's not a secret. The whole town knows about it. But, it's such a source of pain…." Empathy filled Grace's blue-gray eyes. "I know something about pain, how long it takes for a person to heal."

Chloe waited while Grace struggled over repeating Evan's past.

"Evan was married."

An involuntary gasp escaped before Chloe could stop it.

"And he had a five-year-old son. Robin and Sean were his life. Evan and Robin were high school sweethearts, then both went to the University of Texas, too. They knew they were meant for each other from their first meeting. They were married a short time when they learned they were expecting a baby. I don't know of any child that has ever been more anticipated and loved since conception. Their family was the ideal I wanted for myself. I think a lot of other people felt the same way."

Trying to assimilate the revelation, Chloe remained silent.

"To surprise Robin for her birthday, Evan arranged a vacation for the family in Hawaii because Robin had always wanted to visit there. They had honeymooned at Catalina because it was closer and Evan had to get back to the university for his master's studies. Anyway, they flew to Hawaii and stayed on one of the smaller islands. On the second day of their trip, they went to the beach. It was a gorgeous, out of the way area. And there was only one place to rent umbrellas and that sort of thing. Evan walked down the road to rent life jackets, chairs and a float for Sean. While he was gone, Sean got away from Robin and ran out into the water."

Chloe paled, feeling herself shaking inside.

"Robin wasn't much of a swimmer but she went in after him. Because it wasn't a crowded spot there wasn't a lifeguard on duty. Warning signs were posted, but Evan hadn't expected Sean to dash into the water on his own. Evan was only gone a few minutes, but the waves were huge, ferocious. The people on the beach noticed and tried to help, but Robin and Sean were swept out too far."

Chloe held one hand over her mouth.

"Evan dove in after them, but it was too late. The people there said he fought like a madman to get to them, finally retrieving their bodies. But it was too late. They couldn't be resuscitated."

"How awful!" Chloe whispered, tears gathering in her eyes.

"Evan blamed himself. He had planned the vacation. He had left them alone while he went to the rental stand."

"But it wasn't his fault!"

"He can't get beyond that day."

"I think…" Chloe began haltingly. "…that's what I see in his eyes."

Grace nodded. "His heart is broken. And so is his faith."

Chloe stared, unseeing, into the black depths of her coffee cup.

"My experience is different, but I found myself in the same place with my faith. It's difficult to…reconnect." Absently, she rubbed the scar on her hand. "Evan's been surrounded by people who care for him ever since the accident." Grace sighed. "I had to find my path myself, to accept. I couldn't understand until then. I thought the Lord was punishing me, abandoning me. I honestly don't know if that's how Evan feels." She placed her scarred hand over Chloe's. "But his pain must be mixed with fear. How can he love again? Especially a vulnerable child?"

Chloe couldn't begin to imagine the depth of his pain. "Why didn't he just tell me?"

"Maybe there's a tiny part of him that *wants* to accept Jimmy. He's a good and caring man. I suspect it was easier to say no by phone or letter. Seeing the little guy in person must have torn him up."

"He didn't show it.…" Chloe met Grace's concerned

gaze. "It must have been awful trying to keep that inside, especially since I've done everything I could to push Jimmy in his direction."

"Evan's bent, but not completely broken. It's that strength he has to hold fast to."

Chloe was shattered. What about Jimmy? His future? At the same time, her heart ached for Evan. And he'd never shared one word of his pain. "I probably would have gone right back to Milwaukee if I'd known."

A certain wisdom gathered in Grace's eyes. "The Lord knew that."

Had Mr. Wainwright? He had told her that Evan was single, not widowed, with no mention of the son he had lost. Had her boss hoped that Evan would see past his pain to take in another child?

"I'll pray for all three of you," Grace promised. "The Lord doesn't want little Jimmy to be alone, either."

Drained by the enormous discovery, Chloe found herself tearing up again. "I would appreciate that. I have some praying of my own to do. What if I should never have come here? Maybe, knowing this, I should go back now."

"And Jimmy?"

That was the killer. And Chloe couldn't help wondering if Evan needed Jimmy as much as the child needed him.

Chapter Ten

Gordon refused to let anyone off the hook, insisting they all gather in the parlor to decorate the tall native pine tree. Ned had hauled down several boxes of ornaments, lights, tinsel, and beading from the attic.

The living Christmas tree had been grown by a local horticulturist, Bret Conway, who avidly practiced conservation. He and his wife, Samantha, operated a family nursery. And each year, they delivered the tree, then picked it up after the new year. Gordon had been one of Bret's first customers for his living trees and now theirs was a tall, full, beautiful specimen.

"Does it get bigger every year?" Jimmy asked.

"Sure does," Gordon replied. "And we don't have to cut down another tree every year. The planet needs all the trees it has and then some."

"That's what my daddy said."

Evan watched their exchange, pleased that Jimmy seemed more relaxed. But that very fact worried him equally. His gaze roamed over to Chloe, who had been studiously avoiding him since the night of the hayride. She seemed quieter than usual.

Following Gordon's suggestion, she was carefully unwrapping ornaments that had been in his family longer than Evan had. The oldest were hand-blown glass, some imported from Germany and Poland. Others had been made by various family members. Those varied from childish paper cutouts to elaborately decorated salt dough, even a few crocheted snowflakes.

When she reached the one he both anticipated and dreaded, Chloe paused. It was a paper star that Sean had pasted his last photo on. People had always said that Sean was Evan's spitting image. Perhaps that's what Chloe would believe—that it was a photo of Evan. She studied it an overly long time, then placed the paper ornament by itself on a nearby table.

Her cautious attention to that particular handmade ornament made him wonder. Had his father spilled his guts? Wouldn't surprise him. Telling Chloe all about Evan's unfortunate past. Staring at Chloe deliberately enough to cause her to notice him didn't work. She avoided his gaze. Was that because she now knew more? Or because she regretted the kiss?

Eating breakfast and leaving for the office before the others came downstairs, then making certain he and she never met at work, along with skipping family dinner had kept them apart. If Chloe had wanted to confront him, Evan hadn't been available.

Jimmy watched as each ornament came into view. Some caused him to raise his eyebrows, widen his eyes, or light up.

Chloe selected a bell made from tin and handed it to Jimmy. "Why don't you ask Uncle Gordon where to hang this?"

"Anywhere he wants," Gordon replied. "We just put

them up wherever they look good. And, we usually add a few new ones each year." He smiled, remembering. "Evan's mother did have a strict rule about stringing the lights, though. Have to start at the top of the tree. Made me restring them more times than I can count."

Evan knew his father was missing her. "And, she made *us* untangle them."

"They had to be the first thing on the tree," Gordon added.

Chloe lifted the lights from a second box. "Funny how they seem to tangle themselves just sitting in the box."

"Really?" Jimmy asked, peering inside.

She smiled gently. "No. We're usually in more of a hurry to get the lights back in the box than when we take them out. So, they're easier to tangle."

"Oh."

A magical fairy that tangled the lights was probably more exciting, Evan mused.

Chloe held up one string of lights, starting to straighten it out.

"Why don't you help her, son?" Gordon suggested. "Jimmy and I can get out the garlands."

Reluctantly, Evan rose. "Want me to take those?"

Chloe kept her gaze on the lights. "I could use some help."

Still reluctant, Evan sat on the opposite end of the couch. It might be his imagination, but the lights were more tangled than ever. To reach the cording, he had to slide over one cushion closer. Chloe fumbled with the string, unable to find a starting point. Reaching to find it, Evan's hand collided with hers. As quickly, she pulled back, as though stung.

This time she didn't meet his eyes, instead trying to avoid them. Oh, yeah. Something was up.

Thelma bustled into the room, carrying a large bowl. "Who's going to string popcorn?"

Chloe glanced up at her.

"You're elected," Thelma decreed. "It's not hard, just pull a needle and thread through a piece at a time."

"My mother taught me," Chloe replied, accepting the popcorn.

Jimmy ran over and peered down at the overflowing dish. "Can I have some?"

"Sure."

He popped a piece in his mouth, chewed, then frowned. "It tastes funny."

Thelma grinned. "That's cause it doesn't have any salt or butter. You don't salt popcorn you're going to string. Makes it crumble. And the butter... well you can just imagine how hard it would be to string it all greased up. There's another bowl in the kitchen, one I made for you to eat. Want to go get it?"

"Does it have the good stuff?"

She plopped her hands on her hips. "I said it was for eating."

Jimmy grinned and took off for the kitchen.

As he did, Chloe used the excuse of the new chore to leave the couch and settle in a chair, placing the bowl of popcorn on a side table. Threading the needle Thelma had provided, Chloe began stringing the cooled popcorn.

With the fire blazing in the tall limestone fireplace, it could have been a Norman Rockwell sketch. But they weren't united. Odds and ends, all of them. He and his father, widowers. Jimmy orphaned. Chloe… Yes, what about Chloe?

Evan finally got the lights untangled, then strung on the tree. Gordon and Jimmy joined him, ready to hang ornaments.

Thelma came back into the parlor. "I'll string the rest," she told Chloe, picking up the bowl. "You go help the others with the ornaments."

"But I can—"

"Go on."

Chloe didn't hurry, finally edging behind Gordon.

Spotting her, Gordon pulled Chloe forward. "Grab an ornament."

She hesitated, then withdrew a small crystal angel. Evan barely contained his surprise. His mother's favorite ornament. Chloe reached upward. His gaze followed. She affixed the hook, then slowly met his eyes. Hers were filled with something he had never seen before. Evan sensed she wanted to turn away, wanted to run.

Seeing how Chloe had woven herself and Jimmy into their lives, his blood chilled. People close to him didn't fare well. And, Jimmy was becoming too comfortable, too attached. It wasn't right. The child would be crushed with disappointment when Evan had to send him home. Despite Chloe's tenacity, that would still be the end result.

His heart twinged, but he had to ignore the temporal feeling. Jimmy would be better off in a two-parent home, one not fraught with tragedy and guilt. Watching Chloe, Evan knew it was time to tell her so.

The homey warmth of the evening resonated in Chloe's thoughts. A memory maker, her mother would have called it. Seeing Jimmy's happiness. Appreciating all the family times that had been experienced in the Mitchells' house. Especially knowing the pain Evan carried.

How did he bear to perform the same traditions he had shared with his wife and son? Chloe couldn't get the picture of Sean out of her thoughts, his sweet face, his bright eyes. A child who should have had a long and wonderful future. No wonder Evan had resented her sudden appearance on his doorstep.

But could he overcome the past? Build a future with Jimmy?

After pouring a cup of Thelma's spiced cider, Chloe turned around. And met Evan's glower.

It was time, Evan reminded himself. Time to set things straight.

"What's wrong?" Chloe asked.

"You. And Jimmy."

She hesitated, fiddling with a mug. "Your father—"

"Regardless of what he says, this isn't going to work."

Chloe's face filled with distress.

"There's no time in my life to indulge Wainwright's whims. I'm trying to keep a business alive."

She opened her mouth, then closed it as quickly.

"Oh, I appreciate you pitching in at the office."

"I wanted to," she rushed to say.

"Even so, you need to find another option for Jimmy."

"It's a cruel time to—"

"You think I'm cruel? Every day Jimmy's here, you're giving him false hope."

Chloe looked stricken.

And that bothered him far more than it should. "I've

had my say." Unable to watch her despair any longer, he turned on his heel and left the kitchen. Once back in the entry hall, Evan expelled a deep breath. The confrontation had affected him more than it should. He started toward the staircase, then stopped. Pain mixed with guilt, then multiplied. Why did Wainwright have to disregard his wishes in the first place?

Sighing, Evan turned back to the parlor. Everyone had cleared out earlier. Only the lights on the tree lit the room. But he could have navigated the parlor blindfolded.

He stopped next to the table with Sean's paper ornament.

"I made it for you, Daddy!"

"All by yourself?"

"Mommy helped."

"It's great, big guy."

Evan swallowed, then picked up the small piece of construction paper, tracing his fingers over Sean's photo. *I miss you, son. I always will.*

With the greatest care, he carried the precious ornament over to the tree, gently hanging it high on the top branch, close to the angel topping the conifer, her wings stretched out to protect all beneath them. "Sleep well, little angel. Daddy loves you."

Pushing the back of his hand against his lips, he stopped their trembling. But nothing could deter the tears stinging his eyes.

Chloe straightened the quilt on Jimmy's bed, pulling it up to cover his shoulders, tucking it in snugly the way he liked. Elbert had fallen on the floor, no doubt when Jimmy had kicked the covers askew. Despite his progress, Jimmy was still a small boy in a home he knew wasn't his own.

Tucking Elbert next to Jimmy, she sighed. Part of her wished she hadn't learned Evan's terrible secret. Her empathy was overtaking her objectivity. It wasn't just Evan's future, she kept reminding herself. It was Jimmy's. But could a man who had lost so much have anything left to give?

Crossing over to the bay window, Chloe looked out into the street. A tree in the window of a neighboring house caught her eye. It was quiet, families all tucked in for the night, children sleeping, adults easing into the later hours.

Would she ever have a family of her own? A child to tuck in bed? A husband to love? Her gaze strayed toward Jimmy. He had attached himself to her heart—it was no longer just empathy.

The lights in the tree across the street winked in the muted darkness. Closing her eyes against the reminder, she acknowledged what else was building in her heart. More than empathy for Evan. Far more.

Chapter Eleven

Evan's cell phone rang. Seeing it was his father, he answered quickly. "Hey, Dad."

"Didn't see you at breakfast."

No. And that way Evan hadn't seen Chloe or Jimmy.

"I'll take your silence to mean yes. Church school called. They asked if we could supply them with a boulder to use in their school play."

Evan frowned. "Don't they usually make them out of papier-mâché?"

"Not when children are sitting on them. It's for the little shepherd boy when he sees the star."

"Right. How big a boulder do they need?"

"The shepherd boy is probably six or seven. Principal said it's usually a first grader."

"Okay, Dad. When do they need it?"

"I told them today."

Sighing, Evan counted to ten.

"Of course," Gordon continued. "I suppose I could try and lift it myself...."

Pure blackmail. "I'm not that far from the quarry." Evan checked his watch. "Will an hour or so work?"

"Sounds good. Rehearsals start after school today."

"Okay."

"Son?"

Evan waited.

"I'll try not to volunteer you for anything else." Gordon paused. "Today."

Clicking the phone off, Evan smiled for the first time since his talk with Chloe. It didn't take long to drive to the quarry and load a decent-sized boulder along with a flat dolly to transfer it inside the school auditorium.

Funny how schools all had that same smell—chalk and cafeteria food combined with stale gym socks. Having attended the school himself, Evan knew his way around. He pushed the dolly over wooden floors, the weight of the boulder causing them to creak. The noise was going to make it difficult to execute a quick drop and run without anyone noticing him. He glanced around. Class must be in session since the halls were empty. Maybe the getaway was possible.

Children's voices emerged from the open doors of the auditorium. A teacher clapped her hands. "I need the lamb and camel."

Two youngsters bounced up to the stage. The teacher showed them where they would stand. Both stepped outside of the chalk circles she had drawn. "Children!"

Amused, Evan pushed the dolly to the stage. Lifting the heavy boulder, he carried it up the three short steps.

The teacher paused. "Evan! That must weigh a ton."

It *was* getting heavy. "If you'll tell me where it goes..."

Flustered, she looked around. "Well... the night of the play it needs to be in the center of the stage, but it would be in the way for the rest of the performance."

Evan carried the boulder to the far side of the small stage. "It can be moved to the center on the night of the play."

"You'd do that?" the teacher exclaimed. "That would be wonderful!"

He hadn't intended to offer, but submitted to the inevitable. "Fax the date and time over to Mitchell Stone." The boulder in place, he turned around. And stared at Chloe. Who was supposed to be out of Rosewood by now.

Chloe stared back.

"Evan!" Jimmy hollered, running onto the stage.

"No running," the teacher chided.

"Guess what? I'm gonna be the shepherd boy. I get to sit on the big rock!"

Evan looked into the youngster's eager face and couldn't disappoint him. "Congratulations. I hear that's a big part."

Relief flooded Chloe's face.

Had she completely forgotten what he'd told her? That it was time for her to return Jimmy to Milwaukee?

"Jimmy," the teacher called. "Let's try out that big rock."

While he did, Evan pushed the dolly off the stage, then headed straight for Chloe. He nodded his head toward the door. "I'll see you outside."

Tailgate down, he lifted the cumbersome dolly into the bed of the truck. Despite the noise, he heard Chloe's hesitant steps coming up behind him. Evan whirled around. "What did you do? Jimmy's already in too deep and now he's got a part in the school play?"

"*I* didn't give him the part."

"You also didn't tell him no."

She gaped at him. "Why don't you do that? Tell a thrilled little boy who just got one of best parts in the play that he can't be in it?"

"That's your job, not mine."

Chloe shook her head. "Oh, no. You want to crush his spirit, then you'll have to do the dirty work." Stomping off, she didn't look back.

Evan slammed the tailgate shut. How had he lost control of his own life? Angry, he forced himself not to speed as he drove to his only refuge—work. At least Chloe was occupied at the school and wouldn't be there.

His office fronted Main Street and he always left the blinds open so the natural light could enter. Standing by the window, Evan watched pedestrians walking the elm-lined street. Mothers with preschool-age children, two aging men clinging to their canes, an elderly couple arm in arm. It was easy to imagine Chloe as part of the tableau, walking along, her hand gripping Jimmy's.

Evan sighed. Sometimes it was difficult to live in a place with so much happiness. Especially now that he was on the outside looking in.

Someone knocked lightly on the door frame.

He didn't turn around. "Come in."

"Evan." Perry's voice was somber.

Pushing the kaleidoscope of images from his mind, he faced his friend and colleague. One look told him it was trouble.

Perry gripped the back of one armchair. "The financing."

Evan knew what was coming, but he couldn't believe it.

"Fell through."

There was nothing to say. A million things to say.

"Any other avenues?"

"I've been on the phone all day." Perry sighed, then pulled back the chair, sitting down. "I have a few more places to try."

"But you don't expect any better news."

Perry couldn't hide his discouragement.

"How much of the big order can we complete without it?"

"Evan—"

He waved away the words. Barely a dent. He'd known before he asked. "Contract penalty?"

Perry met his gaze. "It'll wipe out everything that's left."

Evan turned back to the window, seeing everyone going on as though nothing had just tipped the world. "How long can we make payroll before we notify TEX-INC?" He ran his hand up his forehead, then through his hair.

"It won't be long."

Christmas was closing in. If he could stretch the funds until it was past… "Work up the figures."

The other man's footsteps echoed over the granite floor as he left.

Refuge? Now this one was crumbling. Soon he would be a man with no safe harbor. And people he had known all his life were going to be without jobs. How was he going to tell them? Evan remembered the solace of turning to the Lord for direction. His own personal war hadn't ended. But, could he keep up the battle when so much was at stake?

Chloe read Jimmy his favorite story twice, then three others before he nodded off. Now she tucked Elbert close. Jimmy didn't stir. He had fallen asleep hours earlier, but she couldn't stop checking on him.

What would happen if Evan remained steadfast about his decision? For all that she wanted to protect and nurture Jimmy, she didn't have the means. Even if she found the money for a babysitter, her time wasn't her own. Jimmy would end up being raised by the sitter.

The ache in her heart resonated. And what about Evan? Was he doomed to live alone, without love, without hope? She had pushed and fought against it, but he, too, had broached her defenses. Why? Of all the men in the world she could have fallen for? Why Evan Mitchell?

Taking a last, long look at the sleeping child, Chloe returned to her room. The fire was banked, her cup of Thelma's spiced cider long empty. But she was still restless. Thoughts continued spinning, encroaching. Gordon had been excited to hear about Jimmy's part in the Christmas play. Since Evan hadn't been there for dinner, she had been spared his displeasure.

The mantel clock struck midnight. It was pointless, unnecessary, but she wondered why Evan wasn't safely at home. Surely if there had been an accident at the quarry, Gordon would have been informed. In a town like Rosewood, the word would have spread quickly.

Chloe edged the curtain aside so she could look out into the street. There was something comforting about the tidiness of the quiet neighborhood. As she ruminated, Evan's truck came into sight. It was the old truck she and Jimmy had ridden in with him. The beater rumbled to a stop near the end of the driveway. Strange that he didn't park it in the garage. Continuing to watch, she saw him climb slowly out of the driver's side, then just as slowly approach the bench that curved around the ancient oak out front.

Straining to see, she wondered at his behavior. Evan always walked briskly, energetically. Now he slumped down on the bench. Worry hit like a well-placed arrow. Something was wrong.

Disregarding the hour, Chloe grabbed her sweater, glad she hadn't changed from her warm slacks yet. Skipping lightly down the stairs, she reached the front door. Caution prodded. What was she doing?

Refusing to listen to the inner warning, she stepped outside, quietly crossing the winter-dried lawn. A few feet away from Evan, she slowed, but didn't stop. "Evan?"

He raised his bleak face.

Immediately, her heart thudded in fear. "What is it?"

Evan only looked at her.

The fear intensified as she sat beside him. "Evan?"

"You know just when to hit, don't you?"

"I'm not here because I want something," Chloe implored. "I was worried when it got so late. Then... I saw you from the window. I can tell something's wrong."

He searched her face, his guard dropping. "Wrong is an understatement."

"The business."

"Good guess."

"No guess. You worry about your employees as though..." She almost said *children.* "As though they mean the world to you. It has to be something concerning them."

The soft gas lights illuminated his expression. "The big order we got from TEX-INC—we can't fill it."

"Maybe they'll negotiate a later delivery date. They took time choosing their supplier. Surely—"

"It's not the delivery. Our financing fell through."

Shocked, Chloe tried to fathom the implications. "Surely your bank has done business with Mitchell Stone for decades."

"Make that closer to a century. The local bank didn't have the funds in this economic climate. We found a big national bank, thought it was a done deal."

"There are more banks!"

"With the same criteria. We've lost money for the last four years, not a banker's dream."

"You can't just give up." She searched her mind for alternatives.

Evan laughed bitterly. "Easy to say."

The difficulty of her own life for the last decade surfaced. "Hardly. Yours isn't the first business to falter. And you're not the only person to face difficulties. But you have to believe you can turn things around!"

"Believe? You *are* new here."

"What? So you're going to cave, let all your employees fend for themselves. I'm sure each of them will find a great paying job, be able to keep their homes, feed their children—"

"Stop! I've been fighting this battle for years. You waltz in here and—"

"*Waltz?* Did you actually say *waltz?* I came here scared to death for myself, for Jimmy, for everything that means anything to me. And now, I'm getting to know the people who work for you, liking them, wondering how they'll cope." Her chest heaved with fury and frustration. "And what about Gordon? He'll be devastated. He cares as much about these people as you do! And—"

Evan held up one hand. "I can't take another *and*."

Her anger deflated. Drained, she sat silent. No bird sang in the night to fill the quiet, no cars passed, no dogs barked.

"I suppose one of us should jump on a white horse, put on some armor," Evan said finally.

Chloe leaned back against the bark of the sturdy oak. "I'm not that good with horses."

He turned, scrutinizing her. "An hour ago I wouldn't have given ten cents toward taking another shot."

"Does that mean you're not giving up?"

"How did you do that? Turn everything around?"

She looked down, fiddling with her hands.

Evan stopped the motion, curling her hand in his larger one. Chloe swallowed, all too conscious of the nearby light that revealed her features, possibly even her feelings. He leaned closer. She'd thought her heart thudded before. Now it nearly jumped from her chest.

His lips touched, then covered hers. Sensation raced through her as though day might never dawn again, that she must take her fill this very instant.

Evan cupped the back of her head, twining his fingers in her long, loose hair. Somewhere not far away, a cat meowed loudly. But it was too late. Nothing could distract her now.

Chapter Twelve

Chloe studied the latest pile of correspondence regarding TEX-INC, taking notes on each key point. The growing stack of refusals from the banks was disheartening. But she had an idea. One of their law firm's clients was a large, privately owned bank, where Mr. Wainwright also sat on the board of directors. She prayed they could extend a loan that would save Mitchell Stone and its employees' jobs.

As a bonus, if Mr. Wainwright helped Mitchell Stone, Evan might reconsider his position on Jimmy. She didn't think of it as buying their way past his defenses. But if Evan didn't have the constant worry about the fate of his employees, he might be more open to an emotional commitment.

Swallowing, Chloe knew she was avoiding her own emotions. Evan's kiss lingered in her thoughts, nagged at her conscience. What was she doing kissing a man she couldn't possibly have a future with?

Logging the last of her comments in her laptop, Chloe didn't notice Viola until she was standing beside her desk. "Oh, hi."

Viola glanced at the computer.

"I'm just used to taking my notes this way. Beats shorthand any day."

"Shorthand?"

Chloe realized her slip. "Typing fast is probably my strongest office skill."

"I don't know. You caught on to our file system in no time."

"Like I said, I know my way around the office."

"Right. In a law firm. Perry mentioned that's your background."

Chloe couldn't lie to this woman. So she nodded.

"Legal secretaries make pretty good money. Guess estate reps must do even better." Viola smiled, deposited a small stack of papers on top of the incoming tray and left.

That was close. She didn't need to complicate things now. Chloe scribbled a note on her desk calendar so she'd remember to check back with Mr. Wainwright the next day.

She glanced at her watch—an hour until she picked up Jimmy. Enough time to phone Mr. Wainwright. Pushing the *away* button on her phone, Chloe gathered her purse and sweater, then grabbed the laptop. Fingers mentally crossed, she prayed that Mr. Wainwright would fall in with her plan. Because reading the correspondence had about convinced her it was the only option left.

Viola handed Evan several invoices to approve. "These are going to start flying in now that we have that big order."

Evan didn't look up. "Uh-huh."

"We've all been praying for an answer," Viola continued, "because we're worried about you. Taking everything on yourself the way you do. Well, anyway, everyone's relieved. We had been talking about taking cuts in salary, benefits, whatever it takes to keep things going. Anyway, if we have more going out on this order faster than it comes in, we're willing to make those cuts. And you don't have to wait for the next staff meeting. We've talked about it, so anything you need from us can get done in a New York minute."

Evan stared, unseeing, at the invoices. "It's not the employees' responsibility to prop up the business."

"Pish posh. You're family, Evan. And you've always taken care of us. Don't you think we want to do the same for you?"

His throat clogged. "We have the best people in the world right here at Mitchell Stone."

"And the most diversified."

Emotion was clouding his brain. "Diversified?"

"Like Chloe. Who knew we'd have a former legal secretary doing our filing?"

Legal secretary? Wainwright's legal secretary? Evan searched his mind, trying to remember if he'd seen her name on any of the correspondence. Chloe said she was an estate representative. He frowned. She'd also made that comment about not having the funds to keep her mother at home like he could.

Evan had believed from the beginning that Chloe accepted the assignment strictly for money. But then she'd broken past his initial misgivings, proving to be more than just some moneygrubber. Was he wrong about that, too? Had she been lying to him all this time?

"I really like her," Viola added just before she left.

Shoving aside the invoices, he strode to the file room. Empty. The away button flashed on Chloe's phone. Her desk calendar was askew. Nearing close enough to make out the letters, Evan read her notation. Slowly raising his eyes, he couldn't help wonder. Had Chloe been reporting to Wainwright each day? From Evan's own office?

Disappointment flooded him. And betrayal. But what had he expected? He had betrayed Robin.

Worse, he'd allowed himself to believe.

The wheels were in motion. Chloe had extracted all the information she needed on Mitchell Stone from the records and accounting files. Mr. Wainwright agreed it was a sound proposition and that he would present it to the loan committee. And, since Mr. Wainwright held a lot of sway in the private corporation, the odds of getting the financing were excellent. Her hopes were high, but she hadn't yet told Evan. She feared what might happen if the plan didn't work out.

Now she sat next to Grace in the school auditorium, watching the kids rehearse. Grace's daughter, Susie, was playing a sheep in the scene right after Jimmy's.

He only had a few lines, but Jimmy practiced them over and over each afternoon and evening, wanting to be sure he remembered each and every word on the big night. By now Chloe, along with Thelma, Ned and Gordon, also knew Jimmy's lines since he practiced on all of them. Everyone agreed to come to the performance and Jimmy grew more excited as the play approached.

"Could they be cuter?" Grace asked in a quiet voice, watching her daughter.

"Thanks for keeping an eye on Jimmy. Knowing

you're here makes it easier to leave him at school each day."

"I haven't done anything, really. And I intended to help you get settled in. It's sort of a Rosewood tradition."

"I don't know how long I'll be here," Chloe admitted. "If Evan sticks to his decision, I'll be taking Jimmy back to Milwaukee. Of course, I'm hoping Evan will change his mind." She tried to keep her voice steady. "In any case, I'll be going back."

Grace looked at her searchingly. "Haven't you found a pretty good reason to stay?"

"Am I that transparent?"

"Evan's a good man. It's going to take time, but he'll get past what happened. I don't believe he wants to be alone forever."

Chloe wished it didn't matter so much. "Even if he could… I have to go back and take care of my mother. I'm all she has."

"Families make adjustments all the time."

"Not that kind of adjustment. I don't know if I told you, but when I go back, I'll be attending law school. Marquette, if I can get in there."

"Wow." Grace absently rubbed the scar on her hand. "I didn't picture you pursuing another career. I kind of thought you were ready to tackle raising a family."

Chloe hadn't confided in Grace. She'd promised Mr. Wainwright she would keep his secret, that she would only tell the whole story when it was necessary. Chloe needed a friend, someone to discuss her confused feelings with, but she wasn't accustomed to breaking promises.

The financing matter, however, wasn't a promise. "I

did something. And I'm hoping it'll help Evan's business. Now, I'm also hoping he won't be mad since I didn't consult him first."

"It would be easier to give an opinion if I knew what you were talking about."

Chloe outlined the basics. "When I had the idea, I didn't really think about any resentment Evan might have that the money would be coming from Mr. Wainwright's bank. I just wanted to help."

"Evan will no doubt realize that. After all, he helps people all the time. It's in his nature."

"Maybe you're right. I didn't think about it that way."

"I'll pray for you, Chloe, and for Evan and his employees."

Chloe sensed she would need Grace's prayers and all of her own.

Evan stood by the window in his office until he saw Chloe park out front. He waited, giving her time to reach the file room before he walked down the hall. She stood midway between the incoming table and her desk, looking around.

"Expecting more information?"

She whirled around, her brow furrowed.

He took one step inside the now immaculate space. He had removed all of the loose filing, the papers that told the tale of Mitchell Stone's situation.

"What happened? Did Melanie come back?"

"You're good. I'll give you that." Evan walked closer. "The innocent look, the nearly convincing confusion."

"Apparently not that good. I don't know what you're talking about."

"Haven't you been talking to Wainwright lately?"

The truth flashed across her face. "I was going to explain—"

"That you've been reporting to him ever since you got to town?"

"Well, of course, I've checked in, but—"

"Like a good secretary."

The color drained from her face. "Mr. Wainwright didn't think you'd take me as seriously if—"

"So you've been lying since we met."

Chloe drew in a shaky breath. "I did as Mr. Wainwright instructed. I work for him, yes. As his private secretary. But, when I agreed to bring Jimmy, my position changed."

"To a far more lucrative one?"

Indecision flashed in her clear eyes. "Let me explain—"

"I don't understand why you want all the inside information on the business. That piece doesn't fit. Wainwright can't blackmail me into taking Jimmy."

Chloe looked genuinely appalled. "Blackmail? With what?"

"With whatever you've gathered that you emailed to Wainwright."

Chloe's gaze flickered back to her laptop sitting on the desk. "You went through my personal computer?"

"What are you really doing here, Chloe?"

She blinked. "I thought I was helping." Pain darkened her eyes and she bit down on her lip. "That was my intention. But you're right. Mr. Wainwright did make me an offer that, as they say, I couldn't refuse. If I got you to agree to be Jimmy's guardian, made sure that he was happy here, Mr. Wainwright promised to raise my salary and pay for law school. I wouldn't have to work any longer, but getting paid, I could make it through law school in the normal three years." She pushed the hair off her forehead. "Obviously, I have nothing to do here any longer. I'll leave my laptop so you have enough time to read everything you want. I do need it back, though." Pausing, she took another breath. "And I'll need your final decision about Jimmy."

Before Evan realized her intent, Chloe pushed past him, running down the hall and out the front reception area.

Viola walked up behind him. "Is something wrong?"

Everything. Absolutely everything.

She couldn't breathe. Having no place to run, Chloe had driven to the school, then remained in her rental car. Had she just blown Jimmy's future? Why had she told Evan in such a clinical manner?

Because his words hurt so badly.

Leaning her head against the steering wheel, she felt the tears roll down her face, wetting her shirt. How would she tell Jimmy?

Horrified, another thought hit. What if Evan wanted them gone before Jimmy could play the little shepherd boy?

She'd ruined everything. And, Evan didn't even know the truth. Deep in her heart, Chloe couldn't regret asking Mr. Wainwright to help Evan. It was the right thing to do. But the price was greater than she'd expected.

Someone knocked on her window and she jumped.

Seeing it was Grace, Chloe rolled down the window.

Grace took one look, then opened the door. "Come on."

"But—"

"My kids are in the library for the next hour. Let's get out of here."

Chloe stumbled out of the car and Grace gripped her arm. "My car's right over here." With the kindness of a sister and the sternness of a mother, she got Chloe seated in the car. Leaving the school, she drove to the café on Main Street. "It's quiet this time of day. Most everybody's already eaten breakfast and it's too early for lunch."

"Grace, really, it's not necessary."

"You're the color of a shucked oyster. It's necessary." Grace guided her inside, choosing the farthest booth in the rear. She grabbed a paper napkin from the holder and passed it across the table.

Chloe wiped her cheeks. "I'm not usually this weepy."

"I'm guessing you have good reason."

Biting her lip, Chloe nodded.

"Did Evan overreact?"

"In a way." Chloe repeated her exchange with Evan. "I didn't even get to tell him why I was calling Mr. Wainwright." Her voice started to shake. "But when he accused me of blackmail…"

A waitress approached. "Two hot teas, strong please."

The woman disappeared and Chloe tried to pull herself together. "And I didn't explain why the money's so important." She told Grace about her mother's illness, the cost of the care facility.

Grace leaned forward. "Tell me more."

And Chloe did, detailing her financial situation. "I can't believe I acted so stupidly. I thought about myself instead of Jimmy. I was indignant for both of us, but I could have handled it better, not alienated Evan.

Oh, Grace, what if Evan makes us leave before Jimmy's play?"

Grace covered Chloe's hand with her own. "Evan is not an unkind man. You've seen how he protects the people he cares about. He wouldn't deliberately hurt Jimmy. He may not have thought about the play in the last few days, but he can't forget about it completely. He got corralled into moving the boulder during the performance."

"I don't think reminding him about that will improve his mood."

Grace smiled gently. "There are a lot of reasons for having friends."

"Yes."

"One of them is to divert the knight so you can slay the dragon."

Chloe blinked.

The waitress brought the tea, caught Grace's expression and disappeared.

"Let me talk to him first," Grace explained. "Right now you're both raw, in pain. I'm not. I won't fall apart if Evan loses his temper, says something he'll regret. And I won't hold it against him." She picked up her cup. "Now, drink your tea while it's hot."

Chloe reached for her cup. "You never impressed me as being the bossy sort."

"Only with people I care about." Grace sipped her tea. "I'm going to need this. Dragons can be scary."

At the end of the work day, Evan sat in his office. Chloe hadn't returned. Hadn't called. He sighed, mentally going over her words for at least the hundredth time. Hearing a soft knock, he looked up.

"Evan?" Grace Brady stood in the doorway.

He stood. "Come in."

"Do you have a minute?"

"Sure."

She sat in the chair opposite his and folded her hands. "I know it's been a rough day."

Evan lifted his eyebrows. *She did?*

"And I'd like to talk to you about Chloe."

Instinctively he stiffened, his defenses kicking in.

"When Chloe told you about Mr. Wainwright's offer today, she didn't tell you why she accepted."

"It's pretty obvious."

"You'd think so, wouldn't you?" Grace's gentle manner was deceptively unnerving. "But did you question why Chloe needed the money so badly?"

"Same reason everyone wants money, I suppose."

Grace leaned forward. "She's not like everyone. And she doesn't want the money—she *needs* it. Has Chloe told you about her mother?"

Evan frowned. "She's in a nursing home."

"No. She's in an extended-care facility because she has severe chronic pulmonary disease and can't be on her own."

"Okay."

"Have you thought about how Chloe pays for the home?"

"I assume she's paid well."

"Not that well. It takes every penny she makes to pay the facility and their rates are constantly rising. Evan, Chloe lives in a cheap one-room efficiency because she refuses to allow her mother to be placed in a state-run facility. Chloe's out of choices. Mr. Wainwright's offer is the only option she has. Her father's dead. Her younger brother barely makes enough in the military to support his young family. So, her mother's care is completely on Chloe's shoulders."

Evan listened.

Grace met his gaze, her own imploring. "What would you do? What if you were the only one Gordon had to count on?"

"That doesn't explain why she's passing on all our financial information to Wainwright."

"No." Grace unfolded her hands. "It doesn't."

When she didn't say more, Evan prompted her. "So?"

"I'll leave that for her to tell. When Chloe wondered about you, we, all your friends, surrounded you with a wall of protection. Now, Chloe deserves the same wall."

"Because she has something to hide?"

"Did *you* have something to hide?"

He didn't reply.

"Of course not. Evan, consider the woman you've grown to know. Does she have any of the qualities you think you've discovered? Is she uncaring? Selfish? Does Jimmy mean nothing to her?" Grace rose. "I know you have a lot to think about and I'll leave you to it. Just remember, you're not the only one who's hurting. And certainly not the only one who'll be hurt if you do something rash."

An image of Jimmy's eager face flashed in Evan's mind. As quickly, he thought of Sean, how he would have done anything to spare him pain.

But what was Chloe hiding? And why did her deceit cut so deep?

Chapter Thirteen

Tied in knots, Chloe waited for the other shoe to drop. That night at dinner she sat next to Jimmy, ready to protect him if there was an outburst from Evan. Gordon looked at her oddly, but didn't say anything. To her relief, Evan didn't make an appearance. She really didn't want to play out the entire scene in front of everyone.

After dinner she read to Jimmy until he was sleepy, then tucked him in, ferociously guarding his room through the night. She didn't even change into her pajamas and robe, wanting to be prepared.

By morning, bleary-eyed, her throat gravelly, she braced herself.

But nothing happened. Again, Evan was absent.

On nervous autopilot, she drove Jimmy to school, then waited until Grace's free period. Digging in her purse, she found Grace's cell number and phoned. They agreed to meet in the empty auditorium.

Watching anxiously, Chloe was relieved to see that Grace was smiling as she slipped into the closest seat.

Grace's concern filled her face. "How are you holding up?"

"I guess I'm not really sure. I haven't seen Evan since the... since we talked yesterday."

"I'm not surprised."

Chloe's brow furrowed. "Really?"

Grace searched her eyes. "In spite of what happened yesterday, you know what kind of man Evan is."

Looking away, Chloe gripped the handle of her purse. "And now he knows what kind of person I am."

"You can't go down that road. If Evan understands anything, it's family. Your reasons for taking on this job are honorable. And, I've seen how you are with Jimmy. He's not an assignment anymore—you care for him like a mother."

"This is so silly," Chloe wiped away the sudden tears. "I haven't cried this much in years. Now I'm the Trevi fountain."

"Love does that to a person."

"I do love Jimmy," she admitted.

"Just Jimmy?"

Chloe met Grace's steady gaze. "I'm certainly not the kind of woman Evan wants in his life."

"You're so sure?"

"I told you before. Even if he did, I have to go home. Besides, right now I'm the last person in the world Evan wants to see."

Grace remained quiet a few moments. "I'm guessing you don't want to go back to his office to help out anymore."

"The welcome sign's been removed."

"Would you like to volunteer here? The younger grades can always use adults to help with reading, that sort of thing. Or in the library—even grading papers would be appreciated."

Chloe thought about it. "I do need to stay busy."

"Let's get some coffee in the teacher's break room, then why don't you stick with me today?"

Glad for the reprieve, Chloe agreed. "Oh, Grace. Was Evan furious when he found out why I'd contacted Mr. Wainwright?"

"Guess you'll find out when you decide to tell him."

"You didn't?"

"He needs to hear it from you. I just told Evan that he had the wrong idea about the money Mr. Wainwright offered to pay you."

Absorbing her words, Chloe rose, following Grace from the auditorium. So, she still had to face Evan. Something told her he wouldn't be any happier about the second portion of her news than he'd been about the first.

In the spring, Lark's meadow was a stunning mix of bluebonnets, bright orange paintbrush and golden coreopsis. Now it stood fallow, the wildflowers tuckered down for the winter, the grass withered, yellowing. Yet, to Evan's way of thinking, it was still beautiful in a different way, standing solid, nestling the seeds of the perennial flowers. It was in its keeping mode. Just as he was.

Evan looked upward, into the sky, searching the heavens. It had been so long since he'd whispered a prayer or even believed God was listening. Yet, now his heart told him he needed to try, to seek the light in his darkness. "I still don't understand about Robin and Sean. But this time I'm not asking for me. Lord, these are good people and they need Your help. There aren't other jobs for them to get. You know that. And

You know that the older ones will be the worst off. I've poured everything I've got into keeping the place alive and I won't be able to help them. But You can. At least that's what I always believed." Evan felt his throat working and he paused. "I'll accept whatever direction You guide us in." Again he had to stop, to fight against the shaking in his chest. "And, I'll try to understand why You took my boy so soon." Evan bent his head as he appealed to the Lord's gift of grace. Around him, the wind whistled, picking up faded petals, scattering them upward and away. Taking his plea, Evan prayed silently. And bringing back hope.

Chloe kept busy between volunteering at school in a few classes, and with the Christmas play.

Then she helped Thelma prepare and deliver numerous Christmas baskets. No one was overlooked. Shut-ins, the people from Thanksgiving dinner, others on their own, aging couples, and some large families. In addition, a basket was prepared for each employee and his or her family. Chloe felt the most emotion when they reached Melanie's house. The woman threw her arms around Chloe in a spontaneous hug, thanking her for keeping her job available. Proudly, Melanie showed her the new baby who happily kicked his chubby legs in greeting.

Now, the play wasn't far away. It was held in the week school let out for Christmas break, giving families time to gather.

And they were gathering. Chloe had seen some unfamiliar faces in the stores recently, Rosewood descendants who had moved away, but returned to celebrate with their families. If Rosewood were her home, Chloe mused, she would never leave. It had everything. All except one very important person, her mother.

In numerous phone calls, her mother assured Chloe that Christmas was celebrated fully at the care facility, that old friends might visit, that she would be completely all right. But Chloe couldn't stop worrying.

Combined with waiting for Evan's confrontation, she was on edge when her cell phone rang. Seeing that it was Mr. Wainwright's private number, Chloe answered on the first ring.

"Mitchell's loan has been approved," he began without wasting time on small talk.

Relief flooded her. "That's wonderful. Thank you, Mr. Wainwright."

"What about Jimmy? Has Mitchell made his decision?"

Chloe bit down on her lip. *Not officially.* "Not yet. Mr. Wainwright, if he does say no, will the loan be withdrawn?"

"No. I won't blackmail the man. And Jimmy certainly wouldn't have a happy home under the circumstances."

She closed her eyes, remembering Evan using that same awful word. *Blackmail.* "Thank you."

"Let me know as soon as you can about Jimmy."

Agreeing, she bid her boss goodbye.

Now she just had to tell Evan.

Evan stared at the pile of envelopes stacked neatly on his desk. Christmas bonuses. Each and every employee had returned what most certainly could be their last bonus. Their sacrifice touched him greatly. While they were all paid well, each could use the money to provide Christmas for their families.

Hearing a stir in the hall, Evan glanced up. Chloe stood hesitantly in his doorway.

He rose, staring while she reached his desk and faced him. Belatedly, his voice returned. "Sit down."

She did, perching on the edge of the chair. "I suppose you wonder why I'm here."

Evan sank down into his own chair, wondering that and so much more.

"I want to explain why I collected the information about Mitchell Stone." Chloe swallowed visibly. "When you told me that the financing fell through and that you didn't believe you could secure it anywhere else, I had an idea." Glancing down, she took a deep breath. "I remembered that one of our clients at the law firm is a privately owned bank and that Mr. Wainwright is a member of the board there. After I got all the data together, I called him and asked if he thought the bank might finance your deal." She heard Evan's sharp intake of breath but didn't dare stop. "He agreed to present it to the loan committee. And…" She took a deep breath. "I heard back from Mr. Wainwright. The loan's approved. You have your financing. No strings attached."

You have your financing.

Lord, can this be so?

Chloe scooted forward another inch or so. "As I said, no strings attached. The loan isn't dependent on your answer about Jimmy. Mr. Wainwright…and I…know that wouldn't only be unfair, it wouldn't be in Jimmy's best interest."

Evan tried to collect his thoughts. "Are you sure you told him how large a loan we need?"

"I confirmed it with Perry.... Mr. Perkin."

"Perry didn't say anything."

"I didn't tell him why I needed to know," she admitted. "I didn't want to raise any false hopes, just in case...." Chloe opened her purse and pulled out an envelope. "Mr. Wainwright had the loan package faxed to me. The contact person and phone number at the bank are on the cover letter."

For once in his life, Evan could not think of a single thing to say. Chloe had just presented him with the means to save his business, his employees. And, the first time he had prayed since the accident, the Lord had answered loud and clear. He had forgiven Evan's railings, blame, accusations of betrayal. In His grace, He had taken care of His children.

It was too much to take in at once.

"Well, then." Chloe stood. "I have to get back to the school. I'm helping out with the rehearsals for the Christmas play."

She reached the doorway before he found his voice. "Chloe."

Pausing, she turned back to face him.

"You don't know what this means."

Her eyes darkened and a surprisingly sad smile tipped her lips upward slightly. "I think I do." Spinning around, she hurried out of his office.

Evan watched even when he couldn't see her any longer. Still mesmerized, his gaze fell on the neat envelope sitting on his desk. Emotions crowded faster than shoppers at a discount sale. Why hadn't she told him when he first confronted her?

If Grace hadn't explained the reason Chloe had been so desperate for money, he *still* wouldn't know about her sacrifices. As the impact continued reverberating, Evan picked up his phone, knowing there was one thing he could do.

A few nights later, Chloe was surprised when Evan appeared for dinner, his mood calm. Jimmy chattered at him, pleased that he was there.

After they ate, Chloe expected Evan to disappear into his study. Instead, he accompanied them into the den while Jimmy told him every tiny detail about the play.

"And Susie Brady's gonna be the lamb. But *I* get to sit on the big rock. I'm the only one who does in the *whole* play."

"I'm the one who gets to move that boulder," Evan reminded him.

"So you'll be there?" Jimmy asked excitedly, his eyes lighting up.

"Of course. Would I miss seeing you play the shepherd boy?"

Chloe nearly dropped her cup of cider. Perhaps her imagination had run amuck. Evan couldn't have actually said he was attending the play.

Jimmy bounced in his chair. "Do you want to see my costume?"

Inwardly Chloe groaned. She had hoped to herd Jimmy upstairs before he latched on to Evan.

"Sure." Evan leaned back in his chair.

Jimmy ran from the room, his sneakers hitting the stairs in rapid succession.

Immediately, Chloe felt the pressure of Evan's gaze. She hadn't been alone with him since the day in his office when she'd told him about the loan. Since then she rationalized that he wouldn't choose that particular time to get into the subject of her deception. Not when he'd been presented the critical financing on a platter. But nothing was stopping Evan now. *Except possibly his father.*

Gordon emptied his pipe, then placed it in his lips without adding any tobacco.

"Running low on tobacco, Dad?"

"Just need it for thinking."

"Anything in particular?"

Gordon hesitated, then glanced up at the portraits lining the mahogany walls. "Just missing your mother."

Chloe sighed. She certainly was missing hers.

"Chloe?" Evan asked.

She jumped. Embarrassed by the reaction, she felt her cheeks flushing. "Yes?"

"Does Jimmy need help with his costume?"

"Just with the head covering and belt. The staff he'll carry that night is stored at school."

Only minutes later, Jimmy pounded down the stairs. As Chloe predicted, he wore the one piece shepherd's robe and carried the accessories. He ran straight to her for help.

Smiling, she adjusted his cotton hat and tied the rope that served as a belt. Then she winked. "All set."

He grinned and turned to Evan. "I get to carry this stick thing while I talk."

"Do you know all your lines?"

"I should say so," Gordon replied for him. "He's practiced all afternoon, every afternoon, since he got the part."

Evan's expression grew reflective, almost nostalgic. Chloe guessed he was missing his son.

"And everybody's coming to see me," Jimmy declared. "Thelma's gonna make a special cake."

"Sounds good. Thelma makes the best cakes in town. Maybe the world."

"It's gonna be chocolate and have lots of frosting. Thelma said," Jimmy confided.

Looking at and listening to the child she had come to love as her own, Chloe hoped the night of the play wouldn't be the last that she and Jimmy stayed in this house. Or the last they were together.

Chapter Fourteen

"It's bona fide." Perry plopped the financing contract on Evan's desk.

"Legal opinion?" Evan asked.

"Combed through word by word. It's solid. No balloon payment, no prepayment penalty. The terms are better than the deal that fell through." Perry studied his friend. "I don't know how Chloe pulled this off, but it's a gift straight from heaven."

Took the words right out of his mouth.

Perry looked at him. "Do you want to give the official go-ahead?"

Evan expelled a deep breath, then shook his head. "I thought our next official statement was going to be…"

"I know." Perry thumped the edge of the desk with his fist. "Probably isn't the best time to say this, but I've been thinking it a while now, so I might as well. The day Chloe and Jimmy showed up on your front porch was a gift, too."

Evan swivelled in his desk chair. "It's complicated."

"Ouch."

Turning back to Perry, Evan frowned. "What's that supposed to mean?"

"It's a cop-out. Life *is* complicated. You know that better than most people." Perry narrowed his gaze. "Are you really going to let her slip away?"

"How do you know she's interested?"

"Unlike you, I'm not blind." Perry shook his head in two rapid nods of disbelief.

"Message received."

"Same message—part two. Don't waste any more time."

Evan couldn't keep the sardonic tone from his voice. "That all?"

"I'm sure I can think of plenty more."

"Do me a favor."

Perry grinned. "Stop thinking?"

"Nah. Keep reminding me."

The night of the play was clear and cool. Although snow wouldn't blanket the hill country town, it hadn't blanketed Bethlehem either. Parents, siblings, students and interested community members filled the school auditorium.

Evan was backstage, waiting until it was time to move the boulder. And, ridiculously, he felt nervous. What if Jimmy forgot his lines? What if he got scared? Didn't want to go on? The teacher had the children lined up in groups, in order of appearance. So it was difficult to talk to him with the other kids around. And Jimmy was one of the last to go on.

As the play began, the older kids did well. Some kindergartners and first graders froze, a few cried. And Evan's nerves accelerated. Then it was time for him to move the boulder. The lights dimmed, the curtain closed and Evan quickly crossed the stage, lifting the large rock to the center.

A few parents, waiting to reassure their children, crowded into the space where he'd been waiting. The side drape blocked the stage while Evan found a new spot. When the main curtain rose, Jimmy sat on the boulder, alone. Evan sucked in his breath, mentally reassuring Jimmy that he would be all right.

The large star, constructed by the high school art department, hung at the highest point. It lit up suddenly, eliciting murmurs of admiration from the audience.

Jimmy stood, the curved staff by his side. Gazing up at the shining piece of scenery, Jimmy's face was radiant. Then the words he'd so diligently practiced poured out. "Papa! Papa! Do you see the star?"

Frozen with pride, a surge of love overwhelmed Evan, amazing him. He didn't think he had that much love left in him. Evan thought he'd given all of it to Sean and Robin. But his heart expanded, telling him there was room for Jimmy. Mindless of anyone who might see, he let the tears fill his eyes.

Blind. Perry was right. He hadn't seen what was in front of him. None of it.

Someone gasped near him. Evan didn't want to tear his eyes from Jimmy, but shifted slightly, just in time to see Chloe withdrawing her hand, then quickly walking away. Had she been about to comfort him? Did she care that much?

A group of children crowded close, ready to go on next. Evan had to move so they could get past him. In the confusion, he missed seeing Jimmy as he left the stage. Several older high school boys carried scenery, blocking the exits.

Evan waited, then finally eased out the back door. It didn't take too long to circle the school, then come back in through the front. The play had ended and the crowd was breaking up, some pausing to chat, others waiting for their children.

Dodging small groups, he made his way to where he had seen Chloe sitting. Gordon, Thelma and Ned visited with the Markhams. Jimmy ran from the stage to Chloe. She knelt, giving him a huge hug. Getting closer, he could hear her praising his performance.

."You were the very best one!"

He bounced on his dark sneakers. "Really?"

"Really!" She hugged him again. "The very, very, very best."

Jimmy hugged her back hard before finally letting go.

"You haven't told me what you want for Christmas yet, big guy."

"A family."

She leaned her head against his, caramel and dark twined together. "Me, too."

Evan stopped, struck by their words. The star on the stage twinkled, beaconing its message of hope. And he wondered if he dared believe.

Hanging the phone up slowly, Evan sank back in his chair. The normally comforting feel of the den didn't help. Jimmy's grandparents in Egypt were ready to step up and take guardianship. They planned to enroll him in the same school Spencer had loathed. They hoped to spend some holidays with Jimmy. Just as they had intended to with Spencer.

Cousin Spencer had always been so excited when he got to Rosewood. And the night before he returned to school he always cried himself to sleep. Years had passed, but the memories had never left. Evan remembered his parents' discussions about Spencer. They had always hoped to convince his parents to let him stay permanently in Rosewood. But they insisted Spencer's education was paramount. His feelings hadn't been.

Evan's throat closed, imagining Jimmy crying himself to sleep, longing for a family. The family he was wishing for right now. The family Chloe wanted.

Now he had to tell her what Jimmy's grandparents wanted. Pushing his own want aside, Evan couldn't help wondering if family would be the deciding factor. Or, if Wainwright's offer would win out in the end.

Sitting at the kitchen table, Chloe carefully cut some beautiful burgundy foil paper. She and her mother had always made gift wrapping an event, finding the most unusual papers, creating beautiful ornaments to place on the packages. Then hot cocoa and cookies.

This year, Christmas was going to be a post office event. She'd mailed her mother's presents. The home's director had repeatedly assured her there would be a celebration that day. Thinking of it, Chloe wanted to cry.

Her brother couldn't help. Chip apologized, but there was no way he could afford the trip. Just sending a gift had strained their tight budget.

Jimmy ran into the kitchen, Bailey on his heels. "Ned said I could help him in the shed if you say it's okay."

"Sure. Be careful and mind Ned."

He skipped out the back door in seconds.

Chloe hoped Ned would like the gloves she'd bought for him. They were a quality leather pair that he could wear to church. She fitted the paper beneath a box. Hearing the door from the dining room open, she was glad the gloves were hidden. She liked all of the presents to be a surprise for everyone. It had been a family tradition. "If you need the table, Thelma, I'll be done in a jiff."

"I don't need the table," Evan replied.

Surprised, she glanced up at him. "I just assumed—"

"Jimmy's grandparents called."

The blood seemed to drain from her entire body. Hands slack, she dropped the scissors.

Evan ignored them. "They're ready to take guardianship."

Appalled, Chloe stared.

"Unless I do," Evan finished. He walked to the window, staring out back. No doubt Jimmy and Bailey were in sight.

"Are they coming back? To the states?"

"Only long enough to enroll Jimmy in school. Seems they have to meet with the university board about the grant for their dig. So, they can kill two birds with one stone. Direct quote."

Chloe thought she was going to be sick. "What did you tell them?"

"They're going to call after Christmas, confirm their plans."

So Evan hadn't refused, hadn't said he was going to accept the guardianship.

"What do you think Wainwright will say?"

Chloe jerked her face up, unable to believe what

she was hearing. "Wainwright?" Truly sickened, she jumped up. "So that's what's bothering you? You think Mr. Wainwright will pull your financing if Jimmy's grandparents take him?" Holding back her tears, Chloe ran from the kitchen, up the stairs and into her room. *Her* room. A guest room in a house she had hoped would be Jimmy's home. Disappointment in Evan cut to the bone. She had been praying that he would grow to love Jimmy. Perhaps she should have prayed for him to get a heart.

Evan looked over the quarry's last safety inspection. Everything had been up to standard. But with the huge order to work on, he didn't want to wait another month to conduct the next one. With Christmas only two days away, a few office employees had taken off, but most of the quarry workers were in place.

"I thought this new deal had stone coming out of most all of Mitchell's quarries," Dilbert Dunn, their longtime stone mason, commented.

"It will. But every site has to be checked."

"Not due yet."

"Better early than late. I'm not compromising anyone's safety," Evan insisted.

"You're the boss, but it could wait until after Christmas."

Decisions. Everyone wanted him to make decisions. As though they were as easy to make as flipping a coin. "You can leave, Dilbert. There are enough guys here to manage."

"Haven't missed a safety test yet. Not going to miss this one."

If Evan had a smile anywhere in him, he would

have grinned. But there wasn't an ounce of humor to be found. Chloe's accusation rang in his ears. And, if she was that quick to accuse him, she couldn't possibly feel the way he'd hoped.

Dilbert plucked a clipboard from a peg on the wall of the utilitarian office. "Better run a check on who clocked in today."

While Dilbert compared time cards to his list, Evan stared off toward the dusty limestone pit. Only two days until Christmas. And then he had to face Jimmy's grandparents alone. Because Chloe would be packing for home.

Chloe sat in the porch swing, remembering her one evening with Evan on this same porch, wondering how she could have been so wrong about him. She thought she had seen tenderness, understanding and kindness in him. Was it an illusion? Worse, a delusion of her own making? Had she infused him with characteristics he didn't possess?

A vision of him on the night of the school play flashed in her thoughts. She hadn't imagined the openly raw emotions as he watched Jimmy, nor the tears. Seeing how deeply he was affected, Chloe had wanted to comfort him, even reached out a hand to do so. But, knowing how private Evan was about his feelings, she stopped at the last moment.

Who was Evan? The man who was moved to tears watching an orphan play a shepherd boy? Or the one who coldly announced that Jimmy's grandparents were going to claim him?

The back door creaked as it opened and Gordon

stepped out. "Well, hello there. I thought I was the only one who liked to sit outside in the winter."

She dredged up a faint smile. "Cool air can be bracing."

He looked at her more closely. "That was said like you need it."

Chloe shook her head, not wanting to worry the older man. He had consistently been kind to her since they met. Thoughtful and caring, his concern for Jimmy was genuine.

"Mind if I join you?" Gordon asked.

She scooted over to one side so he had room to sit. "Of course not."

The swing creaked as he sank down. "This old swing's a great place to think." He chuckled. "And watch the kids. Evan was a pistol. And he always had friends around, enough to be more than a handful to keep under control." They rocked quietly for a while, then Gordon continued, "We wanted more children, but weren't blessed with another. Evan had so many friends, it seemed like he didn't miss having siblings. Now, I wonder."

"I don't see my younger brother often anymore. Now that Chip has children, his family's his focus."

"That was Evan—the family man," Gordon explained. "When Sean was born, everything clicked in place for him. It was the role Evan had been waiting for all his life. That's when he expanded the business, the legacy for Sean. Oh, that's not why the company's in trouble now. The economy's responsible for the business problems." He paused, glancing out over the immaculate yard. All the fallen leaves had been raked into piles, then burned in an old steel drum barrel. The climbing roses, now bare of beautiful blossoms, rustled in the light breeze. "Hope this wind doesn't pick up."

"I've prayed that Evan might come to care for Jimmy," Chloe confessed. She couldn't bear the thought of him being hurt. Closing her eyes, she pictured the confusion and betrayal in Jimmy's face when she told him they would be leaving, that he would be living in a boarding school.

"And you don't think Evan does?" Gordon furrowed his brow, studying her closer. "Can't you see it? The way he watches Jimmy when he thinks no one can see him? The longing to let go of the past, take a chance? The fear that if he does, something will happen to Jimmy. Evan puts on the mask of being tough, caring only about business, but you have to know by now that's not all there is to my son."

Chloe bent her face down, thinking of all the people at Thanksgiving dinner, people whose lives Evan had touched, improved, cared about. "Then why is he willing to let Jimmy go to Spencer's parents?"

Shocked, Gordon scrunched his eyebrows down. "That can't be true."

The wind increased, ruffling her hair. "They called yesterday, told Evan they're ready to accept guardianship. They plan to enroll him in boarding school."

"Like Spencer?" Gordon asked, appalled.

"Exactly."

"Now that they're older, maybe they plan to return to the states, be closer to him."

Chloe emphatically shook her head. "That's just it! They plan to stay on the dig. Oh, and they hope to spend a few holidays with Jimmy."

"You've got to be wrong about this," Gordon objected. "I know Evan. He wouldn't do that to the child. He may be afraid to voice his love since he lost Sean, but, if anything, he's more empathic than ever with kids."

She sighed, wishing that were true. "He's more worried about what Mr. Wainwright might do about the financing than he is about Jimmy's grandparents."

Gordon looked confused.

"Did Evan tell you that the original loan for the company's big new order fell through?"

"No."

"He probably didn't want to worry you. Anyway, I had the idea of hooking him up with my boss. Mr. Wainwright sits on the board of a privately owned bank. Mitchell Stone got the loan it needs through him. It's enough to save the company. Now, that's all Evan cares about."

"Was the guardianship issue a provision of getting the loan?"

"Well, no." Chloe bit down on her lower lip. "Actually, there aren't any strings attached. It's a straight-out business loan with good terms."

"Then his consideration of what Wainwright thinks can't be motivating Evan." Gordon frowned. "Are you sure it's not a little closer to home than that?"

Now, Chloe was confused. "What do you mean?"

"My, you really haven't been paying attention. Jimmy isn't the only person Evan studies when he thinks no one's watching."

Chloe blinked.

And Gordon chuckled. "Evan can't keep his eyes off of you."

"But he's always so gruff!"

"You know Evan. Would you expect him to show up with flowers and chocolates?"

Not really. Especially in his own house. "Still, Gordon, I think that's wishful thinking."

"You haven't done any of your own?"

She had indulged in too many thoughts of how it would be to have Evan as her husband, Jimmy as her son. But that was wishing, not real life. "I have," she admitted. "But mostly for Jimmy. It would kill me to see him shut away in some boarding school. And he worships Evan. They should be together."

"And you?"

Her lips trembled before she got them under control. "My life's complicated. It's also back in Milwaukee with my mother. Besides, I think you and I both must have caught the same wishing bug."

"It's not contagious," Gordon said kindly. "Chloe, do you think your mother would want to be responsible for your unhappiness?"

"Of course not! But—"

He held up one hand. "As parents, what we want more than anything in the world is our children's happiness. That's what makes us happy. And, Chloe, I'm guessing you haven't considered the changes you could make."

Chloe choked up. "I can't make my mother well. And I won't desert her."

Gordon looked as though he wanted to say more. Instead, he expelled a deep breath, looked out again over the yard and gardens, then frowned. "The wind's a lot stronger."

Her mind still muddled, Chloe pulled her sweater tighter. "Maybe a storm's coming."

"Did Evan tell you what time he's conducting the test?"

"Test?"

"It's a safety inspection. This one's not due yet, but Evan wants to make sure everything's safe before they start on the big order," Gordon explained.

Confused, Chloe looked at him in question. "Does the wind have any bearing?"

"They'll be setting charges. I never like doing that in the wind. It's not supposed to affect the timing or the detonator, but when we do a full-out test, I want clear, calm weather." Gordon checked his watch. "I'm going to call Evan, see when it's planned."

"Will he postpone it if you ask?"

Although Gordon still looked concerned, he smiled encouragingly. "Chloe, he's not perfect, but he's a good son."

Slightly ashamed, she nodded. "Of course. I'm just emotional today." A thought struck her. "What if he's already doing the test?"

"I'll make that call." Gordon disappeared in the house.

Suddenly worried, she followed.

Chloe left so quickly she didn't hear the rustle in the bushes beside the porch or the flash of blue jeans as they disappeared into the shed.

Dilbert glared into the rising dust. "I don't know, Evan. Your dad always wanted clear weather when we tested."

"Are you about done checking the time cards?"

"Considering the weather, I say we double-check. And run a radio check before we start."

Evan sighed. "I've got the time." His mind was full

of the distressing call from Jimmy's grandparents and Chloe's unexpected, wounding response.

"You sure Mac said he was taking off?"

Trying to remember, Evan shook his head. "I'll go check with Bud." The foreman always knew exactly who was on duty in case of an accident. "Double-check with the office. Viola will have his vacation slip if he put in for time off." As he walked out of the shed, Evan noticed that the wind had increased since he'd arrived. The dry hill country air couldn't tamp down the dirt and dust from a strong wind. Usually, rain accompanied their storms, alleviating much flying debris.

Evan found Bud checking the detonator. "Is Mac working today?"

"Nah. Took off."

"Dilbert's worrying like an old lady," Evan explained. "He's checked the time cards twice."

Bud rattled off the names of the men who were in the quarry. "Tell him I know what I'm doing."

Dilbert and Bud had an ongoing rivalry that wouldn't end while either was still alive. Luckily, it never got in the way of doing their jobs. "So, we're set?"

"Yep."

Evan thought he heard something. "You hear that?"

Bud shook his head. "Nah. Probably an echo from the canyon."

"Right." Evan realized he was picking up on Dilbert's anxiety. No place for it in his business. And, right now, blowing up the side of a hill suited his mood just fine.

Chapter Fifteen

Gordon pushed Redial again. Again, after a few rings, Evan's cell phone went to voice mail. "He's not picking up."

"And no one's answering at the little office out there?" Chloe asked, her worry escalating.

"The shed just has one line and it's busy. Dilbert always fusses when we've talked about upgrading the place. All the workers have radios, which has worked out fine so far."

Ned knocked on the door frame.

Gordon waved him inside.

"Is it okay for Jimmy to be out riding on that old bike? He tore out of here like his pants were on fire. Now the wind's getting fierce."

Fear hit Chloe harder than any wind could. "When? When did he leave, Ned?"

"Better than half an hour ago. Right after he played that little joke on you."

"Joke?" Gordon asked.

"He hid next to the back porch so he could jump out

and surprise you." Ned looked from Gordon to Chloe. "Didn't you see him?"

"No." Chloe stared at Gordon. "But he probably heard us." Trying not to panic, Chloe quickly calculated how long it would take a seven-year-old to bike to the quarry. Not nearly long enough. "Can you keep trying the shed and Evan's cell? I'll go to the quarry." Running, she grabbed her keys from the entry hall table.

She jumped in the rental car and sped off. "Lord," she prayed. "Please keep Jimmy and Evan safe." It was the middle of the day and last-minute shoppers clogged the road. "And let me get there in time."

But time accelerated, zooming as she remained clogged to a crawl in the quagmire of holiday traffic. The entire time she continued to pray, imploring the Lord to watch out for both Mitchells she loved.

Gordon pushed Redial repeatedly, praying for Evan to pick up. Tuned into his family's needs, Evan never ignored a call from home. Gordon's heart stilled. What if something had already happened? *"Lord, I know his faith has wavered… please let my boy know You are watching over him. Keep Jimmy safe so that You might deliver him to Evan's arms."*

The whipping wind dried the sweat from Jimmy's face and arms as he pedaled faster and faster toward the quarry. He couldn't let Evan get blowed up like Mommy and Daddy. His tummy felt funny and his chest kept pounding like it might burst.

He hadn't wanted to come so far from his house to live with Evan. But now he liked Evan a whole bunch. And he liked Uncle Gordon and Thelma and Ned. He wanted Chloe to never leave. But she looked sad now. Like she had a bad secret.

Jimmy wanted Evan and Chloe to be happy. His chest pounded. He didn't know why Mommy and Daddy had gone to heaven, but Chloe said they were always watching over him. Maybe they would watch over Evan, too.

Not sure whether they were watching right now, Jimmy pumped the bicycle as hard as he could. The quarry was just around the next bend. He didn't want Evan to go away to heaven.

A car honked behind him. Jimmy didn't turn around. Mommy and Daddy said they were just going to work. Then they never came home. Jimmy pedaled harder, his legs burning. He wanted Evan to always come home to him.

Evan listened while Viola named all the quarry workers who had opted for a vacation day. "Okay, Vi. Dilbert's uneasy about today's test, so I figured I'd better be sure. Yeah, I know. I don't *have* to do the safety check today." Putting down the landline, Evan shook his head.

"We could wait until after New Year's," Dilbert reminded him. "We'd have a full crew."

"Dilbert, if I didn't know better, I'd think you're trying to spook me."

The older man shrugged. "Just like to listen to my gut."

Evan wavered for a moment. It wouldn't kill him to wait. But he wanted the test over with. Mostly, he wanted to fill the hours. Empty time with nothing to occupy him left his mind open to thoughts best left alone.

What if he hadn't pushed Chloe away? Had told her

of his burgeoning feelings? Evan looked upward, vibrantly aware of the Lord's answer to prayer. Through Chloe, the Lord had opened a door Evan would never have tried.

Evan left the shed, Dilbert muttering behind him. The wind didn't bother Evan. He'd always found it exhilarating.

As he walked, Evan wondered if Chloe's response could have been a defensive one. Had she felt as wounded as he did? Even a good woman could lash out under the right circumstances.

Out of sight from the small office shed, Evan stopped, bending his head. "Lord, I've faltered. I wouldn't humble myself before until I had no choice, when I thought my people would lose everything." Evan's throat worked. "I made a vow to my wife, Lord. And I meant it forever, until I died. Chloe's changed everything, Lord. She doesn't take, she gives. Only I haven't given back. I keep hurting her instead. Lord, is that what I'm meant to do? So that I can remain faithful to Robin? You know she was a good woman. And, I don't think Robin would want me to hurt Chloe. I need Your guidance, Lord. I need to know what I should do about Chloe and Jimmy. He's in my heart for good now. I'm afraid, Lord. What if I lose him, too? I ask for Your help, Lord, to guide me on the right path."

The dust swirled around his boots. Looking slowly up into the sky, Evan noticed that the sky was graying, the clouds darkening. If he was going to get the test done, he'd better hurry.

Chloe couldn't believe it. Since she had arrived in Rosewood, the streets had never been so full. More like lazy country lanes, even the road leading out of town was normally nearly empty. Had the entire world flocked to the tiny hill country town?

Honking, she considered leaving the car, running the rest of the way. But Jimmy could pedal far faster than she could run. *Lord, he's just a little boy. Please don't take him away. I will do everything to make sure he's happy. I will do anything You guide me to do. Just keep him safe, Lord, please.* She wiped away the tears, then pulled around the car blocking hers, speeding ahead. *Please, Lord.*

Gordon dialed Evan's cell number, listening to it ring, hanging up when it reverted to voice mail. *Where was he? And why wasn't he picking up?*

"Thelma! Ned!" he hollered.

Ned came on a run, Thelma only a few feet behind.

Gordon held out both hands. "We need to pray. For Jimmy and Evan, Chloe, too. I'm afraid there's going to be a terrible accident at the quarry."

Thelma clasped his hand, her eyes filling with tears. Ned gripped his other hand. Closing his eyes, Gordon bent his head. "Lord, we beseech you. Our boys, Evan and Jimmy, and our girl, Chloe, are heading into danger. Please keep them safe so that they might be together again under our roof safely in the arms of those who love them." His voice faltered. "Lord, we ask this in the name of Your Son, the one who saves us all."

Slowly unclasping hands, Thelma crumpled against her husband. And Gordon didn't bother to wipe away the tears. All that he loved most was now in the Lord's hands. He could only believe his heavenly Father would protect them.

* * *

The charges were set. Dilbert had triple-checked employees until Evan finally stopped him. "Everyone's accounted for. The weather's only going to get worse. Let's get this done, then knock off, and everyone can go home. This close to Christmas, people have plans."

Dilbert shook his head, sighed loudly, then slumped on to the stool. "You're the boss."

"You act like you haven't been here through dozens of these tests."

"I've had my say," Dunn retorted, muttering under his breath, slamming the clipboard back on its peg.

Evan pushed in the mike button on his radio set. "Bud. It's a go."

The landline rang suddenly, competing with the whistling wind. Dilbert reached out to answer the call.

"Leave it," Evan told him. "If it's important they'll call back." Picking up his hard hat, he set it firmly on his head, gesturing for Dilbert to do the same.

Muttering, Dunn complied.

Evan picked up his binoculars, zooming in first on the explosives, then the detonator. Swinging around, something glinted off to his far left. The sun was hidden by the clouds. Puzzled, Evan focused on the bright spot. Moving the binoculars up, his heart stilled, his face froze. Desperately, he pushed the radio button. "Abort!"

Static buzzed back in reply.

Flinging the binoculars to the floor, Evan ran from the office shed, legs pumping, heart bursting, mind praying. Jimmy jumped off his bicycle, running toward him.

"No!" Evan shouted, running faster than he ever had.

But the wind swept his words away.

And Jimmy ran toward him even faster.

Evan increased his speed, adrenaline kicking in, hurtling him toward his little boy. Barely slowing as he reached Jimmy, Evan scooped him up, pressing Jimmy to his chest and running away from the blast. He nearly cleared the red-marked danger line when the blast shook the ground, echoed to the canyon and back, and flung Evan to the ground. Holding his body over Jimmy's, Evan formed a protective barrier. The strong wind carried some residual bits of debris, but mostly a huge cloud of dust from the blast.

A car screeched to a stop only a few feet from them. Jerking upward, Evan bent to thrust Jimmy from this newest danger.

Chloe pushed open her car door, hitting the ground at a run, tears streaming down her face as she reached for them.

Picking up Jimmy with one hand, he reached with his other arm to encircle Chloe, pulling them both into his embrace, silently vowing to never let them go. He had asked the Lord for a sign. Had there ever been a clearer one?

Chloe knelt, checking over Jimmy, reassuring herself that he wasn't hurt. Evan pulled her back up, needing to hold on to her, to both of them.

"I thought...." Chloe bit back a sob. "What if you hadn't seen him?"

"I did. That's all that counts." Evan stroked her silky hair, breathing in the clean scent, knowing he would never forget it. Closing his eyes, he silently thanked the Lord, knowing He had saved them.

Jimmy still shook as he hung on to Evan. "I thought you were gonna get blowed up like Mommy and Daddy."

"Oh, sweetie!" Chloe reached for him, but Evan was quicker, picking the child up and holding him close.

"That's not going to happen to me, Jimmy. I'm here now and I'm always going to be here for you. I want you to live with me, be my son."

Jimmy threw his small arms around Evan's strong neck, holding on for all he was worth. Evan held him close, then lifted his face, catching Chloe's gaze. He had made one commitment. Would another be in his reach?

Gasping, Dilbert reached him. "I thought you were all goners for sure!"

"Dilbert, if I decide not to listen to you in the future, just knock me out with my own hard hat."

"I ain't pleased to be right," Dilbert spit out between repeated gasps. "I tried to get Bud on the radio..." He paused for another deep breath. "But it was too late."

Evan clapped the older man's shoulder, seeing how gray he was beneath his leathery tan.

Bud rushed up, one arm grasping Dilbert's. "You all right, you old fool?" For all their bickering, Bud was as pale as Dilbert.

Other quarry workers surrounded them, checking for injuries, most looking shaken, many shocked. All looked relieved when it was certain no one had been hurt.

Humbled by their concern, Evan knew he had much to be thankful for. Meeting Chloe's eyes once more, he realized how very, very much.

Chapter Sixteen

The light in Jimmy's room was dim. Exhausted, he had fallen asleep soon after eating his dinner. Thelma had fussed over him, using the corner of her apron to wipe her red-rimmed eyes while she offered to cook any and everything he might want. Too tired, emotionally and physically, to care, he had agreed to a bowl of chicken and dumplings. But he didn't eat much, instead leaning against Evan for a while, then Chloe.

Evan had helped Jimmy with his bath, then sat with him while he settled in for the night. Evan continued hovering until he was absolutely certain Jimmy was asleep and content.

Chloe had given Evan space, knowing he needed to reassure himself that Jimmy was really, truly out of danger, that he was safely ensconced beneath the Mitchells' roof. Evan was reluctant to leave, finally forcing himself to go.

Now, Chloe watched as Jimmy slept. Although she had tucked Elbert at his side, Jimmy hadn't reached for him as he usually did. Having an actual human to count on had relieved some of his fear, perhaps all of it. She stroked his dark hair, memorizing each feature, holding fast to this memory.

Stars filled the windswept sky. The storm had moved on, after bringing a light rain to wash the last of the dust away. A fresh start, Chloe mused. Utterly, inescapably grateful for Jimmy's safety, she thought she saw one of the stars blink. *Thank You, Lord, for everything, for keeping them both safe, for opening Evan's heart.*

The star twinkled and Chloe's throat closed. Evan's heart had opened for Jimmy and she was more grateful than she could have ever thought possible. Now that Jimmy had a guardian, one who loved him, her precious child would no longer need her. It was what she wanted, what she had brought Jimmy to Rosewood to find. Although she had told herself it would be difficult to say goodbye, Chloe hadn't imagined the loss now swamping her.

Jimmy would also have Gordon, Thelma and Ned, who clearly loved him as well. And Rosewood was a wonderful place for any child to grow up in. He had caring teachers, friends at school, an inspiring church and caring church family. Now that Evan had committed himself to being Jimmy's guardian, he wouldn't hold back. As in everything, Evan would be on full throttle, ensuring that Jimmy would be an incredibly happy child.

Heart brimming with love, Chloe glanced down at him, sleeping so soundly, so peacefully. This sweet boy would never cry himself to sleep because he was lonely, and all his holidays would be filled with family and tradition. The kind of tradition she had secretly dreamed of, imagining the years stringing out before them like a sparkling garland on the tallest Christmas tree.

The door to Jimmy's room eased open. Thelma stuck in her head, followed by Ned, peering over her shoulder. "Is he okay?" Thelma mouthed soundlessly.

Chloe nodded.

Both smiled back, then left as silently as they had come.

Yes, Jimmy would be encased in more than enough love for one small child. But, he would also be loved from afar because Chloe knew she would always carry him in her heart. This, her first, most precious child.

Jimmy slept deeply, unaware that she watched over him, memorizing the shape of his small nose, the way his eyebrows scrunched together when he was concentrating, the bright light of his soul that shone in his winsome eyes. Gently, she stroked his dark hair again, hoping to leave the tiniest imprint in his consciousness so he wouldn't completely forget her.

Gordon opened the door, crossing silently to the bed. "You won't get a minute's sleep with all of us checking on him," he whispered.

Unable to speak, she stepped back, allowing him access. Gordon would be a wonderful grandfather—loving, caring and fun. It was the best ready-made family she could have hoped for.

"I'll get out of your way," Gordon whispered, patting her back. "Our boy's just fine."

Chloe managed to keep a neutral expression until he left. Then she sank in to the wood rocking chair adjacent to the bed. Earlier, she had moved the chair from its usual spot in the corner so she could sit by Jimmy.

Bending her head she prayed silently. *Dear Lord, please help me show Jimmy that I know he's in the right place. Give me strength. Don't let me show my sadness, my need to stay close. I want what's best for him. But I'll need help, Lord. More help than I've ever needed before.*

Christmas Eve dawned bright, filled with people, noise and mysterious but enticing aromas from the kitchen. Refreshed by a full night of sleep, Jimmy bounced up, ready to tackle another day.

He ran through the open door to Chloe's room. "Chloe! Chloe!"

She turned to him with a smile, determined not to allow her sleepless night and anguish show. "Hey, big guy!"

"I got it already! My family!"

"Yes, you did! I'm so happy for you, Jimmy." So happy that she wanted to die, knowing he and Evan would never be hers.

"And you!" he responded, grinning.

"Me?"

"Sure. Now we're all a family." Jimmy grabbed her neck, his thin arms hugging hard.

Don't cry. Don't cry!

He pulled back. "Can we go see the outside Jesus?"

She mentally translated. "The live nativity?"

"Uh-huh. Uncle Gordon said they'll be there as soon as it's dark. And that it gets dark faster now. Please!"

"Unless Evan has something else planned, I think he'll agree."

"They have a *real* donkey and a lamb. Not like Susie Brady playing the lamb in our play."

Chloe smiled. "That's great. But you know the animals aren't the most important part, right?"

"It's the birthday for Jesus. He was borned where my star is."

"So, what else do you want to do today?"

"Evan's taking me to the store." Jimmy stopped. "It's kind of a surprise."

"Christmas is full of surprises." She pushed a bit of hair from his forehead. "Good surprises. You have fun today, okay?"

"Okay." He bounced on his sneakers, ready to start.

Chloe wasn't sure if she could hold her smile in place any longer. "Head on downstairs. I'll see you a little later."

"Thelma made French toast."

"Sounds delicious."

Jimmy skipped through the doorway, then quickened his pace down the hall to the staircase, finally pounding down the stairs.

Chloe heard voices and the closing of the front door. Moving to her window, she edged the curtain back, seeing Evan and Jimmy walk to the truck. Evan had his arm draped around Jimmy's shoulders. They were a perfect match, as she had known they would be.

Watching until the truck was out of sight, she turned around, looking at the shelf in her open closet where her suitcase was stowed. Although she had more presents to wrap, Chloe wanted to pack while Jimmy was out. He didn't need to watch the process. It was going to be hard enough to say goodbye. When she did, Chloe wanted to be set to flee to her car, to make the break as painless as possible for Jimmy.

Grabbing the empty bag, she laid it on the bed, then opened it. Originally thinking her visit would most likely last only a few weeks, there wasn't too much to gather. Pulling open a dresser drawer, she lifted out the jeans and shirt she'd bought for the hayride. She thought of Evan's kiss, the regret that pained him. Holding the items close, she remembered the sweet smell of fresh hay, the laughter, the moonlight, the feelings Evan had brought to life.

Before she could collapse in tears, she shoved both pieces into the suitcase. Folding the rest of her clothes, Chloe dropped them inside, not caring what wrinkled, not caring if the stuff even made it back to Milwaukee. She left out her nicest dress for Christmas Day.

Although she tried, Chloe couldn't get a reservation out for either Christmas Eve or day. She could at least have spent the holiday with her mother. Thinking of Mom alone was worrying Chloe more and more. And she needed to be gone. To allow Evan and Jimmy to bond, to begin their new relationship. Booking one of the few seats left out of San Antonio for the twenty-sixth, she would remain in Rosewood as shortly as possible.

Chloe opened another dresser drawer, withdrawing the last of her gifts for wrapping. Realizing the paper and other supplies were still in the storeroom off the kitchen, she gathered her strength, and tried to squelch her feelings.

Downstairs, she hesitantly pushed open the swinging door to the kitchen. Smelling the French toast Thelma had mentioned, she spotted a note on the table: *"French toast and bacon in the warming drawer. Syrup's on the counter. Make your own coffee."*

Chloe smiled faintly. The note didn't need a signature. Reading it was like having Thelma standing there, speaking. Having no appetite, Chloe put her gifts down on the table and took Thelma's advice, making a fresh pot of coffee.

Back in the storeroom, the paper had been orderly returned to the shelf. Chloe didn't need much to wrap the few remaining gifts. A lace handkerchief for Thelma, a freshly sealed package of cherry pipe tobacco for Gordon, a children's bible for Jimmy that she had inscribed to him, and a paperweight for Evan, made from his own quarry's limestone. Viola and Dilbert had helped her retrieve the small piece she needed. Dilbert had volunteered to cut the stone for her, then inscribe Evan's initials. Chloe's fingers lingered over the paperweight, then traced the lettering on Jimmy's bible.

"Thought I smelled fresh coffee," Gordon declared as he pushed open the swinging door to the kitchen, sniffing in pleasure. "Thelma always leaves me to my own devices until supper on Christmas Eve. Personally, I think she turns into one of the elves while she's out." He filled a mug. "Did you get some?"

Chloe shook her head, afraid to trust her voice.

"You made it, I'm happy to pour." Snagging another mug, he poured more fresh coffee and carried both mugs to the large oak table. "Looks like you're busy. Am I going to be in the way?"

"No." Chloe's voice was raspy. To cover it, she sipped the coffee, forgetting how hot it would be.

"Whew. Must have asbestos-lined innards." Shaking his head, Gordon added cream to his own mug.

Chloe placed one hand over her scalded mouth.

"Chloe? That burned, didn't it?" Rising, he grabbed a glass, put a few ice cubes and milk inside, and rushed it back. "Here, drink this. It'll help."

Obediently, she sipped the cold milk. It did help, but for the life of her, Chloe couldn't dredge up a smile.

Concerned, Gordon studied her. "It's not just the hot coffee. You look like you lost your best friend."

Realizing the milk was no disguise, she set it on the table. "No. Not my best friend."

Gordon leaned back in his chair. "Jimmy."

"I'm so pleased, beyond pleased, that Evan has finally accepted Jimmy as his own." Chloe lifted her face, fierceness burning in her eyes. "And I wouldn't change that for anything in the world."

"And you?"

"I've done my job." Expelling a deep breath, she looked back down.

"It hasn't been a job for you for quite a while now." Gordon squeezing her hand encouragingly. "And, it's not over."

"Afraid it is. I won't lie and say it's not killing me to leave Jimmy."

Gordon's kind, wise eyes searched hers. "Just Jimmy?"

"There's that wishful thinking bug again."

"Oh, Chloe. You've been able to see so much, learn so much while you've been here. Don't stop now."

She couldn't make Evan love her. Certainly couldn't make him stop missing his late wife, nor could she ever take Robin's place. And she couldn't say any of that to Gordon. "Thank you for the milk. I'd have never thought of it for a burned mouth."

He squeezed her hand again, then released it, leaning back to sip his cooling coffee. Chloe was grateful he didn't press her any longer. She couldn't bear it.

By five o'clock that afternoon, the Mitchell family had assembled in the entry hall. Everyone wore warm coats, gloves and hats. Chloe wore her warmest slacks and shirt, covered by the sweater she'd brought.

Evan turned the knob on the front door, then paused, turning around. "Whoops. Jimmy, I think we forgot something."

Jimmy nodded enthusiastically. "Uh-huh." He pulled out a small, gaily wrapped package, then handed it to Chloe. "Surprise!"

"It's a family tradition," Gordon explained. "Everyone gets to open a gift on Christmas Eve."

Chloe looked around. No one else was opening presents. But she didn't want to appear ungracious. With Jimmy about to burst, she unwrapped the box, peeled back the tissue paper and found a lovely pair of brown leather gloves.

"You can put 'em on now!" Jimmy urged, still smiling brightly.

"Great time for it," she agreed.

"I'll snip the tags," Thelma offered, producing a pair of scissors.

They had planned well.

"While she's doing that, open this one." Gordon handed her another box.

"You said *one* gift."

"One, two, who's counting?"

"You guys…" This time, she unwrapped a snug-looking ivory hat. "Very well coordinated, very appreciated. Thank you, Gordon."

Thelma held out a slim, rectangular package.

"Thelma, not you, too!"

"Open it or we're going to be late," Thelma instructed gruffly, her eager eyes giving away her pleasure.

A hand-knitted scarf in an array of colors from a

golden caramel to deep brown rested in the folds of tissue paper. "Oh, Thelma… It's gorgeous. You must have spent hours making this."

"A body's got to stay warm," Thelma replied, trying unsuccessfully to disguise her delight.

Impulsively, Chloe hugged the older woman, who returned the gesture with a fierce hug of her own. "Guess I'd better put it on," Chloe said shakily, looping the lovely scarf around her neck. "Wow. I'm all set."

"Not quite," Evan objected.

Chloe wasn't sure where he'd hidden the large box he now extended to her. "Evan?"

"Just an early gift."

Hands trembling, she slipped off the silver ribbons, then unwrapped the delicate mauve and silver paper. Still shaking, she lifted the lid and set it aside. Chloe was almost afraid to open the pale pink tissue paper that nestled the gift. With everyone looking on, she pushed back the paper. Reverently, she smoothed one hand over the soft material inside. A winter-white cashmere coat, almost too beautiful to wear.

"Let's see it," Gordon encouraged.

Carefully picking it out of the box, she held it up for everyone to see. A circle of pleased, enchanted faces met hers.

"It's not just for looking," Evan reminded her, gently taking the coat from her hands, holding it for her to put on.

Chloe slid one arm into a sleeve, turned to get the other. Evan fitted it in place, his hand lingering on her arm. Even though she tried not to, she glanced up as he stood so very close. His eyes burned with something she'd never before seen in them.

The little group was quiet as they watched and waited, but Chloe still couldn't break her gaze with Evan.

"Do you like it?" Jimmy asked, unable to contain his excitement any longer.

"It's…" Chloe cleared her throat, bogged down in emotion so rich it filled each of her senses, seemed to exude from every pore. "It's beautiful. The most beautiful gift I've ever received."

Evan remained silent, watching.

Chloe gradually returned to earth, then caught sight of her tight circle. "All of the gifts, I mean." She touched the scarf. "I've never received such a bounty of thoughtful, generous, lovely gifts. Thank you…everyone."

The live nativity was a highlight of Rosewood's Christmas celebration. A rural community, they had privy to all the animals that must have attended that first holy night.

Shepherds, along with the three wise men, flanked the stable. Mary and Joseph looked to the crèche.

"There's no one in the crib," Jimmy whispered to Evan.

"Because Jesus was born on Christmas Day," Evan explained. "This is the night before, when everyone waited for him."

"Oh." Jimmy watched the adults portraying Mary and Joseph. "Is that His mommy and daddy?"

"His earthly parents," Evan replied, knowing Jimmy would learn the full meaning in time.

Jimmy gripped his hand. "Are you my earthly daddy now? Since my first daddy's in heaven?"

Evan felt his love for Jimmy swell. "Yes."

"Then is Chloe my earthly mommy?"

Evan hoped so. With every fiber of being, he hoped to convince her to stay. He'd seen her shutting down, withdrawing. But he couldn't blow this chance. The Lord had given him a second family, and, in His wisdom, left that last chore to Evan. Kneeling down, he whispered close to Jimmy's ear, "That's what we need to pray for tonight. You understand?"

Jimmy nodded fervently, then whispered back, "I love Chloe."

His eyes misted, but Evan controlled his voice. "I love her, too."

Standing back up, his hands remained on Jimmy's shoulders as they joined the crowd in singing "Silent Night."

One of the deacons, Robert Conway, began to read from the second chapter of Luke. "And, lo, the angel of the Lord came upon them, and the glory of the Lord shone...."

The familiar words washed over Evan as he silently prayed for just one more glorious event.

Chapter Seventeen

Having left the lights on, the Mitchell house looked warm and welcoming as they returned from the live nativity. Chloe had attended similar services before, but this one touched her deeply, knowing she had so much to be grateful for.

Following the others, she wondered why Gordon and Evan were walking toward the front while Thelma and Ned disappeared inside the back door. Since Jimmy held tightly to her hand, Chloe let him choose the course.

As usual, the door wasn't locked. Once inside, Chloe glanced down at her warm coat, unable to resist touching the sleeve one more time. While she did, Jimmy unclasped her hand. The room seemed unusually quiet. Lifting her gaze, Chloe stared straight ahead. A wing-backed chair that normally resided in the parlor had been moved to the hall. Gordon and Evan stepped aside in opposite directions, revealing the chair's occupant.

Tears blurred Chloe's vision. "Mom?"

"Merry Christmas, sweetheart."

Chloe rushed across the hall, burying her face against

her mother's shoulder as she had done as a child. Barbara stroked her daughter's hair, patted Chloe's back.

Raising her head, Chloe shook it in disbelief. "How...."

Barbara smiled gently. "Your friends. Grace's Aunt Ruth flew up to Milwaukee to get me. Then we flew back together and she drove us here."

Thoughts whirling, Chloe studied her anxiously. "Your oxygen?"

"I used the portable concentrator while we traveled. Grace's husband arranged for a home concentrator that the Mitchells put in a room for me."

"We have a guest suite downstairs on this floor," Gordon explained. "Set it up for my mother when she couldn't climb the stairs anymore. Had it renovated so it's got everything she might need."

Despite her joy, Chloe couldn't shed her anxiety. "And, you're really okay, Mom?"

"I'm better than okay." Barbara smiled tenderly. "I'm with my family for Christmas."

Turning to Evan and Gordon, Chloe looked at them for answers. "How did you arrange all this?"

"Well, now," Gordon began. "First of all, it was all Evan's idea. He's had it planned since..." Gordon scratched his head. "Better than two weeks, I believe."

Chloe's gaze settled solely on Evan, her voice low. "Weeks?"

Meeting her gaze, he nodded, his own dark eyes still filled with that unidentified emotion.

"How did you even know how to contact my mother?"

Grace's Aunt Ruth walked toward her from the side of the hall where Thelma and Ned were also standing.

"Grace said she had a time coaxing the name of the care facility from you."

Totally overwhelmed, Chloe couldn't take it in. "Grace?"

"Evan called her to help him arrange everything. She talked to me. Next thing we knew, your mother and I were having a fine time traveling back to Rosewood. Didn't we, Barbara?"

"Very fine," Barbara agreed brightly.

"I don't know what to say," Chloe began, then paused. "Yes, I do. Earlier, I thought I'd received the most beautiful gift ever." She looked directly at Evan, mentally urging him to understand. "I was wrong. *This* is the most beautiful gift. And the most special anyone has ever given me."

While the others talked in low rumbling voices, she watched Evan's eyes. While she still couldn't read his thoughts, she sensed he understood her gratitude. And perhaps even more.

After Barbara had changed and climbed into bed, Chloe sat on the edge of the mattress, holding her mother's hand. "You took your nighttime medicine, right?"

"You've triple-checked all my meds and both oxygen machines. I feel wonderful, sweetheart."

"You look good," Chloe admitted. "Sorry to fret so, but honestly, Mom, you continue to amaze me."

Barbara chuckled quietly. "And you don't?"

Surprised, Chloe waited for her to continue.

"Sweetheart, you've made a whole new town full of friends, a new family—"

"Whoa. Friends, yes. And the Mitchells treat me wonderfully. But *you're* my family."

"Family grows, expands. That's how it's supposed to be."

Chloe swallowed, unwilling to worry her mother. Jimmy was Evan's now. And Evan... wasn't hers. "I'm so glad you're here. I have so much to tell you." They had already been talking nonstop for more than an hour after the group scattered and they were left alone. Chloe glanced at the clock on the nightstand. "But, it's late. You must be tired after the trip and all the excitement. I know I am."

"You know me too well."

Kissing her forehead, Chloe then rose. "Evan's sleeping in Jimmy's room tonight on the spare bed. So I'll be in the next room." The Mitchells still had a bed in the tiny adjoining space where a nurse had once stayed. Anticipating Chloe's intention, Thelma had made up the single bed. She had also brought down pajamas, robe, Chloe's best dress and all her gear from the upstairs bathroom.

"Honey, I don't want to cause more trouble for anyone."

"Trouble?" Chloe swallowed against tears of truth. "You have never been a moment's trouble, Mom. I wouldn't have things any other way. Sleep well."

"You too, sweetheart."

She turned the dimmer to low, then eased into the spare single bed. Knowing the Lord had differing paths for everyone, Chloe was grateful to have her mother here. It was going to be difficult enough to leave. It would help having Mom by her side.

Still, Chloe couldn't quash the pain that cratered in her heart as she thought of leaving Evan and Jimmy. Burying her face in her pillow, she muffled the sound. And wept into the night.

Pleased, Chloe watched tentatively as Ned pulled out his dress gloves.

"Me, too. Gloves, I mean, not a hankie. I can wear these to church."

"And cover up those leathery hands," Thelma added, then leaned over to kiss her husband's cheek.

Gordon was equally pleased with his gift.

Jimmy ripped the paper from his present. Chloe hoped he wasn't expecting a toy or video game. But when the bible was revealed, he smiled. Then he rushed over for a huge hug. "Thanks."

Chloe fought tears, wanting to never let him go. "I'm glad you like it, sweetheart."

"I can take my present to church, too!" Then he scrambled down, returning to Evan's side.

Evan opened presents from Ned and Thelma, then reached for Chloe's. Holding her breath, she waited for an excruciating few moments while he unwrapped it.

Once out of the box, Evan palmed the paperweight, examining all the edges.

"It's a paperweight," she explained. "Well, I guess you can see that. It's made out of limestone from your quarry. I guess you can see that, too," Chloe babbled, unable to stop the growing flow of words. "You probably have everything in the world a person can make from limestone, and out of your own quarry, too. I just thought, since you have an office, and then the study, here, maybe you could use one." Eventually, the flow reduced to a trickle. "Or not."

"I don't have another thing in my life like it." Again his eyes took on that unusual intensity, one she hadn't yet deciphered. His voice deepened. "Thank you."

Barbara patted Chloe's shoulder.

Evan handed her a small, slim box. "Merry Christmas."

Baffled, Chloe drew her eyebrows together. "But you already gave me my present."

"Just open it."

Trying not to let the shaking of her hands show, she opened the gift. Inside was a string of beads which matched her eyes. Stunned, she lifted the exquisite necklace. "Evan, it's beautiful! But it's too much!"

"Not for you."

She caressed the smooth, hand-carved jade. "Thank you."

The bustle continued, the noise level escalating. Yet all Chloe could hear were Evan's words, and wondered what they meant.

The dining room table was crowded with people. A second table held more, just as it had on Thanksgiving. But Perry volunteered to move so that Barbara could sit next to Chloe.

Although Evan would have liked to sit beside Jimmy, he remained in his usual chair at the opposite end where he could view everyone. Barbara was even nicer than he'd hoped. He could see the resemblance, physical and personality-wise with Chloe. True to her word, Barbara hadn't breathed a word of his surprise. Chloe's expression had been worth every phone call, every niggling detail.

Now, though, Chloe's expression was no longer happy. Eating little, she alternately clasped her mother's and Jimmy's hands. Evan knew he hadn't voiced his feelings for her yet, but surely she sensed how he felt. Did she need a sign?

A sign as clear as the one he had received? A glint

on Jimmy's handlebars on a sunless day shrouded in dark gray clouds? An explosion that could have taken them all?

Or just the words he had locked in his heart? Even there they stumbled. How could he possibly pour everything he felt into mere words?

"Great dinner as always," the elderly man on his right said, his hand shaky as he held on to his water glass.

"Thanks, Elmer. Glad you're enjoying it. How 'bout you, Clem? Getting enough to eat?"

"And then some, Evan." Clem lifted his fork in approval, his hand not shaking quite as much. But then he was two years younger than Elmer. Both were past ninety.

Evan could picture himself growing that old with Chloe at his side. But first, he acknowledged silently, he had to say the words.

After dinner ended, guests lingered for a while, then gradually dispersed to their own homes. This was usually Chloe's favorite time of day. The five of them had retreated to the parlor. Thelma threatened to lock the kitchen door if any of them, other than Ned, tried to help her clean the kitchen and wash dishes.

The fire burned at just the right level, warming the room, the flames dimly lighting rather than jumping. The short stack of logs in the oversize fireplace spit occasionally, then retreated to a comforting crackle. And Barbara was within a hand's reach. Jimmy sat at her feet, playing a new video game Gordon had given him. The tree, still redolent of its fresh pine boughs, twinkled in the early evening.

Mom and Gordon were getting on well, enjoying

each other as contemporaries. It occurred to Chloe that having people one's own age to talk with was important. Her mother was in her late fifties. Most of the people in her care facility were much older. Did she miss having friends her own age close by? She would have to check into that once they were back.

The pain jabbed again as it had each time Chloe thought of returning to Milwaukee. The city had always been her home. Now she felt like she was being shipped to the far edges of the planet.

Jimmy jumped up. "I'm gonna go get the picture of me in the play and show it to your mommy."

"She'll like that." Chloe watched him scamper out of the room, his energy apparently boundless.

"I hate to put an end to a wonderful day, but I think I'll go to bed," Barbara said. "Jimmy can bring the picture to my room."

"I'll help—"

Barbara waved away the offer. "I can get there on my own. Stay, enjoy yourself." Clutching her small, light oxygen carrier, she left.

Worried, Chloe watched.

"She's only one room away," Gordon reminded her gently. "But she's got the right idea. I'm done in myself. Good night, young people."

Achingly aware that only she and Evan remained in the parlor, Chloe drew herself up, trying to disappear in the depths of the chair.

Evan rose and grabbed a poker, stirring the deteriorating fire. "Your mother's a fine woman."

"You won't get an argument out of me."

Replacing the poker, he turned. "Is that a promise?"

Chloe stared at him, the only sound between them the lingering, last gasp crackling of the fire.

"How come your suitcase is packed?" Jimmy demanded, running to a stop in front of her.

"What?"

"I saw it!" His lips wobbled. "On your bed. Like you're going somewhere."

"Jimmy, Evan's going to be your guardian. You have a wonderful home here with him."

"But why are *you* going?"

Evan walked close. "Yeah. I'd like to know that myself."

She gaped at him. "What?"

"I said I want to know why you're leaving."

Chloe gestured haplessly at Jimmy, silently imploring Evan to help her. But he didn't.

"My job's done. You know that."

"Nuh-uh," Jimmy protested. "*I'm* not done."

Again, Chloe beseeched Evan with her eyes.

He shrugged. "Jimmy's right. We're not done with you." Evan walked to within inches of her chair. In a swift movement he pulled her up from the chair, holding her next to him.

Chloe's throat was dry, clogged. "You're not?"

"Are you arguing with us?" Evan asked, his face so close to hers, she could see the depths of his eyes, could feel the whisper of his breath.

"I...." Words failed to pass through the acres of emotion crammed into the small space of her throat.

"Chloe, will you stay? Marry me? Mother Jimmy? Make us a family?"

The heat of his breath eased over her cheek, hovered near her mouth. "Marry?"

"Yes!" Jimmy jumped up and down. "Marry us!"

"I want to."

"That's all I need to hear." Evan cradled the back of her head, his fingers laced between strands of her hair.

"But I can't."

For a moment the room silenced. Not even the fire dared make a sound.

"Why not?" Evan demanded, his face so close to hers she could feel the thrust of his chin against hers.

"My mother. I can't leave her." The dam of emotion burst, flooding her heart, spilling her tears. "You don't understand. I've never wanted anything so much, to be with you, to have Jimmy as my own, but I can't! Don't make me choose!"

"You don't have to choose."

Confused, Chloe shook her head. "Of course I do. I'll never leave my mother on her own."

"What if your mother moves to Rosewood? In here with us?"

"Here? She has to have someone in the house with her all the time. She can't—"

"There's always someone here," he replied gently. "Thelma, Ned, my dad, you, me, Jimmy. And, if by some miracle, not one of us can be here, we have lots of friends and neighbors who can help."

Did she really dare hope? Muddled, she tried to think of all the reasons it wouldn't work. "My mother might not *want* to live here."

"Funny. She told me she'd be very happy to move to Rosewood, to be close to you and your family."

"But, when—"

"When I knew, *finally* knew, I couldn't live without you. Barbara's excited by the idea. You two can spend a lot more time together that way. Unless you really want to go to law school?"

"Law school?" she echoed. "Why... No, I don't care about going to law school. That was just a way to support my mother. And Mr. Wainwright was going to pay..." Chloe stopped abruptly. "Does this mean you trust me now? Really trust me?"

Evan took her hand and placed it on his chest. "With all my heart."

She felt tears slipping down her face. Evan carefully, gently eased them away with his thumb as he had once before. He touched her lips with the same thumb, tracing their outline. Angling his head, he claimed her lips, sealing their promise with his own.

Sated, Evan pulled back slightly. "Is that a yes?"

Breathless, she spoke against the fullness of his lips. "Yes! Definitely, yes!"

"Yes!" Jimmy hollered, jumping beside them.

Bailey barked, circling them with his tail wagging.

Yes, my love. Yes.

"How did we ever put a wedding together this fast?" Chloe asked her matron of honor.

Grace shrugged. "Helps having a wedding gown designer right on Main Street who could whip up a dress." The owner of the shop had jumped in to help, finishing a winter-white gown she had already begun sewing. "Not to mention the Conway Nursery growing flowers all year round." They had chosen deep burgundy roses, creamy calla lilies and hand-gathered swags of evergreen. The owner of the local bakery hadn't even blinked when asked to produce a fully decorated wedding cake. Grace swished the skirt of her long, emerald green gown. "Didn't hurt that I had my own dress, too."

"And I was already in town," Barbara added with a twinkle in her eye.

"I can't believe Ruth talked you into bringing your best dress."

Grace chuckled. "We just seem mild. Our family's actually pretty ruthless."

Ruthless in running every errand, delivering invitations by hand, arranging with the pastor to have the church on New Year's Eve morning, collecting candles to light the sanctuary, enlisting friends with catering and decorating skills.

Mindful of the dress's large train, Chloe turned to her mother. "Are you really sure? Really, really sure you want to move here?"

Barbara threw back her head, laughing. "Good thing I have plenty of oxygen with me. Yes, my dear, for the thousandth time, I am absolutely, positively, one hundred and ten percent sure. Why wouldn't I be? I can see you every day, watch my grandson grow up."

Chloe smiled, thinking of how instantly Jimmy had bonded with her.

"And," Barbara continued, "you're happy. Truly happy. Do you know how long I've wanted that for you?"

Tears misted.

"Now don't start that," Barbara insisted. "Or I'll be weeping buckets."

Grace sniffled. "Me, too."

Chloe turned back to the mirror, wiping her eyes with the newly embroidered hankie Thelma had pressed in her hand that morning. Her new initials, CMM, were stitched in blue on the cotton square. Something blue.

She had piled her tamed curls on top of her head, securing them before adding a delicate headband encrusted with pearls that Grace provided. Something borrowed.

Barbara rolled forward in her wheelchair, then extended her hand, holding a single strand of heirloom pearls. "I wore these on my wedding day, and so did your grandmother."

Touched, Chloe picked up the delicate necklace. "But how did you know?"

"Ruth was *very* helpful," Barbara said with a straight face. Then her lips trembled, giving away her feelings.

Chloe reached down to hug her tightly. "Thank you, Mom."

"You'll pass them down to your daughter one day."

"Daughter?" Beautiful thought. Chloe put them to her neck and fastened the clasp. Something old.

Grace held out a small jewelry box.

"Grace, what—"

"Just open it," Grace chided gently.

Overwhelmed, Chloe opened the case, revealing a pair of pearl earrings. Ones that were the same shade as the aged pearl necklace. "I've never seen anything like this. Not just that you've planned so perfectly, coordinated it beyond belief, but your generosity. Everyone's."

Grace smiled. "I'm glad they match so well."

Fastening them to each earlobe, Chloe blinked away another threat of tears. Something new.

Notes from the organ floated into the bride's room. Chloe turned, facing Grace and her mother. "Sounds like the music before the main event."

Noah knocked on the door. "Grace? Susie's ready."

Grace's husband had watched their daughter, who was to be the flower girl, while the women helped Chloe dress. Accustomed to being quiet in church, five-year-old Susie held her basket obediently, shyly smiling.

Jimmy wasn't to be the ring bearer, though. Evan had chosen him to be the best man, to stand beside them while they exchanged vows.

Gordon had agreed to walk Chloe down the aisle. She had been torn, wishing her mother was strong enough for the task. But Barbara insisted she preferred to sit in the traditional position of the bride's mother in the front pews.

Barbara broke into her thoughts. "I'd better go. I'll need that extra bit of time." One of the ushers was going to help her into the pew, then move her wheelchair to the foyer until after the service concluded.

Chloe bent, kissing her mother's soft cheek. "I love you, Mom."

Barbara met her gaze. "You are the dearest daughter in the world. Be happy, Chloe."

Grace adjusted the simple satin bow on Susie's pale green dress. Then she knelt to check Chloe's train on the whipped up dress. A vintage-inspired satin and tulle Cinderella gown with a sweetheart neckline, fitted bodice, long sleeves and a chapel-length train that spread out behind her elegantly.

Chloe clutched her bouquet of hand-tied, deep red calla lilies. "It's *really* real."

"You look beautiful," Grace murmured.

"Because I have a beautiful friend."

Grace looked ready to choke up. Instead, she blinked

away the tears and took her daughter's hand. "Ready, ladies?"

Rosewood's Community Church was more than one hundred and fifty years old. The intricate stained-glass windows allowed the morning sunlight to illuminate the hand-tooled wooden pews, the clusters of fresh roses and calla lilies, and the guests in the congregation. The sunbeams' warmth coaxed the fragrance of both the roses and evergreens to scent the air. Candles flickered in arched brass holders flanking the nave.

Gordon met Chloe in the marbled foyer. "You look beautiful, *daughter*."

She took his arm, clinging to him for support. "So do you."

Grace knelt down beside Susie when the ushers opened the tall, wide doors to the sanctuary. "Now, sweetheart."

The delicate girl, who looked so much like her mother, took small, careful steps as she dropped red rose petals on the wide center aisle.

Grace smiled brightly, then turned and followed her daughter. When she reached the altar, the organ music grew louder as it began trumpeting the traditional wedding march.

Chloe stepped around the door, seeing the fully decorated church for the first time.

Gordon squeezed her hand and whispered, "Ready?"

Nodding, Chloe took the deepest breath of her life. They started up the aisle when she saw her mother stand, the traditional custom to signal the rest of the guests to do likewise. Looking into the faces of the guests, she realized many of them were familiar. From school, church, the office, even the holiday dinners.

Nearing her mother, Chloe met her proud, pleased gaze. Then she met another set of eyes.

And was glad she had taken that deep breath because she thought she might not be able to take another.

Evan stood tall and proud. His thick, wavy hair had been tamed, his crisp white shirt emphasized his tanned, compelling features. That strong, stubborn jaw, aristocratic nose, those mesmerizing midnight-colored eyes.

Without effort, Chloe glided from Gordon's arm to Evan's. Turning toward him, she thought she might drown within the emotions written on his face.

The pastor began speaking and while Chloe listened, she caught Jimmy's attention, sending him a smile his very own.

"Will you, Chloe Marie Reed, take this man, Evan Sean Mitchell, to be your lawfully wedded husband, to have and to hold from this day forward, for better or worse, for richer, for poorer, in sickness and in health, to love and to cherish from this day forward until death do you part?"

This time nothing crowded her throat or conviction. "I do."

The familiar words continued, seeming to fly by as fast as the wedding preparations themselves.

"I now pronounce you husband and wife. You may kiss the bride."

Chloe felt Evan's tender kiss lingering. Then he took her hand, caressing the engagement ring he had presented her, one that had been his mother's. He had purchased a new wedding band to slide beside it, to signify their new union.

Again the organ music soared, all stops pulled out. They turned to greet their loved ones.

"Mr. and Mrs. Evan Mitchell," the pastor announced.

They stepped down the wide, wooden stairs. Chloe looked up at her new husband. Reading the request in her eyes, they paused at her mother's pew. Embracing her, Chloe gave thanks for all the Lord was showering upon them.

Gordon rose from the other side of the aisle, extending a hand to Jimmy, then crossing over to wait with Barbara while the new couple continued down the aisle and out into the foyer.

Thelma mopped her face with her new handkerchief and Ned reached over to borrow the damp hankie.

Chloe and Evan could only see each other and the love that flowed as swiftly as the now fast-moving river. Because winter had officially arrived in Rosewood. Just as Chloe had done.

Before dashing out to a shower of soap bubbles and confetti, Evan took her hand, pulled her close. "That was I *do* I heard back there?"

Her lips eased into a wide smile before meeting his. "Yes. Most definitely yes."

Tender, possessive, protective, Evan's kiss reflected all.

"I love you, Mrs. Mitchell."

The future opened in front of them like a fertile hill country meadow. "And, I love you, Mr. Mitchell. One more promise?"

"Anything."

"Tell me again on our fiftieth anniversary."

Evan's smile flashed, his eyes full of tenderness. "Don't make me wait *that* long."

Their laughter blended like the vines of a climbing rose, then was muted by the kiss that sealed their promise. And grew to the skies.

Epilogue

The following Christmas

Jimmy Mitchell hovered over his two-month-old baby sister, tucking on a teeny pink bootie she had kicked off. "Gracie won't keep her socks on."

Chloe and Evan exchanged an amused glance while Gordon snapped a photo of the quartet that now made a complete, loving family.

"That's so you'll keep checking on her, son." Evan crossed over to the cradle.

Obviously pleased, Jimmy shrugged. "In that case, it's okay."

Evan ruffled his hair. "And that's what makes you a good big brother."

"I'll say so," Gordon chimed in. "And that's what every little girl needs."

Barbara spread open her arms. "How about a hug for Grandma?"

Jimmy ran over, fitting into her big hug. Barbara's face glowed when he perched on her lap. Her health had been improving steadily the past year and she hadn't had pneumonia once during that time. Grace's husband, Noah, had connected them with an excellent pulmonary specialist and Barbara's health was better than it had been in a decade. She still had COPD, but the dry hill country weather was far healthier for her than the humidity in Milwaukee, a city bisected by a river and bounded by one of the great lakes.

Chloe had tried not to worry, but it was a longtime habit, difficult to break. So Evan called in an electrician who had installed alarm buttons in Barbara's suite. Chloe ordered a medical alert necklace that Barbara always wore, but hadn't needed to use.

Gordon captured Barbara and Jimmy in another shot. Gordon and Barbara had become good friends as well, generously sharing their grandson. Together, they had surprised Chloe and Evan by decorating the house for the holidays with both white and burgundy-red calla lilies, boughs of evergreen, and deep burgundy roses, reminiscent of their holiday wedding.

The living Christmas tree was even taller, filled with all the traditional ornaments and sporting new ones for both Jimmy and Gracie. Jimmy had two, one proclaiming him the best big brother, the other declaring him the most beloved son. Gordon and Barbara had collaborated on a small wreath for Jimmy's bedroom door. Instead of pinecones or the normal greenery, they made it from similarly sized replicas of sports balls—soccer, basketball, baseball, football. And, an emblem at the base announced that he was their number one grandson.

Sensitive to Gordon's late grandson, Sean, Barbara had suggested a different phrasing, but Gordon insisted. Jimmy needed all their love and support in his new family.

For Gracie, a tiny pair of pink porcelain booties were inscribed with her name, date of birth. Chloe watched as she and Jimmy gooed at each other. Her heart was so full, she was surprised it didn't burst.

Jimmy and Evan had bonded so tightly, no one would ever guess he was adopted. Chloe had taken him into her heart even sooner and Jimmy was truly hers in every way. He had blossomed as well in the previous year. She and Evan had adopted him immediately after their honeymoon in San Antonio.

Neither had wanted to travel far, and few other places were as romantic as the nearly century-old walkways nestled against the banks of the San Antonio River, a story below the city itself. Magical year round, it was a fantasy during the holidays. Festooned with twinkling white lights, the waterway carried boats that glided slowly beneath bridges, evoking a sense of incomparable romance. Not that Evan and Chloe needed the setting.

She glanced at her husband of one year, still marveling that he was hers. His pain had subsided after he placed it in the Lord's hands. Renewing his faith had revived his life, his generous heart, his willingness to love without boundaries.

Someone rapped the knocker on the front door. It was still fairly early on Christmas Day, but the family had opened all their presents. Most visitors wouldn't arrive until their traditional midday meal.

Thelma hopped up first. "Early for guests." She opened the door, her tone changing completely. "Well, come on in."

Chloe recognized her best friend's voice. Grace, her

aunt Ruth, Noah and Susie chattered while they strolled into the parlor.

"Merry Christmas!" Chloe rose from the sofa. "I didn't know we'd get to see you today!"

"And miss my namesake's first Christmas?" Grace replied with a swift hug. "Ah, there she is!" Grace walked quickly to the cradle, stopping first to greet Jimmy. "Hey, big brother. You still liking your sister?"

"Yeah." Jimmy ducked his head. "She's okay."

Grace grinned. "Going to keep her then?"

"Uh-huh."

Reaching the cradle, Grace peered down. "I'm not quite sure how we managed to have the three most beautiful children in the world." The baby held up one hand and Grace offered her pinky finger which Gracie latched on to. "She's getting really strong."

Susie tiptoed next to her mother. Fascinated, she stared into the cradle. "Is our baby going to be that little?"

Chloe stared at her friend, hoping Grace's prayer had been answered.

Grace patted her still flat tummy. "I imagine so."

Chloe rushed to give her a hug, while Evan pumped Noah's hand in congratulation.

"Ruth Stanton!" Barbara declared. "Why didn't you tell me?"

"Promised I wouldn't," Ruth replied with an apologetic shrug and nod toward her niece.

Barbara and Ruth had become fast friends. Ruth urged Barbara to join the ladies auxiliary and picked her up each week to attend the meetings. In between, they had lunches both out in town and in the house. Many afternoons were spent playing dominos, gin rummy or hearts. Barbara still had to carry her portable concentrator, but Ruth treated it as just an extra purse. They had purchased a power scooter so Barbara could *walk* through town with her friend.

And, as Evan had predicted, they had yet to need extra help to ensure someone was always in the house with Barbara. Using the lighter wheelchair Chloe had suggested, it was always easy to pack the chair in the back of a car. So Barbara attended church regularly, including special events like the live nativity the previous evening.

Barbara winked at Ruth. "I'm happy for all of you." The much prayed for pregnancy was a blessing Grace and Noah had wanted for some time.

"Between us, we'll have four little ones to spoil." Ruth patted Susie's back.

"And I'm the oldest," Jimmy bragged.

"You sure are, big guy." Evan scooped him up, flinging him up over his head, making Jimmy giggle.

The blessings continued to flow, Chloe thought. Mitchell Stone had revived due to the large order they had been able to produce. Everyone's jobs were safe. The company was doing so well that Melanie, the woman Chloe had stepped in for, didn't have to return to work. Instead, they were able to hire her husband for a different position and Melanie was ecstatic to be home with her children.

Grace reluctantly retrieved her hand when the baby's eyes closed. "She gets prettier every day."

"Just like her godmother." Chloe and Evan had readily agreed to name the baby after Chloe's best friend because, without her, they might not have had a happy ending. Grace had been pivotal in negotiating the tricky issues that divided them. And, she'd been instrumental in successfully bringing Barbara to Rosewood. Grace had filled Ruth in on everything so that Barbara would be prepared for what she was walking into.

"Do you suppose we've started a tradition?" Grace mused. "Having new babies for Christmas?"

"I can't imagine a better one." Chloe squeezed her friend's hand. "I'm so happy for you."

"I've pretty much been waltzing on air since I suspected. I just didn't want to say anything too soon."

"Your timing's perfect." She chuckled.

"What?"

"Just thinking that one day Gracie will wear Mom's pearls on her wedding day, too."

"She's a bit young," Grace teased.

Chloe rubbed the emerald ring on her right hand. Evan had given it to her when Gracie was born. For Christmas, she had received the matching earrings. He continued to spoil her and she loved every moment.

As though he knew her thoughts, Evan met her eyes from across the room. It had been that way since their wedding day, their unspoken communication of each other's needs.

Weaving through their small crowd, speaking to guests on the way, Evan and Chloe met near the fragrant Christmas tree. There was one other ornament that also adorned the tree. A bride and groom, hand in hand, beside a manger cradling the holy babe.

The Lord had brought them together, blessed them beyond measure and continued to hold them in His hands. Looking around the room at all the dear faces, Chloe was so thankful she had to bite back a tear.

"What is it, my love?"

"I'm just so happy," she sniffled.

Evan took her hand, absently polishing the deep green gemstone on her finger. "We've got a lot to be happy for." His life was changed forever. Hope replaced longing, love conquered pain. He put an arm around her waist. "I wasted a lot of time being angry."

She touched his cheek. "The Lord has plenty of patience."

"He needed it with me."

"He knew you were worth it." Chloe smiled tenderly. "So did I."

Evan kissed her long, slim fingers, warmed as always by the sight of the gold band encircling her left ring finger. *What if she hadn't persisted, had accepted his refusal?*

Chloe's hair fell long and loose, the waves cascading over her shoulders, resting full and thick on her back. He would always remember the first silky touch of her curls, the sight of her moonwashed lips, their softness when they kissed for the first time. "I love you more every day," he said quietly, so only she could hear. "No, every minute."

"You're determined to make me cry," she replied, placing her hand on his chest, atop the beat of his heart. "I believe this is mine."

"Always."

Gordon snapped his camera. "Now, I need you two over by Jimmy and Gracie."

Barbara had removed Gracie from the cradle, coaxing her awake with Jimmy's help.

Amused, Evan held his wife's hand as they approached their children. Sitting side by side on the couch, Evan plunked Jimmy on to his lap while Chloe held the baby.

"Smile," Gordon instructed.

Instinctively, Chloe and Evan turned to each other with tender smiles. Gracie cooed and Jimmy grinned.

Gordon clicked the camera, captured the moment. "Perfect picture."

"Perfect family," Evan replied.

He didn't mind as his father shepherded everyone into various groups for all the photos he wanted to take. Then Gordon set the timer and everyone crowded together for a shot of the entire family. Grace, Noah, Ruth and Susie were now family, too. They could fill a new album with just the ones Gordon would shoot this day.

Evan reached again for Chloe's hand. "Always," he murmured, lowering his mouth to hers. Not a whisper of air separated them. And Chloe leaned into his kiss, lingering, loving, wishing the moment would never end.

Just as their marriage. It had taken wing on the tail of the Christmas star. And, now, it glowed, growing brighter, stronger, more heavenly. "Always."

* * * * *

FAMILY BY DESIGN

Many daughters have done nobly,
But you excel them all.
—*Proverbs* 31:29

For Erica Endo, daughter of my heart.

Chapter One

Maddie Carter forgot to breathe. Her hand, swallowed by the doctor's larger one, rioted in unexpected reaction.

Dr. J. C. Mueller smiled and she gaped, unable to think of anything coherent to say as he turned to her mother, Lillian.

"So, Mrs. Carter, I understand your G.P. recommended you meet with me." He winked. "Of course, I am the only neurologist in Rosewood."

Maddie stumbled on her way to the extra chair in the examining room, righting herself quickly, hoping he hadn't noticed.

How had she forgotten this man? True, he'd been three years ahead of her in high school, then he'd gone to Baylor, while she'd attended the University of Texas, but still… She couldn't stop staring. Tall, broad-shouldered, with a shock of thick dark hair, mesmerizing brown eyes and a cleft in his chin that begged to be touched.

J.C. flipped through the thick pile of pages in her mother's chart, detailing the history of strokes that had brought on early onset dementia. He put down the folder, picking up Lillian's hand, placing two fingers over her upturned wrist.

Maddie couldn't still her heartbeat, instantly remembering the strength of his long fingers, the touch that tickled even her toes.

"Mrs. Carter, your vital signs are excellent."

Pleased, Lillian smiled. "Thank you, young man."

"I'd like to run a few tests, nothing invasive."

"Have I met you before?" Lillian questioned, puzzled.

"I grew up here in Rosewood," J.C. responded patiently. His wide smile was easy, kind. And his gold-flecked brown eyes sparkled.

Maddie's own pulse increased. *Good thing he wasn't recording hers.*

"How about you, Mrs. Carter? Are you from Rosewood originally?"

Maddie recognized the pattern to the handsome doctor's questions. He wanted to see if her mother could remember and verbalize her recollections. Lillian's worsening symptoms had prompted their G.P.'s referral to a specialist.

"My mother was born here," Lillian mused, her pale blue eyes reflective. "My father came from the Panhandle, near Amarillo. But he took one look at her and knew he wanted to stay." Smiling, she looked up at the doctor. "Love will do that, you know."

"Yes, ma'am," J.C. agreed, stretching out his long legs.

Immediately, Maddie wondered if he was married, engaged. Surely some smart woman had snagged him long ago.

"So you raised your family here," J.C. continued. Lillian's short-term memory was nearly nonexistent, but she remembered quite a bit from the past.

"My Maddie, yes."

J.C. glanced in Maddie's direction to include her in the conversation. "Just one child?"

"One perfect daughter," Lillian declared proudly.

Maddie felt her cheeks warming and shrugged an embarrassed apology to the doctor.

He grinned. "And why mess with perfection?"

"That's how we always felt," Lillian agreed with a vigorous nod as she turned to stare at her daughter.

J.C. mimicked her action.

Maddie immediately wished she'd remembered to wear lipstick. And what had she been thinking when she'd chosen this rumpled blouse and skirt? *That her mother had let the bath water run unchecked until it overflowed. And Maddie had been zooming on full speed to get the mess cleaned up so that they could get ready for the appointment. Their small home had only one bathroom and Lillian could have easily slipped on the tile floor.*

Self-consciously, Maddie smoothed her full cotton skirt, remembering she hadn't done a thing with her hair. In fact, she'd pulled it back in a messy ponytail. Just add the braces she'd once worn and she would look as geeky as she had in high school. Trying not to flush more, Maddie smiled feebly beneath their inspection.

"Maddie should have her own tea shop," Lillian continued.

"Oh, yes?"

Maddie squirmed. "Just an old dream."

"Nothing of the kind," Lillian declared. "She should

set up right on Main Street, smack dab in the middle of town."

"Let me know when you're ready," J.C. gazed at Maddie. "I happen to have a building...well, actually it belongs to my young niece. And it desperately needs a tenant. Be a great place for a tea shop." Turning back to Lillian, he extended his hand. "Mrs. Carter, I've enjoyed our visit and I'm looking forward to seeing you more often."

"I should think you'd rather visit with my beautiful daughter," Lillian guilelessly replied.

Lord, a hole, please. Underneath this chair, just big enough for me to disappear.

"I'll see you both on your next visit," J.C. replied without missing a beat.

Rumpled, crumpled and thoroughly embarrassed, Maddie rose, ready to end their consultation.

But the doctor wasn't. This time he spoke directly to her. "My nurse will set up the tests." He held out a paper. "Just give this to her." He scribbled on a second sheet of paper. "And I want to adjust your mother's medications."

"Thank..." Maddie cleared the embarrassing croaking in her voice. "Thank you."

"My pleasure."

She sincerely doubted that, but smiled. "Mom, should we go home? Have that cup of tea?"

"Maddie makes the best tea in the world," Lillian announced, this time her voice not as strong. She weakened quickly these days.

J.C. opened the exam room door, allowing them to precede him. Maddie wasn't sure how she knew, but she was almost certain that J.C. continued watching as they left. She had a wild impulse to look back, to see. But there wasn't any point. Her social life had ended when her mother's dementia had begun. And mooning over a handsome doctor would only make her long for what wasn't in her destiny.

"Maddie?"

"Yes, Mom."

"I have a yen for some tea. What do you think?"

That she needed to put longings out of her head. This was her reality. "Sounds good."

Lillian patted her hand, having completely forgotten Maddie's words only minutes before. J.C. wouldn't be part of her own future, but Maddie was fiercely glad he was in her mother's. At the rate she was deteriorating, otherwise, Lillian might lose her grip on even the distant past.

Chilled by the possibility, Maddie gently squeezed her mother's delicate fingers. They were the last remaining members of their family. It didn't bear thinking how dreadful it would be should that tiny number be halved.

J.C. stared after his departing patient. Well, her daughter, actually. Not that he'd forgotten a detail about Lillian.

Or Maddie. Refreshing. The one word summed her up completely. From the sprinkle of freckles on her smooth skin to the strawberry-blond wisps of hair that escaped from her bouncy ponytail. His gut reaction to her had come out of nowhere. That door had been closed since his ex-wife's betrayal. Now with everything else in his life...

The intercom in his office buzzed. "Dr. M?"

"I'm here, Didi."

"School's on the phone."

He sighed. His nine-year-old niece, Chrissy, wasn't adjusting well after the deaths of her parents. It had been a blow out of the blue. His sister, Fran, and brother-in-law, Jay, had been asleep when carbon monoxide had leaked out of the furnace. Chrissy, their only child, had been at a friend's pajama party for the night.

"Dr. M?" Didi called again.

"Yeah, I'll get it." Reluctantly he picked up the phone. "Doctor Mueller?"

J.C. readily recognized the principal's voice. They'd spoken often since the tragedy. "Yes, David?"

"You need to pick up Chrissy."

Frowning, he checked his watch. It was only eleven in the morning. "Now?"

"There's been another... incident."

Chrissy, once a model child and student, had been acting out. "Surely she doesn't need to come home this early in the day."

"Afraid so, J.C." The principal dropped the formalities. "She started a fight with two other girls. One is in tears, the other had to go home because we couldn't calm her down. J.C., you're going to have to figure out how to get Chrissy back under control."

J.C. rubbed his forehead, feeling the onset of now near-constant pain. He'd easily diagnosed himself. Stress-induced migraines. Losing his only sibling had been a devastating blow. He and his older sister had always been close. She'd been the one always looking out for him, the one who had comforted him when they'd lost first their father, then not long afterward their mother. And she'd kept him propped up during his divorce. Without her...

Fran had been his pillar. Illogically, he wanted to speak to her, so she could tell him how to deal with Chrissy.

Opening the day's schedule on his laptop, J.C. saw that he could steal an hour by switching one consultation. After asking Didi to make the arrangements, he drove quickly to the nearby school.

Chrissy sat in one of the chairs in the office, her arms crossed, her expression mute. But her posture and body spoke for her. Sulky. From the top of her head to the tips of her crossed feet.

She didn't meet his gaze while he talked with the secretary and checked Chrissy out of school. But once in the hallway, her footsteps dragged.

J.C. couldn't be mad. Under her rebellious expression was a hurt little girl overwhelmed by pain and loss. He placed one hand on her shoulder as they walked side-by-side, both silent as they approached the car.

Chrissy pulled off her backpack and flung it on the floor. Along with the clicking of seat belts being fastened in place, they were the only sounds until he turned the key in the ignition. J.C. drove out of the school parking lot before he spoke. "You'll have to spend the afternoon at the office."

Chrissy stared out the window. "I'm old enough to stay by myself."

Thinking how vulnerable she was, he kept his tone light. "I'm not sure *I'm* old enough to stay on my own. At any rate, you'll have more space to spread out your books in Mrs. Cook's office."

Chrissy snorted.

J.C. glanced over at his niece. She still stared out the window. The only time she reacted positively was when they passed Wagner Hill House, the building on Main Street that had contained her father's business. It had sat undisturbed since Jay's death.

Thinking it might help Chrissy, J.C. decided to drive by his sister's house. Although he kept putting it off, he needed to sort through the house, make it livable again. Maybe Chrissy would settle down if she could live in her home again. He didn't mind giving up his tiny apartment; it was just a place to sleep really.

Turning on Magnolia Avenue, he saw Chrissy straighten up.

Pleased she was finally showing interest in something, he pulled into the driveway.

As soon as he turned off the vehicle, Chrissy began shrieking.

"No! I won't go in! No! No!" Sobs erupted and tears flooded her cheeks. "You can't make me!"

Horrified, J.C. tried to calm her. "What is it, Chrissy?"

"The house killed them!" She blurted out between staggered sobs.

Her distress was so intense J.C. didn't try to reason with her. Instead, he quickly backed out of the driveway, then sped from the neighborhood. Once past the familiar streets, he pulled into a space in front of the park. Unhooking his own seat belt and then Chrissy's, he gently guided her from the car to a bench beneath a large oak.

Still shaking from the remaining gulps of tears, she allowed him to drape an arm over her shoulders. When she was tiny, he would have popped her in his lap, pulled a dozen silly faces and made her giggle. He felt completely ill-equipped to comfort her now.

Patting her arm, he waited until the last of her hiccupping gulps trailed to an end. "I'm sorry, Chrissy. I wouldn't have gone to the house if I'd known it would upset you." He paused. "I was hoping it would make you feel better."

She shook her head so hard that her light brown hair flew unchecked from side to side. "I never, ever want to go there again."

"After some time—"

"Never!" she exclaimed. Her lips wobbled and a few new tears mixed with the wash of others on her cheeks.

J.C. patted her knee. "I thought you might like to live there again, get out of my scruffy apartment."

"No!" she cried again, burying her face against his shoulder. "I can't!"

J.C. imagined he could hear the child's heart actually breaking. "Then you won't." He would have the contents packed for storage, then rent out the house in case she changed her mind later. "And if it starts bothering you, we won't go by the print building, either."

Chrissy pulled back a bit so she could look at him. "It's not the same."

"No?"

"Daddy's work didn't hurt them. It was the house."

Logic wasn't a factor. Just the raw feelings of a wounded child.

"Okay, then."

"We could move in there," she suggested hopefully. "To Daddy's work."

The first floor of the building had been occupied by the business. And there were two apartments above it. Jay's parents had lived in one until they passed away.

"No one's lived in those apartments for a while," he explained. More important, they wouldn't have any immediate neighbors. Even though his bachelor apartment was small, at least in his complex, Chrissy was surrounded by people. He didn't like the idea of her being alone in a big building on Main Street when he had to make night calls at the hospital. A few proprietors lived above their businesses, but not in the building next to them. And the Wagner Hill House was on a corner next to a side street that bisected Main, so there wasn't a second adjoining neighbor.

"We could fix up the apartment," Chrissy beseeched, kicking her feet back, dragging them through the grass. "And live on top of Daddy's print shop." The apartment was above the business on the second floor, but he knew what she meant.

Blair, a nurse who worked at the hospital, lived in his apartment complex and so far J.C. had asked her to listen for Chrissy when he had to leave her. But it wasn't a comfortable situation. He worried the entire time he was away. What if Chrissy woke up and was scared? What if there was a fire? The possibilities were endless. But he couldn't hire live-in help to share their small space. As it was, he was camping out on the sofa so Chrissy could have the only bedroom.

And babysitters weren't pleased to be phoned in the middle of the night. The few who had reluctantly responded once didn't respond again. Not that J.C. blamed them. Who wanted to get up at two or three in the morning to babysit, not knowing if they would have to stay an hour or the rest of the night? What they really needed was sort of a combination housekeeper and nanny who lived in. But Chrissy had run off every single one he had hired, resenting anyone she thought was trying to take her mother's place.

"I'm afraid we can't live in the Main Street building."

Chrissy sniffled. "Then are we going to stay in your apartment?"

J.C. glanced up at the cloudless sky. Rosewood's tranquility had always been a peaceful balm. But now he wasn't certain there could be peace anywhere. *Lord, we need your help. Chrissy deserves more than just me. Please help us find the answer.*

Sighing, Chrissy leaned her head against his arm, her soft weight slumping dispiritedly.

Please, Lord.

Chapter Two

 ❧

Maddie pulled one of her numerous tins of tea from a shelf in the pantry. "Sure you don't have a preference?"

Samantha Conway, Maddie's best friend and one-time neighbor, shrugged. "Surprise me. How many blends have you made now? One hundred?"

"Afraid not." She placed the tin on the table. "I have ideas for twice that many and space for less than thirty." Collecting two porcelain cups and saucers she added them to the table.

"So, did your mother like J.C.?" Samantha questioned.

"You were right all along. I should have taken her sooner," Maddie admitted. Samantha had raved about J.C. ever since he successfully treated her paralysis. Now Samantha walked with only a cane. She had been urging Maddie to see him about Lillian's worsening symptoms long before their G.P. had made his recommendation. "He's already ordered new tests and altered her medications." Swallowing, Maddie remembered the touch of his hand when he gave her the slip of paper.

"Earth to Maddie," Samantha repeated. "Something on your mind?"

"Of course not." Trying to sideline her friend's curiosity, Maddie got up and retrieved the electric kettle. Pouring water into their cups, she set the kettle on a trivet.

"Um, I hate to complain," Samantha began, "but we don't have any tea in our cups."

Maddie shook her face in tiny rapid nods. "Where's my head?" Because she used loose tea leaves to make her own private blends, she also used individual cup strainers. She put one on each of their cups, then added a scoop of tea leaves. She'd made so much tea over the years that she didn't need to measure the amount.

Samantha fiddled with her cup. "You sure you're okay?"

"Why?"

"For one, the strainer's sitting over the water, so I'm guessing the tea leaves aren't actually wet and…" She looked intensely at her friend. "The water's cold."

"Cold?" Maddie frowned. "It can't be cold. I just got it from the kettle." Poking her finger in the cup, she expected a hot jolt. *Cold water and limp tea leaves. Great.* "I hope the kettle's not broken." But as she checked the adjustments and made sure the base was plugged in, Maddie couldn't remember if she'd actually pushed the On button.

"Okay, give," Samantha urged. "You forgot to put the *tea* in the tea? And then you forgot to turn on the kettle? That's not like you."

"I suppose it's been a stressful day." She recounted the mishap with the morning bath water, how flustered she'd been trying to get them to the appointment on time. "I felt like my accelerator was stuck," she explained. "Filling in all the forms like a maniac as fast as I could, trying not to cause more delay…"

Samantha leaned back, studying her. "Just the letdown after an adrenaline rush?"

"I suppose so."

"Funny. You have at least one crisis a week with Lillian, but you've never offered me a cold cup of water that hasn't even swum close to a tea leaf."

Maddie waved her hands. "Then I'm having an off day."

"You haven't told me what you thought of J.C."

Maddie willed the sudden warmth in her neck to stay there and not redden her face. "He was fine."

"Fine?"

"Nice, then."

"Nice?"

"At this rate we'll be chattering away all day," Maddie observed with a wry twist of her lips. "I told you that Dr. Mueller ordered several tests and he's altered Mom's medications. He thinks one may be sedating her instead of treating the dementia."

"Um." Samantha studied her intently. "And that's all?"

Maddie fiddled with the worn tablecloth. "It was just our first visit."

"You plan on going back?"

"Of course!" Maddie replied in an instant. Inwardly grimacing, she slowed her words. "Providing Mom does better on the new medications." The kettle whistled. Relieved, she rose to get the hot water, using the excuse to try and straighten her muddled thoughts. Taking a deep breath, she returned, carefully pouring the steaming water into their cups. "I should have noticed that there wasn't any steam before. So, would you like some cookies with your tea?"

Looking truly concerned, Samantha drew her brows together, then pointed to a plate of lemon bars. "I brought these, remember?"

"Of course!" She clapped both hands over her reddening cheeks, then sank into her chair. "Not. I've been in a fluster since I got home."

Worry colored Samantha's eyes. "Is there something about Lillian's condition you haven't told me?"

Maddie shook her head. Thank heavens her mother was enjoying her regular afternoon nap and couldn't overhear. Lifting one shoulder in a half shrug, Maddie stared down at the delicate pink roses edging her saucer. "It's so stupid, it's not worth repeating really."

Samantha leaned forward. "If it's got you this upset—"

"I wouldn't exactly call it upsetting. Well, maybe. Depends on what you—"

Rapping the table with her knuckles, Samantha cut off her words. "Spill it."

"I thought… I think Dr. Mueller is…well, attractive."

"Downright handsome to be precise. How can this be a surprise? Surely you've seen him around town?"

"Mom's doctor is in an old building downtown, not in the hospital where Dr. Mueller works. Thankfully, we haven't had to be at the hospital much."

"Still…" Samantha stopped abruptly. "Sorry. Of course I know you don't get out enough. I just thought that somehow…" She brightened. "But you do like him?"

"He's nice."

"Don't start that again. And you can call him J.C." Samantha wriggled her eyebrows. "He's single, you know. Well, divorced actually."

"Divorced?"

"I don't know the details, but I understand it was bad."

Maddie wondered why any woman would let him go. Silly, she didn't know a thing about him. Other than that smile, those eyes... Abruptly, she shook her head. "Honestly, Sam, you're the last person I expected to matchmake. We're seeing him so he can help Mom, not so I can develop a crush." The word was barely out of her mouth when Maddie wished she could draw it back.

Samantha blinked.

"Bad choice of words," Maddie tried to explain.

"Accurate is more like it." She smiled more gently. "Hit that hard, did it?"

Her embarrassment waning, Maddie plopped her chin on one outstretched hand. "Stupid, huh? I'm old enough to know better."

"You're not *that* old," Samantha objected. "Besides, I don't believe in an age limit on falling in love."

"Whoa!" Maddie protested. "Who said anything about love?"

Samantha grinned. "Puppy love?"

"I had my chance. I picked taking care of Mom instead. It's what I want." Maddie wasn't only loyal, she couldn't imagine shuttling her mother away because it was more convenient.

"It doesn't have to be a choice." Samantha patted Maddie's hand. "Lillian wants you to be happy."

"And a man deserves a woman who can devote herself to him and the family they create. I'm not that woman." Although she'd never regretted her choice, Maddie sometimes dreamed of a life with a loving husband and children of her own. It wasn't her destiny, but the fantasy was harmless.

"You just haven't met the right man yet," Samantha insisted in a gentle, yet confident, tone.

"Forgetting Owen, aren't you?" Maddie's high school, then college sweetheart, they'd been engaged when her mother had suffered the first of many strokes. Lillian had only been in her forties at the time, young for the onset of the neurological nightmare that had stolen her short-term memory.

Samantha's expression was steady. "He's a rat. What kind of man asks you to choose between him and your mother? He knew what was going on, how painful it was for you to give up everything."

Maddie tried to interrupt. "But—"

"But nothing. I know you'd make the same choice again, but asking you to put her in a nursing home…" Samantha shook her head angrily. "And it's not as though he was new to your life, didn't know your history."

Stroking the silken smoothness of the porcelain cup, Maddie remembered Owen's unyielding stance. "I did think he might understand. We were going together when my dad passed away."

"He also knew you didn't have any relatives to share the load." Samantha's fierce loyalty didn't waver. "Total rat."

Maddie reluctantly smiled. "That's a little extreme, don't you think?"

"Nope." Loyal to the end, Samantha didn't give an

inch. "And J.C.'s about as different from Owen as a *rat* is to a cat."

"I wouldn't have thought it until you came back to Rosewood, but you're a romantic, Sam. Just because you and Bret got back together after nearly a decade—"

"That was fate," Samantha insisted. "And real, genuine, honest love. It wasn't a reunion, it was a new start."

"I imagine Owen's got his hands full with his business." His family had money, and Owen had stepped into the enviable position of entrepreneur with none of the struggle most young business owners faced.

"Hmm. And, yes, I know, Bret's running his family business, but it wasn't stuffed with cash."

In fact, it was almost failing when Bret took the helm. "No comparison, Sam. I agree. When we were younger I didn't think Owen was that affected by having...okay, everything. He just seemed to take it in stride. But when he got older..." He wasn't the boy she'd fallen in love with.

"Hey, I'm sorry." Samantha's voice changed to one of concern. "I didn't mean to stir all that up. I guess I just thought...well, J.C.'s such a great guy, and you're my best friend..." She smiled encouragingly. "I still think your life's going to change because of him—he's going to help Lillian and that'll help you."

"It's not as though I don't daydream myself. And you're right. If he can help Mom..." Maddie smiled. "That's all I ask." *Because her other dreams were just flotsam in the ether. And as likely to materialize.*

True to his word, J.C. began Lillian's tests with a noninvasive CT scan. Officially called computed tomography, it could detect a blood clot or intracranial bleeding in patients with a stroke. And the scan aided in differentiating the area of the brain affected by the disorder.

J.C. had prescribed a light sedative so that Lillian could lie still. Forgetting where she was, otherwise Lillian might have tried to move, skewing the test results.

The test took only about thirty minutes, but Maddie paced in the waiting room. She didn't want her mother to wake up disoriented and scared. The technician had assured her that he would watch out for Lillian during the scan, but Maddie couldn't stop worrying.

"She's all right," J.C. announced quietly from behind her.

Maddie whirled around. The carpeted waiting area had camouflaged the sound of his footsteps.

Dressed in scrubs, he acted as though it was normal for him to deliver the news, rather than the technician.

Maddie began to shake, fearing the worst. "Was there a problem?"

He stepped closer, his eyes flickering over her trembling limbs. "None whatsoever. I didn't mean to alarm you. I just got out of surgery, thought I'd pop in and check on your mother."

Relieved, Maddie exhaled, her chest still rising with the effort to breathe normally.

J.C. took her arm, guiding her to a chair. "You're going to have to take it easy."

Perched on the edge of the chair, she stared up at him.

"CT scan's about the mildest procedure your mother's going to have. You'll sap your energy if you get this upset about every test."

Suddenly Maddie could breathe. And stand. Nearly nose to nose with him. "I know you're an excellent doctor. Samantha Conway is proof of that. But don't presume to tell me how to react. I've been caring for my mother for years. I know she gets confused and scared..." Maddie's trembling increased. "And I won't let anyone make that worse."

"Good."

Maddie blinked.

"A dedicated caregiver is the best medicine any patient can have." J.C.'s tone remained mild. His gold-flecked brown eyes were more elusive. "I'll call you when I have the results. Should be about two days." With a nod, he left.

Maddie wasn't certain what to think. Plopping the palm of her hand against her forehead, she wished she could travel back in time a few minutes. This doctor was a road of hope for her mother and she'd just insulted him. Refusing to consider that her defensive reaction could have anything to do with her attraction to him, she bit down on her thumbnail.

Catching sight of the technician, she tried to shove the thoughts away and decided it would be easier to tame an infuriated horde of wasps.

J.C. strode down the familiar corridors toward his office. The sandy-beige walls were lined with portraits of the hospital's founders and patrons. But he wasn't looking at any of them. He wanted to kick something, preferably himself. Maddie Carter had been on his mind since the day they'd met. He'd sensed an empathetic soul. One who could understand what he was going through.

A tall, slim man in a white coat plopped himself in J.C.'s path. "Someone put cactus needles in your scrubs?"

J.C. immediately recognized the voice. "Adam."

His colleague and friend Adam Winston tugged at the stethoscope looped around his neck. "I don't normally drive into tornados, but from the look on your face, I think you might need some help getting out of the storm."

"Just a mild gale." J.C. exhaled. "Put too much thought into a nitwit notion."

"Why don't I believe that?"

"Don't you have rounds?"

Adam shrugged. "Not for another hour." Amiable, persistent, often brilliant, Adam wasn't going anywhere without an answer.

J.C. summarized his two meetings with Maddie. "That's it," he concluded.

Adam's knowing look was both confusing and annoying. "Uh-huh."

"Don't try to make something out of this."

Whistling, Adam winked, then briefly shook his head. "I don't need to. You've got that covered."

J.C. clenched his teeth. Realizing he had, he made himself relax.

"Hasn't it occurred to you that this woman's under just as much strain as you are?" Adam continued. "When she saw you instead of the tech, she probably thought her mother had suffered another stroke. Wouldn't be the first time a test triggered one."

"I'm sure she's stressed."

"Are you? Have you checked out the situation? Does anyone help care for the mother? Or is she on her own?"

Remembering that Lillian had said Maddie was an only child, J.C. didn't reply.

"If she's the full-time live-in caregiver, you know

she could be ready to crack." Adam twirled the end of his stethoscope.

J.C. hadn't asked about the details of Lillian Carter's care. Had he done what he'd despised in others? Judged without knowing the facts? Worse even, judging at all?

Chapter Three

J.C. pulled into the semicircle driveway at the front of the Rosewood Community Church school. He was late. Again. Didi had picked up Chrissy a few times for him, but she was busy. Besides, he couldn't expect his employees and friends to sacrifice any more than they already had.

The school was nearly deserted. Only the teachers' cars remained in the parking lot and a few kids were kicking a ball on the playground. Chrissy sat on the steps, clutching her backpack, looking lost.

Poor kid. First she felt deserted when her parents died; now she felt just as abandoned by him. Turning off the car, he got out to meet her halfway. Her face was more than sullen; fear and vulnerability were just as apparent.

"Chrissy, I'm sorry. No excuses. I'm late."

Although she tried to control it, her lips wobbled. "I know."

"How about a big chocolate shake at the drugstore?" The old-fashioned marble fountain was one of Chrissy's favorite places.

"Uh-uh," she replied, shaking her head.

J.C. would have reached for the child's backpack so he could carry it to the car, but she still clutched it like a lifeline. She'd had the backpack with her at the pajama party, untouched by the poisonous carbon monoxide. Untouched by what had changed her life forever.

J.C. wished he could think of something to distract her, to ease the pain from her face. But fun hadn't been on the agenda for quite a while now.

Chrissy settled in her seat, scooting forward suddenly, pulling up a bag that was wedged beneath her. "What's this?"

"Some trial medications for a new patient. I've been meaning to drop them off…" But every time he thought about it, he pictured Maddie's anger.

"Why don't we go now?"

He stared at his niece. "You *want* to go?"

She shrugged. "Nothing else to do."

Except a mountain of dictation, articles, more work than he wanted to think about. "Right." But the stop would distract Chrissy. "Nothing else to do."

The Carter home wasn't far. J.C. had copied their address on the sample bag. Located in one of Rosewood's oldest neighborhoods, the house was an unimposing Victorian. Neither grand nor tiny, it spoke of the families that had inhabited it over the generations. The yard and flower beds were tidy, the porch and driveway well swept. But he noticed the aging roof and the peeling paint on the second-story fascia and gables.

An aged but inviting swing flanked two well-worn rocking chairs on the wide porch. It was quiet as they climbed the steps, then knocked on the outer screen door.

Within just a few moments the door swung open.

Taken aback, Maddie stared at him, then collected her voice. "Dr. Mueller, I wasn't expecting you." Her gaze shifted to include Chrissy. "Hello."

Chrissy ducked just a fraction behind him. J.C. put a reassuring hand on her shoulder. "This is my niece, Chrissy."

"Good to meet you, Chrissy." Maddie pushed the screen door back. "Come in. I just put the kettle on."

Chrissy looked up at him in question.

J.C. patted her back. "Actually, we just stopped to drop off samples of a new medication for your mother."

"Do you have time for tea?" Maddie asked, not a bit of the anger he remembered anywhere in sight.

He glanced down at his niece. She didn't look averse to the idea. "I guess so. Thanks."

"Mom's in the living room," Maddie explained, leading the way from the small entry hall. She glanced at Chrissy. "In a house this old, they used to call the front room a parlor, but ours isn't the elegant sort."

Looking intrigued, Chrissy listened quietly.

"Mom? Dr. Mueller stopped by to have tea."

Lillian sat in a faded green rocker recliner. Seeing her guests, she brightened. "I love meeting new people!"

"This is Dr. Mueller's niece, Chrissy," Maddie began.

Lillian clapped her hands together. "Oh, my! You look an awful lot like my Maddie when she was your age." She patted the chair next to hers. "Come. Sit."

Chrissy's normal reluctance dimmed and she crossed the room. "I thought you knew my uncle James."

Lillian smiled. "Perhaps I do. You'll have to tell me all about him."

Chrissy looked at him, then turned back to Lillian. "He's a doctor. And he's *real* busy."

J.C. flinched.

"I imagine you stay busy with school." Lillian's gaze landed on the ever-present backpack. "Just like my Maddie, always did her homework straightaway."

Chrissy stroked the pink bag and halfheartedly shrugged. "Sometimes."

Lillian's eyes glinted with mischief. "Sometimes we baked cookies first or built a playhouse."

"You built a playhouse?" Chrissy asked in wonder as Lillian dug into the purse that was always at her side.

Lillian produced a roll of Life Savers and offered them to Chrissy. "Sure did. My father thought a girl should know how to use a hammer and a saw. He liked to make things with his hands, so he taught me in his workshop."

Chrissy swallowed. "My dad did, too."

Lillian patted her knee. "Sounds like we had wonderful fathers."

Strange. It was as though somehow Lillian sensed Chrissy's father was gone, as well.

J.C. heard a whistle from the other side of the house. No doubt the teakettle. Considering, he watched his niece, saw that her attention was entirely focused on Lillian. Pivoting, he followed the sound of the fading whistle to the kitchen. A carpet runner covered the oak floor in the long hall; it also muffled the sound of his footsteps.

He paused beneath the arched opening to the kitchen. Maddie was scurrying around the room, pushing strawberry-blond hair off her forehead with one hand, reaching for a tray with the other. Seeing that it was perched on one of the higher shelves, he quickened his pace. "Let me get that for you."

Whirling around at the sound of his voice, she looked completely, totally, utterly flustered.

"Guess I need to stop doing that. Coming up from behind, surprising you."

Her throat worked and her blue-gray eyes looked chastened. "I feel terrible about how I reacted the other day. It's just that Mom's gotten so fragile, and..." Moisture gathered in her eyes and she quickly wiped it away. "I'm so afraid that the next stroke..." Again her throat worked, but she pushed past the emotion. "I know she needs these tests—"

J.C. lightly clasped her arm. "Being a caregiver is the most stressful job I can imagine. Do you have enough help?"

"Help?" Maddie nodded. "Samantha relieves me so that I have some extra time when I run errands, but she has her own family to take care of. Neighbors and people from church sit with Mom, too, when they can."

He'd reread the file and knew that Lillian was widowed. With no siblings, did that mean that Maddie was the sole caregiver? "It's important that you have time for yourself."

She laughed, a mirthless sound. "Hmm."

Spotting the cups on the table, he took her elbow, guiding her to the table. "Let's sit for a few minutes."

"But your niece—"

"Is taken by your mother. Best Chrissy's acted in a while. Tea smells good."

Distracted, Maddie glanced at the tabletop. "It's probably the vanilla you're smelling."

J.C. sat in the chair next to hers. "Who else helps you take care of Lillian?"

"Just me."

J.C. knew that endless caregiving could suck the life from a person. And Lillian had required home care for nearly a decade. "Have you lost some of your relief help?"

"Never had any." Picking up the sugar, she offered it to him.

"But when do you have time for yourself?"

She lifted the porcelain strainers from their cups. "I don't think of it like that. This is my life, my choice. It's hard for other people to understand."

"What about before Lillian's strokes? You must have had plans."

An indecipherable emotion flashed in her now bluish eyes and then disappeared. Had her eyes changed color? Or was it a trick of the light?

"That's the thing about the future," Maddie replied calmly. "It can always change. So far, mine has."

Since J.C. had witnessed that she wasn't always a serene earth muffin, he sipped his tea, wondering exactly who the real Maddie was. "This is unusual. Don't think I've ever tasted anything quite like it."

"The tea's my own blend," she explained.

"How did you come to make your own tea recipe?"

She chuckled, some of her weariness disappearing. "Not just one recipe. I blend all sorts of teas."

"Same question, then. How did you start making your own tea?"

"I've always been fascinated by spices. I can remember my grandfather telling me about the original spice routes from Asia and I could imagine all the smells, the excitement of the markets. So my mother let me collect spices and we'd make up recipes to use them in. Then one day I decided to add some fresh nutmeg to my tea."

Her cheeks flushed as her enthusiasm grew. "Mom always made drinking tea an event—using the good cups, all the accessories. Anyway, Mom bought every kind of loose tea leaf she could find so I could experiment. For a time our kitchen looked like a cross between an English farmhouse and a laboratory. After college I planned to open a shop where I could sell all my blends." She leaned forward, her eyes dreamy. "And I'd serve fresh, hot tea on round bistro tables covered with white linen tablecloths. Oh, and little pastries, maybe sandwiches. Make it a place people want to linger...to come back to."

"The tea shop your mother said should be *smack dab in the middle of Main Street?*"

"Oh, yes."

"Did you ever get a shop set up?"

Maddie shook her head. "I was investigating small business loans when Mom had her first stroke, the major one. Luckily, I'd graduated from U.T. by then."

"Have you considered starting the business? Using part of the profits to hire someone to stay with your mother while you're working?"

"Our funds aren't that extensive. I took enough business classes to know I'd have to factor in at least a year of loss before we'd show any profit. Or just staying even. Doesn't leave anything for caregiver salaries. Besides, Mom's happy with me."

"Don't forget I've got a building that needs a tenant if you change your mind. Plenty of room for a shop and tearoom." He swallowed more of his tea. "What about the senior center activities we talked about? That would fill several hours a day."

Maddie's smile dimmed. "As the first step toward a nursing home?"

"Nothing of the kind. If Lillian responds to her new medication, she could well enjoy spending time with people her own age."

"Her friends have been loyal," Maddie objected. "People stop by fairly often to visit her."

J.C. studied the obstinate set of her jaw. "But not to visit with you?"

Maddie looked down, fiddling with the dish towel still in her lap. "People my age have young families of their own to take care of."

A situation he knew only too well.

"It's difficult for someone who's never been in this position to understand," Maddie continued. "I'm sure you're busy with your work... and it probably consumes most of your time, but I can't walk away from my mother. It's not some martyr complex. It's my *choice*."

"And sometimes there isn't a choice."

Maddie scrunched her eyes in concentration. "Your niece? Chrissy? You said something about how she was behaving. Is there a problem?"

J.C. explained how he'd come to be his niece's guardian. "I don't blame her for acting out. She's lost everyone she loves."

Unexpectedly, Maddie covered his hand with hers. "Not quite everyone."

He stared at her long, slender fingers.

"Dr. Mueller? J.C.?"

"Sorry." He pulled his gaze back to hers. "Chrissy's been fighting with some of the girls at school, her grades are slipping." And she was miserable.

"What about your babysitter? Do they get on well?"

"We've been through a parade of sitters and housekeepers. Can't keep one."

Concern etched Maddie's face. "Can I help? She could spend afternoons with us. Does she go to the community church school? We're in easy walking distance."

"Don't have enough on your plate?" J.C. was dumbfounded. Maddie claimed she wasn't a martyr, but…

"It's what we do."

He felt as blank as he must have looked.

"You know, here in Rosewood. She's a child who needs any help we can give her."

It was how J.C. had been raised, too. "Maybe from people who have the time. You're exhausted now. I'm not going to add to that burden."

The fire in her now stormy-gray eyes was one he remembered. "It's not a burden. I realize my situation isn't for everyone, but it works for me. And I have enough energy to spare some for Chrissy."

She was pretty remarkable, J.C. decided. Even more remarkable—she didn't seem to realize it.

Chapter Four

J.C. stood in front of his sister's closet in her far-too-quiet home. Fran's things were just as she'd left them. Not perfectly in order; she was always in too much of a hurry to fuss over details she had considered unimportant. No, she'd lavished her time on her family, especially Chrissy.

A cheery yellow scarf dangled over an ivory jacket, looking for all the world as though Fran had just hung it up. Anyone searching through the rooms would never conclude it had been a scene of death. Instead, it looked as though Fran, Jay and Chrissy could walk in any moment, pick up their lives.

Fran would be laughing, teasing Chrissy and Jay in turn, turning her hand at a dozen projects, baking J.C.'s favorite apple crumble, inviting friends over.

There hadn't been an awful lot of time to ask why. Why had they perished? Especially when each had so much to give. Caught up in trying to care for Chrissy, the questions had been shelved.

J.C. was on borrowed time even now. He had thought he could make some sort of inventory of the house so that he could set things in motion, have the important contents stored, the house rented. But he couldn't bring himself to even reach inside the closet.

Other people survived loss. As a doctor, he'd seen his share and then some. But how did they take that first step, put the gears in motion? Fran had managed when their parents passed away. She had thoughtfully sorted out mementos for each of them, things she had accurately predicted he would cherish. Now, he needed to do the same for Chrissy.

His friend Adam suggested hiring an estate service, one that could view everything with an eye to its current or future value. To J.C., the process sounded like an autopsy. Backing away from the closet, he tore out of the room. Striding quickly, he passed through the living room, then bolted outside. Breathing heavily, he sank into the glider on the porch, loosening his tie.

The breeze was lighter than a bag of feathers, but he drew in big gulps of air. He'd never been claustrophobic, but he felt as though he'd just been locked in an airless pit. He pictured Chrissy's stricken face. Maybe it wasn't so illogical that she wouldn't step foot in the house.

Lifting his head, he leaned back, his gaze drifting over the peaceful lane. School was in session, so no kids played in the yards or rode their bicycles in the street. A few houses down, Mrs. Morton was weeding her flower bed and a dog barked. Not that there was much to bark at. Extending his gaze, he spotted a woman pushing a wheelchair on the sidewalk across the street. The color of her hair stirred a note of recognition.

Maddie Carter? Shifting, he leaned forward, focusing on the pair. It was Maddie, pushing Lillian's wheelchair. Although Lillian could walk, she tired easily.

Combined with the mental confusion, he understood why Maddie chose to use the chair.

They were within shouting distance when Maddie glanced across the street. Recognition dawned and she leaned down to say something to her mother. Walking a few feet farther, Maddie detoured off the sidewalk via a driveway and used the same method to reach the front of Fran's house.

Trying to tuck his emotions beneath a professional demeanor, J.C. walked down the steps.

Apparently he wasn't completely successful.

"What's wrong?" Maddie greeted him, her eyes filled with sudden concern. Today her eyes picked up some of the green of the grass, rendering them near-emerald.

J.C. straightened his tie, but couldn't bring himself to pull it into a knot. The strangled feeling from being in Fran's house hadn't dissipated. "This is my sister's house."

Understanding flooded Maddie's expression. "Are you here by yourself?"

J.C. nodded. "Chrissy won't come back."

"What can we do?"

He glanced at the wheelchair. "Your hands are full enough."

Maddie patted Lillian's shoulder in a soothing motion. "My mother always enjoys visiting new places." She met his gaze. Both knew most anywhere other than her own home was now a new place for Lillian.

The older woman smiled at him kindly. "Young man, you need a bracing cup of tea."

Apparently even his patient could see his distress. "I don't have the makings for tea."

"We do," Lillian replied, craning her head around and up toward Maddie. "Don't we?"

"Yes, but maybe Dr. Mueller would like to just sit on the porch."

"Well, now, I'd like that myself," Lillian replied.

Shedding his own worries, J.C. offered his arm. "Would you care to sit in the glider?"

She giggled, a young, fun sound. "I always have."

As he helped her rise from the wheelchair, J.C. imagined she'd had a fair share of male attention in her youth. In ways, he could see an advantage in having only partial memories. Hopefully the bad ones faded and only the good stayed.

Once Lillian was settled on the glider, he pulled two rattan chairs close, offering one to Maddie. With the glider set in gentle motion, Lillian's eyelids fluttered near closing.

"What was it?" Speaking quietly, Maddie tilted her head toward the house. "Inside?"

J.C. thought of a dozen noncommittal answers. "Everything."

"It was hard after my dad died," Maddie sympathized. "You said Chrissy won't come back?"

"Completely freaked out when I tried," he replied in an equally quiet tone. "Said she never wants to come back, that the house killed her parents."

Maddie's forehead furrowed. "Were you thinking of moving in here, so Chrissy would have all her familiar things?"

"That and because we're two people living in a one-person tent. So to speak," he explained. "I have a small one-bedroom apartment and it's not good."

"And you're certain Chrissy won't change her mind?"

"Absolutely."

Maddie hesitated. "Are you going to sell the house?"

"Thought about renting it out in case Chrissy changes her mind in the future. But right now… I can't rent it with all of my sister's belongings still inside."

"That's what got to you," Maddie murmured. "There's still a sweater and bathrobe of my dad's in Mom's closet."

The dog down the street barked again. And Mrs. Morton crossed the street to talk to her neighbor.

J.C. barely knew Maddie. Funny to be having this conversation with her. But none of his friends could really empathize. Some had lost a parent, but no one had lost everyone. Certainly no one else had the crucial role of caring for the sole survivor.

Maddie swiped at her wayward hair. He liked the way it sprang back with a mind of its own. "Do you have anyone to help you go through your sister's belongings?"

He shrugged one shoulder. "No one else will know what's important."

"Not necessarily," she objected mildly. "Thinking of things in categories could help. You can decide if there's a special garment, like my dad's sweater, you want to save. If not, then it doesn't take a personal eye to empty closets. Same is pretty much true for the kitchen with the exception of heirloom pieces. Furniture can be sorted through, or just stored for now. Jewelry, papers, other keepsakes can be packed and labeled for when you feel it's time to decide about them."

J.C. sighed. "You make it sound reasonable—"

"It is if you'll accept help."

"It's not a job I can ask anyone to tackle."

"You didn't ask. I'm offering." With her back against the cloudy gray exterior of the house, Maddie's eyes had changed again. But this time the gray held no storm warnings. "Before you mention my mother, she'll come with me. I'm guessing there's a comfortable chair and a television. It'll be an outing for her that isn't tiring."

"For her, maybe not. But you—"

"I can't believe I look that fragile," Maddie declared. "To hear you talk, I'm so delicate it's a wonder I don't blow away in the breeze." She held out one hand as though testing the air. "Even in this breeze. You, of all people, should know how good it makes a person feel to help someone. I'd like to help. You're doing Mom a world of good. I can already see small improvements. Besides, you and Chrissy need to be able to move on. Once this house is rented to another family, it won't seem so scary anymore."

"A friend suggested hiring an estate service," he admitted.

"That might be taking it a tad too impersonal. Do you recall grilling me about who helps with Mom? Now, it's my turn. Who helps with Chrissy? Who can sort through the house? If that's you, will it be between appointments and surgeries?"

"And I thought I felt bad being *inside* the house."

She laughed, tipping her head back, allowing the laughter to gather and spill like a bright waterfall. "Touché."

Somehow, his dread had disappeared.

Maddie held out her hand, palm side up, her eyes still dancing. "I'll need a key."

"I'm a little nervous," Maddie admitted, fitting the key in the lock.

"You should be." Samantha rolled her eyes. "I still can't believe—"

"Other-may," Maddie resorted to pig Latin to remind her friend of Lillian's presence.

"Oh, now you remember."

"I never forgot." The key to Fran's house turned easily and Maddie pushed open the door. "Mom, you like getting out, don't you?"

Lillian smiled. "I like new places."

Samantha rolled her eyes again. "And it'll be new for a month of Sundays."

Maddie elbowed her friend. "I thought you liked J.C."

"I didn't expect you to take on organizing his life."

Maddie flinched. "Do you think he feels that way? And quit rolling your eyes before they fall out of your head."

"The only one here out of her head—"

Maddie grasped the handles of her mother's wheelchair and pushed her inside. "How about some TV, Mom? The cable's still on, so you can watch a movie or Animal Planet."

Lillian considered. "Have I seen Animal Planet before?"

She watched it every day. "I think so." Flipping through the channels, Maddie put the TV on an old movie her mother had seen dozens of times. Fortunately, it was new to her each and every time. Uncapping the thermos of tea she'd brought, Maddie poured some in a cup and placed it on the table next to Lillian.

She caught up to Samantha in the hallway, where she stood, leaning slightly on her cane as she studied family pictures grouped over a console table. "Seems hard to believe they just went to sleep and never woke up."

"I don't know J.C. well enough to say this, but I think he feels the same way."

"As though he might wake up one day and find out it was all just a bad dream." Samantha shook her head. "That's how I felt about Andy." Samantha's brother had died in a plane crash, ending his young life far too soon.

Maddie linked her arm with Sam's. "What we're doing, it's a good way to give back."

Sam's voice thickened. "Yeah." When she had returned to Rosewood paralyzed from a fall, she'd nearly burned down her parents' entire home. She succeeded in destroying the kitchen. But friends and neighbors had stepped up, rebuilding it, making it even better than before. And in the process, she had reconnected with her old love and now husband, Bret. Sam cleared her throat. "Where do you want to start?"

"Master bedroom, I think. J.C. insists on hiring someone to move the boxes once they're packed, so I'd like to retrieve the jewelry for his safety deposit box. Then I thought of recording an inventory." She held up her cell phone. "I can shoot photos of the big pieces to J.C., let him decide what to keep."

They entered the carpeted master bedroom, feet sinking pleasantly into the deep pile. The four-poster bed looked as antique as the fireplace it flanked. In the curve of the bay window was a cozy reading area.

"Nice," Sam murmured.

Maddie walked to the open closet, seeing what J.C. had, instantly understanding why it had been so difficult. Although Maddie hadn't known Fran, remnants of her personality remained.

"What does he want to do with the clothes?"

"Donate them. But I thought we might find one outfit that we'd tuck away for Chrissy."

"Wonder if Fran kept her wedding dress," Samantha mused.

"Oh, Sam! That's perfect! You old softie, I said you'd turned into a romantic."

Samantha grinned. "Okay. So we're both hopeless."

The doorbell rang. A young man sent by J.C. to deliver packing boxes offered his help. Maddie showed him to the dining room where he could assemble the flat cartons.

"Efficient," Samantha commented, sitting on the bed, folding clothes. "You're right. Emptying this room first will make it easier for J.C. The longer we put off clearing Andy's room, the worse it was."

Maddie crossed the room to the dresser, then slid open the top drawer. A vintage leather jewelry box sat inside. "I'm guessing Fran inherited her mother's jewelry. Two generations of mementos for Chrissy."

"Poor kid. I can't imagine losing my parents now… but when you're nine years old?" Samantha smoothed the lines of the dress she was folding. "Still, I can't help worrying about you. Even though you always act chipper, I know the constant caregiving gets to you. And now this…"

Maddie turned to speak, but Sam cut her off.

"I know, I know. Helping people makes you feel better. But face it, even you have to admit this is a depressing chore."

The jewelry box still in her hands, Maddie stroked it absently. "If you could have seen his eyes…"

Samantha sighed. "It's my own fault. I just didn't

expect you to wind up…" she waved her hands around "…here."

Maddie thought of J.C.'s face, the bleak expression, the unexpected spark of hope. Swallowing, she wished it hadn't meant so very much to her.

Chapter Five

Adam sat on the edge of J.C.'s desk, flipping through the messages on his cell phone.

"Your office must miss you," J.C. told him drily as he signed a stack of insurance forms.

"Let Didi come to work for me and I'll stay out of your way."

J.C. grunted. "Last I heard, she's still loyal."

"Yeah. You have the women hooked."

J.C. wagged his head in disbelief. "A whole harem."

"What about the patient's daughter? Maddie?"

Feeling an unwanted burst of protectiveness, J.C. looked up. "What about her?"

Adam flung out upturned hands. "Give."

J.C. fiddled with his pen for a moment. "She offered to close up Fran's house."

The joking demeanor faded. "Wow."

"That's what I thought. I was at the house, felt like I was going to lose it and Maddie stopped by."

"Out of the blue?"

"She was taking her mother out on a walk and spotted me on the porch. We talked about Fran's things. Maddie said it would be harder the longer I left it."

"What about the estate people?"

J.C. sighed. "I know you were trying to help, but it sounded so...cold. Maddie's going to take an inventory, get things packed for storage so I can rent out the house."

"Good plan. Then if Chrissy wants it later..."

"That's what we thought."

"We?"

"Lay off, Adam. Maddie's just trying to help because she's grateful that her mother's improving."

"Uh-huh."

"You need to get married, get off the romance radar."

"Because that worked out so well for you?"

J.C. winced. "There are downsides to having old friends. They know too much."

"Sorry. You know I get jittery about the marriage thing."

"Guess you haven't met the right woman." J.C. held up one hand before his friend could jump in with an obvious reminder. "And neither have I."

Adam raised his eyebrows. "Maybe you have, my friend."

J.C. frowned.

"Maddie sounds like someone worth getting to know."

"Ah, just what I need in my upside-down life."

Chuckling, Adam looked smug. "You said it."

A few weeks later, J.C. glanced around the near-empty rooms of his sister's house. "You're amazing!"

Surprisingly, Maddie blushed.

The quaint sign was charming, taking him aback even more than all she had accomplished.

"You sent a lot of help," she reminded him, not quite meeting his gaze as she fiddled with one of the few remaining cartons.

"Still…" He shifted, taking in how much had been accomplished, how his sister's belongings had all been tucked away.

"I did think of something else." Maddie finally lifted her eyes. Today they were as blue as her sapphire-colored blouse. "Even with another family living here, from the outside the house looks the same. If you had it painted in a new palette, one that doesn't even resemble the gray, it would seem very different."

J.C. hadn't even considered the exterior. "I don't know much about picking out colors."

Maddie smiled, causing the dimple in her cheek to flash. "That's the easy part."

Wanting to study her face, her soft-looking lips, he nodded. "Such as?"

She brushed a lock of hair from her forehead. "Um… yellow would be pretty. A daisy shade of yellow. White trim. Because the front door is mostly glass…" Her voice trailed off.

J.C. realized he was staring, not listening. "Sounds good."

She brightened. "I don't want you to think I'm meddling. I have this habit of over-organizing things, people, well, most everything."

Her dimple moved when she spoke, a punctuation mark to her smile. As he watched, it gradually disappeared. What had she just said?

Maddie's smile faded a bit.

And J.C. marshaled his thoughts. "You were saying?"

"That I meddle."

"Thank the Lord you do." She paled and he instantly realized she'd taken his words the wrong way. "Helping, not meddling. I'd never have guessed Fran's house could be packed up so... quickly."

"And the painting?" she prodded.

"Great idea." Her eyes were incredibly blue. "Maybe blue?"

"With the yellow? Or just a light shade of blue?"

"Definitely not light," he murmured, captivated by the depth of color in her eyes.

"Well, we could get some samples, look them over." Maddie twisted her hands.

J.C.'s gaze followed her action when he abruptly remembered the last time he'd been entranced by a pretty face and mesmerizing eyes. His ex-wife had been pretty, as well. On the outside. "You still haven't told me how much you'll take for doing all this."

Her eyes clouded and that enchanting dimple disappeared. "I did it to help you, not to make money."

"But..." He waved around, again stunned by the emptiness. While it was a relief to have the job done, the house no longer held the reminders of Fran's life. Facing Maddie again, he couldn't keep a sliver of bleakness out of his voice. "It was a big job."

Maddie's voice, too, was quiet. "For me it was Dad's fishing pole. Mom gave it to his best friend. Logically, I knew Dad was gone, that he wasn't coming back, but when his fishing pole was in the shed, leaning against the wall, it almost seemed like he'd stroll back in, whistling, ready to tie new flies."

She got it. Completely. "Yeah."

"When everything's done...if you do decide to change the look of the exterior, it might help Chrissy to see it's just a house."

His niece had been campaigning to live in the building on Main Street. "She'd kick and scream all the way here. And *I'm* not ready for that."

"Think about my offer."

He blanked, looking at her in question.

"To watch Chrissy in the afternoons."

"Still not enough to do?" he asked wryly.

"Actually, Chrissy kept Mom entertained the day you visited. That means more time for me to get things done."

He was skeptical. "You forget, I *know* Chrissy. Much as I love her, right now she's acting like a pain."

"Understandably."

"It's easier to be understanding from a distance," he warned her, thinking of Chrissy's refusal to do any homework. He'd wrangled with her for more than an hour and had gotten nowhere.

Maddie laughed. "Isn't everything? Keep the offer in mind. I'm not going anywhere."

Sobered, he wondered. In his experience, that's exactly what women did.

The phone jangled loudly. J.C. bolted upright, reaching for the receiver before the noise could wake Chrissy. Momentarily forgetting he was sleeping on the couch, he overshot the mark and slammed his hand into a lamp that crashed to the floor. Grabbing the side table so that he wouldn't land on top of the broken glass, he smashed his toes into the unyielding wood base.

Muttering under his breath, he finally reached the

phone. Bad car accident on the highway, possible spinal fracture. Flipping on the overhead light, he glanced at his watch. Nearly two in the morning.

J.C. dressed quickly, then wrote a note for Chrissy. Still uneasy with leaving her alone, he stopped at Blair's apartment, knocking quietly.

Yawning, she rubbed her eyes. "I'll try to listen, but I pulled a double yesterday and I'm beat."

"Sorry I woke you."

She yawned again. "Me, too."

"Thanks, Blair."

Still yawning she closed the door.

Once at the hospital, J.C. rushed to the trauma area. Fortunately, the situation wasn't as dire as he expected, but it was still over two hours before he neared home.

Red lights flashed from an ambulance, strobing eerily in the darkness. Grabbing his bag, he ran toward an EMT. *Chrissy! Had something happened to her?* "I'm a doctor." Panting, he caught his breath. "What's the situation?"

"Heart attack. Nurse that lives here gave him CPR. Touch and go, but she kept him alive."

"Nurse?" *Blair?* J.C. skirted the back of the ambulance, catching sight of Blair, then reaching her on a run. "Where's Chrissy?"

Blair looked distracted. "In your apartment I imagine. Had my hands pretty full here."

"Sorry. Of course." He pushed one hand through his thick hair. "Saved his life, I hear."

"Hope so."

J.C. loped across the lawn toward his apartment. Even from a distance, he could see that the overhead light in the living room was on. Not breaking his stride, he burst inside. But the living room was empty. With the lights on, his earlier tangle with the lamp looked ominous. "Chrissy?"

No answer.

The bedroom light was off, but he could see the mound of little girl beneath the covers. He switched on the lamp. "Chrissy?"

Muffled cries penetrated her covering.

Gently he peeled back the duvet. "It's okay."

"Uh-uh." She cried harder.

"I know one of the neighbors got sick, but it looks like he'll be all right."

"You weren't here!" she accused.

"There was an emergency—" J.C. started to explain.

"The sirens came and everything!"

Logic couldn't overcome her fear. "I'm here now."

Chrissy burst into a new round of tears. It was too late. And it wasn't enough. Worse, he couldn't promise it wouldn't happen again.

J.C. glanced at Lillian Carter's chart. "No nausea or decreased appetite?"

Maddie answered for her mother. "Nope. If anything, she's eating a bit more."

"Now is that something we tell handsome young men?" Lillian fussed, then smiled at J.C. To Maddie's surprise he didn't smile back. Wasn't like him. Not at all. Lillian smoothed her skirt. "You bake a lot of sweets. They're hard to resist."

"I do have a sweet tooth," Maddie admitted.

Again no reaction from J.C. Had they somehow irritated him? "Everything all right?"

"Hmm." Distracted, he glanced up from the chart. "I'm sorry, what?"

She frowned. "I said, is everything all right?"

He shrugged, then exhaled. "Not really."

She searched his expression. "Chrissy?"

J.C. explained the emergency call and his neighbor's heart attack.

"That's dreadful!"

"Chrissy's inconsolable."

"Of course," Lillian spoke up, surprising both of them. "A child must always feel safe. It's the parents' job to make sure of that."

Maddie wanted to wince for him. Still... "It's hard to hear, but true. J.C., you need help. And frankly, Mom and I could use the babysitting money."

"In the middle of the night?" he responded.

"Middle of the night, morning, after school, whenever we're needed. We don't exactly have a schedule carved in stone. You can drop Chrissy by if you get a call in the night. It's not ideal, but it's far better than leaving her alone."

He glanced at Lillian. "You have more to consider than just Chrissy."

"Do you have any tea, young man?" Lillian questioned, apparently now off the subject at hand.

J.C. sharpened his gaze. "No, Mrs. Carter, but I'm pretty sure your daughter does." He pushed the office intercom. "Didi? Could you bring in a cup of coffee for Mrs. Carter?"

"Sure, boss."

There was a soft knock on the exam room door, then Didi pushed it open. As she brought the coffee and tray with creamer and sugar, J.C. took Maddie's elbow, steering her to the other side of the room.

"Have you thought any more about your tea shop?"

Puzzled, she shook her head. "You know I can't—"

"You want a shop. I have a building that needs a tenant. More important, I have a niece who needs someone besides me in her life. She looks at every housekeeper and nanny I've hired as a threat, someone set up to take her mother's place. But she likes you. She likes Lillian." He glanced over at the older woman. "You have to admit your mother couldn't threaten a bug."

"But—"

"Chrissy wants to live in the building on Main Street."

Maddie blinked.

J.C. told her about the two apartments above the business level. "They haven't been lived in for a while. Jay's parents lived in one until they passed away. Then Jay used them mostly for storage the past few years, but both could be made livable without a lot of work."

"Even if that was a viable option, Mom can't handle stairs."

"Jay had an elevator put in for his parents."

Maddie glanced over at her mother who was busily chatting with Didi about African violets. "Even so…"

"It would be an enormous help to me. You and your mother are right. Chrissy should feel safe. With you directly across the hall, she would."

"We have our house…" Maddie tried to think of all the considerations.

"You mentioned needing money. Renting it out would give you a nice income. Not to mention what you make in the shop."

"I've told you, I don't have the money to start a business."

"Let me be your silent partner. Wagner Hill House has been a worry. I don't want it rented by some cheesy tourist outfit or chain restaurant. And if the building sits empty too long, it won't be good for the town."

Overwhelmed, Maddie stared at him. "Just like that? Up and move? Start a business with no money?"

"Just like that," he replied calmly. "What are your concerns?"

"Endless. My mother—"

"Would benefit from more interaction with people. That's a medical opinion."

She waved her hands in the air. "Fixing up the apartments."

"I have friends in the contracting business. Next."

"Renting out our house."

"I have a friend in real estate."

She plopped her hands on both hips. "Don't tell me, you have a friend in tearooms, as well?"

His eyes softened a fraction. "I hope so."

Her heart did a little two-step that dried her throat. "It's so much to take in."

"It's trite, but every journey begins with a step. Think Sam might stand in for you while we take a look at the apartments?"

"I suppose, but—"

"Good. How about tomorrow morning?"

"Tomorrow?" she couldn't keep the shock from her voice.

The smile she remembered was back on his face. "Unless you want to see them tonight?"

By morning, Maddie decided she was out of her mind. A sleepless night only confirmed the diagnosis. Now, a few hours later, Sam was perched on one of the kitchen chairs while Maddie turned on the electric kettle.

"I think it's a great idea!" Sam nibbled on a cookie. "I hope you plan to stock these. I could eat a dozen by myself."

Maddie rubbed her forehead, wondering why she'd given in to J.C.'s suggestion to phone Sam and set up the late-morning meeting. "You've just put at least a dozen carts before the horse. The more I think about J.C.'s idea—"

"Then stop thinking. Maddie, he's right. It's a good solution for all of you. J.C. needs help. Chrissy needs some stability in her life. Your mother will blossom— you know how she loves company. And you..."

"Can't finish that one, can you?"

"Actually I can, but you're too prickly right now to listen."

"Prickly?"

"You're not a martyr. I know that. But you're refusing to think beyond today. You're cutting corners now. How many are left? Do you see the cost of living shrinking in the next decade? And even though we don't want to think about it, Lillian's medical expenses could rise significantly. A business could give you the means to make sure you can take care of her. And, stubborn friend, what's wrong with *you* having some happiness? Pursuing your dream?"

Maddie swallowed. She'd purposely pushed their financial future to the corners of her thoughts, hoping that somehow it would work out. "And if the business is a big flop?"

Sam shook her head gently. "I doubt that's possible.

But if it did, we'd be here for you—your friends, your neighbors."

Sighing Maddie plunked down into a chair across from her friend. "This is all going too fast. I barely know J.C."

"That could change," Sam suggested hopefully.

Maddie swallowed. That was about the scariest part of the whole venture.

J.C. was highly aware of Maddie's reluctance. He'd all but dragged her from her house. Feeling like a used car salesman, he'd talked up the place during the short drive to Main Street. Now, he inserted the key in the lock. Unused since Jay's death, the building seemed to echo with the loss. Jay's employees had scattered. Some were old enough to retire, the rest had found other jobs when the company closed. Without Jay's networking, the place would have crawled to a halt, so J.C. had chosen the only practical option.

Still, their footsteps rang in the emptiness.

"What happened to the equipment?" Maddie whispered.

"Sold it." His voice seemed unnaturally loud in the quiet. Finding a multiple light switch, he flipped all the levers. Fluorescent lights glared overhead. Seeing Maddie wince, he turned all but one off. "You'd have to imagine it without the commercial additions." He pointed toward the walls on the east side. "The original moldings are still in place. Jay updated the lighting and wiring for his business. But Wagner Hill House was built in the 1890s."

Maddie glanced around uncertainly. "The wood

floors are still good." She stared upward at the ugly drop ceiling.

"The original's still under those panels. Be easy to restore. Of course you have to look past the dust."

Just then she sneezed.

"*Way* under the dust."

"Seems more suited to a different sort of business." She halted in front of a stack of boxes taller than she was. "Not really a tea shop sort of place."

J.C. pointed to the original bay window that faced Main Street. "Picture it without the signs and printing displays. You could put up some kind of curtains, I imagine."

"Hmm." Maddie studied the large window. "European," she murmured. "That's the feel I always wanted. Plastered walls."

Helpfully, he gestured toward the original plastered walls. "They're still in good shape."

"Maybe..."

"Plumbing's good. You can reconfigure it however you want."

Maddie frowned. "Sounds expensive."

"That's where your silent partner comes in."

"I'd never be able to pay you back!"

"Look at it this way, Maddie. No matter who I rent to, I'm looking at renovations."

She looked at him suspiciously. "Are you sure?"

"Yep. And the improvements are a write-off. Just clearing the rest of the junk out of here will make a big difference. You'll see."

Pivoting, she studied the space. "It would, actually."

"Let's take a look at the apartments. The elevator's

in the back and there are two sets of stairs, one up front and one in the rear."

Reaching the front stairway, Maddie smoothed her hand over the curved bannister. "Lovely woodwork. Don't see this in modern buildings."

Her eyes were dusky gray in the muted light. Despite the reluctance in them, he spotted a vulnerable flicker of hope. He wondered how her face would look lit up with another emotion, a more personal feeling.

"Something wrong?"

Shaking his head, he smiled. "Just thinking of possibilities."

Upstairs, they entered the first apartment. Furniture shrouded in sheets were ghostly reminders of past occupants. J.C. opened long, heavy drapes that hid blurry windows. "Needs updating, of course."

"And a good clean." Maddie pulled a drop cover off the kitchen counter, revealing a beautiful dark green marble. "These are nice."

"I know in general the whole building looks dismal—I haven't spent any time here since Jay and Fran died. But Chrissy's right. It doesn't have the sad feeling their house does."

"Once it's cleared and cleaned, it will look a world better," Maddie encouraged. "Any place that's abandoned looks it."

"Guess we can take turns encouraging each other," he teased.

She grinned, then sobered. "True, but I don't want you to feel you have to bail me out. I know our situation isn't the best—"

"Agreed. Mine, either. Pooling our resources can fix that." He shoved the drapes open as far as they would go. "Imagine once the windows are clean, the walls have a fresh coat of paint, the place won't look so grim."

"I don't suffer from lack of imagination," she confessed. "Just the opposite, I'm afraid. I can close my eyes and see the shop of my dreams. I can also see the price tag. You're offering to be incredibly generous, but—"

"What? You'll go on the same way until you run out of money? Chrissy will get sadder, more out of control?"

Concern colored her eyes and blue now tinted the gray. "You're pushing my softie buttons."

"Is it working?"

"You swear that helping Chrissy will actually offset the cost of renovating the building? Of setting up the business?"

He fashioned the fingers of his right hand into the Boy Scout pledge. "Yep."

"I've always been a sucker for Boy Scouts."

"Really?"

Maddie suddenly looked embarrassed. "They're nice to old people." She gripped the strap on her shoulder bag. "Well, since we've decided, I guess we'd better break the news to Chrissy and my mother."

Apparently she didn't want him to press her personal buttons. "Right. I'll talk to Seth about the renovations. He can arrange for the cleanup, as well. I can talk to Paul Russell about leasing your house, if you want."

"So we're really doing this?" Worry pushed the blue from her eyes, rendering them the gray of clouds just beginning to darken.

"Yeah, we really are."

Chapter Six

Maddie added another note to her growing list. It still didn't seem real, but Paul Russell was already sending prospective tenants over to look at the house. His wife, Laura, had volunteered to come along and visit with Lillian whenever Paul showed the house. Maddie hated to depend on so many people, but the offer was helpful because she needed to make some measurements in both the new shop and apartment. Because of Chrissy, speed was imperative.

She'd told her mother about the plans, but like anything new that happened, Lillian couldn't retain the information. However, as usual, she loved having company.

Laura held up the tea cozy Lillian was crocheting. "I love this yarn. It feels soft enough for a baby."

Maddie mouthed *thank you,* then waved goodbye. With Laura chatting to her mother, Maddie hopped in her car and sped to Main Street. Ever since she'd agreed to the arrangement, a seed of excitement had begun blossoming. As she pulled into one of the diagonal spots out front, she saw window washers set up to clean the second-story windows. J.C. wasn't wasting a minute.

The bay window had already been scrubbed, all the old lettering removed, as well. Gleaming in the noonday sun, the glass practically winked an invitation. And she realized that the neglected limestone had been power washed, as well. Suddenly it was easy to imagine her shop, with its wide awning, pots of flowers and bistro tables out front.

Unwilling to build her hopes too high, she hesitantly opened the front door. The clutter was gone and workmen were pulling down the ugly ceiling panels. More dust and debris were being generated, but in a good way. The newly cleaned window allowed the light to pour inside, illuminating every nook and corner.

The kitchen should be in the back, centered so it had easy access, she decided. And shelves of tea blends should be off to the right so the inside tables could be placed front and center, beckoning guests to linger.

Dust motes floated through the sharp sunbeams, enticing her to spin slowly around in the near-empty room. The workers' voices faded as she imagined customers sharing the latest news, laughing as the tea worked its magic, carrying away the stress of the day.

As she revolved back to where she'd begun, she met J.C.'s gaze.

How had he come to be there? she wondered. She hadn't heard his footsteps. Lost in her thoughts, she'd forgotten she was smack dab center in the work area. Trying to recover some of her aplomb, she gestured toward the rear. "Just thinking about how everything should be laid out."

"Must have been good thoughts," he replied, the flecks in his brown eyes seeming to sweep right through her.

"Place is shaping up," she blurted. "The window—" pausing, she pointed to the bay window as though he might have missed it "—looks great. I can picture the awning, the tables out front."

"Just stopped by to see how it's coming. Seth says the bones are so good that it won't take long to fix things up. Have you talked to him about what you want?"

Want? She never thought about what she wanted. It occurred to her that since J.C. had come into her life, the possibility had flirted with her good sense. Was it somehow possible? Could what she wanted somehow be able to happen?

"The plans," J.C. reminded her. "I told Seth you choose the design, the materials, whatever you want. The shop and the apartments."

"Yes, the plans." She landed back on earth with a mental thud loud enough to shake away her wanderings.

"Do you know Seth McAllister? The contractor?"

"I don't think so. The name's familiar..." Glancing up toward the second story, she tried to shake off the distraction J.C. caused. "I haven't thought too much about the apartments, mostly just the shop so far."

"Seth says the plumbing and electric are all in good shape. As you saw, the kitchens and bathrooms in the apartments are, shall we say, quaint?"

She grinned. "I'm used to quaint. Oh, about Chrissy's bedroom—how about letting her have a big say in the decorating?"

J.C. shrugged. "Fine with me. I know even less about decorating girls' bedrooms than raising them."

"Her favorite color's purple. A soft lavender would really freshen her space."

"You can paint the whole thing purple," he agreed.

Looking into his eyes she sensed he wasn't thinking one bit about color. "I might just do that."

"Okay."

He definitely had something else on his mind. "Something going on?"

J.C. hesitated, which he seldom did.

"There you are!" a man called out. "I've had more luck chasing down prairie dogs."

J.C. turned around. "Seth. You need to meet Maddie, she's the one who'll be calling the shots."

"Not really—" she began, shaking the stranger's hand. "Nice to meet you. I just stopped by to take some measurements."

"Have time to look at the preliminary plans?" Seth carried tall cylinder rolls of paper in his hands. "I have a few configurations, but everything's changeable at this stage."

J.C. cupped her elbow and she swallowed at her unexpected reaction.

"That's Maddie's cue," he was saying. "All I care about is having two bedrooms in my apartment so I don't have to sleep in the living room. My spine's close to being permanently bent in the shape of a sofa."

J.C. took his hand away and immediately she felt disappointed.

"I'd better get back to the office," J.C. explained. "Got a full roster waiting."

Seth nodded in his direction, then turned to Maddie. "So," Seth began, "I hear we're going to build a tearoom and shop."

She pulled her gaze away from J.C.'s retreating back. "Yes…" Her voice was hoarse so she cleared her throat.

"J.C. told me about the general idea, but I imagine you're the one with the specifics." He chuckled. "My wife, Emma, always has the specifics."

Despite the storm of issues clouding her mind, the name penetrated. "Emma? Emma McAllister?"

"The very same."

"She owns the costume shop! My mother and I volunteered one year to make costumes for a school play." It had been the last year Lillian could concentrate long enough to complete even a small portion of a project. Maddie had assembled all the costumes in the final stage, but her mother had enjoyed prepping sleeves and tunics.

"Emma's assistant manager runs the shop now. Our kids keep Emma pretty busy these days."

"Of course." Other lives moved on, changed. Her own had been static so long that she often forgot that things were no longer the same for everyone else.

Seth placed a plank over two sawhorses to create a desklike area to spread the plans on. "These are computer-generated, so feel free to scribble away." He handed her a drafting pencil.

For a few moments she studied what he'd designed. "Is this a counter?"

"I'm thinking marble. Not big enough to compete with the old one at the drugstore." Rosewood's drugstore still held the original marble fountain from the last of the nineteenth century. The ice-cream creations produced at the area's oldest operating soda fountain lured people from the entire state.

"Hmm. I do want an old-world look for the shop. Maybe Carrera marble?"

He agreed and she went on to explain the custom shelving she wanted to hold jars of loose tea blends and numerous accessories. She envisioned decorating with all the teapots she'd wanted to buy but never had room to store.

"I agree with the location for the kitchen," Seth said as he penciled in a note. "Cutting-edge restaurants these days want to put the kitchen on display, but I didn't think that would work in this setting."

She laughed. "I like to cut the crusts off my sandwiches in private."

"And J.C. said you want to keep the original walls."

Nodding, she walked closer to see them in the sunlight, running her hand over the ageless plaster. "After they're painted, I want to apply a glaze. That won't take too long, will it?"

"Nope. Won't change our target completion date. I know how important it is to get the place renovated as soon as possible. Wouldn't want to leave my kids alone at night, either." Seth glanced again at the plans, making another note. "Place should look good. Emma can't wait to visit once you're up and running. Of course she'll have to drag the kids along."

"Kids?" Maddie mused, her thoughts whirling.

"Yep. They're her appendages."

Like most young women. "Seth, do you think we could work in a spot that would accommodate a few small tables—kid-size? Mothers would probably enjoy the convenience." Her mind flew into hyper-speed. "And maybe even little tea parties for birthdays. If we could fit it close to the corner for my mother, she'd love it. She adores children and they take to her."

Seth scribbled a few notes on the plans. "Don't see why not. Thinking of any built-ins for that area?"

Maddie rubbed her forehead. "I don't know yet."

"I'll work up another set of plans with the additions. Before the final decisions, we have plenty of demolition left to do. With the exception of plumbing and wiring, some things can be decided along the way."

Relieved, she exhaled. "That's good to hear. My mind's pretty full."

"Imagine so. What with setting up a business, moving, it's a lot to take on." His kindly gaze was calming.

"Thanks for understanding." She sensed it would be easy to work with Seth, which would ease some of her worry. Glancing at the now-vacant space where J.C. had stood, Maddie also sensed some of the anxiety was only going to increase.

"Are we really going to move to Dad's building?" Chrissy persisted.

She had asked the same question dozens of times since he'd told her about his plan. J.C. glanced up from the notes he was typing on his laptop. "I know I haven't done that great a job so far, but I've never lied to you."

"I didn't mean that." Chrissy picked at her light brown hair. "It's just that…"

She hadn't been able to count on anything since her parents' deaths. "Seth is working as fast as possible. We can stop by and see the progress if you like."

Chrissy tipped her head, considering. "Nah. That's okay. I kinda think I'd like to see it all fixed up." She didn't look completely convinced.

"What is it?"

"How come Maddie's going to move there? I mean, she's not family or anything."

Oh, she was definitely something. "I explained to you about how she's wanted to open a tea shop and that she and her mother need help."

"Oh."

"What?"

Chrissy shrugged. "Mrs. Lillian's pretty cool."

J.C. pulled his gaze from the computer. "This move will be good for her. With her type of dementia, inter-action with people helps."

She frowned.

"Having you around will help her," he explained.

"She never tells me what to do."

Lifting his eyebrows, he studied his niece. "We all have rules and boundaries we have to live by."

She stuck out her lip.

"Your parents gave you rules."

Chrissy's lip wobbled, but her voice remained bel-ligerent. "They were my *parents.*"

And that was the rub. Having a bachelor uncle as her only viable relative wasn't helping. He and Chrissy had always gotten on well together. But that was when he was her fun uncle, not her full-time guardian. "Do I make you follow more rules than they did?"

She shrugged.

It would be the most he'd get out of her on the sub-ject. She had resented every nanny, housekeeper and babysitter he had hired and her behavior had driven each one of them away. He had explained over and over again that they weren't intended to replace her mother, but she refused to cooperate. "Chrissy, would you like to design your own room?"

Her brow scrunched in wary concentration. "What do you mean?"

"Maddie mentioned that she'd like your help in planning it."

"What about Mrs. Lillian?"

"I imagine Maddie could bring her mother along to add her ideas."

Chrissy studied him, then finally nodded. "I guess that'd be all right."

J.C. hid a grin. His niece looked intrigued. Good. When she saw that it was real, maybe she could begin the journey back to who she had been. He'd had another call from the principal. Chrissy was close to failing two subjects. He hated to think how he was letting his sister down.

True to his word, Seth and his crew were making great strides with the renovation. At J.C.'s request, Maddie and her mother had picked up Chrissy from school and taken her with them to Wagner Hill House. The girl waited while Maddie unloaded Lillian's wheelchair and got her settled into it. Together, they entered through the tall front door.

"Wow," Chrissy murmured as she took in all the changes on the first floor. She clutched her pink backpack tight.

Even though she was not a child and hadn't lost both parents, Maddie clearly remembered the loss of her own father. The feeling reinforced how all-consuming Chrissy's loss had been. She stopped beside the child. "It's pretty different. What do you think?"

Craning her head to look up, Chrissy tried to take in all the changes. "The ceiling looks kinda good."

"I think so, too," Lillian chimed in. "How did it look before?"

While Maddie explained, Chrissy strolled around the converted space, finally coming back to stand beside Lillian.

"The machines are all gone," Chrissy said in a small voice.

"Of course," Lillian replied. "Maddie doesn't need machines to make tea."

Maddie watched Chrissy, hoping the child wasn't too overwhelmed. "Do you think your parents would like the changes?"

Chrissy shrugged. In the same small voice, she replied, "Maybe my mom."

"Everyone should enjoy tea," Lillian responded. "But it's usually women you'll find in a tearoom."

"Hopefully, because I'm selling loose tea blends, we'll get a few male customers, as well." Sensing the apartments would be less emotional for Chrissy, Maddie led them over to the elevator. "This is sure going to come in handy."

"My grandma used the elevator," Chrissy volunteered. "But that was a long time ago."

It was an unlucky stroke of fate that had also left Chrissy without grandparents.

"Would you like to push the button?" Maddie asked. "I haven't used this elevator yet."

Obligingly Chrissy pushed the button going up.

Maddie noticed a button marked *B*. "Does this actually go down to the basement?"

"Uh-huh. There's not much down there, though."

"Probably the furnace," Maddie mused.

On J.C.'s instructions, the apartments had been cleared. Although there was still some familiarity to her grandparents' place, J.C. had worried that it, too, contained memories of people Chrissy loved. He wanted a fresh start. Seth had suggested that after rebuilding the kitchens and bathrooms, they keep the original oak floors in the living, dining and bedroom areas. The other rooms were all in good shape, needing only a fresh coat of paint.

The main entry doors to both apartments were propped open, as well as the back ones that led out from the kitchens. Maddie followed as Chrissy walked into the apartment that had been her grandparents'.

"It looks so different." Her voice was still quiet but held a note of surprised interest.

"The kitchen and bathrooms will be all new." Maddie leaned down next to her mother. "We'll have a wheel-in shower in your bathroom. There's so much space, we each get our own private bathroom." One of the advantages of the old building, the apartments were generous in size. Seth confirmed that adding extra bathrooms would also add value to the property. "Oh, and Mom, the doorways will all be widened."

Chrissy looked back at Lillian. "That's good."

Maddie smiled, seeing the kindness J.C. had always insisted the child possessed. She had sensed the quality was there, but it was heartening to see her old traits reemerging.

"We don't need anything fancy," Lillian began. "But it never hurts to shake things up."

Unexpectedly Chrissy giggled.

Lillian had broken the tension in a way Maddie couldn't have managed.

"You're right, Mom. I'm excited about having a new kitchen."

"Imagine what you can brew up, then," Lillian replied tartly. "Maybe even some magic."

"Magic?" Maddie chuckled deprecatingly. Her mother meant romance. Not much chance.

Lillian wheeled her chair toward the large front window. Reaching the sill, she glanced out. "We'll be right in the center of the action."

Chrissy giggled again, lingering beside Lillian, relaxing.

Maddie noticed buckets and wall cleaner sitting in one corner. Glancing upward, she saw what looked like smoke stains on the ceiling. Unless there'd been a fire... She looked closer at the wall. The finish was smooth, unlike the other plaster walls. As she tapped lightly, the sound went from solid to hollow. Intrigued, she wondered what laid beneath the surface.

Lillian and Chrissy headed toward the first bedroom. Reluctantly, Maddie left the discovery behind.

"Is this going to be my bedroom?" Chrissy asked, crossing over to the window seat.

"Your uncle said for you to choose."

"This one," she decided, scooting deeper into the window nook.

"Good choice," Lillian declared. "Nothing like a window seat to read a good book."

"Or to dream in," Maddie added quietly.

Chrissy's gaze darted toward hers, a flash of understanding in her eyes.

Maddie smiled, but Chrissy turned away, her defenses back up.

Not taking it personally, Maddie glanced around the room. "Tell me again what your favorite colors are."

"I used to like pink," Chrissy replied.

Maddie hid her smile. Nine years old and trying to be twice her age. "Me, too. Do you remember telling me that you like purple?"

"I guess."

Maddie had gone to the hardware store for color chip samples and she pulled one from her pocket. "What do you think of these shades?"

Chrissy glanced over. Then, drawn by the sample card, inched closer. Finally she pointed to one of the colors at the top of the card. "That one's okay."

"With crisp white trim?"

"I guess."

"She'll need curtains," Lillian inserted as she dug in her purse. "And a new bedspread."

"And furniture," Maddie added.

Chrissy's determinedly sullen expression vanished. "I get new furniture?"

"Your uncle wants you to pick all new things."

Lillian beamed, offering a butterscotch Life Saver to Chrissy. "Aren't you a lucky girl?"

Maddie winced inwardly at her choice of words, but Chrissy didn't seem to mind. "*All* new?"

"That's what he said."

Slowly Chrissy twirled in the center of the room, Lillian watching in delight.

Maddie met her mother's gaze. It was probably her imagination, but it seemed as though she glimpsed a bit of the past in Lillian's nostalgic gaze. Maybe, just maybe, J.C. was right. This move might be good for her mother. Sending a silent prayer toward heaven, she held the hope close.

Chapter Seven

A month later, Maddie stood in front of her new shop watching as the awning was being installed. The Edwardian building suited the furnishings and accoutrements she'd chosen. As the fabric of the awning unfurled, her eyes swept over the exquisite lettering: *Tea Cart.*

Perfect.

Inside, she had envisioned elegant, delicate, inviting. Hoping to achieve that look, she'd brought many of the furnishings from home. The collection of family antiques that she and Lillian had simply considered furniture mixed with new pieces. With Chrissy's agreement, she'd brought a small table to sit beside the front door. It would hold menus and mints.

A van pulled into one of the parking places on the street. Maddie turned, recognizing Samantha's business van, Conway's Nursery. Sam climbed out of the driver's seat, then headed toward the rear of the van.

Curious, Maddie followed.

Sam propped open one of the rear doors, then reached inside. As Maddie watched, Sam pulled out a charmingly weathered terra-cotta pot filled with what appeared to be a miniature Christmas tree.

"Dwarf Alberta spruce," Sam explained, touching the soft grass-green needles. "It'll look like this year-round. No dead-brown in the winter."

"Sam, it's gorgeous, but I didn't buy—"

"Housewarming present," Sam replied briskly. "And you can refuse until you're hoarse, but it won't do you any good."

Knowing her friend meant business, Maddie gave in gracefully. "It's lovely. Thank you."

Sam plopped the container in Maddie's hands. "By the door, I think."

Maddie decided her friend was right. The dwarf spruce looked perfect by the door. She turned to say so and noticed that Sam hadn't emerged from behind the van. "Sam?" Not getting an answer, she returned to see that her friend had the other rear door propped open, as well.

Sam held a matching container. "For the other side of the door."

"But—"

"So this doesn't take all day, look inside."

Cautiously Maddie peered into the van. The floor was filled with all sorts of container plants. "And?"

"They're for you."

"I really can't—"

"You never let us help you as much as we'd like with Lillian. I know you think Bret and I can't spare the time, or should use it to be with each other, but we'd like to help, really help."

Wordless, Maddie stared at her friend.

"So, you going to help me get them positioned?"

"I—" A rush of emotion choked her throat.

Sam took the opportunity to plop the second container in her hands. "The other side of the door."

While Maddie carried the matching spruce to the door, Sam pulled several other containers forward. "Just grab what's next," she instructed, carrying a hanging wire basket filled with overflowing gardenias and jasmine. Despite her cane, she managed almost effortlessly. "I want to set things out before we hang these, see if how I designed it works as well as it did on paper."

Maddie moved the remainder of the potted evergreens from the van, marveling at each species, loving the way they were coming together.

"*Koreana.* Also known as Korean boxwood, although the chain nurseries don't always label boxwood correctly. The California Korean boxwood is a completely different animal, so to speak." Sam traced her fingers over one of the glossy dark leaves. "You said you wanted a European look, so I tried for something between an English cottage garden and an Italian terrace." The boxwood spilled over the pot, draping over the aged terra-cotta to touch the brick pavement.

Maddie frowned. "I don't remember ever seeing anything like these at your nursery." Conway's specialized in native species.

"Computer and a phone—a person can order most anything these days. The flowers are all local, if that makes you feel better."

Maddie grinned. "I'm not the one committed to conserving our corner of Texas, as you and Bret phrase it."

Sam muttered something under her breath as she repositioned the white cedar. The delicately textured bluish-green foliage was a breathtaking contrast to the boxwood. "Why don't you make yourself useful and grab a ladder. I need to position the climbing ivy. Once we get it attached, I don't want to have to move it."

"Aye, aye." Maddie knew exactly where the stepladder was because she'd used it constantly over the past few weeks to stock her shop. Taking the ladder outside, she set it up quickly. "This thing's become another appendage." She loved the look of the scaled-down Christmas trees. "How tall do these get?"

Sam turned to the four-foot plants. "These are fairly mature shrubs. Takes thirty-five years for them to grow to seven feet."

"Wow. Individually the plants are great. All together, they're gorgeous. I had planned to add plants at some point, but I wouldn't have known how to design anything like this."

"That's why I'm the botanist," Sam replied with a cheeky grin. "How much longer until your grand opening?"

"I'm not sure. We're concentrating on the apartments first so we can get Chrissy settled. Mom and I have a tenant for the house and we've been packing for the last month. A lot will go into storage, which is fine. And I cherry-picked the antiques I want to use in the shop. It's all still hard to believe."

Samantha's smile softened. "It is, isn't it?"

"What are you doing?" a loud male voice intruded.

Startled, both women turned to stare at Owen Radley, Maddie's former fiancé.

"I asked what you're doing," Owen demanded, his thick body bristling.

Maddie squinted, then shook her head, feeling she needed to clear her vision or her mind, maybe both.

He had cropped his blond hair so short, his scowling face looked rounder than she remembered. The years hadn't been especially kind. She didn't remember the deep creases beside his thick lips, or the lines around his pale blue eyes. "What?"

"That's what I asked you." There was nothing soft in his face or voice. When he was younger, Owen had been sensitive. Apparently, after years of being in the business world, he had abandoned any such notions. A small part of her mourned its passing. "Well?" he insisted.

"Well what?"

Impatience flashed in his eyes, pulled down the corners of his mouth. "What's wrong with you, Maddie? I asked what you're doing."

"Why does it concern you?" Sam interjected.

"I wasn't speaking to you," he replied abruptly. "What's between Maddie and me isn't any of your concern."

Samantha raised her eyebrows, then swung her gaze to meet Maddie's.

Knowing exactly what her friend was thinking, Maddie heard the echo of Owen's words. *What's between Maddie and me.* "Owen, what are you talking about?"

He waved to the new awning. "Tea Cart is what you planned to call your tea shop," he accused.

She wondered at the anger that had him bristling. "Of course."

"So what's all this about? Has your mother passed on?"

Maddie flinched, hearing Sam gasp at the same time. Ice formed amid the unexpected hurt. "No."

Owen's frown deepened, and Maddie noticed the

well-defined grooves in his skin that indicated he frowned often. "Then I don't understand."

"There's nothing to understand. I'm opening my tea shop."

His dark eyes narrowed. "You said you were devoting your life to taking care of your mother."

"I am."

Owen gestured to the shop. "This isn't a *small* conflict of interest."

Aggravated, she wondered why he had happened along to spoil her day. "Look, Owen—"

He glanced pointedly at Sam. "Does your friend have to hang around?"

Samantha leveled a glare that would have stopped bigger men. "Definitely."

"I expect an explanation, Maddie. When your bodyguard isn't around."

"I don't—"

But Owen was striding down the sidewalk.

"What blew the rat in?" Samantha wondered aloud.

Maddie shook her head. "No idea. I haven't seen him in…" She tried to think. "It's been so long I don't really know. *Explanation? Owen* wants an explanation?"

"Maybe you should send him to J.C."

"I can defend myself."

Samantha grimaced. "J.C.'s a neurologist, and Owen definitely needs his head examined."

Maddie chuckled in spite of herself. "I'm not sure J.C. would appreciate the referral."

Sam stared down the street. "He gives me the creeps."

"I was having such a good time…" Maddie shuddered. "You know that old expression—feels like someone's walking on my grave?"

"He'd be doing a jig." Sam frowned. "I don't like this."

"I'm sure it was a one-time hit-and-run."

Sam didn't stop staring at his retreating figure. "I'm not."

Reluctantly, Maddie joined her gaze. Owen was almost out of sight. She intended to make sure he was also out of mind.

J.C. stacked the last of the day's boxes in one corner of his bedroom. Seth had enlisted a second contractor and together their crews had worked in record time. The apartments were nearly ready. With Chrissy still crying herself to sleep each night, it wasn't a moment too soon.

Straightening up, he heard a noise from across the hall. Because no air-conditioning or heat was running, it was especially quiet in the building. J.C. glanced at his watch. Eight in the evening. All the workers should be gone. He'd left Chrissy with Maddie and Lillian. More curious than concerned, he crossed through his apartment and saw that the door to the other apartment was now open. Funny, he distinctly remembered it had been closed.

He hadn't locked the front door of the building, but crime was a nonissue in Rosewood. The most that ever happened were car accidents and teenage pranks. There had been one case of arson, but that had been solved and the culprit was behind bars.

Footsteps echoed over the oak floors, then a light flickered on.

Was someone just curious? But why poke around at night?

Hugging the wall, J.C. glanced inside. Nothing.

Thud.

Sounded like a box was dropped. Almost immediately, he heard something being dragged across the
floor, something relatively heavy. J.C. wasn't innately
suspicious, but what was someone up to? It couldn't be
a workman; they were all gone for the day.

He still wore the soft-soled shoes that he'd had on
during his hospital rounds. They made it easy for him
to move silently as he closed in on the bedroom where
the noise came from. Suddenly the light flickered off.
Maybe he hadn't been as quiet as he thought.

J.C. stepped away from the wall, intending to block
the intruder. As he did, he crashed into a body much
softer than he expected.

A feminine scream made him jump back.

"It's J.C."

"What?" Maddie's breath was short, fear prickling
her voice.

"It's me. J.C."

"Why are you creeping around in the dark? You
scared the life out of me." One hand pressed against
her neck, the other against the wall.

"Last time I saw you was at your house, remember?
Watching Chrissy?"

Her breath was coming back, but her eyes were still
wide. "Yes, well, Sam and Bret came over. They're with
our *ladies*. Sheesh. I thought I'd take the time to bring
a few things over that I didn't want to move by truck."
She pointed into the living room. "That vase has been
in our family forever."

"I'm glad you weren't still carrying it. I have a feeling it might have landed on my head." Seeing the humor
in the situation, he grinned.

She hesitated, then smiled, as well. "I guess I looked pretty ridiculous jumping out of my skin like that."

He tagged her wrist. "Looks intact."

Maddie chuckled. "You're okay for a boogeyman."

"Did you get all your *fragiles* moved?"

"Pretty much. Some of Seth's guys took the rest of the stuff marked for storage today. House looks...not bare, but unsettled. Then in two weeks..."

Moving day. They had plenty of volunteers lined up. Adam had even rearranged his schedule to help. J.C. wanted to move in immediately, but he had a full surgery schedule on Friday, which meant the coming Saturday was out. He was on call and had to be there for his postoperative patients. "Ready?"

"It's more change than I've experienced in a decade," she admitted.

"Is that bad?"

Maddie shook her head. "A little daunting."

"I'd offer a comforting cup of tea, but..."

She laughed, the reservation in her expression fading. "That part is amazing."

Her radiant eyes were a deep blue. And her lips parted in a smile, lighting up the rest of her face. Wanting to reach out and touch the curve of her cheek, he checked the motion, tucking his hands behind his back.

"I have a nearly finalized copy of my menu," she told him, heading toward the living room. Several paintings were stacked against the wall.

He nodded toward them. "Part of your *fragiles?*"

"My dad painted. Not professionally, but well, I think. I wanted to make sure nothing happened to them."

Bending down, J.C. picked up the one on top. Studying the canvas, he was surprised to see a portrait of a young Lillian. He sorted through the remainder. Most amateurs painted landscapes or still-life groupings. Not the late Mr. Carter. His subjects seemed to all be people. Grasping the next picture, he recognized a young Maddie. She must have been about sixteen. A very sweet sixteen.

A thud made him look up. Maddie was marking the wall.

"Let me help you with that," he offered. "Did you bring molly bolts—wall anchors—for the heavier paintings?"

She put down the hammer, then picked up an unopened package. "Yep."

He restacked the pictures he was holding and retrieved the hammer. Tapping on the wall, he looked for Maddie's markings.

She caught his elbow. "I'm not sure about this wall. I don't think it's...normal."

"In what way?"

Maddie knocked on the wall, starting as high as she could reach, then downward. It sounded solid at first, then he heard a hollow ringing. "It doesn't sound right, does it?"

"I never saw the apartments when they were lived in. We donated the paper stored up here, but even then I just took a quick glance around. Maybe something's been walled over."

Her expression brightened. "Like maybe a fireplace?"

"I suppose so. Why don't you check?"

Maddie blinked. "Knock a hole in the wall? I couldn't do that."

"I can." He tapped on the wall, but hit a solid structure.

"I think it's lower." Maddie stepped closer.

He swung the hammer, extending it out farther than he intended.

Maddie swivelled to avoid the claw end of the hammer, but started to slip on the newly polished floor.

Seeing that she was about to fall, J.C. reached for her. But the same slick floor tripped him up, too. Together they crashed into the wall. The ancient plaster connecting to the Sheetrock fractured under the pressure. As they tumbled, crumbs of falling plaster along with Sheetrock dust covered them. Pieces of the demolished Sheetrock rained down.

Afraid that Maddie would get hurt, J.C. pulled her close, shielding her from the landslide around them. Immediately aware of her softness, he caught his breath. Up close, he could smell the soft scent of apple blossoms from her hair. Silky hair slid beneath his hands.

His breath deepened. As though in accompaniment, hers did, too.

Arms still wrapped around her, he was close enough to see the blue in her eyes darken, her lips opening in a silent sigh. Tipping his head, he reached to close the distance, to see if her lips were as soft as they looked.

Unable to keep her reaction under control, Maddie pulled away. Trying to rein in her breathing, she jumped up. Disappointment flashed in J.C.'s face. But it disappeared so quickly Maddie wondered if she'd imagined it.

Although dust still sifted from the wall, she spotted what looked like granite. Using it as a distraction, she brushed some of the dust away, uncovering pinkish-red granite. "It *is* a fireplace!" she blurted out, scooting even farther away, hoping to disguise her awkward response to him.

"So it is. Good call."

Nervously, ran her hand over what remained of the wall. Sheetrock still clung to some of the stone, but the large fireplace was open. Over six feet tall, J.C. had to crouch to get out of the fireplace. Emerging, he swiped at the dust that coated his jeans.

My, his legs were long! Catching herself watching too intently, Maddie dusted her own cotton trousers again, even though she'd already wiped most of the debris away. She didn't know what to do with her hands or which way to look. Every direction seemed to contain a glimpse of J.C.

"I hope Seth won't be upset with what we did," she said in a strangled voice.

"Won't be too much work for his guys." J.C. ran his fingers over the jagged edges of remaining Sheetrock. "It'll look better with plaster."

"Do you suppose there's one, a fireplace I mean, in your apartment?"

"Probably."

She could tell he didn't want to talk about fireplaces, but she wasn't about to address her reaction to him. "I guess it would be too much to hope there's one downstairs."

"Did you check the walls?"

Maddie shook her head, not caring about fireplaces, either. "J.C.?"

"Yes?"

What was she going to do—blurt out her thoughts?

"Oh...nothing. Went out of my head. Guess I'd better get going."

"What about the paintings?"

"Paintings?"

He pointed to the pile of her father's portraits.

Feeling her cheeks go hot, she felt like an idiot. "We don't have to hang them now."

J.C. tilted his head in question.

"I mean...it will look different with the fireplace exposed. I'll have to think about where to put them. Are you going to see if there's a fireplace in your apartment?"

"Suppose so."

"Do you need any help?" she asked, even though she didn't want to repeat the experience. She might not be able to hide her response a second time.

"I can do it on my own."

"Oh. Of course." *Ridiculous, the letdown feeling.* "Then I'll say good-night."

Nodding, he walked out of the apartment to cross the hall. And Maddie couldn't help wishing he had asked her to stay.

Chapter Eight

$\sim$

After lunch at the café a few days later, J.C. decided to walk to what would soon be his new home. Although he'd tried to push Maddie from his thoughts, she remained there. Why had she reacted as she had? True, he was skeptical about another relationship himself, but Maddie had acted as though she'd touched fire, jerking away so abruptly.

Now that it was too late to undo their arrangement, he wondered if he had made the right decision. She would be living across the hall. And Chrissy would be spending a lot of time with her, further complicating things.

J.C. took a deep breath. There wasn't an alternative. Chrissy needed this. And for all he knew, Maddie had her reasons for backing off so quickly.

Activity at Wagner Hill House flurried. J.C. drew his eyebrows together as he watched the scene. Maddie stood out front and a man held her arm possessively. Walking closer, J.C. recognized him. Owen Radley. The guy had an ego the size of his family's fortune.

J.C. could hear the sound of voices. If he kept approaching, he'd walk right into the middle of the duo. Pausing, he strained to make out their words. Owen repeated Maddie's name in a raised voice. But her tone didn't match his.

Watching closely, his protective instincts kicked in, surprising him. Maddie wasn't his responsibility. Still, he itched to yank Owen's hand from her arm.

Just then, Maddie stepped back and Owen loosened his grip. She rushed inside her shop. Owen strode quickly away in the other direction. J.C. wished the man had come toward him. He wanted to see his expression, witness whether Owen had a claim to Maddie.

The fact that he did halted his steps. J.C. didn't want those feelings again. His jaw tightened, remembering his ex-wife, Amy. Her cheating had nearly killed him. Once she left, he'd filled his life with his work and family. Pushing the inevitable loneliness to the back of his mind, J.C. had decided being lonely was preferable to the torment of betrayal.

Maddie had never mentioned Owen Radley. His gut tightened. Evidently, she had secrets of her own. As J.C. watched, the other man stopped next to a Cadillac Escalade, got in and roared off.

Memories hit like a bitter taste, unwelcome, hard to get rid of. His ex-wife had possessed two faces, one that charmed, one that bit once he was lulled. He had dreamed of a family; Amy wanted only what made her happy—his money, her *interests*. Interests that he eventually learned consisted mostly of other men. She had bad-mouthed J.C. to her friends, claiming he was cold, uninterested in her. He supposed it made her cheating seem more acceptable to her way of thinking.

J.C. had been drawn to Amy because of her large

personality and contagious sense of fun. He hadn't realized that both camouflaged a self-obsessed narcissist.
The betrayal still cut deep. So deep he hadn't allowed
himself to trust another woman. He had been so certain he knew Amy before they married, that she was
the person he wanted to be with for the rest of his life.
The scars she inflicted remained, reminders of how
blind he'd been.

Lifting his gaze, J.C. stared down Main Street, Ow-
en's flashy car now gone. Turning on his heel, he left
the Wagner Hill House behind, wishing he could leave
his thoughts as easily.

The first floor of the building was swept clean. It
wasn't long now until moving day. Nervously, Maddie
studied Chrissy's expression. Maddie had brought over
an old painting which had hung in the living room of
Chrissy's former home. The impressionist style scene
was lighthearted—a Victorian couple dining in the dap-
pled sunshine beneath the leafy branches of a chest-
nut tree.

Not seeing any consternation, Maddie touched the
gilt frame. "I love the composition—that they're eating
at a small round table." Pointing toward the partially assembled tearoom with its eclectic mix of tables where
customers would hopefully soon be sitting, Maddie
smiled. "Seems as though it was meant to be."

"I guess so."

Maddie knelt down. "Chrissy, if you don't want it
here, I'll take it down. I hoped it would be a good memory, something that makes you feel at home."

Chrissy nodded. "It's okay."

Worried about her next surprise, Maddie offered her

hand. "Will you come upstairs? I have something else to show you."

The child glanced in Lillian's direction where Maddie had set up a small television to keep her occupied. "Will Mrs. Lillian be okay?"

Touched by Chrissy's concern, Maddie squeezed her hand. "We'll only be a few minutes."

Given free rein by J.C., Maddie had chosen more contemporary pieces for his apartment. She hadn't wanted to drown Chrissy in the past, but she did want the home to feel cozy, so she warmed the walls with a classic but modern sage-green that complemented the oak floors. Maddie wasn't sure if he would, but J.C. had opened up the fireplace and it made a perfect focal point for the room. Above it, Maddie hung a family portrait of Chrissy and her parents.

Not letting go of the child's hand, Maddie nudged her to look up over the mantel.

Feeling her hand tremble, Maddie drew Chrissy closer. "It's completely up to you whether the picture stays."

Chrissy stared, tears gathering in her eyes.

"Oh, sweetheart, I didn't mean to upset you! I'll take it down."

Maddie reached for the portrait and almost immediately Chrissy snagged her arm. "I miss my mommy and daddy."

Heart breaking for her, Maddie enveloped the child in a hug. "I know." Smoothing her light brown hair, Maddie wished she had more comfort to offer, something that could ease the pain.

Minutes passed before Chrissy pulled away, wiping at the tears on her cheeks.

"We don't have to decide about the portrait today."
Chrissy sniffled in reply.

"Shall we go check on…" Maddie had almost said
her mom. Quickly she changed the term. "Mrs. Lillian?
I brought sandwiches. Maybe she'll be hungry." And
hopefully, Chrissy would eat, too. There had been so
much change in her young life that Chrissy could seldom be coaxed to eat enough, and she had lost far too
much weight for her small frame.

Back downstairs, Chrissy checked on Lillian, who
produced a roll of Life Savers, then companionably offered one to the girl. Maddie's worry eased a fraction.
They were an unlikely pair, but Chrissy had latched
onto Lillian. And Lillian responded in a way that made
her seem a little more like her old self. If a stranger were
to drop in at that moment, they might suppose that Lillian was fine. An incredible blessing.

Nearly as remarkable was the coming together of
her shop. The shelves that Seth's carpenter built were
exactly as she had envisioned. Apothecary jars filled
with her own blends mingled with classics like Earl
Grey that she had recently ordered. Tea shops were on
the rise just as coffeehouses had once boomed. So her
suppliers carried enough varieties to please anyone she
could imagine.

Seth had built out her mother's nook perfectly. It
wasn't far from the fireplace he had unearthed. And
with plenty of room to pull up extra chairs, Lillian
could interact with customers and friends. And next to
that space was the one designated for the children's tables. The more she'd thought about it, the more Maddie
wanted to offer tea parties for the younger set. She had
already planned on carrying a line of sodas and other

drinks as well as tea. And on the final menu, she had included kid-friendly sandwiches and desserts.

Among the teapots and mugs, Maddie had interspersed smaller versions for the children. As a young girl, she'd prepared many a tea party for her parents, friends, dolls and stuffed animals. She wasn't certain little girls still enjoyed having tea parties, but she gave in to the whimsy. If they caught on, she planned to offer "dress up" costumes and cake for birthday celebrations, the ultimate little girl's tea party.

Maddie glanced at her favorite purchase, a gleaming French 1940s iron-and-gilt rope three-tier tea cart, which would soon be filled with pastries and delicate sandwiches. Samantha had helped her find it online. Afraid that the cart might break in the shipping, Maddie had been delighted to see that all three glass shelves arrived intact, the frame unbent. *But what was that sitting on the top tier?*

Her menu? But it wasn't just a copy of her finalized menu. Framed in dark cherrywood, matted to match the ink, this was a piece of art. Instantly she remembered something J.C. had said after he'd admired the line sketches she had drawn on the menu. *When the menu is all set, you need to put up a framed copy.* She glanced again at the cart, but there was no note, no indication of how the piece had been delivered.

Easing her fingers over the delicately scrolled frame, Maddie wondered. And held on to a wish she had no business courting.

J.C. stopped by the Wagner Hill House after his hospital rounds a few evenings later. His last patient was an elderly man with rapidly advancing dementia.

Reminded of Lillian, his thoughts turned far too easily to Maddie. The previous evening he had dreamed of Maddie and Owen Radley. Amy wove her way in between the two and his dream launched into a full-fledged nightmare. Although he carried the mistakes of his past with him every day, they hadn't enveloped him like this since his divorce.

Pushing open the front door, he noticed it wasn't locked. But the shop area was dark, the workers all gone. Last person out probably just forgot to lock it. Having grown up in a house that never had locked doors, it didn't bother him. Baylor Med in Houston had taught him that that wasn't a safe practice in the city, but this was Rosewood.

J.C. shifted the box he held and flipped on the light over the stairwell along with the second-floor hall light. Only days away from fully moving in, he wanted to see the final product. With most of their stuff packed, Chrissy was staying with Maddie and Lillian this last week until the move. From what he could get out of his niece, she seemed to like her new room.

The doors to both apartments were closed but not locked. Pushing open the one to his place, J.C. deposited the box on the dining room table. The living room was dotted with color, a far cry from his beige apartment.

Glancing past the kitchen, he saw that the doors were gone from the old butler's pantry. Curious, he switched on one of the lamps. Tucked into the spot was a scaled-down but complete study. Although accustomed to doing his paperwork on whatever bit of space was available on the coffee table or kitchen counter, he had needed a home office for years.

J.C. ran his hands over the smooth beech surface

of the desk. What could have been a dark hole was light because of the wood and glass choices Maddie had made. *Why had she taken the time and trouble to convert the butler's pantry to a work area for him?*

His mind full, J.C. ambled out into the hall. He intended to enter only his own apartment, but his fingers closed around the doorknob of Maddie's place. Swinging open the door, he was met with silence. *What had he expected? Maddie? Waiting for him to just stumble by?* Feeling ridiculous, he turned to go.

Click.

It was a quiet sound, nearly inaudible. Had he imagined it? J.C. listened again.

Nothing.

A footstep whispered in the dining room close by. *Must be Maddie.* Not completely sure whether he wanted to run into her, he hesitated. Remembering how he had scared her before, J.C. flipped on the light switch, blinking at the sudden change.

Eyes focusing, they landed on the last person in the world he expected to see. Owen Radley. "What are you doing here?"

"I could ask you the same thing," Owen countered.

J.C. angled his head in disbelief. "I don't think so."

Owen's eyes narrowed into ugly lines. "Unless you own the place—"

"Actually, I do."

Owen didn't like being crossed and didn't mind showing it. "You *don't* own Maddie Carter."

J.C. felt a tic in his jaw and forced himself to be still. What was Owen implying? That he had a hold on Maddie?

Owen stood his ground, his posture and gaze a clear challenge.

J.C. didn't have a claim to Maddie, but he didn't have to allow Owen in the place. "I was just locking up."

Owen frowned, obviously resenting J.C.'s tone. Instead of replying, he pushed past J.C. and out the door.

Staring after him, J.C. wondered if Owen and Maddie... She had never said anything about him, still... The other man's attitude implied that Maddie *was* his business. He glanced at the short distance in the corridor between their apartments, and hated the sinking in his gut that told him he would learn soon enough.

Moving day was exhausting, but at the same time exhilarating. No longer running between Wagner Hill and the Carter home, Maddie would be able to devote more time to her shop, get it ready for her grand opening day. There wasn't that much left to do, but she wanted to make it perfect.

Even though friends were helping, J.C. had hired some men to carry the heavy furniture up the stairs. Maddie asked them to set up the beds first, including the extra twin bed in her own room that was for Chrissy whenever she stayed over. By the end of moving day, Maddie wanted to be certain everyone was able to sleep in his or her own bed.

Lillian was at Samantha's for the day because the stress of the move would be overwhelming. Maddie hadn't purchased any new furniture for their apartment, intending to set it up to resemble their home. Familiarity in their surroundings was important with Lillian's dementia. Blessedly, her mother still recognized her own home and possessions.

While the movers left to take a short break, Maddie quickly put sheets on all the beds, then added blankets and pillows. Nothing worse at the end of a grueling moving day than to find they were camping out instead of curling into their beds. As a final touch, she plumped the small heart-shaped pillow that her father had given her mother on their first anniversary.

"What's that?" Chrissy asked.

Startled, Maddie whirled around. "I didn't hear you come in. Whew! Um, this? It's a special pillow Mrs. Lillian likes to put on her bed."

"Oh."

"Is everything going all right at your end?"

Chrissy shrugged. "I guess."

"How about your room?" Maddie had drawn a scaled sketch of just where everything should be arranged so J.C. could tell the movers.

A sliver of interest pricked the girl's eyes. "It's okay."

"Need any help?"

"Nah."

"I'm planning to come over and make sure everything is set up right once all the furniture is delivered. That okay with you?"

The resolute lines in Chrissy's face eased. "Yeah."

She was trying so hard to be all grown up, but she was just a little girl. Impulsively, Maddie smoothed her ponytail. "I'm excited about being neighbors."

Chrissy snubbed the toe of her shoe at the floor. "Where's Mrs. Lillian?"

"She's at my friend Samantha's. You've met her."

"When will she be back?"

"Later today after the movers have gone."

Relief flashed in the child's eyes. "Good."

"My feelings exactly."

Chrissy lifted her face, her expression a trifle less guarded. "Does she like going to Samantha's?"

"Yes, but when she's tired she likes to be home. That's why I wanted to finish her bedroom first."

"How come you didn't get new furniture?"

If only life were that uncomplicated. "What we had is fine."

Chrissy scrunched her forehead in concentration. "The apartments are way different."

"Because people are different," Maddie explained. "My mother is comfortable in the furniture she picked out years ago. She'll have lots of new to get used to down in the shop."

"Oh."

Maddie glanced at her watch. "Are you getting hungry?"

Chrissy shook her head.

The child never wanted to eat. "What about your uncle?"

"I dunno."

Maddie needed to continue putting things away, but Chrissy had to eat some lunch. "Why don't we go check?"

Chrissy didn't reply, but she followed Maddie across the hall. Poking her head into the kitchen, Maddie felt a tap on her shoulder and let out a squeal before she saw that it was J.C. "You gave me a start."

J.C.'s expression flickered.

Instantly, she wondered if he, too, was remembering their encounter on the night they crashed into the fireplace.

"Looking for me?"

"Yes." Realizing she sounded breathless, Maddie calmed her voice. "Chrissy should eat some lunch."

J.C. pointed to the dining room table. "Ordered from the café. Just sandwiches and chips."

Maddie felt unreasonably nervous around him. "Then I'll leave you to it."

"I ordered enough for all of us."

"Oh." She noticed three paper drink cups, as well. The chairs were scattered around the spacious table and she was suddenly very glad that the old apartments were so large. Unlike most new ones, these had been built when families gathered around the table for every meal. So the dining room wasn't an abbreviation linked to the living room. Instead, there was plenty of room for them to spread out. Which Maddie did, taking the chair at the far end of the table.

"We've got ham and cheese, roast beef and pimento cheese," J.C. told her.

"Anything's fine." Maddie directed her attention to Chrissy. "What's your favorite?"

Predictably the child shrugged.

J.C. handed Chrissy a sandwich. "Ham and American cheese with mayo on plain white bread." Then he offered Maddie the other two sandwiches.

"Really, I don't care."

"You choose."

He seemed to be challenging her. Deciding she must be overly tired from not sleeping the previous night and imagining things, she opted for the pimento cheese. But J.C.'s eyes remained on her as she unwrapped the sandwich. Her own appetite dried up under his scrutiny. Chrissy glanced sideways at her, so Maddie made an effort. Although the pimento cheese sandwich was tasty, she felt as though she was trying to swallow cardboard. Unaccustomed to the intensity in his gaze, she wondered what could have caused it. Sipping soda from her cup, she tried to wash down the bite of sandwich. "Just think, not too long and we'll have cucumber sandwiches and tea right downstairs."

Chrissy looked at her blankly.

"Not just cucumber," Maddie rushed to explain and fill in the awkward silence. "We'll have all kinds of sandwich fillings. And pastries. And tea, of course." Both J.C. and Chrissy stared at her. "All kinds of teas," she ended lamely. She needed a bracing cup of her strongest blend. What was up with J.C.? Fiddling with the chips, she wished someone or something would fill the yawning void of silence.

"Eat your sandwich," J.C. instructed.

Maddie's head whipped up, but she saw that he was speaking to Chrissy who had taken only one bite.

"I'm not hungry," she complained.

"Probably because we forgot to bless the food," Maddie blurted, needing the prayer that began all her meals. Needing the Lord's guidance to get her through this unknown minefield. "J.C.?"

Hesitating only a few moments, he set his sandwich on the table, then clasped his hands together. "Dear Lord, please let us be thankful for this nourishment. May it strengthen us in all ways and fortify our resolve. In the name of your son. Amen."

"Amen," Maddie echoed.

But Chrissy didn't join in. Maddie wondered if the child had been counseled by their pastor, if she was receiving the comfort of fellowship. Her own connection to the Lord was what had gotten Maddie through losing her father. She missed going to church. After Lillian's first stroke, Maddie had tried to continue taking her to worship services. But Lillian's attention wandered and often she forgot why they were there, speaking aloud during the sermon or prayers. The pastor visited weekly, but it wasn't the same as being part of the loving body of worshippers.

J.C.'s cell phone rang, sounding especially loud. "Hello." He listened for a few moments. "Right here." He handed the phone to Maddie.

"Hello?" She heard Sam's voice and felt some of her tension dissipate. "Is Mom okay?" Listening to Sam's assurances, she sneaked a glance at J.C. and realized he was listening. Sam offered to keep Lillian entertained as long as needed. "You're sure? Okay, then. We'll be ready for her by evening."

"She's going to be gone *all* day?" Chrissy questioned.

"Well, until things are a little more settled."

"You expect to get everything settled by tonight?" J.C. quizzed. The words were tame enough, but the undertones in his voice were anything but ordinary.

What was he getting at? It seemed the walls of the large apartment were shrinking, boxing her in. Swallowing, Maddie wished she could set time back. Back before they had found the fireplace. Back before the kindness in his eyes had turned to distrust.

Chapter Nine

Maddie worked like a madwoman to get every last knickknack in order. Lillian was fine with the new apartment, for the most part not realizing she was in a different place. She wondered at the elevator every time they used it, but that, too, was forgotten quickly.

Once Lillian had gotten to the apartment on moving day, Chrissy seemed to relax. Maddie knew the child felt that everything she had or wanted was always taken away, so Lillian's reappearance was an apparent comfort. While the duo played checkers or rearranged the large dollhouse that had been Maddie's as a child, she was able to concentrate on final details in the shop. Her grand opening was set for Friday and Saturday. Not that she expected it to be all that grand, but it was the official kickoff.

In choosing the days, she wanted stay-at-home moms to be able to stop by on Friday because many of them spent Saturdays with their husbands. For people who enjoyed coming downtown on Saturdays, she hoped her new sandwich-style advertising board that sat on the sidewalk would entice the crowd. The fair weather held and she placed inviting tables outside beneath the aged elms that lined Main Street.

By Friday, Maddie felt like a child on Christmas morning. Would people respond to this different sort of shop? Had she gone overboard on the old-world café look? Did people in Rosewood even drink tea? The sandwiches would be made to order, but she'd baked long into the night to prepare the pastries, petits fours and tiny cakes. Now, she looked at them as though alien invaders filled the glass-fronted display case. What had she been thinking? What man would want one of the delicate little jam tarts? Or mincemeat tartlets? She pictured large manly hands trying to grasp them and decided the whole idea was insanity.

Brewing fresh coffee for non-tea drinkers, she set out small pitchers of rich cream as well as vintage salt cellars filled with sugar. A curiosity, that's what her shop would be. People would shake their heads at the *Carter Folly.*

"Are you open yet?" Emma McAllister asked. Smiling, she held the hands of her two youngest children. "I'm so glad you picked a weekday for the launch."

"Yes, yes, of course." Maddie ran her hands down the sides of her apron, willing them to be still. "You can sit anywhere you want. I have a few child-size tables next to the adult ones in that corner." She pointed. "In case the kids would like to have their own little table."

"Perfect. A few friends are going to meet me and I'd love a grown-up table."

Soon Emma's *few* friends crowded the shop, ooh-ing and aahing over the sweets in the display case, then ordering some of everything. Almost all of them also purchased tea blends to take home.

From her nook, Lillian visited with more people than she had seen in years. She couldn't remember names, but she enjoyed the interaction. People dropped in all day, even in what Maddie had expected to be the lull time. Chrissy popped in after school and promptly claimed her spot beside Lillian, engrossed in all the activity.

By five-thirty, when Maddie turned the Open sign to Closed, she was joyfully exhausted. "Can you believe the turnout?"

Lillian nodded vigorously. "I always said you ought to open your shop."

Maddie kissed her mother's delicate cheek. "And you were right."

"Will it be this busy all the time?" Chrissy asked.

"Probably not," Maddie answered realistically. "It's a novelty right now, but that's okay. I never expected to have steady traffic like the café does." The local dining spot was open before dawn and stayed open until well after the dinner hour. But the café had a small staff, not a sole proprietor. Those hours weren't feasible for either her type of business or life. Lillian needed a relatively early dinner because she went to bed soon after. And Maddie wasn't going to neglect her mother in favor of the Tea Cart. "Chrissy, I bet with all the commotion, you didn't get to your homework."

"We did numbers," Chrissy mumbled.

Numbers? Looking closer, Maddie saw a completed math homework sheet.

"Mrs. Lillian helped," Chrissy admitted.

Her mother had always been a whiz at math. Funny how she could remember to calculate but didn't have a clue what she'd eaten for breakfast. "That's great. I didn't want the opening to interfere with your school-work." Chrissy's performance at school had improved slightly but was nowhere near the straight A's she used to bring home.

"Are we going to have cake for dinner?" Chrissy asked.

Laughing, Maddie shook her head. Delighted that the child had any interest in eating, she smiled. "Knowing today would be crazy, I made lasagna. Just have to warm it up."

"Uncle James isn't home yet."

Being the city's sole neurologist, J.C.'s hours weren't predictable. He could come home promptly at six or in the wee hours of the night. "Lasagna reheats well."

"A lot of times it's better the second time around," Lillian commented.

"Why don't we go upstairs, get things going? I'll stick the lasagna in the oven. We can pick out a DVD to watch or a game to play."

Chrissy fetched Lillian's wheelchair from where it was stashed nearby. The child was becoming territorial about Lillian, which pleased Maddie. Maybe it was the transition Chrissy needed to accept supervisory adults other than her parents. J.C. and Maddie had offered countless times to help Chrissy with her homework and she always refused; yet today she had allowed Lillian to help. Apparently she didn't view Lillian as a threat, someone who would take her mother's place. Each step, no matter how minuscule, was a step. Although Chrissy might not realize it, Maddie knew the Lord was watching over her. His plan had given them all renewed hope.

While Chrissy pushed Lillian's chair toward the elevator, Maddie's gaze strayed out the window onto

Main Street. J.C. wasn't anywhere in sight. Remembering his strained behavior the past few weeks, she wondered if the same was true of him. Was he feeling hope? Or regret? Regret for allowing her this much access in his life?

"Are you coming?" Chrissy called out.

"You go ahead. I have to put some things away, but I'll be up in a few minutes." However, after the elevator doors closed, Maddie didn't move, instead holding a dishcloth as she stared outside. And hated the lump forming in the pit of her stomach.

J.C. had debated staying late at the office, catching up on notes, but he knew it was a delaying tactic that wasn't fair to Chrissy. He'd barely seen her for five minutes early that morning. The entire building had been in a mild frenzy as the Tea Cart prepared for the big launch. He could have stolen a few minutes to stop by, but he'd chosen to extend his hospital rounds.

Stepping inside the shop, J.C. saw that Maddie had left two lamps aglow on each side of the main room, just enough to softly illuminate the tidy area. The light above the stairwell was also left on. For him?

Knowing he couldn't delay any longer, J.C. mounted the steps. The door to the Carters' apartment was ajar. Reaching his own, he saw a note tacked near eye level. *Lasagna for dinner. Chrissy's with us. Maddie*

He pushed open the door. The last specks of light from the sunset had faded. And the apartment was dark. Suiting his mood, J.C. didn't turn on a lamp. Enough light from the corridor spilled inside so that he could see the furniture. Dropping his briefcase on a chair, he shrugged out of his jacket, loosened his tie and pulled it off.

Voices from the other apartment drifted toward him, small snatches of conversation, a little laughter. Feeling too much like a sulky schoolboy, J.C. forced himself to cross the hall. In a glance, he could see the table was set for four. Looked like they hadn't eaten yet.

Maddie spotted him first. Although smiling, she looked hesitant. Chrissy and Lillian were engaged in what appeared to be an intense checkers match.

"No moves left!" Chrissy announced triumphantly. She glanced up just then, noticed him and quieted.

He couldn't allow his reservations about Maddie to affect how he treated his niece. "You still the all-time checkers champ?"

A small smile emerged.

"I hope you're hungry," Maddie added. "Not that the menu's a surprise. I put that in the note. We have salad and garlic bread, too."

J.C. wondered why she sounded so nervous. "So how'd the grand opening go?"

"Good. Lots of people. Of course there won't be that many people every day. The shop's a novelty right now. And I'm not sure the menu's male-friendly. Little sandwiches, little desserts, little…" She swallowed. "Little stuff…you know."

She didn't usually prattle like this. He glanced across the room. "Did everybody cope well?"

"Mother enjoyed all the company and Chrissy fit right in. That was after school, of course. Because today's Friday and she had school. She won't tomorrow because it'll be Saturday and…"

J.C. looked back at Maddie. "Something wrong?"

"No, no. What would be wrong?" She gripped her apron as though she expected hurricane-strength winds to tear it away.

"Good."

"Dinner's ready. We kept it warm—the lasagna, I mean. Warm salad wouldn't taste good unless it was German potato salad or maybe a wilted salad that's supposed to be warm. Oh, and the garlic bread, it's warm."

Because Maddie looked ready to burst out of her own skin, he nodded. "You all could have eaten without me."

She waved toward the pristine china on the table. "No bother."

Looked like she'd gone to enough trouble, especially after the adrenaline-draining day. She had to be tired. "You cooked. I'll clean up."

"But—"

"Let's eat first, argue later."

"We don't have to argue—"

"Did you say something about lasagna?"

"Oh! Yes. It's vegetarian. Mom? Chrissy? Dinner's ready." She glanced at J.C. "I'll just grab the salad and pitcher of tea."

When Chrissy was in hearing distance, he leaned close, whispering. "What's up with Maddie?"

Chrissy shrugged, her usual helpful self.

Wouldn't do any good to question Lillian since she couldn't remember the day.

He gestured to Chrissy. "Let's wash our hands."

She rolled her eyes but complied. Once his own hands were clean, too, they rejoined the others. Maddie fussed over the table settings, repositioning the serving dishes.

After he recited the blessing over their meal, J.C. accepted a hefty portion of the fragrant lasagna. "So, how many people did you have at the shop today?"

Maddie dropped the offset spatula she was using to serve the main dish. Recovering, she dabbed at the sauce that had spilled on the yellow tablecloth. "I don't know exactly. Emma McAllister was the first customer. Sam was next. She wanted to be the very first one, but Emma got here a little before the actual opening time. Of course the door was unlocked and it wasn't a big deal that she came early." Maddie finally paused to breathe. "And she brought the twins. They sat at one of the kid-size tables."

J.C. began to wonder if she'd swallowed a tape recorder that she couldn't turn off. "Was business steady then?"

"All day. It was amazing. I kept waiting for the lull." This time when Maddie paused, she seemed to actually collect her thoughts before she resumed speaking. "It's a novelty for Rosewood."

"And it fills a niche. The town's never had an eatery that's targeted for women. Café's good, but not all feminine."

She frowned. "So the men won't like the Tea Cart at all?"

"Didn't say that. But you told me yourself that more women tend to frequent tea shops. It's not easy to find a new target market these days. Everything's saturated. You came up with something new for the town."

Her cheeks flushed a light pink. "I suppose it's hard to believe it's really happening. I dreamed about opening this shop for so long..." Maddie reached over, covering Lillian's hand. "Mom always believed it would work."

Lillian smiled but she looked tired. "Maddie can do anything she sets her mind to."

"Did you get a nap today?" J.C. questioned.

When Lillian looked blank, Maddie answered for her. "No. And she's usually in bed about now."

He frowned. "You shouldn't have waited dinner on me."

Chastened, Maddie looked down. "I just thought..." She cleared her throat. "You're right, of course. I was only thinking of myself."

Feeling as though he had kicked a puppy, J.C. laid his fork down. "I didn't mean that."

Maddie's lips trembled slightly before she firmed them together in a grim line. "I need to keep my priorities in order. Mom is my top priority." She looked down at her own untouched plate. "You should eat the lasagna while it's hot."

Noticing that Chrissy was staring at him, J.C. picked up his fork. "This is good, isn't it, Chrissy?"

"You haven't tasted it yet," she pointed out.

Wincing inside, he loaded his fork. "Dig in."

While he chewed, Chrissy picked at her food, finally edging a little bit of lasagna on her fork.

"It's really good," J.C. declared.

Maddie kept her gaze on her own plate.

Feeling even worse, J.C. searched for something, anything to say. "You'll probably have an even bigger turnout tomorrow."

Maddie blanched, then looked at Lillian.

J.C. belatedly realized he had said exactly the wrong thing. "I'll be around tomorrow so Lillian and I can hang out while you're in the shop."

Still looking wounded, Maddie stared at him.

"What do you say, Lillian?" he asked.

"I'm tired, Maddie."

Looking even more guilty, Maddie pushed her chair back. "Come on, Mom. Let's get you ready for bed. I'll bring in a cup of warm milk."

Lillian's shoulders drooped as Maddie led her away.

"Jiminy…" Chrissy muttered.

"What?"

"You don't know?" she questioned, wide-eyed.

J.C. knew all right. He had managed to ruin the celebratory dinner. Not to mention causing Maddie to feel as though she had neglected her mother. He just hated that his nine-year-old niece had figured it out before he had.

The following morning, the shop was packed within fifteen minutes after opening time. It seemed that all of Rosewood had turned out to see the newest business on Main Street. A quirk, Maddie kept telling herself. Even when Samantha stepped behind the counter and pulled on an apron so she could help. Between them, they could barely keep up with all the orders. Lillian came down for a while, then J.C. took her back upstairs. Still feeling like the worst kind of daughter, Maddie fretted about Lillian until Samantha popped upstairs to check on her.

"She's fine," Sam reported. "Watching a little TV, drifting off."

"Does she look tired?"

"Maddie, stop it. So, one day out of how many? Thousands? You focused more on yourself than your mother and she got tired. That is in no way a terrible thing. Not to mention, if J.C. had gotten back from work sooner, dinner wouldn't have been so late. I think I need to have a talk with him and—"

"No! That'll just make things worse."

"This arrangement is supposed to help all of you, not just him. Did you complain when you kept Chrissy overnight because he had to go to the hospital? No. It won't hurt him to help out."

Exasperated, Maddie stared at her friend. "Do I have to remind you who funded this shop? Who's letting us live here for free?"

Samantha grumbled beneath her breath, then solidly met Maddie's gaze. "Fine. He did a good thing, but you can't feel indebted forever."

"Business probably won't be this steady after the newness wears off anyway."

"So now you're hoping your business fails?"

"No, I just need to clone myself."

"Or hire someone to help when you can afford it. Meanwhile, I'll volunteer."

"You can't do that."

"Want to try and stop me?" Samantha retorted.

"I've already imposed too much. You've watched Mom a lot lately."

"I wouldn't have made it when I came back to Rosewood if the whole town hadn't pitched in and helped, you included. Let me give back, just a little."

Maddie guessed she would never be able to convince her friend otherwise. "Not too much, though, okay?"

Samantha grinned. "I'm not punching a time clock."

"Yes, but—"

"Maddie!" Sam grabbed her arm, her grin gone. "Look."

Owen stalked toward her as though he owned the shop.

"Will you watch the counter?"

"Yes, and if you need backup, holler." Sam lifted her cane as though it was a sword.

"That *probably* won't be necessary." Maddie stepped from behind the counter, suddenly feeling vulnerable, uncomfortable in her own place. Realizing that, she straightened her shoulders.

Without asking, Owen took her elbow, steering her toward the door.

Maddie tried to shake off his grasp, but he tightened it further. Not wanting to cause a scene, she waited until they were outside on the sidewalk. Yanking her arm away, she glared at him. "What do you think you're doing?"

"Better question. What do *you* think you're doing?"

Bewildered, she gaped. "What are you talking about?"

"You couldn't marry me because your mother was your first concern. Forget that we were engaged, planning a wedding. You called everything off because of her."

She blinked. "Why are you bringing all this up now? It's ancient history."

He flung his arm in the direction of the shop, then stood far too close, his face in hers. "Really? What do you call this?"

Jerking her head back, she retreated, needing more space between them. "It's my tea shop."

"Exactly!" Triumph filled his voice. "The one you couldn't open because of your mother."

"So?"

"What's wrong with you?" he demanded, his voice gritty.

Appalled, she wondered what was wrong with him. A week ago he'd tried to talk to her again and she had escaped when his cell phone rang. Fortunately, she thought to lock the front door so he couldn't follow. He had knocked, then rattled the doorknob, finally leaving. She had thought it would be the last of him.

"If you can open a shop, you can get married!"

"Owen, it's been years. You didn't even try to keep in touch." She didn't remind him that he was the one who issued the ultimatum.

"Because you insisted your mother was more important." The way his voice curled when he said *mother* made it sound like an ugly word. "Clearly that's not true."

Still confused, she wasn't sure what he wanted to hear. "If you want to be friends—"

"Friends?" he snarled.

Maddie took another step backward. "Then what?"

Reaching into his pocket, he pulled out a ring, the two-carat, emerald-shaped diamond she had returned to him.

She shook her head. "Surely you've moved on?"

"Don't you have that backward?" Again, he flung his arm toward the shop. "You're the one moving on."

"Owen, I don't know what this is about, but I'm in the middle of my grand opening." She turned away from him.

"This isn't over." The anger in his voice made his words sound like a threat.

A chill traveled up her spine. Irritated, she shook her head, dismissing him. She whipped open the door, but refused to give him the satisfaction of running inside.

"What did he want?" Samantha demanded, in full mother bear mode.

"I'm not really sure. Apparently he's still mad because I've opened my own business."

"It doesn't have anything to do with him!"

"You and I know that, but I'm not sure Owen's playing with a full deck. He's acting as though our engagement was on hold all this time."

Frowning, Samantha looked out through the front window. "That's kind of scary."

"No, sad maybe."

"I don't know…"

"Probably just a power thing, Sam. What's really sad is that I didn't see one atom of the man I used to know."

"Just be glad he's out of your life."

Maddie glanced out the bay window. She hoped Sam was right.

Chapter Ten

Spring in Rosewood elicited fields of wildflowers at the outskirts of town and the blooming of multihued azaleas in nearly every garden in town. Sudden downpours of rain could trigger flash floods in the arroyos, but sunshine filled Sunday's sky.

Lillian's new medications were working pretty well, enough so that Maddie decided it was time to try taking her mother to church again. J.C.'s schedule was clear and he offered to drive. His SUV was more suited to carrying four adults and a wheelchair than her small Honda.

When they arrived, Chrissy dragged her feet, dawdling as they walked into the Sunday school building. Maddie placed a worn, familiar Bible in her mother's lap. It was one thing Lillian had never forgotten. Maddie decided to stay with her mother in the older ladies' class. If she coped well, Maddie hoped Lillian could interact with the other members. As the hour passed, Lillian's attention wandered, but she was content.

Afterward, Lillian chatted with the ladies as they strolled toward the sanctuary. A few lingered, matching their pace to the wheelchair. Hoping her mother wouldn't tire, Maddie found places at the end of a pew close to the back, then folded the wheelchair so that she could lean it out of the way. But she wanted it close in case they needed a quick escape. Lillian could still forget where she was and talk out loud, interrupting the service.

Maddie soon forgot her worry, distracted when person after person came to greet them and comment on the new shop.

"We knew it was going to be a smashing success." Samantha beamed, winking at Maddie.

Emma McAllister was only a few feet behind. "It really is super, Maddie, and we've never had anything like it here in Rosewood."

Which is what J.C. had said.

Chrissy slipped into the pew, crossing past Maddie to sit beside Lillian. J.C. was right behind her. Not expecting him to climb over two adults, Maddie asked the others to scoot down. They did but didn't leave as much space as Maddie would have liked. When J.C. sat beside her, his arm pressed into hers. At first she couldn't tell if the warmth that swamped her was coming from him or from the flush she felt.

Holding herself rigid, she didn't move when he reached for a hymnal, brushing against her, then settling back in place. Belatedly, she realized she could stop holding her breath. Feeling ridiculous, she lectured herself. *They were in church. He just happened to be sitting next to her. Just like any other member of the congregation.*

But he wasn't just any other member. He was her business partner, landlord, the man who caused her pulse to quicken, her thoughts to meander toward romance. Initially worried that Lillian might not make it through the morning service, now Maddie wondered if she would.

Bowing their heads for the opening prayer, Maddie added urgent, silent words, asking the Lord to help her through this hour, to calm her racing feelings. Both the piano and organ played the prelude to the first hymn. As they stood, J.C. offered his hymnal to share. Maddie started to refuse, planning to use her mother as an excuse, but Chrissy had already opened another hymnal and was sharing it with Lillian.

J.C.'s voice was a pleasing surprise. Hitting each note evenly, he sang the words with ease. She wondered why he wasn't in the choir. The thought melded into another, remembering the timbre of his voice when they had crashed into the fireplace. The way it had caused her skin to prickle, to raise her awareness of him.

Abruptly, she tried to step backward. The pew already hugged the back of her knees and she swayed. J.C. immediately caught her arm, holding it until the song finished. Flushing even deeper, Maddie swallowed, wondering how much more embarrassed she could become.

Thankfully, she sank back onto the pew, momentarily forgetting that J.C. was still pressed next to her. Although she had always been able to lose herself in the sermon, today she scarcely heard the pastor's words. She certainly didn't absorb any of them. Maddie tried to put a little space between them by inching toward her mother. Lillian smiled, then patted her knee affectionately, but she didn't budge. To make matters worse, she could see that J.C. was listening intently to the message, not affected as she was.

By the closing prayer, Maddie was ready to bolt out of the pew. She needed and wanted to listen to the sermon. Today had taught her that wouldn't happen unless she made sure she didn't sit by J.C. again. Feeling guilty as she shook the pastor's hand, Maddie silently promised the Lord to behave properly in the future.

Relieved to be away from the jarring sensations, she nearly screeched when J.C. suggested lunch. Her voice came out in a squeak. "I'm sure Mom is tired."

"Lunch?" Lillian responded gamely. "Where?"

Rosewood's café was closed on Sunday like the rest of the businesses.

"There's a new place on the highway," J.C. replied. "A big chain outfit, but they have a good menu."

Maddie tried to refuse.

But Lillian beat her to the punch. "That sounds lovely." She patted Chrissy's arm. "Would you like that?"

For once Chrissy didn't shrug her indifference. "Okay."

Great.

Maddie tried to maneuver in beside her mother. Lillian waved her away. "Let Chrissy sit with me."

J.C. stowed the wheelchair in the back and Maddie reluctantly slipped into the front seat.

After driving about fifteen miles, Maddie couldn't remain silent. "How far is this place?"

"Not too much farther." He glanced at her. "Do you have something else on for today?"

Her lips froze. Of course she didn't. And since he lived across the hall she couldn't avoid him. "Just wondered. I haven't seen this restaurant before."

"Chrissy likes their French fries and cheese sticks."

Even better. A place that served food that would go directly to her hips and stay there.

As J.C. had told her, they drove only a few more miles. The parking lot was packed.

"If we have to wait, I don't think Mom will have the energy," Maddie told him in a low voice, not wanting to be trumped by her mother again.

"Their service is good. Why don't we check it out?"

Wishing she could will his vehicle to peel off in the opposite direction, she kept quiet as they parked. It didn't bode well that J.C. unloaded the wheelchair. Once Lillian was inside, she would no doubt want to stay.

The wait was only ten minutes, all of which Maddie spent plotting to make certain she didn't sit close to J.C.

The hostess led them to a small curved booth. "I'm sorry it's a bit on the small side. But a larger table won't open up for at least thirty minutes."

"It's fine," J.C. assured the young woman.

Maddie silently agreed, not wanting to lengthen their stay. She looked over the compact booth. Lillian needed to sit on the outside. Maddie assumed J.C. and Chrissy would slide into the middle section and she could take the remaining outer position.

"Lillian, why don't we get you seated first," he suggested.

She allowed him to assist her out of the wheelchair and into her spot.

Pleased, Maddie teetered on her heels.

"Chrissy, hop in this side," J.C. instructed.

She complied and Maddie suppressed her grin. However, unaccustomed to wearing her dress shoes, she tilted more than she expected. J.C.'s arm shot out to steady her. The next second he was ushering her into position between Chrissy and himself.

Maddie bent her head. *Why Lord?*

The hostess had remained and she placed menus in front of each of them. "Your server will be here in just a minute."

Maddie grabbed her menu, wanting to decide as quickly as possible so she could eat quickly, then leave quickly. Quickly, quickly, quickly. Yet her attention wandered when J.C. shifted, his long legs stretched out beneath the table and more important, next to her. She tried to scoot over.

"Ouch!" Chrissy complained.

"I'm sorry, just trying to get comfortable," she mumbled, feeling the warmth flooding her face, then grabbing a menu to hide behind.

"Lillian, they make a great chicken pot pie," J.C. suggested.

Lowering her menu slightly, Maddie saw the confusion in her mother's face. Guiltily, she realized she had been more concerned about herself than her mother. All the choices on the menu would be overwhelming for Lillian. "You like chicken pot pie," she encouraged.

"And you can have some of my fries," Chrissy offered.

That brought a smile to Lillian's face.

Watching her mother and Chrissy interacting, Maddie realized how fortunate she was. The Lord had answered her prayers for both assistance and guidance. Financially, they had a solid future. Before J.C.'s offer, she had worried constantly about how they would manage. And she was fulfilling her dream. The shop was a wonder. She couldn't ask for a better situation.

Keeping that thought in mind, she ate her lunch, tried to ignore the flutters J.C.'s proximity caused and made herself concentrate on the good. When they were ready to go home, she couldn't understand the jab of disappointment when J.C. left her side and stood up. Deciding she was more fickle than the storms in spring, Maddie made herself smile.

J.C. took charge of Lillian's wheelchair, Chrissy walking next to Lillian as they crossed the lobby. Maddie paused to pick up mints for each of them.

"Are you here with him?" Owen demanded from behind her.

She turned around, wishing she had seen Owen first so she could have avoided him. "I'm just on my way out."

J.C. glanced back, then turned the wheelchair around so all three of them were staring. Uncomfortable, she waved him on. "I'll meet you at the car." Waiting only until he complied, she lowered her voice. "As I said, I'm on my way out."

"You didn't answer me."

Exasperated, she clenched the mints in one fist. "It's none of your business."

"Of course it's my business!" Owen raised his voice and several people craned their heads to watch.

"You're making a scene."

"You think I care?"

"Apparently not. I'm sorry if you have some mixed-up idea about us, but you need to let it go."

"How can you say that?"

Perplexed, Maddie shook her head. "Owen, I don't know what's gotten into you, but please stop." Not listening to his retort, she fled outside.

* * *

Having stowed the wheelchair, J.C. settled Lillian in the backseat while Chrissy hopped in next to her without any coaching. J.C. helped Lillian buckle her seat belt. "Looks like we're all set."

"You're such a nice young man," Lillian told him. "Like Maddie's young man."

He froze.

"Who's that?" Chrissy asked.

"We just saw him," Lillian murmured. "His name is…" She shook her head. "Did you eat your dessert?"

J.C. recognized that Lillian was tired. It was possible that she was wrong about Owen Radley. Instantly, the image of Owen and Maddie on the sidewalk flashed in his thoughts.

Closing the backseat door, he spotted Maddie rushing toward the vehicle. By the time he skirted the hood to open her door, she hastily climbed inside, looking as though she was fleeing the scene of a crime.

The only conversation in the SUV was Chrissy's chattering to Lillian. J.C. pulled out of the parking lot back onto the highway. His mind racing, J.C. could rationalize Lillian's wanderings as simply fatigue. That didn't explain why he had seen Owen with Maddie before. Was he, as Lillian phrased it, Maddie's *young man?*

But as much as J.C. wanted to ask, he couldn't. Not only was it the wrong time and place with Chrissy and Lillian in the back, but Maddie also hadn't shared any more of her personal life with him. He knew who her closest friends were, but she had never divulged information about any romantic interests. Was that why she had pulled back from him so abruptly when they discovered the fireplace?

Silent until they were close to the outskirts of town, Maddie finally spoke. "Thank you for lunch."

He glanced at her. "It's an interesting place."

She avoided his gaze. "Yes."

Tell me what Owen means to you. The words nearly tumbled out, but he clamped his lips shut.

Chrissy piped up from behind. "I wish the drugstore was open so we could get shakes."

Distracted, he looked in the rearview mirror. "You just ate dessert." Then it hit him. He wasn't having to coerce her into eating.

"I could make shakes," Maddie offered. "We have chocolate ice cream."

Chrissy's favorite. He hadn't noticed that Maddie was getting to know his niece so well. It reinforced his need to know what else he had missed.

Chapter Eleven

The following weeks encouraged Maddie to believe her tea shop could succeed. Not expecting the same volume of business as her grand opening weekend, she had been pleasantly surprised to see that many of the people, primarily women, became repeat customers.

"It's *the* place for ladies' lunches," Samantha assured her.

Maddie had added muffins and cookies from the local bakery to the display case. She had planned on making everything herself, but preparing the tarts, pastries, sandwich fillings and other items on her menu took quite a bit of time. And Lillian still required the same amount of care.

Glancing over to the nook where Lillian chatted with one of the women from her Sunday school class, Maddie silently prayed that her mother would continue to flourish in their new environment.

"She's loving it," Samantha commented, breaking off a bite of a coconut macaroon.

"I've been so blessed."

"You deserve it."

Maddie shook her head.

Samantha tapped her cane. "I'm pretty well versed in the blessings area, you know."

Her friend's recovery had been nothing short of a miracle. When Sam had returned to Rosewood, she had been paralyzed with no hope of recovery. Prayer, determination and J.C.'s expertise had defied that diagnosis. "Yeah, I know."

"So how *is* J.C. these days?"

"Subtle, Sam, real subtle."

"And you're avoiding the issue."

Maddie shrugged.

"Now you're acting like Chrissy. Give."

Chuckling, Maddie picked up the tray of tarts, rearranging the ones that were left. "Sorry to disappoint you, but there's nothing to tell."

"Why don't I believe that?"

"Because you're a hopeless romantic. This time, though, your radar's off." She glanced again at Lillian's nook. Chrissy sat beside her, concentrating on her new project.

"What's Chrissy doing over there?"

"She's making name tags for Mom's friends so she can know who she's speaking to when they come in. See that basket? We're going to keep them in it on the little table by the door."

"Wouldn't it be easier to write them out when people drop by?"

"Oh, these are permanent name tags. Chrissy decided they ought to look like little teapots. So I helped her with the mold, bought the clay, paints and pin backs. And she's making and painting each one."

"Clever."

Maddie frowned. "She's a bright girl."

"Then why don't you look pleased?"

"She's still not doing as well as she should in school."

"I'm guessing that's natural," Sam protested. "I can't imagine how she's coped."

"And she resents anyone who wants to take her parents' places. J.C. said she ran off every nanny, housekeeper and babysitter he ever hired."

Sam looked pointedly at Lillian. "She seems content when she's with your mother."

"I know." Their bond kept increasing and the relationship was helping both of them.

"It's going to take time…bringing your family together."

Knowing that would never truly happen brought a piercing pain. Although Lillian could fulfill the spot of a missing grandparent, Maddie couldn't do the same in a motherly capacity. It wouldn't be fair. When J.C. married, his wife would be the one to step into that role. Watching how earnestly Chrissy was working on the name tags brought a lump to her throat. The child was encroaching on her heart, as well.

Along with her uncle.

Samantha poured a fresh cup of tea. "Let's be grateful for today's blessings. The other will come along in time."

Knowing Sam had read her thoughts, Maddie swallowed. "You're right. The Lord has always watched over us." And even if she wasn't part of Chrissy's future, she could enjoy each and every day with the child while she prepared her own heart for a life without her new family.

By Sunday, J.C. was eager to attend worship service. His mind had been in such confusion that he needed the fellowship, as well as the guidance in the pastor's words. Regardless of where he was, what he was doing, Maddie kept popping into his thoughts. Knowing he should be concentrating on Chrissy's happiness, J.C. wanted to reinforce his commitment and keep the Lord close.

Pulling on his suit jacket, he smelled pancakes from across the hall. Chrissy had gone over while he showered and dressed. They had fallen into a routine of eating with Maddie and Lillian. The only thing he could really cook involved meat and an outdoor grill.

After school each day, Chrissy walked home, spending the afternoons in the Tea Cart. Then she headed upstairs with Maddie and Lillian. If he couldn't leave the office or hospital, they ate dinner without him. Either way, Chrissy was never left on her own any longer. It was an overpowering sense of relief. One that should have made him content. Instead, his thoughts were continually spinning around Maddie and Owen.

The door to the Carters' apartment was ajar as it usually was once the building was locked up for the night and on Sundays. Ever since Owen's intrusion, J.C. made sure they were safely locked in when the shop wasn't open.

Maddie stood at the stove flipping pancakes on the griddle while maple sausage sizzled in a second pan. Must be tasty. Chrissy's plate was nearly empty.

J.C. pulled out a chair, sat down and reached for a napkin. "You better get dressed, Chrissy."

"Uh-uh."

He glanced at his watch. "We don't want to be late."

"I'm not going."

J.C. smoothed the napkin in his lap. "What do you mean?"

"That I'm *not* going," she said slowly, drawing out each word.

"Quit joking around and get dressed."

"You never listen to me," she replied, her lower lip wobbling a tiny bit.

"Of course I listen to you." Baffled, he studied his niece.

"Uh-uh. And I'm not going!" Shoving back her chair, she ran out and across the hall, slamming the front door of their apartment behind her.

Sobered, he glanced at Maddie. She had abandoned the cooking, frozen in place, holding a spatula in one hand as she stared out into the hall after Chrissy.

"She's not happy," Lillian commented. "Someone should talk to her."

J.C. knew who that somebody was. Pushing back his chair, he met Maddie's concerned gaze. She and Lillian remained silent as he left them.

Back in his own apartment, he saw immediately that Chrissy's bedroom door was closed. He knocked softly, but she didn't reply. "I'm coming in," he said in a voice loud enough to carry through the thick door.

Curled in the window seat, Chrissy's arms were crossed in silent defiance. It certainly wasn't the first time she had displayed defiance, but this time he suspected it ran far deeper.

"Pinker Belle," he began, using the nickname he'd coined when she was a baby. He remembered how tiny she had been. Her face pink and crinkling into early smiles, she'd made everyone around her happy since her first day on earth. Funny, he hadn't planned to call her that...hadn't used the moniker since her parents' deaths. For at least the hundredth time he longed for his sister's wisdom. "Want to tell me what this is about?"

"I told you." Her lip wobbled a bit more.

"Your mom and dad loved going to church. I always thought you did, too."

"It's different."

He knew in an instant what she meant.

"God didn't have to kill them," she continued, her voice warbling.

J.C. winced. "The Lord didn't kill them."

"He let them die!" she accused.

Differentiating wouldn't help. "The Lord gave them both life, you, as well. We don't always understand what happens to us, but He loves us, wants the best for us."

"Is the best letting Mommy and Daddy die?" Her lips no longer just wobbled. A wail erupted that broke his heart.

Immediately J.C. pulled her close, patting her back, trying to comfort her. "It's difficult for grown-ups to understand." He remembered the anguish when his own parents had died. "It's especially hard when you're young."

"That's no reason," she sobbed.

Knowing how keenly he felt the loss of his sister, he was all that more aware of Chrissy's pain. He let her cry until the final hiccuping sob was gone and the last of her tears trickled away. She pulled away, then stared out the window.

"Do you remember when your dad wanted to take off the training wheels on your bike?"

She didn't reply.

"You hated the idea…it was scary. He told you that

you had to give it a try. If you really didn't like having them off, he would put them back on for you."

She scowled. "This isn't the same."

"The idea is. I want you to attend church while you search for the answers."

"And if I don't like it, I don't have to go back?"

That wasn't a promise he could make. "We will talk it over again."

She balked. "That's not fair."

He tucked a lock of unruly hair behind one ear. "Chrissy, you want to do what would make your parents happy, don't you?"

Reluctantly she nodded.

"Going to church would make them happy. They believed very strongly that God was in everything we see and touch, from leaves on a tree to puppies to the bluebonnets every spring."

Chrissy took a ragged breath, her red-rimmed eyes puffy from all the crying.

Considering how upset she was, he offered a compromise for the day. "Why don't we go see some of those things today? I'll pack a picnic basket and we'll worship under the sky God created."

"With Mrs. Lillian?" she questioned.

"I can ask. Next Sunday, we'll go to services at church. Now, go wash your face."

J.C. explained the situation to the Carters and they were in instant agreement. Maddie offered to make the lunch. He drafted Chrissy to help gather blankets and lawn chairs so that she would have something useful to do that would distract her.

It took a little time for Maddie to make lunch because her sandwich fillings were all gone from the day before. She had to help Lillian change out of her Sunday dress into a knit blouse and corduroy jumper, then change her own clothes.

But in plenty of time for lunch, J.C. drove out of Rosewood to a perfect picnic area. The town park would have been fine, but J.C. wanted to put Chrissy right in the middle of nature. The glory of His work was always compelling.

As spring gradually advanced toward summer, the days were bright with sunshine and cloudless skies. Buds dotted the flowering trees and the withered grasses of summer were ripe with new shoots, coloring the fields.

Maddie helped him stretch out the hand-tied quilt beneath a canopy of newly sprouted leaves. She turned to glance at Lillian and Chrissy who were sitting side by side watching for white-tailed deer, wild turkeys or jackrabbits to run by on the brush-covered sloping hills.

J.C. saw the concern in Maddie's eyes. He hated to add to the worry she always carried for her mother, but he needed her help.

She set the picnic basket on one end of the quilt. "I'm guessing no one's ready for lunch yet." Some of them had eaten a hearty breakfast not that long ago.

J.C. held the other two lawn chairs, not quite ready to set them up. "I'm worried that Chrissy isn't going to be easily convinced about going back to church."

Maddie's gaze swerved again toward Chrissy. "You can see so much of your sister and brother-in-law in her."

Surprised, he drew his eyebrows together. "I didn't know you met them."

"I didn't. I've been in their house, which gave me

a look into their personalities. But it's mostly through Chrissy. Even though she hasn't stopped acting out, she's thoughtful, considerate. How many nine-year-olds would choose to spend their time with an older woman who has a failing mind? And Chrissy never loses her patience. If Mom rambles, Chrissy just listens." Maddie smiled as Lillian offered Chrissy a butterscotch Life Saver. "Even though Chrissy prefers cherry candy, she always picks out butterscotch when we go to the store because she knows Mom likes it." Maddie lifted her gaze to meet his eyes. "Your sister was like that, wasn't she?"

Exactly like that. For a moment it seemed as though Fran stood at his side, her voice soft. *She understands you, little brother. Don't let her go.*

"I hope I haven't upset you," Maddie continued, her eyes darkening to a grassy green.

"They do change," he muttered, fascinated by her eyes, the delicate blush of her cheeks, the way she pursed her lips when concentrating.

"Excuse me?"

"Yes, Fran was like that."

"So, what are we going to do?" she asked quietly.

It wasn't a presumption, it was who Maddie was. Despite caring for her mother and running a brand-new business, he suspected it hadn't even occurred to Maddie that Chrissy wasn't her problem. "I told Chrissy she could see the Lord in everything around her. If she keeps seeing His wonders…"

"She can believe again," Maddie finished the thought for him.

"That's what did it for me," he confided, thinking of his ex-wife's betrayal, how his faith had faltered.

Questions filled Maddie's remarkable eyes, but she didn't ask.

"It was a while ago," he explained, not wanting to spill the ugly details. Trust wasn't all he had lost. He was ashamed of what had happened, the fact that Amy had tossed away their marriage as though it had been the kitchen trash.

She seemed to understand his reluctance. "We've all had trials that test our faith..."

"Look!" Chrissy exclaimed loudly. "A deer."

Realizing he had walked closer to Maddie than he had meant to, J.C. stepped back. The breeze stirred between them as though missing the near contact.

The expression on Maddie's face seemed to resonate his own thoughts. *Surely not.*

"Did you see?" Chrissy asked. "Maddie? Uncle James?"

"Missed that one." He cleared his throat. "Find me another."

"Uncle James!" Chrissy harrumphed but turned back to scrutinize the hills.

J.C. carried the last two lawn chairs away from the tree, plunking one down beside Lillian, the other by Chrissy. He rationalized that he should spend this time with his niece, not that he needed to put distance between himself and Maddie. This wasn't the time to get lost in his own longings. Yes, J.C. reminded himself, Chrissy needed all of his attention.

Yet when Maddie lifted her face to watch for deer, he studied her profile rather than his surroundings. A rabbit would have to jump in his lap before he'd see it. She was pretty, but he'd known that since their first meeting. It was something more, something he didn't have the courage to explore. Love with all its tricky complications had died for him after his divorce. Anyone with his track record would have to agree. Sure, he used to dream about the one perfect woman he could grow old with. But once the eyes dimmed and the skin lost its youthful freshness, what was left of that woman? Was her heart bigger than the sky? Were her morals higher than the Rockies? And her spirit? Her faith?

As he watched, Maddie entwined her hand with her mother's, giving an encouraging squeeze.

"It's beautiful out here, isn't it, Mom?"

Lillian looked over the budding field, the spring grasses stirring faintly. "Soon the bluebonnets will be gone."

"We can enjoy them now."

Content, Lillian leaned back, settling into the chair.

As J.C. watched, he wondered. And wished it was his hand Maddie held.

Chrissy's birthday was approaching. And she had to decide whether she wanted a party at the Tea Cart or an outdoor gathering. Maddie and J.C. had been taking her on hikes and nature walks for weeks now. Chrissy reluctantly kept her part of the deal and didn't balk at going to church. But she was still a work in progress.

Maddie felt she was, too. Owen continued to annoy her every chance he got, and J.C. continued to ignore her. Well, maybe not ignore, but he didn't interact the way he had. Apparently, she didn't need to worry about her own weakness since he didn't show a shred of interest. Relieved, that's what she should be. Relieved.

Then why was she so disappointed?

Maddie sighed as she wiped off the shop counter.

"Something wrong, dear?" Lillian asked.

"No, of course not." Maddie turned to Chrissy. "Are you leaning one way or the other about your party?"

Chrissy climbed down from Lillian's side and circled around the smaller tables. "Will everybody fit in here?"

"Let's see. There are eighteen kids in your class."

"If we have hot dogs, too, I could invite the boys. They might not come if they think it's a tea party for just girls. And Lexi's brother, Chance, won't come if he's the only boy."

"Good point," Maddie agreed, holding up her fingers to count. "Your uncle, Mom…"

"Lexi and Chance," Chrissy reminded her.

Maddie tapped her two next fingers to include them. "Everyone should fit just fine. And because it's your party, we'll have an extra special menu, all your favorites and whatever little boys will eat."

"Uncle James used to be a boy."

Lillian snickered.

Maddie coughed so she wouldn't laugh, as well. "Then we'll ask him."

"Hot dogs. Definitely hot dogs," James decided. "Pizza's good, too."

"Pizza?" Chrissy's voice quickened in excitement.

It would be a special treat because Rosewood didn't have a pizza parlor. "I could make pizzas," Maddie offered. "I'm guessing cheese and pepperoni would be the most popular."

"I like cheese," Chrissy announced.

"And I like pepperoni," J.C. added the male vote.

"Cheese pizza and pepperoni pizza. Hot dogs, of course. And your favorite cake—one layer chocolate, one layer vanilla."

"With your special frosting," Chrissy chirped.

"Both flavors?" Maddie questioned.

"Uh-huh." Chrissy reached for a dinner roll.

J.C.'s fork paused midair. "Both?"

"It's all butter cream," Maddie explained, "vanilla and chocolate."

Planning parties and menus wasn't his thing. "There'll be enough room for all the kids on a busy Saturday?"

"It'll work best if we plan for an afternoon party. The busiest time is from brunch until the early afternoon."

J.C. couldn't imagine a swarm of nine-and ten-year-olds on a crowded Saturday, but Maddie didn't look even slightly fazed. "I could grill the hot dogs," he offered. They had a garden space in the back of the building. It wasn't large, but there was plenty of room for the grill, a picnic table, chairs and a swing. "What else do you want me to do?"

Maddie pursed her lips. "I'll make a list...not just for you. A list of everything we'll need to get done—decorations, favors, place settings..."

"Presents," Lillian added to their list.

Lowering her glass of milk, Chrissy smiled.

J.C. wiggled his eyebrows at her. "No peeking."

"Uncle James," she moaned. "I'm not a little kid anymore."

Oh, but she was. "Remind me...you're going to be thirty? Forty?"

Chrissy rolled her eyes.

Maddie chuckled and ruffled Chrissy's hair.

J.C. liked it when Maddie relaxed. With the shop closed and Lillian contented, Maddie shed her cloak of worry. Once upstairs in the living area, it was as though the rest of world was locked away.

He sobered, remembering Owen's intrusion. Unfortunately, not *everyone* else was locked out of her life.

Chapter Twelve

⁓

Wanting everything to be perfect for Chrissy's birthday, Maddie decided to make an investment she had been mulling over. Costumes for children's tea parties. She had planned on them when deciding to create the children's corner, but she hadn't bought them right off, having to consider the cost. As it was, buying costumes would stretch her already-mangled budget.

Fortunately, Emma McAllister had continued to frequent the Tea Cart. Before she married Seth, Emma had operated a costume shop, Try It On. Once she was married, she had sold the shop to her former assistant, Tina.

Emma came into the Tea Cart about twice a week while her twins were in preschool, often meeting friends for tea and her favorite tiny hazelnut cakes. Maddie was watching for her, wanting to discuss her idea while Chrissy was in school and couldn't overhear.

Just after ten o'clock, Emma pushed open the door, then inhaled deeply. "Fresh brewed tea and something with cinnamon. Yum."

"Apple tartlets," Maddie explained. "I just took them

out of the oven. It's a new recipe I've made up, so I'm not sure how they'll turn out."

"Can I be your guinea pig?"

"Only if you let me treat."

Emma tsked. "Having been in business for myself, I can tell you that's not very profitable."

"I'm hoping to intrude on your morning quiet time, and actually it is about business."

"How can I argue?" Emma grinned. "From the aroma, those apple things have to be delicious."

Knowing Emma's favorite blend of tea, Maddie filled a teapot with leaves and boiling water. With Lillian happily chatting to one of the ladies in her Sunday school class, Maddie put the pot and cups on a small table nearby. "Is this okay?"

"Perfect."

Back behind the counter, Maddie pulled out the tray of fresh apple tartlets and stacked some on a delicate pink glass dish. She added dessert plates, forks and napkins. Unloading it all on the café table, Maddie stashed the tray.

"Is it okay for me to dive in while you talk?" Emma asked, eyeing the pastries.

"Of course."

Emma took a bite, savoring it slowly, then sighing. "Oh, I wish you hadn't come up with this recipe."

"Too sweet? Needs a touch of salt?"

"Afraid not. Now I have one more goody that'll glide from my lips to my hips."

Pleased, Maddie grinned. "Really?"

"Taste one if you dare." She took a second bite.

"If you don't mind, I'll talk instead." Maddie waved toward the nook filled with small tables. "When I was designing the shop, with Seth's inspiration, we planned an area for kids. As the idea grew, I knew I wanted to host children's parties."

"It would be great for birthday parties," Emma mused. "Girls especially."

"My thought, too. When I asked Chrissy who she wanted to invite, I thought it would probably be all girls, but she wants to invite her whole class. That got me thinking. I'd been envisioning fancy costumes for the girls, hats, gloves, fun things they don't usually have. And when Chrissy mentioned the boys, I thought, why not? For costumes, I wondered about top hats."

"And little vests," Emma mused. "Boys like lots of pockets so we could design them with extra ones. The bow tie could be sewn to one side and attached with velcro on the other."

"It's doable?"

"Sure. Great thing about costumes, you're really only limited by your imagination. We never designed any outfits with special effects like fireworks, but just about everything else, including a dragon whose eyes light up. One of the main customers for Try It On is the local theater." The theater costumes, along with Emma's award-winning designer wedding gowns, had put her shop on the national map.

Maddie quietly clapped her hands together. "Perfect! I want Chrissy's birthday to be really, really special."

"I keep her in my prayers," Emma said quietly. "Such an enormous loss for a little girl."

"Fortunately she has her uncle."

"And you."

Maddie shook her head. "I don't do much."

Emma stared at her. "You're kidding. Chrissy has

improved by leaps and bounds since you've been in her life."

"She's still traumatized."

"Healing takes a long time. I know that from personal experience." Emma had come to Rosewood after being placed in the witness protection program. Formerly a prosecuting attorney, she had been targeted by the brother of someone she had rightfully sent to prison. Out for revenge, the man had tried to kill her by setting her house ablaze. She hadn't been in the house, but tragically her husband and young daughter were. Fortunately, the arsonist was caught in Rosewood when he made a second attempt on Emma's life. Pain had been tempered by her faith, but the loss was still part of who she was. Not turning it into anger, instead she had funneled it into compassion.

Knowing Emma's past, Maddie regretted stirring up any memories. "I didn't mean to—"

Emma patted her hand. "With solid people like you and J.C., Chrissy's on the right road. I can see the Lord's hand in bringing you together."

"I pray you're right." Maddie knew her own contribution hadn't been much, but she was overjoyed that Emma saw a visible difference in Chrissy. "And you can understand why the party is so important, why I want her life to be as normal as possible."

"Of course." Emma set her cup back in the saucer. "What aren't you telling me?"

Maddie traced the outline of the sugar bowl with her fingers. "I had planned to add costumes either a few at a time or later on…."

"Would an installment plan help?"

Leaning forward, Maddie's anxiety spilled out. "I

know it's a huge thing to ask. I can make a deposit. I just didn't know if payments would be something a costume shop offered."

Emma lifted her shoulders. "In special circumstances. That's how I sold the business to Tina. She makes payments. I'll speak to her and we'll work out something."

Maddie suddenly realized she didn't even have a bid on how much everything would cost. It could be far more than her budget would handle.

But Emma anticipated the request. "I'll make some sketches, get Tina's input and ask her to put together a bid." She pursed her lips. "I have some vintage hats, too. Some are at the shop, some at home. The top hats will be easy to make. They don't have to be wedding-quality, especially because the boys will no doubt be pulling them off and jamming them back on. A crushable thick felt fabric might be just the thing."

"I can sew," Maddie inserted, thinking she might be able to hold down the cost.

"In all your copious spare time?" Emma shook her head. "That's about as practical as having high tea in the costume shop. Buttons in the pastries wouldn't be that appetizing."

Chuckling, Maddie was awfully glad she knew Emma. "You're right. Oh, and in the bid… I want Chrissy's dress and hat to be extra special."

"Favorite color?"

"Purple. We painted her room lavender and she really likes it."

"Hmm. Accented with red it's festive, with gold it's glamorous or royal, like a princess. For a ten-year-old girl…" Clearly, Emma's wheels were spinning.

Maddie suddenly remembered Emma's children. "I don't expect you to take time away from your kids to work on this."

"I design costumes for their school plays, anything I get a chance to. The shop's truly Tina's now, so when I can get my hands on a pencil to sketch, watch out!"

Maddie's grateful smile crinkled her entire face. "Wonderful!"

"I'll talk to Tina after I leave here." She reached for another apple tartlet. "But I'm not going until we finish our *experiment* down to the last crumb."

Maddie thought Tina's bid was very reasonable so she paid fifteen percent down on the order. Emma insisted on designing Chrissy's dress and she consulted with Maddie on the details. The end result was a swirl of multilayered lavender chiffon. The puffy sleeves were accented with cutouts edged in dainty lines of gold. She used the same effect on the high collar. It was at once age-appropriate, yet magical.

They assembled different gift bags for the girls and boys. Afterward, Maddie took Chrissy to Barton's shoe store. The owner had special ordered gold Mary Janes to go with Chrissy's party dress. Maddie wouldn't reveal the final dress design, but told Chrissy the shoes would be perfect for her outfit. Intrigued by the shiny shoes and new white tights, Chrissy was appeased.

With Tina's encouragement, they decided that choosing and putting on the costumes would be the first portion of the party. And to make this first, most important party extra special, they would gather at the Tea Cart, then walk down Main Street to the costume shop and change into their outfits. That way, if there were any fitting difficulties, Tina would have all her supplies at hand. Both Maddie and Tina thought the kids would be intrigued by a tour of the costume shop with all its nooks and crannies filled with everything from Little Red Riding Hood to dinosaurs.

Even though Chrissy was trying to play it cool, she was excited about her party. Maddie was pleased with almost everything. Except J.C.

He politely listened to her suggestions. But he didn't share anything or encourage any discussion. She knew it wasn't just her imagination. J.C. had become distant and she didn't know why.

Saturday afternoon, the children swarmed the costume shop, all clamoring to get into their party outfits. The boys were enthralled with the dinosaur costumes Tina had shown them, but the girls were more interested in princess and fairy gowns. Controlled chaos was the best way to describe their time at Try It On.

Chrissy had gotten ready at home, delighted when Maddie and Lillian presented the frothy lavender chiffon dress. The final touch was the hat Emma made. She had pleated the same lavender chiffon on the base, then added deep purple ribbon and delicate gold edging. For whimsy, she attached two jaunty feathers which she had dyed deep purple. Chrissy positively glowed when she looked in the mirror at the complete effect. As the guests arrived, the girls oohed and aahed seeing the magical dress.

For the first time, Chrissy had left the building without her backpack. She didn't even seem to notice she had. It took a while, but once all the kids had their costumes and accessories, they headed back to the Tea

Cart. Crossing her fingers, Maddie hoped J.C. would be pleased. And maybe, just maybe, he would let down at least part of the barrier he had put between them.

J.C. practically flew to the Tea Cart. He had been called to the hospital in the middle of the night for an emergency that had him operating for hours. His patient now stabilized, J.C. was finally able to get back home for the party.

He dashed upstairs for a fast shower, then changed into a fresh shirt and jeans. Taking time only to shave and run a comb through his hair, he was back downstairs in ten minutes. One thing about being a doctor, his internship and then residency had prepared him to get ready in record time.

Exhaling, he saw that the kids hadn't returned yet from getting their costumes. Samantha manned the counter and Lillian sat in her special spot. The children's nook was decorated with tiny white fairy lights along with banners and balloons in Chrissy's favorite colors. A bouquet of lavender, purple and acrylic gold balloons were tied to the chair he guessed would be the birthday girl's. He hadn't pictured anything so festive.

"Looks great, doesn't it?" Samantha asked. The shop was quiet with customers at only three tables.

"Amazing."

"Wait until you see what else Maddie has whipped up."

"What can I do?"

"Light the grill," she replied. "When the kids get here, we'll be too busy to even think."

He thought she was exaggerating. "Little girls aren't all that rowdy. Boys probably won't even show up."

"Oh, you are a dreamer, J.C."

"You think they will?"

"They met here at the shop, remember? They all came."

Frowning, J.C. glanced over at the children's area. "Then we need more space for the party."

She waved her hand in dismissal. "Nope. Maddie thought out every detail. She had an exact count, then planned for a few extras. She's been planning, decorating, cooking and baking ever since Chrissy decided where she wanted her party. She wants it to be extra special."

Because this was Chrissy's first birthday without her parents. "I'll get the grill going, then round up the ketchup and mustard."

"Just the grill. Maddie already fixed a condiment bar for the hot dogs."

He frowned.

"What's wrong?"

"I'm wondering when she had time to sleep," he muttered. "Running the shop, taking care of Lillian and Chrissy..."

"She wants to do this," Samantha replied in a quiet voice. "Surely you know by now that Maddie's happiest when she's giving and caring for others. It's rare... she's rare, and special."

He knew that. Unfortunately, he wasn't the only man with that information.

The bell jangled over the door as two women entered.

"I'd better get back to work," Samantha told him, turning to greet the customers.

It didn't take long for J.C. to light the grill. A cooler sat on top of the picnic table. He flipped it open—the hot dogs. Maddie hadn't left anything to chance. He went back inside just in time to see the shop door fly open. Kids crowded inside, all dressed up. Looking closer, he saw they all looked like little ladies and gentlemen, outfitted for a formal event. Grinning, he wondered how the boys liked that. Then Chrissy stepped forward. J.C.'s breath caught.

His little Pinker Belle looked so pretty. Dressed in what he guessed was any young girl's fantasy dress, there wasn't a trace of sadness in her face.

"Uncle James!" She twirled around. "Do you like it?"

"It's very pretty…" He felt a lump in his throat. "*You're* very pretty."

Chrissy glanced down, looking shy, then tapped her shoes. "I never had gold shoes before."

Or a small but perfect hat. It was obvious everything she wore had been carefully designed. "Perfect for the birthday girl."

She grinned. "Maddie fixed everything. Isn't it cool?"

"Yep." He remembered his feeble effort of simply lighting the grill and suppressed a grimace. Good thing Maddie had picked up the ball, then scored touchdown after touchdown.

As though his thoughts had produced her, he spotted Maddie in the crowd, shepherding the kids inside. He stepped to one side so they could pass. She looked a little flushed but completely in control. Not harried or overwhelmed as he would have been. Glancing up, she met his gaze, then prodded the boy in front of her toward the small tables. J.C. would have liked to read what was in her eyes, but her gaze had darted away too quickly.

"Come on, Chance, there's plenty of room." Keeping her attention on the children, Maddie didn't look at J.C. again.

He wanted to tell her how terrific everything looked, how great she'd been organizing all of this, how grateful he was that she had put a bright smile on Chrissy's face. Instead, he watched as she herded the children to the tables.

"You probably want to get the hot dogs going," Samantha reminded him, nodding toward the back.

"Right." It didn't take long to grill the handmade hot dogs that Maddie had purchased from the local sausage maker. He found bratwurst at the bottom of the cooler, his favorite.

The kids had begun on the homemade pizzas when he brought up the plump, fresh hot dogs. As predicted, the boys dove in. The girls remained fascinated by the tiny sandwiches in the shapes of hearts, diamonds and shamrocks.

J.C. glanced at the condiment bar. As he did, the sketch on the wall above the dispensers caught his attention. Peering closer, he realized the subject was Maddie when she was probably around Chrissy's age. She was sitting at a child-size table. Dolls and a teddy bear sat in the other chairs. Miniature dishes were set on the table. *A tea party?* It must be. The young Maddie was holding a cup midair. Apparently, little tea parties had been part of her childhood. And her father had captured the scene brilliantly.

"Excuse me," Maddie said in a quiet voice.

J.C. realized he was blocking the aisle and moved aside. Before she could escape, he caught her elbow. "Tell me what to do."

Her eyes flickered in astonishment.

"I want to help with the party," he explained.

The emotion in her eyes flitted away. "Um, collect dirty dishes, um, yes, that would help."

Now she seemed plenty distracted. Before he could voice the thought...or anything else, Maddie scurried away, disappearing in the back.

He bused the table, listening to the children's chatter. It was easy to see they were having fun. No doubt the novel type of party would catch on.

Carrying the dishes he'd collected into the kitchen, J.C. paused when he saw the birthday cake. It was a beauty. Lavender and purple around the woven sides, with pink lettering and gold candles. "Wow."

Maddie turned from the sink where she was washing her hands. "So it looks okay?"

"It looks fantastic. How did you get it all smooth on top like that?"

"Fondant over the butter cream frosting," she explained.

"Looks like it came from a fancy bakery."

"Fingers crossed, it tastes good."

J.C. scrunched his forehead in surprise. "You've never made anything that didn't taste good."

Maddie blushed. "I hope the public agrees with you."

"Have you had any complaints?"

She shook her head.

"I think I made a good investment."

Her eyes, now a soft blue, widened. "Investment?"

"As a silent partner."

She blinked, then turned back to the sink. "Good."

Frowning, J.C. wondered what he'd said wrong.

"You can take that stack of dessert plates out to the

party if you'd like," she continued, still not turning around.

"Sure." Each little plate was topped with a scalloped paper doily, like the ones she used for her pastries. She had seen to every minuscule detail.

"There's a tray on the counter with forks. You can stack the plates on it and save a trip."

And get out of her way? J.C. followed her instructions, leaving the kitchen. He set the tray on the counter while he collected more dirty dishes from the party nook. He couldn't very well leave the mess in the shop, J.C. rationalized as he returned to the kitchen. Maddie was checking the candles and it occurred to him that the tiered cake was probably heavy.

After depositing the dishes in the sink, he crossed the room to stand beside her. "I'll carry the cake."

"I'm used to—"

"It's too heavy for you." Surprising her, he lifted it off the counter. Before she could recover, he headed out front, pausing at the counter. "Where do you plan to light the candles?"

"Here is good." She rummaged in a drawer and produced a fireplace lighter, one long enough to reach all the candles without getting singed. Once they were all lit, J.C. headed to the table, Maddie and Sam trailing just behind him.

"Maddie! It's so pretty!" Chrissy exclaimed.

The kids and handful of adults erupted in applause. Maddie's face flushed, then she smiled. The women beamed. They all began singing "Happy Birthday," prodding Chrissy's shy grin.

"Make a wish!" Lillian called out.

Chrissy looked up.

J.C. nodded, then winked.

Maddie smiled. "Yes, make a wish!"

Chrissy closed her eyes for several moments, took a deep breath and blew out her candles.

"Yea!" Clapping her hands, Maddie left J.C.'s side to help serve the cake.

Once all the kids had some cake, she slipped an arm around Chrissy, giving her an affectionate hug before tugging her ponytail.

The curling in his stomach had nothing to do with all the delicious aromas in the shop. It had everything to do with Maddie. The way her eyes crinkled when she grinned, the laughter that was as natural to her as breathing. She had brought joy into their lives when he had thought it was impossible. Was it possible there was even more ahead? Even more to fill his heart?

Chapter Thirteen

The backyard didn't have much of a garden. But in the late spring, scents of neighboring gardens stirred in the mild breeze. The building blocked almost all of the noise from Main Street. In the evening, most people were home, reducing even that small bit of noise. Closing her eyes, Maddie could imagine that she was back at the house she had grown up in, nestled in its serenity. Amazing how much had changed in such a relatively short time. When the year began, she couldn't have imagined she would be running the Tea Cart, living in the Wagner Hill building. She certainly couldn't have imagined the way J.C. had tumbled her feelings, totally uprooted her emotions.

She pushed the wooden swing with her foot, allowing the slow motion to ease her mind. It had been some day. Chrissy's party had been all she had hoped for and more. Seeing her truly smile was such a blessing. Remembering the curt, fractious child she had first met, Maddie pondered the change. She couldn't take the credit. Actually her mother had been the one to breach the child's defenses.

Leaning her head back, Maddie studied the blanket of stars above. She had heard people scoff about the legend of the Texas skies. Although her travels had been limited, she had always studied the night skies, seeing how different the heavens looked. Maybe she was just a Rosewood girl to the bone. The thought made her chuckle.

"What's so funny?"

Startled, she sat up straight, stopping the swing's motion. "J.C., you nearly made me jump out of my skin."

"I seem to have that effect on you."

More than he knew. Certainly more than the rush of fear from running into him in an empty apartment. Far more.

"Can I sit down?"

Scooting farther over to one side, Maddie nodded.

"It's quiet out here at night," J.C. commented as he sat down.

Maddie tried not to think of his proximity, the length of his leg pressed next to her, the muscled arm that met hers.

He didn't say anything for minutes, the creaking of the swing the only discernable sound in the secluded garden. Maddie swiped nervous hands against her skirt as she tried to think of something neutral to say, something that wouldn't make him aloof.

"Quite a party today," J.C. told her.

"I think Chrissy liked it."

"Understatement." He looked up at the sky. "Only gravity kept her attached to the planet. She was floating on happiness all day."

Maddie was silenced by the poetry of his words... the appreciation.

"I didn't realize until today how much work a party is. I don't know how you made the time."

She shrugged. "I'm used to fitting a lot of different things into a day."

"Again, an understatement." He shifted, brushing her arm with his.

She swallowed.

"I almost forgot we have this little garden." J.C. glanced at the border of fuchsia and white azaleas. "I used to wonder why my mother poured so much time and energy into flowers that only bloomed two or three weeks a year. I know some varieties bloom for months, but ours didn't. Looking at them now…"

Maddie's gaze followed his. Between the light on the roof and the shimmer from the moon, she could see the delicate flowers. "The blossoms don't have to live forever. Every time I look at the bushes, I can picture the blooms long after they've fallen off."

"That doesn't surprise me."

She wondered what he meant. "I'm not sure—"

"You always try to see the best in every person and every thing."

Maddie inhaled deeply. "You think so?"

"You don't?"

Her throat dried.

"Maybe it's a Pollyanna complex…" he continued.

Jerking her chin up, she stared at him, wondering if he was teasing or mocking her.

"And maybe you're just a good person."

"I think I like the last description best." She'd intended to make the words crisp, instead her voice sounded husky.

J.C. leaned a fraction closer. "Me, too."

Was it the moonlight? Or the whisper of the stars? It couldn't be her attraction to J.C., the way he made her heart yearn, or her breath to shorten. Swallowing, she closed her eyes tight against the feelings that swamped her.

Yet she still sensed his hand hovering over hers. Along with the exquisite torture of wondering whether he would take it in his. When his fingers curled over hers, she gradually opened her eyes and slowly turned to meet his. Was that promise she saw in them? Afraid to look, even more afraid to turn away, she wondered. And hoped.

And prayed her hope wasn't in vain.

The days flew by. Chrissy, buoyed by a new attitude, continued her nature outings with J.C. and Maddie. Heartened by the success, Maddie suggested attending Girl Scouts again. Together they looked over the list of junior badges and decided to try Camp Together first. Samantha offered her large backyard and Emma brought over a tent.

Chrissy decided to invite Lillian, Samantha, Emma and her best friend, Lexi. Although Lillian couldn't stay in the tent through the night, Chrissy wanted her to have dinner and roasted marshmallows with them. Samantha had prepared her guest room so Lillian could have a comfortable night. Emma planned to stay for part of the evening and then go home to be with her children.

That left Maddie in charge of the girls. She thought of the campouts in her own backyard as a child. Her parents always made them special, memorable. By the time darkness fell, she imagined they were in a faraway, exotic spot. In the morning she was always surprised to find she was still in her own yard. She wanted to make the same kind of memories for Chrissy.

Knowing Chrissy loved beanie weenies—pork 'n' beans with sliced hot dogs—Maddie prepared them ahead, needing only to warm the pot on Sam's grill.

The campout was on Friday night. J.C. had to follow up on two surgical patients from that day, so Bret and Seth did the heavy lifting. They carried the fire pit from the patio so the girls could use it like a campfire, and then they set up the tent. Maddie thought the four-person tent was the perfect size—they could all fit inside, but it was small enough to be cozy.

The fire flickered cheerfully as they began dinner.

Sam took a bite, then lifted her eyebrows. "Beanie weenies, huh? I didn't know what to expect, but these are good."

Emma agreed. "Tastes like baked beans... I've made this and it never turns out...so good."

"Maddie makes it special," Chrissy informed her. "With stuff besides the beans and hot dogs."

Emma shook her head, ruminating. "Obviously it's the *stuff* that makes the difference."

"I just fiddle with the ingredients," Maddie replied.

"Next time you're fiddling, write down the recipe. My kids will be grateful," Emma said, then took another bite.

Smiling, Samantha caught Maddie's gaze, then subtly nodded toward Chrissy.

Maddie could guess what her friend was thinking. Chrissy looked happy, unconcerned, like any other ten-year-old. *Thank you, Lord.* He was bringing Chrissy around, healing her pain, giving her hope. Swallowing, Maddie realized how much the child had come to mean to her. She couldn't imagine how empty her life would be without Chrissy. Her stomach wrenched as she thought of the day J.C. would meet the right woman, get married, no doubt move away.

Samantha leaned close to whisper. "Are you okay?"

"Of course. Just glad we're all together."

Her friend didn't look completely convinced, but she couldn't delve deeper with the circle of women and girls listening.

As the sun set and darkness cloaked their little gathering, they chose sticks from the pile of mesquite that Samantha had collected. The girls were first to push their marshmallows on their sticks and hold them over the fire.

Maddie brought the makings for s'mores and she helped Lexi and Chrissy assemble their treats. She turned to the other women. "S'more?"

"Yes, please," Lillian agreed instantly.

Emma groaned. "I'll have to walk ten miles to wear all this off, but yes, I want one."

Samantha shook her head. "I'm a purist, no graham crackers or chocolate." She held her long stick over the fire. "I like my marshmallows almost incinerated."

Munching on their goodies, the evening quieted around them as neighbors settled into their houses and the already-lazy streets emptied.

"Stories," the girls chanted together.

Lillian eagerly took the challenge first, telling them the story of how Rosewood had been founded by German, Czech and Polish immigrants. Her voice was dreamy as she spoke, remembering tales her parents had passed down to her.

Maddie's heart filled with joy seeing her mother so

happy. J.C.'s treatment had improved her life beyond measure. Another blessing.

Night deepened and the stories segued into the scary variety. Nothing ghoulish, just enough to cause a few goose bumps. When Sam finished her second tale, she nudged Maddie. "Your turn."

Taking a deep breath, Maddie looked at the girls' expectant faces and began.

J.C. opened the door of his apartment. The shop downstairs had been shuttered, closed for the evening campout. Shrugging out of his jacket, he tossed it on the leather club chair. One Maddie had picked out, he mused, surprised the thought had sprung up. It had been a long day of surgery, office calls and hospital rounds. And he hadn't had time to do more than grab half a sandwich. Wandering into the kitchen, he opened the refrigerator. A sticky note with his name was secured to a foil-covered plate. Funny, he hadn't really eaten that often in his own apartment. Maddie cooked all their meals. Breakfast before school and work, dinner when they converged after their separate days.

Accustomed to a welcoming smile and a warm dinner, it was surprisingly quiet in the apartment. He peeled back the foil and stuck the plate in the microwave. When the timer beeped, he carried his dinner into the living room. The chicken enchiladas that Maddie had cooked for him were good, but he didn't have much of an appetite any longer. Considerate of her to think of his dinner when she had the whole campout to get ready.

Picking up the remote control, he flipped between channels, not seeing anything that held his interest. He clicked off the television. Again, the silence was disconcerting. No chatter from Chrissy. No laughter or snatches of murmured conversation from across the hall. Sighing, he realized this was how it would be someday. Chrissy would grow up, go away to college. Maddie…he didn't want to even consider where she might be then. An image of her with Owen Radley flashed in his mind. The man wasn't good enough for her. Not that he wanted to think of her with any other man, either.

Getting up from the club chair, J.C. paced the living room, pausing at the fireplace, remembering how they had discovered the first one in her apartment, crashing through the crumbling Sheetrock. How soft she had felt in his arms. And how soft her hand had been curled in his the night of Chrissy's party.

J.C. knew the thoughts would just torture him. Glancing over at the study alcove she had fixed up for him, he considered passing the evening catching up on paperwork. The thought held no appeal.

The emptiness of his home was as blaring as a siren. He'd lived on his own for years before Chrissy had become his responsibility. And he'd never had any trouble relaxing or finding plenty to do when he was alone. Two books sat on the coffee table, ones he had been meaning to read when he had some spare time. He picked up the text on parenting. Although he had been keen to study it, the pages didn't hold his interest. Maybe something lighter, the novel he had wanted to savor on a lazy evening. Switching books, he concentrated on the words. After ten minutes, he had reached only the bottom of the first page and he didn't have a clue what he had read. *What was wrong with him?*

Getting up, he forgot about the book in his lap and

it thudded to the floor, the sound overpowering in the silence. An image of Maddie's smile flashed in his thoughts. When she was planning this evening's campout, she'd been so excited that a person might have thought *she* was the junior Girl Scout. And she had been disappointed to learn he had to be at the hospital and couldn't attend the first part of the evening.

J.C. glanced across the hall. The door to Maddie's apartment was closed. Normally it was only closed at bedtime. Chrissy ran between both places as though it was one home. He supposed it was…when Maddie was there to make it so.

Maddie drew out her words, building the suspense. Chrissy and Lexi leaned forward, their eyes growing bigger, the light of the fire flickering over their faces. It was just the three of them. Samantha was inside and Emma had gone home. "The old lady had one favorite thing—a quilt she had made as a young woman. She worked for a seamstress who allowed her to keep scraps of the finest materials like silk and satin. The old lady had collected them until she had enough to sew this fine, fine quilt. Her friends and neighbors always admired it. One neighbor in particular was always after her to sell it to him. But the old lady didn't want that neighbor to have it. She sensed he wanted it so he could show it off and she wanted her treasure to be appreciated. One day the old lady fell and hurt her back. Because she didn't have anyone to care for her, she had to move into a nursing home. She wasn't even able to return home to retrieve her things, most especially her quilt."

Maddie paused, thinking that could have been her

own mother's fate. She cleared the lump in her throat. "Knowing this, the neighbor dashed in, took the prize quilt and hid it in his house. He spread the beautiful quilt over his bed, gloating at his success, finally turning off his lamp so he could sleep. His eyelids closed...." Maddie drew out the words slowly, building the girls' expectations. "Just as he was falling asleep, the quilt began to creep, ever so slowly, moving toward the end of the bed. He tugged at it, thinking the fine silk and satin was just sliding because of its slickness. He closed his eyes and the quilt crept away again. Reaching to tug at the quilt, he realized it was out of his reach. His eyelids flew open! And he sat up in bed and watched as the quilt continued creeping until it fell to the floor."

She paused for effect. "Deciding he was being silly, the man fetched a rough woolen blanket to place between his top sheet and the quilt. Settling back down he closed his eyes, determined to sleep the best he ever had, now that he possessed the quilt. Sleepy again, he started to drift off when the quilt ever so slowly began to creep down."

The girls swallowed, their eyes huge.

"He suddenly remembered the old lady's words— that the quilt knew its rightful master and it would never be him...."

Chrissy's mouth dropped open a bit.

"So..." Maddie stared at the girls "...the quilt began to crawl...."

Lexi and Chrissy huddled together.

Maddie lunged forward. "And landed right here!"

The girls jumped back as though expecting the quilt to materialize, scrambling to get away.

Laughing, Maddie hugged them both. "But we know that quilts can't crawl."

"You sure?" a deep male voice asked from close by.

Shrieking, Maddie and the girls leaped as though embers from the fire pit had scorched them.

J.C. chuckled. "Didn't mean to scare anyone."

Chrissy stomped her feet. *"Uncle James!"*

"Sorry, Pinker Belle, I just thought I'd come check on you, see how everything's going."

Maddie clutched her chest, trying to catch her breath. "I thought you had to be at the hospital."

J.C. shrugged. "Got done."

Their small faces scrunched in annoyance, the girls frowned at him.

"Didn't mean to interrupt…" He took one step backward.

Recovering, Maddie shook her head. "You aren't. We were just telling scary stories."

His face eased into a smile. "I heard."

Embarrassed, Maddie flushed, grateful for the darkness that disguised it. "Come sit down by the fire. We have plenty of marshmallows to roast."

"I didn't think I was hungry, but that sounds good."

She frowned. "Didn't you find the plate I left for you?"

"By the time I got home… I wasn't in the mood to eat."

"But you're hungry now?"

"Seems like it."

"We didn't have a fancy dinner, but we have plenty." She crossed the yard to the grill where she'd kept the pot over ebbing embers. "This is still warm." Scooping out a generous portion, she handed him a paper bowl and fork.

J.C. took a bite. "What is this?"

"Beanie weenies," she explained.

He took a second bite, then a third. "This is really good."

"It's pretty simple compared to the enchiladas."

"Maybe so, but it really hits the spot." He finished off the bowl, then asked for another serving which he finished in record time.

Across the campfire, the girls had begun to droop, although they were fighting sleep.

Maddie stuck marshmallows on two sticks and handed one to him. "Requisite dessert for campouts."

"Don't have to ask me twice."

Quiet descended, with only the sparks from the fire pit intruding. Nervous, Maddie tried to think of something to say. Truth was, she enjoyed the deepening shadows uninterrupted by words.

J.C. checked his marshmallow. "Hope this stick lasts long enough that I can practically burn my marshmallow."

"You, too," she murmured. "Samantha soaked the sticks in water so they would last longer."

"Clever."

"I have graham crackers and Hershey bars."

"Maybe on the next one. This smells too good." He turned the stick. "It's just about right."

Mesmerized by the length of his tall, muscled body, she forgot to watch her own stick.

"Whoa!" J.C. moved even closer, grabbing her stick and pulling it out of the fire. "Hope you like them really well-done."

The light flicked over the cleft in his chin, his sturdy jaw-line. And her breath quickened.

He turned toward her. "Do you?"

"What?"

J.C. smiled. "Like your marshmallow well-done?"

Could she really see the gold flecks in his eyes? Or was it night magic?

His gaze lowered and she realized his lips were only a hand span away from hers. Pewter beams of moonlight illuminated his face. *The flecks in his eyes were truly gold.* Forgetting to breathe, she inched closer.

"No!" Chrissy called out in her sleep.

Having forgotten the girls were still across from them, Maddie jerked back. Her throat worked and she struggled to speak, her words coming out in tiny puffs. "The story."

His eyes continued to search hers. "Story?"

"The scary story…about…the quilt. I should check on the girls." She swallowed. "Get them in the tent for the night."

J.C. remained silent, his eyes locked with hers.

Chrissy stirred, her bad dream apparently continuing.

"I have to…" she began.

He exhaled. "I know." But he didn't pull away. His fingers cupped her chin.

She wanted to lean into his embrace…his kiss. Reality hit like a wash of frigid water. What was she doing?

Rising in one accelerated motion, she left his side, rushing to check on the girls. Her back to him, she wiped away the tears she couldn't stop, any more than she could suppress the splintering of her heart. To have him so close, to imagine what it would be like if they could form a family. Knowing it couldn't happen… Tears pooled, wetting her cheeks, ripping open her heart.

Chapter Fourteen

Maddie lingered over the calico pioneer dresses in the costume shop. She could picture Chrissy wearing a small version of the dress at the harvest festival, one that would match her own. Sighing, she pushed the thoughts out of her mind. Chrissy wasn't hers to outfit and it was dangerous to keep going down that road.

Since the night of the campout she was having to remind herself of that every single day, often every hour of those days. What if? she kept wondering. What if?

"You thinking about renting one of those?" Tina asked as she waved goodbye to the customer she had been assisting.

Maddie gave a quick, tight shake of her head. "Wrong time of year anyway."

"Oh, I don't know, women rent them all year long." Tina straightened the bonnet's ties. "So, what brings you here?"

Pulling a check from her pocket, Maddie extended it to her. "My second payment."

Tina held up her hands. "No need."

Baffled, Maddie drew her eyebrows together. "I don't understand."

"Your account's paid in full."

"That can't be." Then she thought of her silent partner. "Don't tell me J.C. paid it off!"

"Actually, I can't tell you anything."

Maddie stared at her.

Tina's face scrunched in apology. "The person who paid said I had to keep it anonymous. I really thought you'd know who it is."

"Well...narrowing it down can't be too difficult." Maddie ran through the abbreviated list. J.C., Samantha, possibly Emma. Realizing Tina still felt uncomfortable, Maddie tried to recover. "Hey, it's a good thing. I'm just surprised and overwhelmed. I love the costumes. I have two more tea parties booked for this weekend."

The worry didn't leave Tina's face. "You sure you're okay with this? I wouldn't have agreed otherwise. I thought it was a nice surprise."

"It *is* a nice surprise," Maddie insisted. She held up the check. "This can go a long way toward increasing the accessory inventory, which is something I've really wanted to do."

Not completely convinced, Tina gave her a half-hearted smile. "In the future, if you still want us to supply costumes, I'll check with you first on anything to do with your account."

Wishing she hadn't made Tina feel bad, Maddie reached out to hug her. "Of course this is where I'll always order my costumes. They are perfect and so is the way you've handled things. Now, don't think about it for another second, okay? Or I'll feel terrible."

Tina's face cleared. "In that case..."

"Come over later for some lunch," Maddie told her, walking toward the door. "I made some killer chicken salad."

"You don't have to twist my arm," Tina replied.

Once out on the sidewalk, Maddie's smile disappeared. What had J.C. been thinking? She wanted...no, needed to make the shop succeed. The start-up money was one thing, but he couldn't bail her out every time she made an investment in the business. What would happen when he was gone and she had to handle things on her own? The thought pierced her very being. Tears blinding her vision, Maddie rushed the rest of the way to her shop, hating that she had to confront J.C.

J.C. dashed up the stairs, eager to get home. Since the night of the campout, when he realized how lonely he was in the empty apartment, he had developed a new appreciation for everything Maddie did for them. And he resolved to put the past behind him. Maddie was nothing like his ex-wife. It had been unfair to compare them.

Shedding his jacket and briefcase in his own apartment, he could hear Chrissy's chirpy voice and the far quieter replies from Lillian. Inhaling the scent of what he guessed was roast chicken, his stomach rumbled.

"I'm winning!" Chrissy announced as he walked into the Carters' entry hall.

Glancing her way, J.C. saw that she and Lillian were playing checkers. "Watch out." He winked. "Mrs. Lillian's pretty cagey."

Chrissy scrunched her nose at him, then grinned.

He followed his nose to the wonderful aromas in the kitchen. "Smells delicious."

"Just roasted chicken and potatoes." Maddie didn't

turn around, adding black olives to a bowl filled with lettuce and sliced tomatoes. "And this salad."

"Do you want me to set the table?"

"Chrissy already did it."

J.C. glanced toward the living room. "Did Chrissy give you a hard time about it?"

"No. She sets the table every day, it's one of her chores."

J.C. had barely been able to get his niece to attend school. He wished Maddie would turn around so he could see her face. Sharp beams of late-afternoon sunlight lit her strawberry-blond hair. Wanting to reach out and touch the soft waves, instead he wandered over to the refrigerator and grabbed a root beer. "What kind of salad dressing do you want?"

"I made a vinaigrette." She finally turned toward him. "Will you tell Chrissy and my mother that we're ready?"

Her face was so expressionless, he started to ask if anything was wrong, then he remembered that Lillian and Chrissy were close by. They were just finishing their game of checkers when he walked back into the living room. Chrissy hopped up and rushed into the kitchen while he offered his arm to Lillian.

"Thank you, young man," she said with old-fashioned gentility.

"My pleasure." When they reached the table, Chrissy was filling the water glasses.

As had become their habit, he blessed the food. Passing the salad around, Chrissy chattered about her day. Lillian picked the black olives from her salad and gave them to Chrissy because they were one of the child's favorites.

Maddie offered the carving knife and fork to him. He sliced some white and dark meat, severing a drumstick for Chrissy. She remained a live wire and Lillian smiled at the child's silliness. But Maddie was unusually quiet. Not silent, just quiet. Maybe she'd had a rough day in the shop. Orders sometimes went amiss and even in Rosewood customers could be cranky.

"Can I have chicken salad in my sandwich again tomorrow?" Chrissy asked.

"If that's what you want," Maddie replied.

"It's yummy." Chrissy turned to him. "Maddie puts dried cranberries in it and it's really good."

"And she uses roasted chicken instead of boiled," Lillian added. "That makes a big difference."

He glanced at the roast chicken they were having for dinner.

Maddie nodded. "It's easier if I coordinate the sandwich fillings to what we're eating for dinner."

"I'm so hungry I could have eaten a plate of boiled cabbage," he replied.

She smiled, but it was a small, reserved smile.

"But I'm glad it's chicken." He stabbed a bite. "How did things go in the shop today?"

Shrugging, Maddie reached for the potatoes. "Fine."

"Nothing out of the ordinary?" he persisted.

A strange look entered her eyes and her lips thinned to a line. "No."

He glanced over at his niece and Lillian. Whatever was on Maddie's mind would have to wait until later in the evening after both had been tucked in bed.

By the time they had eaten and Chrissy reluctantly surrendered the book she was reading, J.C. was anxious to find out what was the matter with Maddie. He tried to think of all the possibilities, but came up blank. He waited what he hoped was long enough for Maddie to get her mother settled in for the night. Chrissy was asleep, so he left only a few lights on, propping open his apartment door so he could hear if she woke up and needed him.

Maddie sat alone in her living room. The television was off and she wasn't reading as she often did.

"Lillian asleep?"

"Yes." She looked up at him. "Have a seat."

Choosing the closest chair to her, he hoped she wouldn't dance around the problem.

"J.C.," she began. Knitting her hands together, she pressed until the tips of her fingers whitened. "I went to Try It On today."

He waited.

"The costume shop," she explained.

"And?"

She glanced down, then pressed her fingers even tighter. "It was a very kind gesture, but you can't keep funding everything."

Baffled, he drew his eyebrows together.

"The costumes," she continued. "I know you paid the outstanding balance in full."

J.C. blinked.

"Tina told me."

"Maddie—"

"It's not that I don't appreciate the thought, but I have to know if the Tea Cart can succeed without a benefactor." She looked pained, upset. "I have to think of the future."

Of the dozens of possibilities that had run through

his mind, this one hadn't even made it to the list. "Before you go on, I didn't pay off the costumes."

"But..." Her mouth remained open, then she bit down on her lower lip. "I was sure it had to be you."

"Nope."

Her eyes darkened. "Then who?"

He wanted to know, as well.

"I'm sorry, J.C. I just assumed..." She shook her head, short rapid nods. "I can't imagine..." She exhaled. "I feel terrible. I've been worried...well, anyway, sorry."

"You really don't have anyone else in mind?" The happiness he'd been feeling the past few weeks drained at an incredible rate.

Slowly she shook her head.

Immediately, J.C. thought of Owen Radley. The man had the money...and definitely the motive. Seeing the remorse in Maddie's eyes, J.C. wanted to discard the thought, wished it away, but it stayed, planted so firmly he knew it was all he would think about. Not even the gray in Maddie's eyes softening to blue could chase it away.

Unable to leave the Tea Cart, Maddie called Samantha who agreed to come over. Two tables of women had come in just after the shop opened and were lingering over their tea and scones. Normally, Maddie would have been delighted with the early business, but she had hoped to have the place to herself so she and Samantha could talk.

Lillian sat at her usual spot, crocheting. Every single day at least one of the ladies in her Sunday school class came by to visit.

The bell over the door jangled and Maddie was relieved to see Samantha. Dispensing with the usual niceties, she waved Samantha over.

Sam sniffed the air. "Is that the cheesecake kind of filling you put in some of the pastries?"

Maddie pulled her behind the counter.

"I was just asking," Samantha muttered. "Don't I even get tea?"

Grabbing the hot water, Maddie dumped in some of the blend she'd prepared for the last customer. "It has to steep, okay?"

"Silly me. I thought that's what we did here—drink tea and—"

"Sorry," Maddie apologized. "Of course you can have some tea. It's just…"

The teasing left Samantha's eyes. "What's wrong?"

"Nothing's wrong. But I do need to ask you something."

"Shoot."

"Sam, did you pay off my account at the costume shop?"

"What gave you that idea?"

Maddie tried to temper her impatience. "I really need to know."

"No, I didn't pay anything at the costume shop."

"You're sure?" Maddie persisted. Samantha wasn't just her best friend, she was also one of the few people who knew about her payment arrangement at Try It On.

"I think I would remember something like that!" She scrunched her brow. "Oh, I bet it was J.C."

Maddie shook her head. "I already asked him. His expression matched yours—clueless."

"Did you just insult me?"

"Funny." Maddie sighed. "Sam, *somebody* paid my account in full."

Samantha started to speak.

But Maddie cut her off. "No, Tina won't tell me. Whoever it was said they wanted to remain anonymous."

Samantha scratched her head. "And you're absolutely positive it wasn't J.C.?"

"He wants to know who did."

A knowing look settled across Samantha's face. "I bet he does."

Samantha and her happy endings. "It's not like that."

"Uh-huh." Then her expression changed to a frown. "Do you suppose it was Owen?"

"Owen?"

"Think about it. He has the money. It wouldn't even put a dent in his wallet. And the weird way he's been acting ever since you opened the shop..."

"That's too weird even for him. Besides, how would he know about my account at the costume shop?"

Samantha's expression remained somber. "I've always heard that rich people have their fingers in every pie. At the least, they know everything that's going on. Your birthday tea parties are being talked about all over town. If I remember right, the last time he came in before Chrissy's party, you didn't have the costumes. And we know he showed up that day and must have seen them. It doesn't take a genius to make the next leap in logic. Try It On is the only costume shop for hundreds of miles."

"It's ridiculous. I told him in no uncertain terms that our relationship is completely in the past. What would he gain from this?"

"A way to worm into your life." Samantha still looked worried. "I didn't want to say anything, but I've been asking around about Owen. Since I was gone from Rosewood for years, I didn't have any idea what he'd been up to. Apparently, he's spent just about as much time away from here as I did. And I got the same answer from everybody I asked about whether he had married, gotten engaged. There hasn't been anyone in his life since you two broke up."

Maddie frowned. "He must have kept it quiet. And maybe the woman lives somewhere else, somewhere he travels to."

"That's not the impression I got."

Noticing that one of the customers was trying to catch her attention, Maddie had to leave the speculation unfinished. Several new customers came in, so Samantha pitched in and helped. Still, it took a while to prepare the new orders. As Maddie was arranging heart-shaped sandwiches on the last plate, Emma stopped in.

Samantha noticed, too, and guided Emma to a table situated away from the other customers.

Maddie hurried, delivering the plate of sandwiches and refilling a few cups. Not wanting to look as though she was pouncing on Emma, she slowed her rapid steps. "Hi. Do you want to start with tea?"

"No. Samantha said you needed to talk. What's up?"

Maddie cringed. "Sam didn't need to say anything."

Emma looked concerned.

"Guess I'll just spit it out." Maddie took a deep breath. "Emma, did you pay off my account for the costumes? Or make some kind of arrangement with Tina so I didn't owe anymore?"

"You mean someone paid it off?"

Maddie's heart sank. "Then it wasn't you?"

"You know what? I bet J.C.—"

"He was the first person I asked. It's really got me baffled."

"Tina must know—"

"Sworn to silence. I already made her feel bad about not being able to tell me." Maddie held up her hands, ticking off each name on progressive fingers. "It's not J.C. or Samantha or you."

Sam jumped in with her suggestion. "I told her I thought it was Owen Radley."

Emma frowned. "I've heard a lot about him." Not being a native of Rosewood she didn't automatically know everyone. But there was something in her tone…

"Like what?" Maddie asked.

Emma fiddled with the salt cellar. "Seth did some business with him. Even though the Radleys have a lot of money to spend, Seth doesn't want to work for him again."

"Owen's been acting weird ever since Maddie opened the shop," Samantha confided.

Maddie sent her friend a pointed gaze.

"Well, he *has!*" Samantha insisted. "They went together in high school and college, even got engaged. When Maddie wouldn't put Lillian in a nursing home, he gave her an ultimatum—her mother or him. Now he acts as though he still has a claim on Maddie."

Worry stirred in Emma's eyes. "People like that can be dangerous. You both know what I lost…" The memory of her murdered husband and child chilled the air. "And that the guy who was after me nearly killed me here in Rosewood. I don't want to scare you, Maddie, but you never know what drives some people."

Maddie hated that she had caused Emma to think about that terrible time in her life. Good grief, she was talking about someone paying a bill, not committing murder. Clearly, she had overreacted. "Emma, I used to know Owen really well. I don't believe he would hurt me or anyone else. If anything, he's just a lot of hot air."

The worry didn't leave Emma's face. "I hope you're right." Briefly she closed her eyes, then swallowed. "And I didn't mean to scare you unnecessarily. But please be careful. I wish I could have been warned."

Maddie took Emma's hand. "I'll be careful. I promise." She made herself smile brightly. "Maybe I have a secret admirer or benefactor. I should be grateful instead of making a fuss. Now, I'm going to get tea for all of us. I've got some of those apple tartlets you like, Emma. Be right back."

Maddie brought the tea and pastries, checked on her customers and kept her smile in place. All the while she wondered. The pit in her stomach told her this wasn't over. What worried her was that her intuition was usually right on. And now it was saying trouble.

Chapter Fifteen

❧

J.C. reworked his schedule so he could take the day off. Chrissy had a school project—to collect aquatic bugs. It was a good opportunity to connect with nature and strengthen her faith. When Chrissy invited Maddie, Samantha offered to take care of the Tea Cart so that she could join them.

Although they'd had a fair-size rainstorm earlier in the week, the sun was bright, the day clear. With underground springs from aquifers populating the land, it was easy to find creeks and streams for Chrissy's school project.

His SUV handled the hilly terrain, still they bumped along. But he didn't mind when Maddie occasionally pitched near him.

"There it is!" Chrissy sang out from the backseat.

J.C. parked and Chrissy practically flew out of the vehicle. He opened the back cargo door and started unloading everything they had packed, which was quite an assortment.

Chrissy held up her list importantly, checking the

first item. "Everybody wore safe shoes." She glanced at them.

Maddie stuck out one foot clad in an old running shoe.

Chrissy looked pointedly at J.C., so he extended his waterproof hunting boot.

She checked the box on her project list. "Forceps?"

J.C. held up three pairs of tweezers.

"I have the magnifying glasses and nets," Maddie offered.

Carefully Chrissy marked those boxes on the paper. "I have the pans to hold the bugs and pencils so we can write down what we find."

"And the list," J.C. couldn't resist adding.

"And the list," Chrissy repeated seriously.

Maddie's gaze slid toward him, her lips clamped shut so she wouldn't laugh.

"Everybody needs to have forceps, a net and a magnifying glass."

Following Chrissy's directions they all swapped until everyone had one of each. Allowing Chrissy to take the lead, they followed her to the stream.

"We have to be careful," Chrissy instructed. "And when you turn over rocks to find bugs, you have to put the rocks back just like they were."

This time J.C. caught Maddie's gaze. Both glanced away so they wouldn't erupt in laughter and hurt Chrissy's feelings.

Wading into the shallow water, they each looked for rocks to upturn. While Maddie concentrated on finding bugs, J.C. found himself concentrating on her. The bright sunshine made her strawberry-blond hair look golden. He liked the casual way it fell over her shoulders and glinted in the light. If they were panning for gold, he'd know just where to find it.

"Uncle James!" Chrissy's eyebrows pulled together in disapproval. "You have to look *under* the rocks."

So he did. Not wanting Maddie to realize he had been studying her, J.C. flipped over a rock. But he didn't slide the net carefully along the sandy bottom as Chrissy had instructed them on the drive to the stream. Instead, he wondered how Maddie felt about Owen Radley. Were they in a relationship? And if they were, why didn't she say something? Was it possible they were keeping their relationship quiet because of Lillian? Maybe Maddie didn't want Lillian to feel like a burden…that she was keeping the couple apart.

But *Owen Radley?* Just thinking about the man left a bad taste in his mouth. Maddie could do so much better. So much…

J.C. didn't hold himself up as some sort of perfect match, but he couldn't stomach the idea of Maddie with Owen. She deserved…she deserved the very best, someone who would not only love her, but cherish her, appreciate every wonderful quality she possessed. The epiphany hit him like a club to the head—it was just how he felt about Maddie. Despite his mistrust, despite her possible feelings for Owen, his feelings had grown.

But how did Maddie feel? If anything at all. An image of Owen's bullying face intruded. Blindly, J.C. reached for a rock, colliding with Maddie who was already holding the same stone. Their hands brushed and he wanted to hold hers close.

Maddie watched him, her eyes a magical mix of blue, green and gray, reflecting the water, the sky, the fields of wild grasses. Vulnerable, they exposed a glimpse into her thoughts. Or was he just imagining what he wanted to see? When she didn't pull away, he absorbed every nuance of her expression, the velvety texture of her skin, the dimple that dared him to kiss her cheek.

If his niece wasn't standing twenty feet from them, he would accept that invitation, learn for himself if her skin was as soft as it looked, her lips as welcoming.

Standing so close, he could see Maddie's throat working, the uncertainty in her trembling hands. *Share your secrets!*

"When we get enough bugs," Chrissy called out, "I have to collect some leaves for extra credit." She pointed toward the sloping hill. "From up there. I have a plastic bag in my pocket."

If he could give in to irresponsibility, J.C. would have suggested she go on her own. But it wasn't part of his makeup. "Okay."

"Did you…" Maddie began, then cleared her voice. "Did you get any bugs?"

J.C. looked down into his shallow, empty pan. "Not yet."

"Oh."

They both knew they weren't talking about bugs, but the difficult words remained unsaid.

"I found a snail!" Chrissy announced.

Maddie continued to hold his gaze.

"I'm going to write it on my sheet."

"Good idea," he replied, his voice raspy.

"Yes," Maddie agreed in a breathless whisper.

"Did you find anything yet?" Chrissy persisted.

Reluctantly J.C. withdrew his hand and straightened up so he could see Chrissy. "I'm still looking."

"I have to collect at least three," she replied. "And a sample of moss if we can find any."

Maddie's hand still shook as she turned over the rock they'd both touched. "Maybe there'll be one under here." But she glanced up at him rather than down at the creek bed.

J.C. didn't want to move, but made himself search for another rock. It took a while, but between them, they found four different bugs that Chrissy could catalog.

Wading out of the stream, Maddie nearly slipped, then righted herself. "I guess my running shoes weren't the best choice. Wrong kind of traction, I guess."

Climbing the slope to search for leaves was a little trickier than it appeared. The rain had softened the soil, making it slippery. Chrissy clambered up like a monkey. J.C. had decent traction with his hunting boots, but he kept his pace slow to watch out for Maddie. On dry ground her shoes would have been fine. But they weren't meant to dig in to wet soil. Near the top, he turned and extended his hand.

Maddie accepted, her soft skin seeming to meld into his. He wasn't sure if the quivering he felt was in her hand or his heart.

"Look! A rainbow!" Chrissy pointed to the sky.

J.C. didn't turn, keeping his gaze on Maddie. "Yes, beautiful."

Her hand definitely trembled in his.

"Come here, you all," Chrissy insisted. "It might go away before you see it."

"I don't think so," J.C. replied so quietly that only Maddie could hear.

With the ever-changing attention of a ten-year-old, Chrissy had abandoned the rainbow by the time they looked toward the sky. She had begun scavenging for leaves. Because it was spring, there were new leaves on the trees and remnants of those that had fallen in autumn and winter. Chrissy seemed determined to collect each and every kind.

"She wants enough to fill a big poster board," Maddie whispered. "It's for extra credit, but she wants it to be the best one in her class."

The fact that his niece did was incredible. Before her turnaround, she had failed two subjects. Maddie's gentle care had healed Chrissy in a way that no psychologist's sessions could have.

"The rainbow really is something," she continued, looking upward. "I think this outing is perfect for Chrissy, for her to feel the connection between the Lord and what He created."

J.C. watched Chrissy twirl in the leaves, then reach toward one of the low-hanging branches. "I can't help wondering whether I should have taken Chrissy to more counseling. If I had, she might have started healing sooner. She didn't want to go and after refusing to speak during the first three appointments, I couldn't see much point in continuing."

"I think you did the right thing," Maddie assured him. "She needed a home, not a counselor. Since she's improving, I can't see reconsidering your decision."

"Back then, especially as a medical professional…"

"You're also her uncle and you'd just lost your sister. Being a doctor doesn't make you immune to your feelings."

"Most people think it does," J.C. admitted. "As though because I've lost patients before, it doesn't bother me when I lose another. It's a big deal every time."

"Your patients should be grateful you feel that way." Maddie's eyes, large and luminescent, filled with empathy. "Look at how you've cared for Mom. I was afraid to hope that she would stop worsening. I know it's not the same as before her stroke, but..." Her lips wobbled. "It's a miracle."

"What's a miracle?" Chrissy questioned.

"I didn't see you, sweetheart." Maddie swiped at her cheeks. "The miracle is how much better Mrs. Lillian is since your Uncle James has been taking care of her." She encircled Chrissy's shoulders with one arm. "And like the rainbow you just showed us, it's a sign of the Lord working in our lives."

Sobered, Chrissy stared at her uncle.

"Do you see it, Pinker Belle?" he asked quietly.

"I think so. I just wish..."

Maddie tightened her hold on Chrissy's shoulders. "Losing someone is really hard. When my dad passed away...it hurt. A lot. But the Lord kept watching out for us, brought you and your uncle into our lives."

Chrissy scrunched her forehead. "I still wish Mom and Dad were here."

"Of course you do! Want to know something? I still dream about my dad all the time, but in a good way. He's always happy, healthy."

"Does he smile?" Chrissy asked cautiously.

"Yes, he does."

"I had a dream sorta like that."

J.C. smoothed her hair. "Your parents would be happier knowing you trust the Lord again."

Chrissy blinked. "I want that."

Maddie took a shaky breath and met J.C.'s eyes. "You can tell the Lord about it in your prayers."

Considering this, Chrissy finally nodded. "Okay." She scampered toward a copse of slender trees.

"There's nothing as simple or complex as a child's thinking," J.C. remarked. "She questions the deepest meanings, yet can accept just like that."

"Life would be a lot less complicated if we could keep that reasoning with us as adults," Maddie mused.

J.C. wished that were true, as well. Then he could understand what was in Maddie's head, know whether he was chasing a fantasy.

"Are you guys going to help?" Chrissy called out.

The moment to ask was gone. He and Maddie headed toward the trees to pick out specimens for the poster. It didn't take very long to fill Chrissy's bag with leaves. She started toward the slope, getting ready to climb down.

"Chrissy, let's go back the way we came. The soil's not all that stable. At least we know what we faced climbing up." He led the way back to the spot above the stream. "I'll go first. That way if anyone takes a tumble, I can block you from falling all the way." The footing was mushy, but J.C. didn't have any trouble. Glancing back regularly, he could see Maddie and Chrissy following. About ten feet from the bottom, he heard an unexpected whoosh.

"Watch out!" Maddie hollered as she slipped.

He turned, seeing that she was sliding toward him rapidly. Planting his feet in a solid brace, he reached out to catch her. Although she was a small person, she was moving fast, far too fast for the waterlogged hillside.

J.C. caught her, but his feet didn't hold in the shifting soil. Clutching Maddie close, they slid the rest of the way, landing at the edge of the stream.

Maddie was in his arms. Finally. Unlike the day they'd crashed into each other in the fireplace, she didn't pull away. She was so close he could count the freckles peppering her nose, touch the softness of her cheeks, feel the whisper of her breath. Like a gift from the heavens, she was the woman he had waited for all his life.

Wanting to never let her go, he didn't turn around when Chrissy hollered, "Whoo-hoo!"

He was near enough to fit his lips to Maddie's, to see if she would reciprocate. Angling his head, he was knocked off balance when Chrissy flew on top of him, tangling her limbs with theirs. Arms, legs and torsos collided, then went askew as they all toppled into the water.

"Are you all right?" J.C. questioned his niece.

She giggled. "Uh-huh."

"Maddie?"

Maddie tried to sit up. "I think so." Rubbing her arm, she nodded. "Just bumped it against a rock."

Ignoring his emotions, J.C. examined her arm. "It's not broken, unless there's a minor stress fracture."

"Really, it's fine," Maddie insisted. "It'll probably bruise. No big deal."

J.C. turned to Chrissy. "Does anything hurt? Legs? Arms? Your head?"

"Nope. You and Maddie were good padding."

The laughter they'd held in all day exploded.

"What's so funny?" Chrissy demanded.

"Nothing, *Stinker* Belle," J.C. answered when he caught his breath. "Glad we could be of service."

She looked at them suspiciously.

"And I bet you collected more leaves than anyone else in your class," Maddie added.

Distracted, Chrissy's suspicion evaporated. "I got four kinds of bugs. Some of the boys were just going to dig up earthworms and try to find ants."

"Do you mean we didn't have to wade into the stream?" J.C. questioned.

Chrissy shrugged. "To find water bugs you do. I thought that'd be way cooler than worms and ants."

J.C. extended a helping hand to Maddie so they could stand. "Ants and worms, huh? Let's hope when she studies astronomy she doesn't have us try to hitch a ride on the space shuttle."

Maddie hummed as she cleaned one of the round tables in the shop. Monday afternoons were usually quiet, but she didn't mind. It was a good day to stock the shelves, check what she needed to order. Glancing out the front window, she saw Samantha and waved, always happy when her friend dropped by.

"Hello, Lillian!" Samantha said brightly. "How are you today?"

"I'm just fine, young lady." Lillian held up her crocheting. "As bright as this red yarn."

Samantha grinned. "And you, Maddie?"

"Sunflower yellow!"

"I think I've stumbled onto a rainbow."

Grabbing Samantha's favorite blend of tea, Maddie allowed herself a dreamy smile.

"Something I said?" Sam reached for two cups and saucers.

"Just thinking about how much fun we had on Chrissy's outing to collect bugs."

Samantha wrinkled her nose. "I love everything in a garden, but I never thought of you as the bug type."

Laughing, Maddie placed Sam's favorite cookies on a dish. "Now, I'd like to see the woman who admits to being the *bug type*."

"Fair point. Want to sit near the window? Or in the back nook? Unless Lillian's expecting company?"

"Doesn't matter."

"My, we are in a good mood." Samantha wiggled her eyebrows. "Anything you want to share?"

"Isn't it amazing how life can change without you expecting it to? In a good way, I mean?"

Samantha's eyes softened. "Like my reuniting with Bret... It's beyond amazing."

"Beyond..." Maddie precariously balanced her burgeoning emotions. "I don't think I've ever been this happy." And she never wanted the feeling to change.

Chapter Sixteen

J.C. was glad for the short lull in patients. The previous week had been packed. Punching up his calendar on the laptop, he glanced at the afternoon lineup. Frowning, he read Owen Radley's name as the first appointment after lunch. He pushed the intercom button. "Didi? Why is Owen Radley on today's schedule?"

There were a series of clicks as she referenced the schedule on her computer. "He made an appointment for a consultation."

"What are his symptoms?"

A few more clicks. "He didn't say. He specified a consultation, not an exam."

"Thanks, Didi." J.C. turned off his intercom. It wasn't difficult to guess what the other man had on his mind, and it wasn't neurological in nature. Glancing at his watch, he saw that Owen would be arriving in minutes. Too late to cancel the appointment. As much as he dreaded what the other man had to say, J.C. also wanted all the facts. He and Maddie had danced around them far too long already.

Didi knocked briskly on his door. "Mr. Radley's here, Dr. M."

Once Owen was inside, she discreetly closed the door.

"Have a seat." J.C. didn't waste a smile or words of phony cordiality.

Owen took the chair closest to J.C. "I'll get right to the point."

J.C. waited.

"I want to buy the Wagner Hill building." Owen opened his briefcase. "My attorney has drawn up an offer." He extended the papers.

"The Wagner Hill isn't for sale."

"Read the proffered amount."

J.C. reluctantly accepted the document, scanning it until he saw the proposed price. It was sixty percent over the appraised value. J.C. was certain of it because an appraisal had been necessary for the estate distribution. "Why the Wagner Hill?"

"How many buildings are for sale on Main Street?" Owen countered, clearly knowing there weren't any.

J.C. didn't believe for a minute that the offer was related to real estate.

"I intend to create a museum of living history, Rosewood's history."

"That doesn't sound very profitable."

Owen didn't blink. "I understand your skepticism. But along with wealth comes obligation. This generation of my family's legacy."

"Understandable, but as I said, the Wagner Hill isn't for sale."

"Would you rather see a superstore in its place?" Owen's already-hard eyes deadened. "Because that's the only other buyer that'll be interested. That or a T-shirt and mug shop that I suspect would draw in the tourists."

"The point's moot. If the building isn't sold, nothing has to replace it."

"Are you certain that's what your niece will decide once she's in charge of her own estate? Young women these days aren't always keen on keeping traditions in place."

"What Chrissy wants to do with the Wagner Hill is her choice and I'll respect it."

Owen leaned forward a fraction. "But are you respecting her estate now? That offer will ensure her financial future. Do you feel comfortable rejecting it out of hand?"

J.C. despised the man's smug expression, but he couldn't deny the truth in his words.

"Why don't I leave it with you for now? I'm sure the best interests of your niece will be your primary consideration." Owen rose. "I'll see myself out."

Even after Owen was gone, his oppressive imprint lingered. J.C. swivelled his chair toward the window, needing air, fresh, untainted air.

The price Owen dangled stuck in his mind as though carved of granite and painted in neon orange. It would do more than pay for Chrissy's education. Owen's offer would allow Chrissy to pursue whatever she might want, a business, travel, a charitable foundation.

And J.C. couldn't dispute the value of a living history museum. The town as a whole had decided long ago that they wanted Rosewood to retain its thriving local economy, encouraging entrepreneurs to keep their businesses. That didn't happen in towns that allowed superstores to invade, undercutting prices, driving small business owners to bankruptcy.

Rosewood didn't welcome a tourist economy, either. It was difficult to keep the integrity of their community when constantly pandering to tourists to keep afloat. Of course, some of their business partially came from tourists, like the bed and breakfast and eating places. But those businesses were locally owned. Many of the tourists they served were regulars who came back year after year because they appreciated the town's inherent difference. Wildflower season bloomed with visitors that they welcomed like old friends. But this... The prospect of changing Rosewood into a clone of other overtaken towns was bitter.

But it was the other factor, as welcome as the plague, that worried him most. How did Maddie play into this offer? Did she know what Owen was up to? That prospect was sickening. The lovely woman who had brought laughter and warmth into his home, his life... Could she have been part of this?

J.C. stayed late at the office, prolonging his arrival home. Although the shop was shuttered, as usual Maddie had left two lamps on, a soft welcoming glow. Locking the front door behind him, J.C. instantly thought of the night Owen had brazenly trespassed.

His feet dragged as he climbed the stairs. Chatter, laughter and cooking smells floated toward him. He had phoned to let Maddie know he wouldn't be home in time for dinner. She always kept a plate for him in the warming drawer of the oven. The night the ladies had all been gone to the campout flashed in J.C.'s thoughts.

Lonely. The heart of the home had been gone and he had desperately missed it.

Swallowing, he wondered how he would ever fare on his own again. Stupid thought! He had lived by himself for years. But that was before he met Maddie.

As usual, the doors to both apartments were propped open. Loosening his tie, he chose to enter Maddie's first. She spotted him and smiled.

Then her gaze landed on his briefcase. "Did you bring a lot of work home?"

He took the easy way out, shifting the case in his hands. "Enough to keep me busy all night."

Her smile remained constant. "Understandable. I have inventory to work on myself."

J.C. couldn't stand making small talk when there was such an important issue to air. "Fair enough. Chrissy—"

"She's helping Mom with her crocheting." Maddie glanced over at them, lowering her voice. "I think everything's coming out circle shaped." She grinned. "Excellent pot holders."

Although he tried, J.C. couldn't force a smile. "Good practice."

Maddie met his gaze. "Is anything wrong?"

He looked at the concern in her eyes, wishing he could see straight through to her soul. "Should there be?"

"Why…no. Of course not." Maddie's smile faded as she tightened her hold on a dish towel.

"Is Chrissy okay over here for a while?"

Her brow furrowed. "Sure."

Unable to hold up his end of the conversation any longer, J.C. left. The prospect of wading through his thoughts was almost worse, but he couldn't fence with

Maddie. She looked concerned, wounded. And despite Owen Radley and all his implications, J.C. couldn't bear to hurt her.

Maddie watched until J.C. disappeared inside his apartment. Although he didn't completely close the door, he pulled it from its propped open position so that barely a foot of it remained open. Why did he want to shut himself away? Torment was written in his eyes, his face, even his voice. What could it be? Thoughts whirling, she considered the possibilities. There literally was no family of his left that could be ill or in trouble. Friends? She would have heard through the grapevine about their mutual friends in Rosewood. Of course, he had friends from college and med school. Maybe...

It struck her. A patient. She remembered J.C.'s words about how losing one hurt just as much every time. Before she could change her mind, Maddie sped across the hall, knocking quietly on his door.

Silence. Then the scraping of shoes as he got up, the footfalls as he approached. J.C. pushed the door open wider.

Maddie placed one hand on his. "I know, J.C."

He stared at her with utter bleakness.

"I'm so sorry. I know how deeply this affects you."

"Maddie?" His voice was hoarse, gravelly.

"Losing a patient... I know how you suffer."

J.C. glanced down.

"I'll keep you in my prayers. I hope you can think instead about all the patients you've helped, like Samantha and Mom. Now, I'll let you be alone. But remember, you don't have to be...alone, I mean. I'm just across the hall." She patted his hand a final time, then turned to cross the hall. Oddly, she thought she felt his gaze on her back the entire time. But not wanting to intrude on his emotions, she kept her face forward, hoping her words had helped.

As the days passed, J.C. couldn't shake Owen's insinuations. Or Maddie's overwhelming concern. Working until late every evening, he made sure he wasn't home until long after dinner was eaten. And each evening she left a special meal in his refrigerator. But his appetite had disappeared.

J.C.'s staff had begun to notice. He waved away their concern. But today Didi had brought him one of his favorites from the café, hoping to tempt him into eating. He had to do something.

Seth McAllister was his only friend who also knew Maddie fairly well. Fortunately, Seth had time to meet with him, so J.C. drove over to his current work site, an old Victorian home, to talk.

The oak-lined, brick-paved street was in the oldest part of Rosewood. Many of the homes were still lived in by descendants of the town's founders. Its permanence resonated with J.C. How would this neighborhood look in twenty years if a superstore took hold of the town? Would it eventually become run-down or deserted because the owners' businesses could no longer compete?

Seth's truck was parked out front. J.C. pulled in behind it. The place was quiet. Plans rolled out on a makeshift table, Seth sat on a crate of tile. He gestured to another one close by. "Pull up an uncomfortable hunk of wood."

"Where's your crew?"

"I told them to take an extra hour for lunch."

J.C. winced. "That wasn't necessary."

Seth unscrewed the lid on a thermos bottle. "I can enjoy an hour with an old friend." He poured coffee into two foam cups.

J.C. straddled the extra crate, then picked up a cup.

Seth sipped his coffee, letting J.C. begin at his own pace.

"Do you know Owen Radley?"

"Why?"

"It's important, Seth."

"I did one job for him. He undercut the price we agreed on, imposed penalties that weren't in the contract, made up restrictions so he could charge the penalties. Worse, he treated my men...poorly."

J.C. told Seth about Owen's offer to buy the building.

"Wagner Hill? Nothing personal, but what does he want with the building? I appreciate the fine craftsmanship, the history of the place, but I'd be surprised if he does." Seth pulled his eyebrows together. "There's more, isn't there?"

"A lot. He wants to turn Wagner Hill into a living history museum of Rosewood and he'll pay plenty for the privilege."

Seth frowned. "That doesn't sound like something he'd be interested in."

J.C. nodded in agreement. "But he has a valid point about Chrissy's future. His offer is sixty percent over the highest appraisal from top market years."

"Jay and Fran left enough money for college, didn't they?"

"With their life insurance."

Seth was quiet.

"So you're wondering why I'd consider the offer?

Why Chrissy would need the money? I don't know that she will. But it would give her any opportunity she could dream of."

"That she won't have otherwise?" Seth shifted his weight and the crate creaked beneath him. "Don't you believe the Lord will give her endless opportunities?"

"That goes without saying."

"Not always."

"For me it does." J.C. exhaled. "There's something else. Owen says he'll make sure we don't get a superstore on Wagner Hill's land, or a tourist shop."

"Funny, I'd have thought bringing a superstore to Rosewood would be right up his alley."

J.C. nodded.

"That's not what's bothering you."

He smiled bleakly. "You always see right to the heart of things. I don't know what Owen and Maddie…if they're in a relationship."

"Not one I've heard about and Emma usually sniffs out that sort of thing pretty well. Claims it has to do with designing wedding gowns, that she's tuned into romance." Seth paused. "Have you asked Maddie?"

"Owen's made…insinuations."

"I bet he did," Seth scoffed.

J.C. stared at the ground. "Do you think she could have planned this buyout with him?"

"Have you met the woman?" Seth shook his head in disbelief. "Think about it. A diabolical plan? First step, taking her mother to you. Of course she'd have to know that you'd offer to help her set up a shop and renovate the apartments. Then, have Owen buy the place? Kind of a stupid plan. Why use all that time and energy if Owen wanted to turn Wagner Hill into a museum? I don't think much of Owen, but from experience, he doesn't throw his money away. If anything, he would try to drive the price down." Seth frowned more deeply. "I don't like the sound of any of this."

"The man's arrogant, but I don't think he's dangerous."

Seth's face was still grim. "I know firsthand that danger comes in all kinds of packages. Even to Rosewood."

"I may be gullible, but my concerns about the danger are more...emotional than physical."

"Don't take things at face value, J.C. Talk to Maddie, find out for yourself how she feels about Owen."

"I don't have any claims on her."

"An even better reason to ask. Maybe it's time you do."

J.C. looked sharply at his friend.

"Even I can see that you're crazy about her. And Emma will tell you I'm usually the last one to know."

Maybe.

But this time, J.C. reasoned, he was the last to know.

J.C. held Seth's advice close for days. If he questioned Maddie, he had to be prepared to share his own past, explain why it was so hard for him to trust. By the end of the week he decided he couldn't put it off any longer and returned home in time for dinner.

Maddie greeted him with a hopeful smile. "I'm so glad you don't have to work late. We've missed you."

Chrissy spotted him. "Uncle James!" Putting down her book, she ran to his side. "You haven't been home in *forever*."

"Not so long," he replied, giving her shoulder a quick hug.

"You missed your turn to pick out what we do on Saturday!" She grinned mischievously. "So I got to pick."

"Hopefully we're not climbing the water tower."

Chrissy giggled. "No, silly."

"Your uncle's probably tired and hungry," Maddie intervened. "Why don't you help me dish up the vegetables?"

J.C. wandered into the living room. Lillian was crocheting something in a fine ivory yarn. Her hands trembled only slightly, a sign that she was holding her own. "Evening, Mrs. Carter."

Looking up, she tsked. "Sit down, you look as tired as week-old bread."

Her words brought a reluctant smile and he sat on the end of the sofa closest to her chair.

Lillian reached into her yarn bag, rustled around, retrieved a roll of Life Savers and handed it to him.

Accepting one, he extended the rest to her.

But Lillian waved him away. "Appears you can use the whole roll."

Even though he knew every facet of her neurological history, he sometimes saw insights in Lillian that defied her medical condition. "What about you and Chrissy?"

She dove back into her yarn bag and pulled out another roll.

Chuckling, he relaxed. "As long as you're covered."

Lillian sniffed, catching the scent of what Maddie was cooking. "Dinner ought to be ready pretty soon, shouldn't it?" She frowned. "Wouldn't be lunch I don't think..."

"Dinner," he confirmed. "Smells good."

"My Maddie's a wonderful cook, always has been. When she could barely see the top of the kitchen table, she wanted to roll out biscuits and stir cake batter. Her father built her a special little set of stairs so she could reach. He was afraid she'd fall off a step ladder."

Chrissy ran into the room. "Dinner's ready! Come on, Uncle James, Mrs. Lillian!"

J.C. got up, then offered his hand to Lillian. Accepting, she leaned on him as they walked to the table. He pulled out her chair, then helped her get settled.

He thought about the blessing while they all assembled. Bending his head, he silently prayed for guidance. "Lord, we thank You for this nourishment, the blessings You bring us every day, for each of our loved ones. Let us appreciate these blessings, and keep in mind You are with us in each step, each day. Amen."

A quiet murmur of *amen*s circled the table.

Glancing up, he met Maddie's gaze. She sat across from him, watching, her eyes simmering with questions. Tonight they were the softest of blues, their dark-rimmed edges making them more luminescent, more enchanting.

"I've read more books than everybody in class except Susan Porter. But she reads *all* the time, even during lunch." Chrissy passed him the basket of rolls. "And she didn't do the extra credit in science."

Lillian winked at her. "You'll catch up."

J.C. felt himself thawing.

"That's right," Maddie agreed. "You made the best poster in class. And your teacher's going to enter it in the science fair."

Chrissy grinned.

The phone rang.

Maddie started to rise, but Chrissy jumped up first. "I'll get it." She scampered into the kitchen and was back in a flash. "It's for you, Maddie."

"I wonder who's calling at dinnertime," she mused.

"Owen," Chrissy replied, reaching for potatoes. "Ra... Ra something."

Startled, Maddie quickly put her napkin on the table and pushed back her chair. "I won't be a minute."

She could take an hour, J.C. told himself. A day, a week, a year. Because he didn't want to hear what she had to say about Owen Radley.

"Owen," Lillian mused. "Maddie's fiancé. Nice young man."

The sinking in J.C.'s gut nearly did him in.

It was true, then. And there was nothing he could do about it.

Except prepare to say goodbye.

Chapter Seventeen

Maddie paced the cobbled walk in the far northern corner of Rosewood's town park. Away from the swings and slides, even the picnic tables, the spot was sheltered by the low-hanging branches of an ancient oak tree. The curving wrought-iron bench beneath the tree was a beacon for couples young and old, a place to sit and hold hands, to declare their love.

Owen's phone call the previous night kept running through her mind. *Meet me at our bench in the park.* Furious over the assumption, she had refused. But then he'd warned her that if she didn't, he would ruin J.C. and Chrissy's futures. She couldn't imagine how, but she wasn't prepared to risk it.

Striding down the walk as though he owned it and every piece of land on either side, Owen arrived. He gestured toward the bench.

"I'll stand," she replied, unwilling to sit next to him. What, she wondered, had happened to the young man she once loved? Had these rotten seeds been in him all along?

Owen sent a proprietary gaze over the bench. "We

spent a lot of afternoons here, talking about our future, planning our lives."

Anger dissolved into pity. "Owen, that was so long ago. We're different people now, too different."

"And J. C. Mueller isn't?"

"Why did you want to meet? You talked about his future and Chrissy's—"

"And yours. Maddie, I want to buy out your lease."

Puzzled, she stared at him.

"For your shop. I'll pay you twice what it's worth."

"I don't have a lease."

Owen frowned. "You rent the place month-to-month?"

"No. It's…" She paused, wanting to say it was none of his business, but she needed to know how he was threatening J.C. and Chrissy. "Why do you want to buy my lease?"

"Because I don't want you to lose your investment."

Truly baffled, she shook her head. "That won't happen. I don't want to hurt your feelings, Owen, but my shop, my business doesn't have anything to do with you."

"Even though I'm buying the Wagner Hill building?"

Shock struck hard and fast. "That's not true!"

"Why do think I paid off your account at the costume shop? To keep you from going further in debt. You're probably not making enough in your tea parlor to cover costs."

Maddie shook her head, hating what she was hearing. "I'll pay back every cent."

"I can afford it. It'll be a write-off when the deal goes through for the building."

"I don't believe you."

"Ask J.C."

She knew J.C. wouldn't agree to Owen's deal. "Last night you said that if I didn't meet with you, it would ruin his and Chrissy's future. What did you mean?"

"I'm paying above market price, way above. You think anyone else would? That child can have an Ivy League education, then anything else she wants. J.C. knows a good deal when he sees it."

She couldn't speak.

"I have different plans for the Wagner Hill. Your tea parlor has to go."

"J.C. won't—"

"Grow up, Maddie. This is business, not personal."

But his tone told her it was. "I don't believe you."

Owen grasped her hand. "You're right, Maddie. We are different people now, better, stronger. You're the only woman I've ever loved."

Her throat was so choked she could barely speak. "I don't even know you anymore."

"You'll enjoy getting reacquainted."

She snatched her hand back. "No."

Satisfaction flooded his expression. "Face facts. You've rented out your mother's house. Your business and apartment will be gone. What then?"

Maddie shook with renewed anger.

"Accept it, Maddie. There's nothing you can do. Nothing."

Aimless and shaken, Maddie got in her car and drove. Owen had to be wrong. Malicious, but wrong. She turned into her old neighborhood, needing to get away from any of the more traveled streets. Tears burned in her eyes, clogged her throat.

Why had she agreed to meet Owen? To hear his lies?

She gripped the steering wheel. All she had to do was ask J.C. He… Would what? Tell her Owen had invented the story? But why would Owen lie about something so easily disproved? Unless it was true.

Maddie pictured J.C.'s face at dinner the previous night. Somber, strained, uncomfortable. And he couldn't get away fast enough once they had eaten. Just as he had avoided coming to dinner all week. She'd had no reason to question whether he genuinely had to work late each evening. Doctors had all kinds of crazy hours.

Reluctantly, she delved into her memory. Remembering, even though she didn't want to, that the week's hours weren't all that crazy. J.C. had arrived home every evening just late enough to be sure dinner was over.

The unwanted thoughts kept attacking. J.C. had to consider Chrissy's interests first. Maddie didn't resent that a bit. But to be speaking and dealing with Owen… To let Owen blindside her with the news…

Tears slid down her cheeks. It wasn't the loss of her shop that she was grieving. The Tea Cart was only one of her dreams. Disappointment wedged its way through her heart. Even though she had lectured herself not to, hope had been sprouting…making her wonder about a future with J.C. Even a family of her own.

She drove as though on autopilot until she turned onto her street, to the house she had grown up in, the house that was leased to another family for two years. Maddie had used the tenants' deposit to paint the exterior. It looked fresh, but not like home. Because it wasn't theirs again until the lease was up.

Maddie leaned her forehead against the steering wheel. How could J.C. have made a decision like this without talking to her? Pulling her home and business out from under her without a word?

Where would she and Mom live? And how would she pay for it? She had already committed the money from renting out their house to the roof contractor. She and her mother could have dealt with another season of catching leaks with buckets, but she couldn't expect renters to do the same.

But that paled next to how she felt. How she had hoped J.C. felt about her. Despite her responsibility for her mother, Maddie had thought perhaps it could be different with J.C. That he was different.

From what? she mocked herself. She'd been out of the dating game since her mother's first stroke. What did she know about men anymore? Worse, what had she ever known? If not for her mother's illness, she would be Mrs. Owen Radley. The thought made her stomach turn. Wrenched with pain, she tried to think of some-where, anywhere to run to. There was only one place.

Ignoring the tears blurring her vision, Maddie drove until she reached Samantha's house. Praying her friend was home, she made herself look away from the gate leading to the backyard where they'd held the campout, where J.C. had almost kissed her.

"Hey! You should have called. I saw you driving up and remembered that we're out of coffee, and..." Sa-mantha halted, stared, then hurried across the porch, wrapping Maddie in a hug. "What is it?" Samantha's voice choked. "Not your mother?"

"No, it's not Mom." Maddie allowed herself to be led inside.

Sam hovered, guiding her to the couch. "Do you want some...water?"

Shaking her head, Maddie swiped at her tears. Then she poured out the whole story. "I just can't believe it, Sam."

"Well, I *don't* believe it. What did J.C. say?"

"I haven't asked him."

"Why not?"

Tears and sobs exploded as though she had pulled a trigger.

"Oh, Maddie!" Sam rubbed her back for a few moments. Then she walked as fast as her cane would allow, bringing back a box of tissues. "I always say the wrong thing."

Maddie took a handful of tissues and leaned her face into it. When the worst of her crying jag ended, she pressed the knuckles of one hand to her lips to stop them from trembling. Taking a ragged breath, she looked at her friend. "It still seems unreal. I got the call from Owen last night…" She willed herself to not start crying again. "Then this morning when I met him…"

Sam stared at her in question.

"He said that J.C. and Chrissy's futures were at stake. I wouldn't have gone otherwise. Good thing I did."

"Good? Maddie, you've got to talk to J.C. He wouldn't do something like this. Certainly not without discussing it with you."

"It's our whole lives, Sam. Not just the shop, but we rented out our house…" She couldn't continue. *And she had given her heart to J.C.*

"You're talking crazy. No one's taking away your home and business. It was J.C.'s idea to back you. Why would he sell to a worm like Owen?"

"I told you—the money."

"No, not J.C."

"He has to think about Chrissy."

"And you." Sam face filled with concern and wisdom. "Don't you see it? He's nuts about you."

Maddie clapped a hand over her mouth, hoping to stop herself from crying. "Wishful thinking."

"Bret and I have both seen it. You two belong together."

"You know that's not possible. Besides, you don't do something like this to the person you love."

"Oh, Maddie, talk to him. Let him clear up whatever this is. Owen has cooked this up to try and get you back. The man has no principles!"

"Which says a whole lot about my judgment."

"Don't say that! You were too young to know what you do now, to see people for who they really are. At the same age, I thought my career was more important than Bret. I thank the Lord every day for the accident, for bringing me back to Him and to Bret."

"Apparently J.C. is no Bret, either."

Sam took her hands. "No. He's James Christopher Mueller. A fine man, a principled man of honor who cares about everybody he meets. He never gave up on me and I'm not going to let you give up on him."

Maddie bent her head, staring down, seeing nothing. "I keep coming back to the same thing. Why would Owen lie? He knows I can ask J.C."

"Maybe he hoped you wouldn't." Sam squeezed her fingers. "And it almost worked. You took the path of logic he hoped you would. Probably thought he could bluff his way through it."

"And what? That I wouldn't figure it out when the building didn't change hands?"

Sam hesitated.

"What?"

"It's possible Owen offered to buy Wagner Hill."

Maddie sucked in her breath. "Then it is all real."

"No, I didn't say that. Just that Owen could be trying to buy the building, to be in control."

"Control?"

"Of you, Maddie. Of you."

Knowing it must be done, Maddie steeled herself to talk with J.C. Actually, she would know just by J.C.'s demeanor if Owen had been telling the truth. J.C. didn't hide his feelings well. At least, she prayed he didn't.

J.C. sat by his patient's bedside. He had operated on her that morning and was optimistic about her recovery from a severe spinal injury. It was quiet in the intensive care unit. Her family had gone to the cafeteria after he assured them that she would sleep while they took a break.

He listened to the quiet but reassuringly steady rise and fall of her breathing, relieved that the procedure had gone well. J.C. had always felt comfortable at the hospital, it was his second home. One he was likely to need again soon. He had been waiting for Maddie to say something, to deny any involvement in Owen's plan. But there'd been nothing, no explanation.

"Doctor?" The nurse acknowledged his presence, then began recording his patient's vitals.

J.C. realized that this wasn't the place to do his thinking. With a nod, he left. The familiar scent of disinfectants was strong since an aide was mopping the floor. Glancing at his watch, J.C. realized it was almost midnight. He'd left a message on the answering machine to let Maddie know he would be late. Chrissy was no doubt asleep in the extra bed in Maddie's room. When she knew he wouldn't be home, Chrissy preferred to stay there close to the others. As much pain as he was in, J.C. couldn't begin to fathom how much it would hurt Chrissy to be yanked out of what she considered her home. When Maddie married Owen, the child wouldn't be part of her life any longer.

His office was quiet, dark. No one left soft lights on for him here. He flipped on the overhead fixture in the reception area, then switched on a lamp on his desk. Everyone had gone home to be with their families, tucked in safe and cozy.

The office was set up to be practical, not cozy. Accustomed to practical from years of being on his own, that had been fine with him. But it didn't exactly say welcome, sit and stay a while.

Sinking into his desk chair, he propped both elbows on his desk and reached to open his laptop. But his hand fell away. Nothing it contained held any interest. Oh, there would be emails from college and med school friends, along with work that always needed to be done.

His fingers grazed the newspaper he had looked at earlier. The local Rosewood paper that was published twice a week was open to the small real estate section. He had circled ads for an apartment and a house. They would need something large enough for a live-in housekeeper and nanny. One that Chrissy would no doubt resent on sight. Truth was, with Maddie gone, he might as well sell the Wagner Hill. His niece's financial future would be secure and Owen's purchase would ensure that the site would never become a superstore.

Bending his head, J.C. rested it against his hands. *How had it come to this? How had he allowed this to happen again?* He was certain he had learned his lesson with his ex-wife. Knowing the signs of betrayal, he was sure they would never slip up on him again, that he would spot them immediately.

But Maddie had crept past all his defenses, made him trust again. *Lord, I am lost again.*

Feeling the Lord's urging, J.C. knew he would need every shred of his faith to make it through this time. Lifting his head, he swivelled his chair so that he looked out into the night. The only cars in the parking lot belonged to the staff and a handful of visitors. He hoped most of the visitors were new fathers staying the night with their wives and new babies, rather than relatives of critically ill patients.

J.C. remembered his plans for children, the vision he'd once had for a family. When they dated, Amy had assured him that she, too, wanted children. Meeting her near the end of medical school, she had seemed so sweet, so kind.

He swallowed. Much like Maddie. But that had changed after they were married. It was as though Amy had morphed into an entirely different person. Would that happen to Maddie? Was she wearing an assumed face? One that would change as soon as she and Owen married? The image scorched his already-tortured thoughts.

He remembered her many kindnesses, the deft touch she had with Chrissy. Instinctively, she had known not to try and step into Fran's place. Instead, she treated Chrissy like a favorite niece, and encouraged her bond with Lillian. How could she have faked that?

She didn't.

Was that the Lord's assurance or his own wishful longing?

The silence surrounding him didn't clarify which it was. Turning around, he stared out the doorway, the solitude reinforcing the emptiness of his life. It wasn't as bad during the day when he was surrounded by colleagues, staff and patients. But the nights…

Exhaling, he tried to close his mind to a lifetime of endless nights. Knowing there was only one thing that would help, he bent his head and prayed. And called on the Lord for help.

Chapter Eighteen

The Tea Cart's birthday party business for children had grown steadily since Chrissy's debut party. Now it was Lexi's birthday. Chrissy had pleaded to help host her best friend's big day. Maddie, still numb, would have agreed to almost anything for the child.

J.C.'s absences told her Owen hadn't lied. He stayed gone long into the nights, never home when he could run into her. Apparently he couldn't face telling her the truth.

Now, knowing Chrissy would also be out of her life, the hole in her heart deepened. She'd had a taste of what it would be like to have a child of her own. And she'd grown to love Chrissy, hoping she could help her past this worst time in her life, then watch her mature and grow into a young woman.

Hovering, Samantha clasped her elbow. "What is it?"

Maddie willed the shimmer of tears from her eyes. "Just thinking how fast kids grow up."

The expression on Samantha's face made it clear she knew there was far more, but she didn't press. "The cake and decorations are beautiful."

"Lexi's favorite color is pink. And I didn't want to repeat the gold." She tried desperately to focus on the setting, to take her thoughts away from herself...the pain.

"It's gorgeous. The tiaras are a nice touch."

"They were Chrissy's idea." Maddie smiled in spite of her distress. "And she insisted that we find one with pink and clear rhinestones for Lexi so it would be extra special. Tina ordered one that was a little larger than the others and switched out some of the clear rhinestones for pink."

"Chrissy's a sweet girl. Nice to see her that way again."

Swallowing around the lump in her throat, Maddie agreed. "She saved all of her allowance so she could buy Lexi a special birthday present." Maddie had contributed the difference so that Chrissy could buy the locket she wanted for her friend.

"Maddie, you haven't told me what J.C. said."

"Sam, he avoids me, doesn't come home until he's sure no one's still up. He has to let us know if he's going to be late so we can take care of Chrissy. But he makes sure he leaves a message on the answering machine so he doesn't have to talk to me."

"You mean you haven't asked him about Owen and the building?"

"There's not any point. I can tell by the way J.C. avoids me that Owen was telling the truth. Then, I was tidying up his apartment and saw..." Maddie drew in a ragged breath. "He had the real estate section of the paper next to his chair. He'd circled places to buy or rent."

"Could be any number of reasons..."

"Even you can't finish that statement." Maddie raised

her gaze, seeing her friend's concern. "It's okay, Sam. I've always known I couldn't have a relationship anyway. Mom's my first priority."

"But J.C.—"

"Needs to move on. I've prayed about it, Sam. He has to do what's right for Chrissy."

"*This* is what's right for Chrissy. You've made a home for her, returned her ability to trust."

Maddie squinted against the pain. "She's given me the opportunity to know how it would be to have my own family. It's more than a fair trade."

Samantha stamped the foot of her good leg. "Maddie Carter, if you don't ask J.C. about the sale, I will."

"You can't."

"Oh, but I can. I'm not going to let you throw away your happiness because of pride."

"It's not pride." Maddie swallowed. "It's reality. You know, that bothersome fact that intrudes on stupid dreams."

"I want you to promise me that you'll talk to J.C., find out what's really going on with Owen."

"There's no point."

"Humor me," Sam implored. "I know this isn't right. It stinks of that rat. Don't let Owen ruin your future. You deserve more." She paused. "J.C. deserves more."

It wasn't a promise Maddie wanted to make. But Sam was only voicing what she had already decided. She did have to talk to J.C., if only to learn why.

And when her life would shatter.

The kids started arriving in the afternoon. Lexi had invited only girls. On the shy side, she preferred a princesslike tea party and didn't want the rowdier boys.

Chrissy nearly popped waiting to show Lexi the special tiara with the sparkling pink and clear rhinestones. It looked perfect with the dainty pink dress Lexi's mother had sewn. Chrissy chose to wear one of the dresses that Tina had created for the Tea Cart. Maddie thought it was endearingly sweet that Chrissy didn't want to steal Lexi's spotlight by wearing her own special lavender birthday dress.

The other guests chattered nonstop as they picked out their dresses and popped on their tiaras. Maddie took mental snapshots, knowing she would never forget this day or the other days she had spent with Chrissy... with J.C.

Even though Maddie had baked a birthday cake, she also prepared tiny pink petits fours in the same pale pastel pink. Their *dress-up* tea party was touchingly sweet. All on their best behavior, the girls drank punch from teacups while wearing their petite white gloves.

Sam, along with Lexi's mother, helped Maddie serve. Lillian had opted to stay in her nook with two friends. Giggles resonated through the tea shop, causing the other few customers to smile. It was easy to imagine being ten years old again, having a fancy tea party with friends.

Concentrating on carrying in the birthday cake, Maddie didn't notice J.C. until she nearly slammed into him. He deftly stepped aside, preventing the crash. Flustered, she muttered an apology.

Glancing up, she caught the concern in his eyes. And...was that distress?

"Need help carrying that?"

Instinctively, she pulled the cake back. "No, I'm good. I'm fine."

He moved to clear the aisle, landing smack dab in front of the sketch of Maddie as a child at her teddy bear and doll tea party. His eyes lingered on the picture, then lifted to catch her gaze. Not so long ago, she would have grinned, shared the moment. Now all she could do was scurry away. If she stayed a moment longer the tears clogging her throat would escape.

Presenting the cake, she mouthed the words to "Happy Birthday," as they all sang, hoping no one would notice. She wanted to be far away, hidden from prying eyes. She had no doubt that Sam would carry out her promise and talk to J.C. if she didn't. The possibility made her nearly faint with humiliation.

Maddie had tried to follow Sam's line of reasoning. Yes, it made sense that J.C. had never shown himself to be the same kind of person as Owen. But the silences, the avoidance. They weren't coincidental.

A huge part of her wanted to never broach the subject, like a child hiding beneath the covers on a stormy night. If she didn't ask, maybe it wouldn't happen. Equally childish.

Chrissy clapped when Lexi opened her present, the pink and silver cloisonné locket. Chrissy looked so happy, so content. And Maddie's resolve dissolved like ice on a hot summer's day. Chrissy deserved the best, everything she could possibly have in her future. She had already lost far more than any child should.

Maddie knew it was wrong for her to hope the building wouldn't sell. Jay had inherited the Wagner Hill from his parents. And although his printing business had done all right, it hadn't made a lot of money. Their home was saddled with a mortgage that about equaled its value.

Fran and Jay had an insurance policy, but nothing compared to what Owen was offering for the building. And who knew what would happen in the next eight years? Would there be enough money for Chrissy's education?

J.C. had poured a lot of cash into creating the Tea Cart. That must have dented his savings considerably. Guilt leached from every pore. While she'd worried about *her* future, *her* feelings, she hadn't really considered all the angles. Regardless of Owen's motives, his offer could change Chrissy's future. That was all that really mattered.

More giggles erupted from the children's corner. She would do whatever it took. And her heart would have to fend for itself.

Waiting through dinner seemed interminable. Chrissy was consumed with retelling every detail of Lexi's party. Her light chatter and Lillian's observations were all that could be heard. Each moment, Maddie wondered if J.C. might finally come home in time for dinner. But when they finished dessert, there was still no sign of him.

Chrissy helped her clear the table and load the dishwasher. Lillian was more than ready to retire by then. Although she had enjoyed watching the girls at the party, it had tired her. And she was more forgetful.

"Maddie, where do I sleep?"

"In your room, Mom. Just like always."

Lillian's eyes were vague. "Is this your house?"

"It's ours," she explained with a pang.

"I don't see my armoire." No, it had been too large to fit comfortably in the apartment, so it was in storage.

"I have your gown and robe." Maddie held them up.

"Good," Lillian murmured.

Maddie prayed that Lillian's worsening symptoms were temporary, only a result of fatigue, not signs of another small stroke. Casually, she reached for her mother's hand, clasping her wrist so that she could take her pulse. Thankfully, it was normal. Still, she uncapped the aspirin bottle and took out two pills. J.C. had told her if she suspected a stroke or heart attack, to give her mother two aspirins rather than one.

Scrutinizing her mother's moves, she saw that Lillian lifted her feet when she walked, a good sign. When it was a stroke, the person tended to drag their feet, unable to lift them properly.

"Mom, do you have a headache?"

"No, honey, I'm just tired."

Another good sign. Still, Maddie knew she had to call J.C. to be sure. She couldn't risk her mother's health.

Just then she heard footsteps in the hall. "Be right back, Mom." Dashing from her mother's room, she sped through the apartment, catching J.C. just before he entered his own place. "J.C."

He turned, looking surprised.

"It's probably nothing, but could you have a look at Mom? She's a little disoriented."

"Sure." Not making any small talk, he followed her back to Lillian's side.

He took her pulse and blood pressure, then checked her eyes with a pin light. "How are you feeling, Mrs. Carter?"

"Fine."

"Mom!"

"A little tired. Maddie's such a tattletale."

"She worries about you."

"That's because she's a good daughter." Lillian smiled tiredly at Maddie.

J.C. didn't reply, instead glancing at the pill case on the night stand. "Maddie, did you give her this morning's medicine?"

"Of course. I always…" The party, all the questions whirling in her thoughts… "I'm not sure."

He picked up the plastic container. "Today's meds are still here."

Maddie bit her lips. What a dumb trick. "I thought I had." She rubbed Lillian's back. "I'm sorry, Mom."

"Can I go to sleep now?"

"Of course." Maddie pulled the blanket up the way her mother liked. "All tucked in, snug as a bug in a rug." Kissing her forehead, Maddie inwardly thanked the Lord for watching over them, for not letting her mistake hurt her mother.

Maddie left the door ajar when they left the room so she could hear if her mother needed anything, then walked with J.C. to the living room. "A few minutes ago I gave Mom two aspirins."

"She missed a dose of her blood thinner so that won't be a problem."

Rubbing her forehead, Maddie still couldn't believe she'd been so careless. "Thanks for checking on her."

"I suppose Chrissy's already asleep here."

Maddie hesitated. "When I didn't hear from you, I thought it was best."

"I was in surgery until late, then I tried to call but some of the lines must be down from the storm."

Blinking, Maddie realized that J.C.'s hair was wet, that some of the rain still dripped from his forehead, creasing his cheeks. She had been so concerned about her mother that she hadn't noticed anything else. "Storm?"

"Pretty wicked one. My coat's drenched." He wiped at the moisture on his bag. "Along with everything else."

"I haven't listened to the news. Didn't realize it's storming."

J.C. shrugged. "Not a good night to be out. Flash flood warnings are out for the whole area. Heard that on the car radio." He turned to leave just as a bolt of thunder hit close by.

"Um, speaking of news..."

He turned back, waiting.

Maddie fiddled with her hands, uncertain how to begin.

"News?" he prompted.

She swallowed. "Yours. News, I mean."

J.C. shook his head. "I don't know what you mean."

"I should have asked you when I spoke with Owen..." Glancing up, she saw J.C.'s jaw tighten, his eyes hardening. She took a deep breath. "He told me about the plans for the building, this building."

"Plans?" J.C.'s voice was dangerously tight.

"Yes, that he offered you a lot of money for it, that you plan to sell."

"It's what you want, isn't it?"

"Me?" Outraged, disbelieving, she wanted to shake him. "Of course. That's why I've worked myself to death, spent every penny I had to open the shop. Now you're pulling the rug out from under us. Or didn't it occur to you that when you sold the Wagner Hill you were also selling my home, my business?" She heard a small clatter, but before she could turn to look, J.C. grabbed her arm.

"*Your* home? What about my home?"

Baffled, hurt, overwhelmed, she stared at him. "I figured you must have plans for another home since you're selling this one to Owen."

"Says who?"

"Well... Owen." She narrowed her eyes. "Are you saying you didn't talk to him about selling the Wagner Hill?"

"I talked to him."

Maddie glowered, pain filling her very core.

"But I didn't agree to sell the building."

"But he said—"

"I don't get it, Maddie. You're engaged to the man. His interests are yours."

"Engaged?" She flung her hands upward. "Years ago, when we were in college."

"You're not engaged now?"

She stared at him in amazement. "How can you even ask that? What engaged couple goes years without seeing each other?"

"How was I supposed to know that?"

"The fact that he never came around should have given you a clue."

J.C. stared into her eyes as though trying to read every particle of her thoughts. "I've seen you with him."

Frowning, Maddie tried to think. "He came to the shop on Chrissy's birthday."

"And you looked pretty cozy out on the sidewalk, and then again at the restaurant that Sunday."

"Cozy? Did you really say *cozy*?"

His lips were tight. "It sure looked that way."

"Then you're half blind. I hadn't seen Owen since we broke up. Then out of nowhere, he got all hot and bothered because I opened the Tea Cart."

"Without any encouragement?"

Anger joined her pain and her chest heaved with suppressed fury. "I've never cross-examined your personal life."

"Not interested?"

"You don't get off that easily. I've given you room, respected what you want to keep private even when I…" Abruptly she halted before she could spill all of her feelings for him.

"When you what?"

Her breathing escalated, her stomach pitched. "Nothing."

J.C. took her hands. "Now *you* expect to get off that easily?"

"No, this can't happen."

"Maddie?" Lillian's fatigued voice barely reached the living room.

"I have to…"

J.C. gently squeezed her fingers. "We're not done."

Maddie sped to her mother's room. "What is it, Mom?"

"Chrissy. Find Chrissy."

"Mom, she's asleep in my room."

Lillian flopped her head from side to side, not lifting it from her pillow.

"I'll check on her real quick and be right back." Dying to finish her talk with J.C., Maddie was tempted to step out in the hall, then immediately return to her mother. But they'd never indulged in even small lies. Quietly, she entered her bedroom. Her own bed was still neatly made. She glanced at the other side of the room where Chrissy's bed was situated. It was empty. Apparently, she was in another room. Moving quickly, she checked out the bathroom connected to her room. Empty. She moved on to the second one. Also empty.

Chrissy must have wanted a snack, Maddie told herself. The light above the stove was on in the kitchen, but she didn't see anyone. Flipping on the overhead fixture, the light blared into every corner. Every empty corner. Maddie's breathing halted. The door from the kitchen that led to the outside hall was ajar.

J.C. followed the sound of her running from the rear of the apartment to the kitchen. "What's wrong?"

"Chrissy's not here, not in bed or any of the rooms." She pointed to the open door.

"She must have gone to her own room in our place." J.C. took the shortcut through the kitchen to the hall and into his apartment. Maddie was only steps behind him. Splitting up, they searched every room. Chrissy wasn't in any of them.

"Of course," Maddie exclaimed. "The leftover party favors are in the shop. She must be down there."

In sync, they rushed downstairs, turning on every light, but no giggling child emerged from the kitchen or the storeroom.

"J.C., where can she be?" A flash of lightning, followed by a boom of thunder emphasized her words. "You don't think she's outside? In this storm?"

Striding to the front door, he grasped the doorknob and it turned easily. "Unlocked."

"She can't have gone far." Another flash of lightning illuminated the dark night sky.

J.C.'s face was grim. "She's a small child in a very large storm."

Maddie sucked in her breath. "We have to find her."

He flipped open his cell phone. "Tucker? J. C. Mueller. Chrissy's out in the storm somewhere. We're leaving now to look."

"The sheriff?" Maddie asked in a strangled voice.

"The more people looking means we find her faster." J.C. pulled open the door, Maddie on his heels. "You need to stay here with your mother."

"Give me your phone."

He obliged.

Maddie punched in Sam's phone number, filled her in quickly, then handed him back the phone. "She's on her way over and Seth will call volunteers to help look for Chrissy." She grabbed a coat from the rack by the door.

Stepping out onto the sidewalk, they were immediately assaulted by a lash of stinging rain. The gutters on Main Street were overflowing, rainwater rushing downhill, spilling over. The wind whipped the rain and hail into sideways slashes.

"Where would she go?" Maddie shouted.

J.C. turned his head, looking first up the street, then down. "Lexi's?"

Piling into his car, they drove as fast as the severely reduced visibility allowed. Lexi's father answered the door. They hadn't seen Chrissy but checked Lexi's room just in case. He and Lexi's mother offered to call the parents of other children in their class.

"Where now?" Maddie asked. Picturing Chrissy floating away in a massive surge of water, she bit back a sob. Not knowing when Chrissy left the apartment, they didn't know how far she could have traveled.

"Back to Main Street. She's on foot." He reversed the car and sped back to the center of town. The stores, bakery and café were all closed. A light was on at the bed and breakfast, but it wasn't a place Chrissy would go for refuge.

Refuge? Had Chrissy overheard them? Horrified, Maddie stiffened. "J.C, when you came upstairs, was the door from the kitchen to the hall open?"

"No."

Maddie closed her eyes. "She must have heard us."

"You said she was asleep."

Rain pounded on the car, hard, heavy, loud. "The storm. It must have woken her."

J.C. slammed his hand against the steering wheel. "She thinks we're taking her home away, that things will be the same as they were before…"

Their eyes met.

Before they had come together as a family.

"Oh, J.C., we have to find her!"

He stared into the ominous night. Then he jerked the car back into gear, driving down Main Street.

Maddie didn't know where he was headed, but she had faith in him. She placed her ultimate faith in the Lord's hands, beseeching Him to watch over Chrissy, to allow them to find her, to bring her safely home. To their home.

J.C. turned, driving in a sharp, short burst. Screeching to a sudden stop, J.C. put the car in Park and yanked up the emergency brake.

Maddie jumped from the car, barely able to see

where they were. Recognizing the town cemetery, she gasped.

J.C. didn't hesitate, striding past the front gate. Maddie kept even with his pace. Sure-footed, he cut through the rows, heading for what must be familiar. Because the rain was pounding relentlessly, obscuring their vision, rendering everything to a seemingly different state, nothing looked as it should.

Not ceasing her prayers, Maddie dogged his lead, afraid she'd lose sight of him, more afraid that they wouldn't find Chrissy.

Reaching one of the outer sections, J.C. finally stopped. Maddie took another step so she could stand even with him.

Huddled against the Mueller family headstone, Chrissy clung to the engravings of her parents' names on the stone, sobbing.

J.C. reached her first, scooping Chrissy up into his arms, pressing her against his chest, shielding her as best as he could from the relentless downpour. "What are you doing here?"

Chrissy sobbed even harder.

Maddie wiped at the water that drenched her small face, her sodden clothing. "Oh, sweetheart, we were so worried."

Unable to speak, Chrissy flung her head from side to side in denial.

"I love you, Pinker Belle," J.C. told her.

"Me, too," Maddie added, wishing she could take back everything the child had heard, return her hard-won security.

Rain pelted the child's stricken face. "Then why is everyone leaving?"

J.C. met Maddie's gaze. "No one's going anywhere."

"I heard you!" Chrissy accused, raw pain filling each word.

"I'm not selling the building," J.C. reassured her. "We're still going to live in our apartment."

"What about Maddie?"

Again J.C. caught her gaze. "That's up to Maddie."

Chrissy fixed her imploring gaze on Maddie.

"Sweetheart, you're part of my life, Mrs. Lillian's life." Praying her words would be true, she touched Chrissy's cheek. "That's not going to change."

J.C. caught Maddie's eyes, locking them in a challenge, a promise.

"Let's get you home," he told his niece. "Home."

Chapter Nineteen

With the same sure direction, J.C. took them back through the cemetery, depositing Chrissy in the backseat of his SUV. He grabbed a blanket from the rear and draped it over her trembling body. Turning on the heater, he drove quickly but not frantically back home.

As soon as they were inside, Maddie took over, guiding Chrissy into a warm bath, then getting her dressed in warm flannel pajamas. While she did, J.C. made hot cocoa. Maddie arched her eyebrows when she saw that he had.

"Hidden talents," he explained while Maddie wrapped Chrissy in a warm blanket.

They took their places on either side of Chrissy on the sofa, while she cautiously sipped her cocoa. Exhausted, emotionally drained, she leaned her head on J.C.'s strong shoulder. Maddie smoothed the child's drying hair, incredibly grateful that she was all right, that they had found her before the storm could sweep her away.

Chrissy handed her uncle the mug, unable to finish

her cocoa. With her free hand, she reached for Maddie's hand and clung on.

Tears stung Maddie's eyes. Tears of gratitude and love.

"Do you promise we'll always be together?" Chrissy asked.

"I promise you'll always be with me," J.C. replied.

Maddie pushed away the dart of pain. He hadn't included her.

"Together," Chrissy said, her voice sleepy.

"Together," J.C. echoed.

Chrissy's eyelids drooped, then drifted shut. Carefully, J.C. eased off the sofa so that he could prop Chrissy's head on the armrest and allow her to stretch out.

"Do you want to take her home?" Maddie asked.

"I want to keep an eye on her tonight. I can't sleep anyway."

Maddie tucked the blanket closer, then reluctantly rose, following J.C. into the kitchen. Again switching roles, he turned on the electric kettle and reached for two cups. A canister of tea sat on the small breakfast table. But she didn't feel like sitting. Or drinking tea.

J.C.'s voice remained even. "Do you still love him?"

Maddie wanted to scream, flail, pound the wall. All too aware of Chrissy and her mother, she couldn't. Tears smarted, but she refused to give in to them. "How can you even ask that?"

"Because I have to know." He no longer looked forbidding.

"Of course I don't."

"And what about me?"

Tears tortured her eyelids, flooded her voice. "You're

a man who deserves a loving wife who can devote everything to her family."

J.C. stepped closer. "And what do you deserve?"

Helplessly she held open her hands.

Taking one more step, he smoothed her hair back over one shoulder. "What do you want?"

Tears snuck out, one by one. "It's not about what I want. I am going to take care of Mom, that won't ever change."

"Of course not," he replied calmly.

She bit her lip. "But until you meet the right woman, I'm where I want to be."

"I've met her." He cupped her chin. "*You're* the right woman."

Irony was like a sword to her throat. "Afraid not. Mom and I come as a package deal."

"So?" J.C. stroked her cheek, savoring the softness of her skin.

"So I can't be that right woman, the one who can devote herself completely to you."

"Funny, I don't remember writing that on my application." His upturned lips were close to hers. "I believe I asked for the woman with the largest heart in the world, who can love her mother, an orphaned child and if I'm very, very lucky, me."

Heart quaking, she felt his breath mingle with hers. "You deserve more—"

He placed two fingers on her lips, hushing her words. "I don't deserve you, Maddie Carter, but I love you. I think I fell in love with you the first day you walked into my office."

Her eyes searched his. "I'll never put Mom in a home."

"Not even ours?"

Breath stuttering, she tried to control her tears.

Gently, he smoothed each drop from her cheeks. "We're a family, Maddie. We might not have planned it that way, but we are, and I wouldn't trade one member for anything in the world."

"I can't believe..."

"Believe."

She traced the outline of his strong jaw. "Did I tell you that I love you?"

His eyes said it all, the gold flecks reflecting each unspoken word.

"I love you, J.C. With all my heart, with every breath I take."

That breath caught as he touched his lips to hers, possessive, loving, completing. And Maddie knew it was for real.

Hammers and electric saws pounded and buzzed; Sheetrock dust and wood shavings littered the floors. Ripping down the exterior walls between the apartments had been J.C.'s idea. Maddie suggested an arched opening for the connection. And Seth found the perfect spot for the exterior door just past the head of the stairs. With some reconfiguring, he was able to create an entry hall, and fashion the two living areas into a den and living room. J.C.'s old bedroom became Lillian's new room, right next to Chrissy's, which pleased both of them immensely. The wall between Maddie's bedroom and Lillian's old one was shifted so they would have a larger master bedroom with an adjoining smaller space perfect for a future nursery.

They were able to stay in the apartments until it was time to alter the bedrooms. Sam and Bret opened their home, inviting them all to stay until the work was done. Seth had a strict deadline. Their new unified home had to be completed by the time they arrived back from their honeymoon.

J.C. offered Maddie the world. She chose Paris. Not having traveled outside Rosewood since college and never having left the United States, Maddie had vacationed in her mind, exploring the Louvre and Musée d'Orsay, walking the banks of the Seine, gazing at the Eiffel Tower, strolling beneath the Arc de Triomphe. Now, she would retrace those imaginary steps with her groom.

Initially, she worried about leaving Lillian and Chrissy for two weeks. But practically everyone in Rosewood stepped up, offering to help. Familiar with the shop, Sam would run the Tea Cart. Chrissy and Lillian would keep to their normal routine, then spend evenings with Samantha and Bret. Each and every one of Maddie's protests was shot down, made null and void.

J.C. took care of her primary concern, telling Owen that he would never sell him the Wagner Hill. Not long afterward, J.C. was contacted by the superstore Owen had intended to build on the site once the Wagner Hill was demolished. The entire plan exposed, and realizing that Maddie was really going to marry J.C., Owen left Rosewood for Dallas where his family's corporate headquarters were located.

Maddie was filled with relief. Not that she had much time to worry anyway. Caught up in wedding preparations, every hour was full to the brim. Emma insisted on designing the wedding gown, but she didn't have to do much persuading.

Still, on the big day, Maddie touched the silk confection reverently. "Emma, it's too beautiful to wear."

Accustomed to dealing with brides, Emma took the comment in stride. Still, her smile was soft. "It's not nearly as beautiful as you are."

"Ditto," Samantha chimed in.

"Maddie is the most beautiful woman in the world," Lillian declared, then patted Chrissy's knee. "And I've got the most beautiful *girl* in the world right next to me."

The sweetness that perfumed the bride's room had little to do with the scattered rose petals and everything to do with the bond between the occupants. It was as smooth as the silk that settled over Maddie's hips, then trailed to cover her bare toes and puddle like a swirl of icing. Long sleeves of soft, delicate lace came to perfect pyramids on each hand. The same lace fitted around her neck and shadowed the silk bodice. Tiny pearls were hand sewn on the waist. The same pearls festooned the veil that flared down her back to trail behind the full-skirted dress.

Samantha clasped her chest. "Oh, my. Maddie…"

Carefully, slowly, Maddie turned to the full-length mirror. "It's this incredible dress."

"Every time she makes one, I think it's the most gorgeous ever," Samantha murmured. "And it is."

"But it's the bride wearing it that makes the dress beautiful," Emma insisted. "You are an exquisite bride, but then I expected nothing less."

"Ditto," Samantha muttered, wiping at a tear.

"Honestly, Samantha, you have become the soggiest, most romantic person I know." Maddie sniffled.

Emma softly clapped her hands together. "Makeup, ladies. We're all be reapplying if you two don't stop."

She glanced at her watch. "Chrissy, it's time for you and Mrs. Lillian to take your places."

While Chrissy wheeled Lillian to the vestibule, Samantha helped Emma adjust the veil so that it fell perfectly over Maddie's loose curls that were softly gathered in an upsweep. "I feel like I'm sending my child out into the world!" Samantha wailed.

"Knowing the kind of friend you are, you'll be a great mom someday."

"Glad you think so." Samantha patted her slim stomach. "Someday's arrived. A few more weeks and Emma would have had to let out my dress."

"Oh, Sam!" Forgetting about her dress or makeup, she pulled her matron of honor into a hug. Sam and Bret had been hoping for some time. "I'm so happy for you."

"You crush Maddie's dress and I'll wish twins on you," Emma threatened.

They all laughed.

Wiggling her bare feet, Maddie slipped on her shoes. "I think that's it."

"Perfect," Emma declared.

"Are you ready?" Samantha asked.

"Oh, yes." She had been ready since the moment J.C. proposed.

Emma opened the wide double doors. Organ music floated from the sanctuary. Now the scent of roses did permeate the air. As a botanist, Samantha had lovingly helped Maddie choose the perfect flowers. They agreed that white roses suited the innate beauty of the aged sanctuary. Nestled among them were exquisite hand-chosen orchids.

But Maddie wanted her bouquet to be a declaration of her love. Flawless scarlet roses. The eternal symbol of love, her love for the man not only of her dreams, but who had made her dreams a reality.

Anxious to see J.C., to begin their new life together, Maddie practically floated to the archway that opened onto the center aisle of the sanctuary. There, waiting to give her away, were Lillian and Chrissy.

Lillian grasped Maddie's elbow, which would ensure she was steady as they walked to the alter. "I know you'll be as happy as your father and I were."

"Oh, Mom." Maddie kissed her cheek.

Chrissy tugged at the waist of her chiffon dress made of the palest of lavenders. She and Lillian, as well as Samantha, wore the same color, their dresses a delicate blush of lavender with just enough color to accent Maddie's gown.

Samantha squeezed Maddie's fingers. "Be happy, my friend." Despite her cane, her steps were even as she proceeded up the aisle, holding a nosegay of white roses.

"Ready?" Emma asked.

Maddie smiled. "Absolutely."

Emma signaled the organist and the familiar notes of the wedding march trumpeted through the sanctuary. With her mother and Chrissy on either side, Maddie felt as though her feet didn't even touch the ground as she walked toward her groom.

Tall, achingly handsome, he was dressed in a black tuxedo and crisp white shirt. The boutonniere he had chosen was also a scarlet rose, one that matched hers. His eyes lit up as he caught sight of her and didn't waver, holding hers as she came to stand beside him.

The pastor began the age-old words, soon asking, "Who gives this woman?"

Lillian and Chrissy chorused, "We do."

Chrissy held Lillian's hand as they sat in the reserved pew.

Gazing at J.C., Maddie wanted to pinch herself, to believe this wonderful man was to be her husband. The pastor's words spilled over her like polished diamonds on velvet.

"Do you take…"

"In sickness and health…"

"Until death do us part."

"I do," Maddie vowed.

J.C. echoed her response.

"I now pronounce you husband and wife."

Their lips met, a gentle kiss of promise. An overture of love flooded them both.

J.C. took Maddie's hand, holding it as though he would never let it go. "Are you ready, Mrs. Mueller?"

A love so overpowering it filled every particle, every pore, sang through her veins. "Are *you* ready, Mr. Mueller?"

J.C. drew her hand to his lips, kissing it softly. "Only for the next fifty years or so."

Music poured from the organ, guiding their first married steps as they traveled down the aisle and into the future created from faith and love, their own family by design.

* * * * *

*When a young Amish woman has amnesia during
the holidays, will a handsome Amish farmer help
her regain her memories?*

Read on for a sneak preview of
Amish Christmas Memories *by Vannetta Chapman,
available December 2018 from Love Inspired.*

"What's your name?"

The woman's eyes widened and her hand shook so that
she could barely hold the mug of tea without spilling it. She
set it carefully on the coffee table. "I don't—I don't know
my name."

"How can you not know your own name?" Caleb asked.
"Do you know where you live?"

"Nein."

"What were you doing out there?"

"Out where?"

"Where was your coat and your *kapp*?"

"Caleb, now's not the time to interrogate the poor girl."
His *mamm* stood and moved beside her on the couch. She
picked up the small book of poetry. "You were carrying this,
when Caleb found you. Do you remember it?"

"I don't. This was mine?"

"Found it in the snow," Caleb said. "Right beside where
you collapsed."

"So it must be mine."

Caleb noticed that the woman's hands trembled as she
opened the cover and stared down at the first page. With one
finger, she traced the handwriting there.

"Rachel. I think my name is Rachel."

Rachel let her fingers brush over the word again and again. Rachel. Yes, that was her name. She was sure of it. She remembered writing it in the front of the book—she'd used a pen that her *mamm* had given her. She could almost picture herself, somewhere else. She could almost see her mother.

"My *mamm* gave me the pen and the book…for my birthday, I think. I wrote my name—wrote it right here."

"Your *mamm*. So you remember her?"

"Praise be to *Gotte*," Caleb's *dat* said, a smile spreading across his face.

"Is there someone we can call? If you remember the name of your bishop…" Caleb had sat down in the rocker his mother had vacated and was staring at her intensely.

They all were.

She closed her eyes, hoping to feel the memory again. She tried to see the room or the house or the people, but the memory had receded as quickly as it had come, leaving her with a pulsing headache.

She struggled to keep the feelings of panic at bay. Her heart was hammering, and her hands were shaking, and she could barely make sense of the questions they were pelting at her.

Who were these people?

Where was she?

Who was she?

She needed to remember what had happened.

She needed to go home.

Don't miss
Amish Christmas Memories *by Vannetta Chapman,*
available December 2018 wherever
Love Inspired® books and ebooks are sold.

www.LoveInspired.com

Looking for inspiration in tales
of hope, faith and heartfelt romance?

Check out **Love Inspired**® and
Love Inspired® **Suspense** books!

New books available every month!

CONNECT WITH US AT:

Facebook.com/groups/HarlequinConnection

 Facebook.com/HarlequinBooks

Twitter.com/HarlequinBooks

Instagram.com/HarlequinBooks

Pinterest.com/HarlequinBooks

ReaderService.com

Toby Potter watched the flames shoot toward the sky as he raced toward the building. "Robin!"

Sirens screamed closer. Toby had been on his way home when he'd spotted Robin's car in the parking lot of the lab. Ever since Robin had discovered his deception—orders to get close to her and figure out what was going on in the lab—she'd kept him at arm's length, her narrow-eyed stare hot enough to singe his eyebrows if he dare try to get too close.

Tonight, he'd planned to apologize profusely—again— and ask if there was anything he could do to earn her trust back. Only to pull into the parking lot, be greeted by the loud boom and watch flames shoot out of the window near the front door.

Heart pounding, Toby scanned the front door and rushed forward only to be forced back by the intense heat. Smoke billowed toward the dark night sky while the fire grew hotter and bigger. Mini explosions followed. Chemicals.

"Robin!"

Toby jumped into his truck and drove around to the back only to find it not much better, although it did seem to be more smoke than flames. Robin was in that building, and he was afraid he'd failed to protect her. Big-time.

Toby parked near the tree line in case more explosions were coming.

At the back door, he grasped the handle and pulled. Locked. Of course. Using both fists, he pounded on the glass-and-metal door. "Robin!"

Another explosion from inside rocked Toby back, but he was able to keep his feet under him. He figured the blast was on the other end of the building—where he knew Robin's station was. If she was anywhere near that station, there was no way she was still alive. "No, please no," he whispered. No one was around to hear him, but maybe God was listening.

Don't miss
Holiday Amnesia *by Lynette Eason,*
available December 2018 wherever
Love Inspired® Suspense books and ebooks are sold.

**Inspirational Romance to
Warm Your Heart and Soul**

Join our social communities to connect
with other readers who share your love!

Sign up for the Love Inspired newsletter
at **www.LoveInspired.com** to be the
first to find out about upcoming titles,
special promotions and exclusive content.

CONNECT WITH US AT:

Facebook.com/groups/HarlequinConnection

 Facebook.com/LoveInspiredBooks

 Twitter.com/LoveInspiredBks

LISOCIAL2018